Praise for "DUPPY

C000154719

"Ronald Haynie h... ....
depictions of the daily struggles of a Harlem man to cope
with his errant grandson who succumbs to the pathologies
around him. Their conflicts and their yearnings become
ours as we helplessly witness their downward spiral to
perdition, but always with the hope of redemption."

—**Warren Wyss,** co-author of "Shadows on Bleecker
Street"

"Ronald Haynie has an actor's ear for dialogue and a clear
eye for detail that breathes life into his characters. In his novel
"DUPPY: Ya Reap What'cha Sow", Haynie weaves a wild and
heartfelt tale of people dealing with the choices they've made in
the past while trying to make a fresh future for themselves."

—**David Surface**, Director, Veterans Writing Workshop

"Brilliant mind...Exciting! Incredibly dark and radical."

Walter Reed aka **Killah Priest** of Wu-Tang Clan
Lyricist / CEO Proverbs Records
KillahPriest.com

"DUPPY: Ya Reap What'cha Sow" is a pleasure following the antics and poignant adventures of Pappy Al and his teenage grandson, Baby Al as they relate in rocky but always heartfelt journeys in Harlem, USA. The author, Ronald Haynie, is an amazing actor and wonderful writer, so the dialogue is pitch-authentic and the characterization truly spot on, with a fast-moving story that will keep you turning the pages. A rich, captivation of inter-generational blending and a touching cultural experience, as you follow Al, the good guy loving protagonist and Baby Al, a classic villain. You can't put this novel down!"

—**Dr. Milton Polsky, Ph.D**., co-chair, the UFT (United Federation of Teachers) Players and Shubert Fellow in Playwriting, Former Professor, Creative Arts, CUNY and NYU, Co-Author of the mystery novel, "Shadows on Bleecker Street"

"Ronald Haynie has written a book that is filled with all the passion and intensity one might expect in a relationship between a grandfather and grandson that has been built upon a lie that has been allowed to fester for years, with devastating consequences for the future. Mr. Haynie has written his story in masterful fashion -- vividly and engrossingly. His characters are well-drawn and the portrait he paints of late twentieth century Harlem will make you feel as though you are actually there. DUPPY: Ya Reap What'cha Sow is a page turner. You will love every page. A great introduction to a fine young writer and, one hopes, a promise of more great stories to come."

—Richard Wesley
Drama Desk Award Winning Playwright and Educator, Chair of the Rita and Burton Goldberg Dept. Of Dramatic Writing and Associate Professor at NYU's Tisch School of The Arts, Screenwriter of "Uptown Saturday Night", "Let's Do It Again", and "Native Son"

THIS NOVEL IS DEDICATED TO THE MEMORY OF:

Bennett Lorenzo Haynie	(1909-1994)
Ola Bell Hemphill Haynie	(1912-1994)
Odessa Knight Roberts	(1912-2009)
Willie Mae Smith Rogers	(1911-2009)
Laura Johnson Marshall	(1918-2011)
Paul "Bunny" Reeves, Jr.	(1936-1993)
Verneshea Reeves	(1940-2011)
Doristine Johnson Jones	(1953-2014)
Curtis "The Almighty Scourge" Ervin	(1968-2012)
Leo Thomas	(1967-1986)
Eleanora Maxwell	(1933-1994)
Dwayne "Cuckoo" Carolina	(1965-1996)
Norris G. Bonner	(1967-1996)
Marcia G. Cecil Carter	(1967-2001)
Randolph S. Shuler, Sr.	(1945-2008)
Carol Shuler	(1946-2011)
Darnell Daja Daniels	(1970-2014)
Cleopatra Mullings	(1967-2014)
Desiree Covington	(1968-2015)
Mary Emma Roberson Jordan	(1920-2009)

Charles Jenkins   (S.I.P.)

Tony Guyton   (S.I.P.)

Nadine C. Brown   (S.I.P.)

Book Cover Designed By: Demitrius "Motion" Bullock courtesy of www.motionillustrationz.com

Book Cover Layout By: Austin Lynch

All Comments, Inquiries, and Correspondence for future purchase for this novel, contact the Author:

Ronald Haynie, P.O. Box#564, New York, NY 10034

Haynie.Ronald@gmail.com (646)535-6170

DUPPY:

YA REAP WHAT'CHA SOW

A Novel

By

Ronald Haynie

FOREWORD & ACKNOWLEDGMENTS FROM THE AUTHOR

Twenty-one years it has taken me to finally publish this work of pure fiction I hope you read and enjoy. With "DUPPY: Ya Reap What'cha Sow", although I have penned a screenplay version converted to a radio drama, that was awarded a third place certificate for a contest; plus the scripted stage version titled "Duppy" loosely based on the work, I now have closure for the original literary slice of life created by me, four drafts and over two decades later. The Almighty sent me this token of love and rescue I refused to give up on, while quite a few folks discouraged me against it, especially because I am not Jamaican. Luckily there is faith, hope, and a higher power, for if I were consumed by the darkness of self-inflicted death, this piece would have never been written, my truth refreshingly so. Also, we can positively learn and benefit from each other's culture. Each one should teach one, share, and learn to share, in terms of culture.

Therefore, I thank The Almighty God first and foremost, and I am eternally grateful to supportive you! Sure I will strive to acknowledge each individual who has positively touched this work in some fashion over the last two decades; from the successful Indiegogo campaign, to the phenomenal stage thespian work, kudos behind the scenes, the novel trailer, many audiences, all of the heartfelt encouragement. This foreword is written within total love, and failure to not mention anyone is not personal, because I am striving to credit the consistent positive support, along with the negative opposition, the small few who would rather not be associated with me or this work. "Haterade" will never quench the thirst of those who choose love and light through hard work, faith, diligence, hope, and positive belief.

Actions do speak louder than words, and when they reveal themselves through love and light, haters still should be acknowledged because people's rejection is God's Protection.

My literary influences of inspiration: I will begin with Zora Neale Hurston, who gave me the absolute courage to write in different dialects, and spell the dialect the way I need the reader to hear exactly what I hear, painting the picture in an auditory sense. From Jamaican patois, to "around the way" street dialect of particular eras, to the vernacular of senior citizens recuperating from strokes with other life challenges, I thank the literary legacy of Ms. Hurston for that.

There is William Peter Blatty and Stephen King aka Richard Bachman. I love the gentlemen for their macabre, gore, and their exploration of the supernatural, the mysticism of the mind, and the brilliance of their writings gave me the encouragement to investigate doctrines versus medical diagnosis, and the reasoning of this combination.

I thank Agnes Nixon and Henry Farrell, for without their works I couldn't have written the domestic family conflicts, or intertwine these stories at the chronological level of consistency.

I thank the songwriters of the Motown Record corporation from the early days of the company, primarily the skilled writings of Brian & Eddie Holland, with Lamont Dozier, which brings me to thank the vision of Berry Gordy Jr., and the entire Gordy Family legacy, for Motown is instilled musically forever into human beings globally.

I thank the infinite literary brilliance of Richard Wright and Ralph Ellison, their works being a huge influence on this novel, in terms of imagery and use of the English language.

Last but certainly not the least, Donald Goines and his literary enormity about life in the streets; yes, the writings of Donald Goines, plus the beautiful stories of Walter Dean Myers. The work of these men encouraged me to tell my story straight, no chaser, with all of the honesty I could muster about the ups and downs of people who reside in metropolises worldwide, faced with the cards inner city dwellers are dealt, hoping for better tomorrows they may never see.

Again, I thank The Almighty God, and Ms. Toya Revo-Du Barry: film director of the novel trailer, for inspiring me, encouraging me to be strong and maintain belief in my own talents. A shout-out to Augustus Publishing, for telling me I have a publishable story. God bless my proofreading team: Jean St. Hill, Duane Gallop, and Michele Girard, thank each of you for your expertise in English, and strength in education.

Much appreciation to the contributors of the Indiegogo Campaign: Denisse Rosas, Edward Mable, Lamont Terrell Covington, Marsha R. Bonner, Michelle L. Madden, Timothy Jackson, Freida G. Jones, Trevaughn L. Bynum, Audrena Russum, Anita John, Carol Johnson, Corwin Smith, Desmond Graham, Dr. Gloria J. Arnold, Laverne Harris-Anderson, Liam Donovan, Madaline McKay, Mia King-Woolley, Uncle Richard A. Robeson, Shaunta Macklin-Benbow, Yolanda Askew, Marsha Borenstein, Arnold Pinnix, Cousin Jeannette V. Chambers, Laura Gift, Dr. Milton Polsky, Rahviance Robinson, Anthony Wyche, Clovia Chisolm, Denise "Mistah" Coles, John Thompson Jr., Karen D. Taylor, Larry Calhoun, Pamela White, Raymond A. Robinson, Sonya Reed-Cato, Suzanne Lamberg, Tasha Paley, Anthony Harper, Barbara Haspel, Brian "Tah" Whitty R.N., Charlotte Balibar, Debbie George, Fred Arcoleo,

George Bacot Jr., Jorel Lonesome, Kevina O'Carroll, Joseph Sellman, Lourdes Ayala, Marjorie Bryant, Mishelle Parks, Monique Andress-Williams, Elena "Mamarazzi" Marrero, Catherine Parsons, Michelle White, Rebecca Lloyd, Adam Glenn, Alphanso Wilson, Andy Torres Jr., Anthony Wills Jr., Bashshir Sultani, Bryan Champion-Thompson, Charlotte Ferrell, Charnae Betton, Cheray Diggs, Geoffrey M. Lee, Joseph Fobbs, Khadijah Muhammad, Natasha Baptiste, Elizabeth Lamboy-Wilson, Nicole M. Lewis, Pamela Washington-Clarke, Patricia Davis, Warren Wyss, Aleathia Brown, Ayesha Depay, Ed Cushman, Linda Gardner, Michelle Anthony, Dave UOG, Frieda Holmes, & Dr. Sylvie de Souza M. D.

Thank you to each actor that has touched this work before an audience live on stage, on the air, currently on film, plus direction, help & encouragement behind the scenes: John Eric Scutchins, Darnell Daja Daniels(R.I.P.), Jim Willis, Kyle P. Carter, Demitrius "Motion" Bullock, Tequan Worthen, Leonardo Benzant, Philip Holland, Bryan Champion-Thompson, Leo Bona-Balibar, Adam Glenn, Robert Siverls, John D. Hendrickson, Russell Rogers, Drego Moore, Jr., Ivelaw Peters, Gervon Robinson, Norma Miller, Francine Brown-Wilson, Dr. Gloria J. Arnold, Mia Anderson, Khadijah Muhammad, Panala Cole-Wilson, Yvonne Delaney-Mitchell, Rosetta L. Gadson, Kimisha Williams, Kimberly Renee Thomas, Shaunta Macklin-Benbow, Sharlesha Williams-Bradford, Monet Dunham, Nadine C. Brown(R.I.P.), Catrina Davis aka Zera Priestess, Runita L. Jones, Renee Williams, Jess Hoffman, Kevin Gonzalez, Boubekeur Benkhoukha, Rachel Young, Demitrius Bullock Jr., Tanisha Moales, Shanese Moales, my goddaughter Tatiana A. Brinkley, Dennis Pressey, Marc L. Abbott, Eric Moreland, Prudence Blackmon, Nikita

Blackmon, Hendrix Xavier, Crystal Hanton, Kenya T. Leach, Denaul M. Jenkins II, Ondre Devonte Carter, Bashshir Sultani, Darnell White, Acy Brown, Joel Smith, Sonya M. Hemphill, Ed Hemphill, Veronica Kirkland, Pastors Charles & Cynthia Williams, George Goss & Audra Moore, Joan Green, Sobrino James Barrett & Reina Dawkins, Mrs. Grace Gregory & Family, Sgt. Marcquell Adin Roy, Seankierre Lyons & Family, Aixa Kendrick, Karen Brown, Kori Galloway, Dionne Spence & The Spence Family, David D. Wright aka Baba Osun Gumi, Saundra Hamilton, Stephanie Toure, John Shaw & Mrs. Joyce L. Dukes-Shaw, Linda Lawton & Family, Rashawn Chisolm, Ivan Rivera, Hector Rivera Jr. & The Entire Rivera Family.

Besides the preceding thank you's, I need to speak on the angelic ancestors to whom this work is dedicated. Originally, the novel was dedicated to my maternal grandfather Bennett Lorenzo Haynie and the beautiful surviving seniors who loved him and supported his transition: Cousin Odessa Knight Roberts, Mrs. Willie Mae Rogers-matriarch of the Rogers-Mallard clan, and Mrs. Laura "Grand" Marshall-matriarch of our extended family, the Jacksons, Marshalls, and the Taylors. I planned to shout out ancestor Alfred Peets, my granddad's friend and former neighbor, whose son Basil found my grandfather's body, and I still say God bless Mr. Basil & Mrs. Irma Peets and the legacy of their families. Then, six months after my grandfather transitioned my maternal grandmother Ola Bell-his wife-was called home. My grandparents preceded a growing list of ancestors, as one by one others transitioned while I continually drafted the work, won the radio award, and performed the stage play. DUPPY: Ya Reap What'cha Sow is not only dedicated to my maternal grandparents, but to other transitioning angels who have encouragingly touched me, the work, and for a few schoolmates who have also gone to heaven before me.

Along with the aforementioned, this novel is dedicated to the memory of Bunny & Verneshea Reeves who let me borrow their books as a child, lots of time spent at Atlantic Towers in the seventies; Doristine Jones, the surrogate aunt I have always needed, and she truly cared about my Mother; Schoolmate Curt Ervin, you are FOREVER DECEPT in our hearts and minds, and Brooklyn is not the same without you; Leo Thomas, you were down to earth, and so cool in Printing High School, and I see you every other day in my mind, gone way too soon, when we were still children; Schoolmate Tony Guyton, when, how, and why did you go so soon; Mrs. Eleanora Maxwell, I have always wanted to do this work for you and your baby boy Mike, you were such a gracious patient and I loved taking care of you; Cuckoo you was good to me during the early drafts, listening while you were sick. You know the character Dwayne is named after you. The famm from LG misses you; Norris Bonner, I think of you every day, and thanks for telling Cheryl about this work. I'm finally publishing it after all these years, and Cheryl & Sandy are still doing their thing too my brother, I know you are watching this; Marcia Cecil-Carter, I'll never forget you and my boy at the stage play premiere of "Duppy". You are always with us; Randolph Shuler Sr. & Carol Shuler, you are one in heaven, and I thank you for your legacy, hard work in the community, and for raising a great family of friends; Brother Darnell Daja Daniels of Maryland, I hoped to see you portray Al Carter more times on stage. The Almighty needed you more as an angel my brother. You are with me as a veteran also; my pretty schoolmate Cleopatra Mullings, Cleo, I just want you back for all of us. I think of you every day, but no more suffering for you, first female angel of my high school class; my

xiii

friend, homie, neighbor, and schoolmate from elementary Desiree Covington, I'll always have memories of you from the block, 995 Gates, and of course P.S. 309. God bless and keep you Desiree; Nadine Brown, when I think of you being gone, it is too surreal, unreal, after sharing many stages with you while you portrayed Barbara Nelson. You will never be forgotten sweetheart. You were no joke, on and off stage! Always real, we miss you; and to my paternal grandparents Charles Jenkins, and Mary Emma Robeson Jordan, Grandma I wish you were still in Wagner Projects after being there many years since the sixties, I love you very much. This story is for you.

Again, I can't stop thanking The Almighty God, and some extra special thank you's again for a few who went above and beyond in their understanding the importance of this piece: My schoolmate brother from Harlem, Edward Mable; my schoolmate, ex-singing partner, and brother Timothy Jackson; Toya Revo-Du Barry & Denisse Rosas, Marsha R. Bonner I can't thank you enough; Michelle L. Rhoden-Madden, we have been friends almost thirty years, I love you; and to my childhood friend from Bed-Stuy, Lamont Terrell Covington, Terrell, you are the greatest.

Thank you for your quotes gentlemen: Dr. Milton Polsky & Warren Wyss, David Surface: you are awesome and welcoming with the Veteran's Writing Workshop; my brother & original neighbor Walter "Killah Priest" Reed-940, 950, 969, 995, plus the brownstones are proud of your success; and thank you my original mentor Richard Wesley for taking me under your wing early on, and always being there during this never ending process of healing. Rachel Ford you were invaluable with your information about the criminal justice system and the NYPD, thank you, Yael, & The Ford Family; Many great thanks to Austin Lynch for last minute formatting on the spot, thanks dude!; Thank you Mr. & Mrs. Demitrius "Motion" Bullock & Family for infinite encouragement; Thank you Dwayne Woods & Francine Leone and Family, Rashad & Liv Clinton and Family, Ishan Edwards & Family, Harry "Pop" Harris and Family, my surrogate older brother Deymond "Deemo Da Pro" Hill and Family(RIP Nana & Ma Dukes), Powerful Poetic Brother & Author Gary Holmes, Dearest Diane Waller & Val McGhee, I love you. Thank you Cheryl "Salt" James-Wray for touching and encouraging the work in its infancy stage thanks to our bond with Norris, you and Pepa are still the consummate female entertainers in hip-hop. Peace to the memory of Onyx, Fred, Trop, (RIP Marlon), and double peace to Sonee Seeza, my godbrother. Triple peace to the actor/director Eric Coleman, and the playwright Ms. J.e Franklin and their families for preserving my talents during my coldest winter ever.

God bless Mrs. Katherine "Kat" Anderson-Schaffner for much inspiration and strength, and The Schaffner Family of Inkster, Michigan, Kymberly Davis of Clinton Township, Michigan; the Ballard/Chapman/Lacey Family, Derek Thornton and The Entire Thornton Family, Eric Martin and The Entire Martin Family & Antonio Dandridge of Detroit, Michigan, Rhonda R. Clayborne-Funderburk of Baltimore, Maryland, Linda L. Pickwood & Family of the Bronx & Brooklyn, thank you all for love.

Thank you to my Mother Diane Elizabeth Haynie for health confirmation, and to my Father Cecil Andre Jenkins for the flash drive formatting to complete the work. Peace to my Uncle Richard Alfred Robeson, and surrogate Uncle Tony Williams of Cincinnati/Blue Ash, Ohio, my Aunts Didi of NC, Jan of DC, and Deborah of Brooklyn; Peace to my brothers James, Cecil, and my sisters Tanya, Tunisia, and

Melissa. Peace to Tujuana Worthen-Council, and to Cousins Twanika D. Harris & Crystal Brown Scudder Weiss; and to my dearest friend Nancy aka Manuela A. Pascual: Thank you for ALWAYS BEING THERE, for over thirty years. Nancy, I love you very much.

I hope all of you enjoy DUPPY: Ya Reap What'cha Sow, now published after twenty-one years of life's peaks, and valleys.

Ronald Haynie August 2015

CHAPTER 1

∗

Al Carter tossed and turned, dreaming dreams of his young life yesteryear on a disgustingly hot spring night. In his dreams he searched for the dancing, true love of his life Mattie Mae, while his subliminal haze was filled with thousands of different sized U. S. flags, fluttering with the identical victory of the red, white, and blue. Some of the tiny hand held flags were frantically waved by many of the soldier's wives, girlfriends, and their loved ones. Like many of his comrades from the "colored" platoons returning home from war, hopefully for the last time, Al simply needed to get home, with the gratitude to be alive, after losing many buddies during combat.

'WHERE IS MY MATTIE MAE? . . . Is she out'chere with the baby wit' all these millions of folks? . . . She cain't have my baby out'chere I reckon! . . . Too daggone hot! . . . Sho' is hot out'chere! . . . Wait now, where is everybody! . . . Where y'all running off to in all dis here heat?! . . . It's too hot! . . . Ain't no shade!! . . . I need some shade! . . . I need some water!! . . . WATER!!! . . .'

Like clockwork, the climate in his bedroom awakened Al, ending his dreams as it did every other hour. Tossing, turning, with approaching dreams filled with the familiar voices of his deceased wife and deceased daughter, his thirst awakened him continuously, prompting him to finish his nearby cup of iced water. The green plastic cup of water was located a mile away, proudly standing on the nightstand while he slept uncovered at the foot of the bed; and even this night, sleeping in briefs only, still provided no relief for a tenement bedroom absent of any means of air conditioning. His pillow-drenched with perspiration-was on the floor once again, after he had blindly retrieved it several times. The windows were raised as high as possible in his bedroom and throughout the entire apartment, with thickening night waves of humidity flowing through by the second, but staying by the minute.

Al Carter tried to keep his eyes shut inside his blackened room dimly lit by the streetlights, but his ears remained open to the current outside sounds of laughter which began to drown out the ticking of his alarm clock. The sounds of the street escalated with its music, occasional fast moving automobiles, male and female voices mixed with profanity, and distant honking car horns. Seems like the higher the streets' temperature, the more the neighborhood and its young people became oblivious to the term "sleep". He hated to be the one to crush their all night hangout dream, to be the one he knew the new breed of children desperately needed in the absence of their unknowing, uncaring parents, or people unaware of the nighttime activities of their offspring. Deep in the midnight hour before sunrise surely wasn't the time for a party and the stoop of his five floor walk-up tenement surely wasn't the place for the festivities.

Licking his gums and remaining teeth inside a sternly clenched mouth, Al stretched and knocked the cup of water off the nightstand with his feet. Sitting up on the edge of the bed, he inched over to turn on the lamp to seconds of temporary blindness. Once his eyes focused on the last of the melted ice cubes sliding aimlessly across the worn linoleum, noticing the hands of time he thought angrily, "A quarter to four? And them rascals downstairs on them steps carrying on! These days, these kids ain't got no home training whatsoever!"

It was a long way down to the asphalt and sidewalk from the top floor of the tenement that housed him and his poignant dreams and memories since the late thirties when he himself was young, yet a bit older than the young people he would now have to scold away from their loitering haven.

Back in 1938, after becoming separated from his mother and younger sisters while the family fled their native Arkansas, Al became a stowaway, eventually making it to New York City, barefoot, via a boxcar of a northern freight train. With a knack for shoe shining, he earned enough pennies upon arrival in Pennsylvania Station, and more pennies came with more shoe-shining around, which would lead to subway trips uptown, with his own brand new shoes to wear. Once he established contact, and was taken in by his Aunt Louise Esther, who had lived in Harlem for several years, he would continue shoe shining until he was drafted into the war. In spite of the circumstances, being separated from the family that he had protected, loved, and who fled the South to Detroit, Al remained with his Aunt Louise in Harlem. Aunt Lou ran her household in a dignified manner and she influenced her nephew Al with dignity and morals as a favor to her estranged younger sister and the rest of the family, with high hopes that they would all be together again one day, a day that would never come again.

Al painfully rose with his usual arthritic pain and drag-limped to the right window, not connected to the fire escape, so he could look down at the nightly sleep thieves. The giant radio blared Parliament's "Flashlight" for the streets to hear, and the Wilkinson kids and their friends who lived in the adjacent tenement happened to be the early morning culprits. The young people and their friends danced to their hearts' content with discotheque energy, without a care in the world.

"Quiet down that noise out there," Al pleadingly shouted. "People need to get up in the morning, please! All this carrying on for God's sake, it's almost morning!"

"It is morning!," one of the guys retaliated, and one of the girls shoved him, walked up a few steps and turned down the radio. "We sorry Mister Carter," she shouted up with a hue of consideration. Al couldn't tell the children apart. He had heard that a few of the Wilkinson kids were respectful.

He returned to bed after relieving himself in the bathroom, desperately wanting to return to the dreams, and his continuous soul search for his wife and daughter. Unfortunately, the dreams never happened. The sun had started to rise, and the flies were already looking for homes to hang out in until their deaths. Flies-all sizes and shapes-periodically entered the screen less windows of Al's bedroom. They buzzed in his face several times just as his alarm clock came to life: 7:00 A.M. Al pondered his early morning activities, wishing for another night's sleep, grumbling each time he had to swat at a teasing fly. Aggravated, he sat up on the edge of the bed, collecting more thoughts to start the routine, breakfast for himself and his thirteen-year old only grandchild Dwayne.

After freshening up with a quick morning bath, relief, the addition of his partial dentures, and the donning of clean pajama pants, he slowly dragged down the long, sweaty hallway of the apartment. He passed his grandson's tiny bedroom with door half opened; and inside the face was unseen, with adolescent foot dangling from his cot-like single bed. Al entered the living room, heading straight to his nostalgic closed top loading stereo set, with eight track tape player and broken turntable that once boasted four different rpm speeds: 16, 33, 45, and 78, with AM radio dials that no longer tuned into stations overseas, on the front of the outside. On top of the closed stereo sat a 13 inch black and white television with a wire hanger connected inside, in place of the broken antenna. Ignoring the television, with the flick of the stereo switch, he tuned into AM news radio station 1010 "WINS", the daily morning ritual.

"The day is Friday, June the 23rd, 1978!"

Outside, the sun began to vengefully beam on the Harlem skyline while inside, he continued from the living room into his kitchen, frowning the moment he opened the refrigerator door. Al fixed his overturned pots and pans filled with leftovers, relieved after receiving a blast of cool air. He reluctantly closed the door, longing for the frost of winter and began preparing breakfast, mumbling to himself.

"Ain't no need in me wantin' it to be wintertime . . . cause we ain't gon' have no heat or no hot water none of the time . . . that ole Baby Al, he done went in that frigidaire last night . . . messing with my neck bones and kidney beans and whatnot, knocking all my stuff over . . . that rascal ain't got a bit a sense."

He dutifully started the meal of grits, scrambled eggs, and sausage, pan of water for coffee, mood changing from somber to cheery the moment he thought of the agenda that lay ahead for himself and his grandson. Whistling as he whisked the eggs, Al eyed the clock on the greasy covered, beige kitchen wall. He turned away and poured the beaten eggs into the frying pan.

"Time for Baby Al to be getting up, today's his big day . . . That rascal shoulda been up on his own by now . . . I know he ain't gon' hear me yelling so I'm'a get on with this food, when I'm done I'll get him up . . . I'm hungry as a hog," he thought, adding additional stirs to the pot filled with grits. Al's nickname for Dwayne was "Baby Al"; a name he had grown attached to since Dwayne was a toddler. In spite of the circumstances that plagued him over the years, a mild stroke that made his left side paralyzed from the thigh down, with his left hand frozen in a clawed fist, Al managed to whip the breakfast into shape within a matter of a minutes. He fixed their plates of food with tall glasses of orange juice, with Maxwell House instant coffee for himself, giving a second glance at the clock in the kitchen, then hearing the time announced from the radio: 8:15.

Al limped from the kitchen through the living room, and down the long hallway to tap on Dwayne's bedroom door. With each dragging footstep into the darkened corridor, he became more anxious to wake up his grandson. Dwayne was set to graduate from junior high school within two hours. The hallway became brighter the closer Al came to the bedrooms.

He gently tapped on Dwayne's opened door. "Baby Al! Time to get up!"

Feeling the urge to urinate again, he quickly limped back into the bathroom, which was nestled between his bedroom and Dwayne's room. Once he finished, Al peeked into his room, frowning at his unmade bed, the overturned cup he never retrieved from kicking it over, and his ancient furnishings that needed replacement. The curtains stood still, and were baking-no type of wind in the outside air-and the heat of the summer steadily approached. A second 13 inch black and white television sat on top of Al's long bedroom dresser with connected mirrors. Next to the TV sat a framed 8x10 family portrait of Al and his deceased wife Mattie, with her arms around Dwayne as a youngster.

"My food's gettin' cold I reckon," Al thought, proceeding back towards the living room. He noticed no movement going on in Dwayne's room, so he banged hard the second time. "Baby Al! Get up in there, boy! Yo food's on the table!" With his last comment, Al continued on to the living room, stopping with sudden pain.

"So busy thinking 'bout this rascal and his graduation I done forgot to take my pill . . . Feel like this body of mine getting' worse, like I cain't even walk without them pills no more . . "

The drag-limp and claw was almost four years old after his mild stroke he had suffered attending his beloved wife's funeral, prolonging her burial.

At the funeral, the entire left side of his body went dead and he fell to the floor right in front of his wife's casket. His bereaved grandson had run frantically through the chapel unable to be contained. During Mattie Mae Brown Carter's home going recessional in the post-Christmas, pre New Year afternoon, Al was rushed to North General Hospital with a stroke on the right side of his brain. He was eventually discharged from the hospital to bury his wife, and then spent weeks in therapy grieving the love of his life, a relationship with Mattie for thirty-eight years, who passed away on Christmas Eve. His Detroit relatives and a few of Mattie's relatives offered to help raise Dwayne, and Al came to the firm decision of taking care of his grandson on his own. He decided that Dwayne was his one true link to the loving family he created and once had. Gwenny had been gone for so long, and now Mattie Mae was no more. Everything with life and its speed had happened so fast; he never felt there were goodbyes; he could never feel them, could never say them. Mattie and Gwenny still existed in his spirit, his mind, and all over his body.

He sat down at the dining room table, shooing the flies away from his breakfast. The table was against the wall, next to the opened doorway of the tiny kitchen, across from the stereo set and TV in a catty direction. The stereo was against a wall that had the window leading to the alleyway, the same alleyway outside the bathroom window and Dwayne's bedroom window. Next to the stereo up in the corner against the wall was an antique, wrought iron three tiered unit filled with framed photos and potted plants, purchased during the fifties. A small, ancient sofa was opposite the stereo, TV, and unit along the opposite wall that extended down the entire hallway of the apartment.

"HEY, BABY AL," Al bellowed after noticing a few green backed flies congregating over his grandson's plate of food at the other end of the table. He chased them away and began eating, savoring each bite of eggs and sausage, fondly remembering the days he spent as the top chef at a counter restaurant inside a prestigious department store. He had been the first black employee in the entire store, starting out in the late forties, post war, post shoe shining. He became the top chef and held onto that position dutifully.

After being forced into retirement with his condition for nearly four years, Al became bored, feeling the wrath of age. He was no longer a strong, sturdy, well-poised, caramel colored man everyone knew, towering over six feet. He had shrunk to 5'10", with a weight of one-sixty. His afro became totally gray, bigger, and thicker. Some of the kids from the block liked to call him "The Jackson Five Grandfather". He permanently used a walking cane in public after his stroke, yet he vowed to carry out his mission: to continue raising the grandson he loved into a fine, strong man. After losing Mattie, and refusing the outside help from anyone, including his out of town relatives, Al assumed total responsibility of the house: the cooking, the cleaning, the washing, etc. It was rough in the beginning because of the stroke, but he managed with the encouragement of Jimmy Robinson, and with the love of Arlene Montgomery, the only two friends of the family he trusted, who were Dwayne's godparents.

Jimmy, Al's younger cooking protégé, would send for Dwayne on occasional weekends and holidays from school to spend time with his wife and the Robinson family in Brooklyn. Arlene would visit when possible from the Bronx; dividing her time between family life and helping Mister Carter manage with Baby Al.

Arlene had been close to the Carter family since the early fifties, becoming best friends with Gwenny Carter, Al and Mattie's daughter, while in elementary. A year older than Gwenny, she had become attached to the Carters while living with her aunt and uncle on the second floor of the building. The two young girls would run up and down the stairs, from the fifth floor to the second, dividing time in between each other's homes. Wearing pigtails and bangs, the energetic youngsters baked cakes, played with their dolls and their doll houses, ruined Mattie's hairpins, combs, and rouge, practicing their "grown up" make up tricks. From jumping rope off and on all day, to homework, to going to the movies around the corner, through all four seasons with all holidays, the loving girls planned to be best friends forever.

The friendship lasted until the day Gwenny was expelled from college. Gwenny, returning home after being raped by a few male students, including her on campus boyfriend, had become another person, lost in an unreachable depression after the campus prank-in a cruel twist of racism-a prank she was blamed for by the faculty; and she was pregnant as a result of this rape, when abortions were illegal. Arlene tried to get through to her friend, but she was never the same again. Arlene vowed to be the best godmother to her girlfriend's baby, even coming up with a list of names for the infant. Gwenny never saw the boy child she produced, and her bond with her best friend Arlene was severed for life, with her last smile painfully fading into the existence of memory.

Al finished his breakfast and coffee while his grandson's plate, complete with a hardening mound of grits with butter, scrambled eggs, with sausage was now cold and the orange juice, lukewarm, with no Dwayne.

Rising to his feet, Al took his plate, mug, and glass into the kitchen. "Baby Al gettin' his tail up right now," Al thought, popping some pills and drinking more orange juice. He began washing away his breakfast remains, still enjoying the news from the living room. "Well, well, well, so they found a satellite in outer space, by the planet Pluto? Lawd have mercy, folk ain't got nothing else to do with they time, and they money?" He snapped out of his news listening daydream the moment he heard the toilet flush.

Bypassing the living room Al entered the hallway with his one-two drag step, hearing the bathroom sink water running as he approached. Dwayne's room was opened, bed unmade; and Al pushed open the already cracked bathroom door, sticking his head inside. Dwayne stood over the sink brushing his teeth furiously.

"Morning Baby Al."

Dwayne glared scornfully at Al, then at the mirror, with his mouth filled with saliva and toothpaste. Spitting out his waste he stated, "What's so good about it?", then he began to rinse his mouth.

"What's so good about it? The good Lord woke ya up this morning boy. He keeps ya," Al grinned proudly, anticipating Dwayne's junior high graduating ceremony. His grandson stared back and smirked at his grandfather.

"Oh yeah? Well good morning then. If that's how it is." He exited the bathroom, looking back at Al giving off a "hiss", a habitual noise he made when he wanted to be cool, mean, or sarcastic.

Al watched the grandson he raised walk into the living room. Dwayne was growing tall, standing at 5'7", wearing a size 9 in shoes and sneakers. People often mistook him for being Hispanic due to his light complexion, bushy eyebrows and straight to curly hair. Gwenny's forehead and chin rubbed off on Dwayne; however Dwayne inherited his eyebrows, nose, eyes, ears, personality, and temper from Arnold Mucci. Arnold was killed during a race riot on the school grounds the same year President Johnson passed the law giving blacks the right to vote in the South, the summer after Gwenny died giving birth.

"This stuff for me?"

Al could hear Dwayne attempt to turn up the living room's drab, low volume, black and white TV that saw better days. In response to his grandson's question, coming up the hall, Al said, "Yeah, it is. Sho' took you long enough to get up. And turn that TV off boy. Cain't you hear I'm listening to the radio?"

Dwayne turned off the television and plopped into his chair, fanned the flies, and took a long swallow of orange juice. His grandfather entered the room and held onto the unbalanced table.

"Our refrigerator broke," asked Dwayne.

"No. Why?"

"Cause the juice is hot."

"Well if ya' would'a got up when I called ya', it Wouldn't BE hot!"

Dwayne hissed, eating a forkful of eggs, then grimacing at the cold taste. "Dag Pappy! Why you let the food get cold like this man? I can't eat this."

Al gave his grandson a dirty look and exclaimed, "Huh? What'cha mean? You should'a got up the first time when I called. I called you plenty! Baby Al, I called ya' a few times, I banged on the door!"

"Pappy, who you know in this world eat cold eggs?" Dwayne took a bite of the cooled, hardened sausage. "Pappy, this is nasty. You losing your touch!"

Dwayne's comment hurt his grandfather's feelings. Al took his art of cooking very seriously and he thought he had done well fixing breakfast for the umpteenth time.

"Look, if it's that nasty, then don't eat it," Al snapped. Dwayne stared down at his cold plate of food. "But, Pappy, I'm'a be hungry! I can't graduate on an empty stomach!"

"Gimme your plate, Baby Al!"

Al took the plate of food into the kitchen huffing and puffing, placing it on the counter, and then he searched for the small tin foil pan he used to heat food. Dwayne walked into the kitchen grinning.

"All I want is some hot food. How would you like eating cold eggs and sausage? Yuck! And hard grits!"

Al struck a match to light the oven, then he dumped the contents of the food into the pan, then he placed his grandson's breakfast in the oven and shut the door. Even though he fussed with him, he hardly ever meant it. Dwayne had been a spoiled brat for so long, thanks to Mattie. Al felt that his rotten ways had to come to an end. He was too old to be a spoiled brat at 13 years old.

"Next time you'll get up when I call you," Al stated while the oven heated, facing his grandson. "Go get washed up. By the time you get dressed the food'll be hot, now get!"

"Thanks, Pappy," Dwayne exclaimed, exiting the kitchen briskly.

Fifteen minutes later, Al had reheated Dwayne's entire breakfast, and he set up the table nicely for the graduate. Al checked the clock again. Time surely was flying, and he was ready to get dressed.

He yelled, "What the hell ya' doin' boy! Back there? Playin' witcha dingaling boy! Get out here! That's how the food got cold in the first place!" He sat back down in his seat, wiping sweat from his brow with the back of his hand. "Hurry up boy!"

Inside the bathroom, Dwayne gave his beckoning grandfather the finger. "Ah, shut up," he mumbled, stepping back to admire himself in his baby blue, three-piece pin striped church suit. He added his matching bow tie; then he licked his thumb tips and brushed his thick eyebrows with them.

"Damn! My suit's the joint, I'm dressed to a "t". I am the joint!," he happily exclaimed; he was ready to take all the girls by storm, removing his suit jacket.

Al wiped more sweat from his forehead, frowning the moment he noticed the food getting cold. Before he yelled again, he could hear the floor creaking, indicating his grandson was on his way up front.

"Pappy, where's the juice," he asked entering the living room.

"Oh, forget it. I cain't remember everything."

"I'm thirsty! You know how hot it is? You need to buy us a new fan." Dwayne walked into the kitchen. Al became angry, "Baby Al, get in here and eat! You gotta get to the schoolhouse!"

There was no answer from Dwayne. Al fell into another scolding mood. He stood holding onto the table, dragged into the kitchen, suddenly taken aback, eyes burning with more anger. In plain sight, Dwayne stood with the refrigerator door open, head cocked back, drinking the ice-cold orange juice from the container. Al was livid, infuriated. Dwayne didn't even notice his grandfather watching. He continued to quench his thirst.

"BABY AL," Al shouted, startling Dwayne. Some of the juice went down Dwayne's windpipe, making him gasp and cough; and he too, suddenly became angry, doing his best to catch his breath.

Al started chastising, "Baby Al! Where and da hell is yo' home training? You know better than that! Where's your glass?"

"You ain't fix it!"

"You right! You thirteen years old, boy! You could'a least fix ya own glass of juice! I done did everything else! I cain't believe my eyes! Drinking stuff out the frigidaire without a cup or glass!"

"So!"

"So? You want me to go upside yo' fool head, boy? Don't you back talk me! Hear?"

They stared at each other. Al held the doorway of the kitchen because of the stroke, putting more weight on his right leg. Dwayne began to pout, noticing his grandfather was still wearing pajama trousers only.

"Don't just stand there! Get dressed," he hollered at Al.

"Ain't gon'e be no graduation this morning Baby Al if ya go on with this mess! I'm gettin' old man! I cain't take it," he fired back.

"Pappy," Dwayne whined.

"This my house boy! Hear? It's been my house since nineteen thirty-eight and what I say go!"

Dwayne hissed and looked at the ceiling while Al continued: "Don't you ever let me catch you drinking from that frigidaire without a cup or glass ever again! And don't you ever back talk me no more! Hear? Huh?"

"I'm leaving, Pappy! It's . . . ," Dwayne glanced at the kitchen clock, "It's almost nine-thirty and I gotta get ready to line up! If you ain't coming to see me graduate, then, don't come!"

Young Dwayne stormed past his grandfather leaving the refrigerator open and the juice on top of the washing machine. Al let go of the wall and limped after him. Dwayne gathered his wrapped graduation cap and gown with suit jacket inside his room.

"Baby Al, wait a minute," Al yelled, coming into the hallway. Dwayne unlocked the top and bottom locks and stepped half way out of the apartment turning towards Al as his grandfather approached.

"Grandma Mattie would be at my graduation, if you didn't make her have all them bad headaches that made her die," Dwayne said and gave off a hiss.

Dwayne pulled the door shut and ran non-stop to the first floor. He jumped from the top step in front of the walk-up tenement he'd known all of his life, 128 West 117th Street. He picked up his cap, gown, and suit jacket from the pavement noticing some schoolmates different ages, some with parents some without; and the ones who were also graduating, proudly walked with their caps and gowns; and there were a few turning the corner at Seventh Avenue.

"Hey," he yelled, running off to catch up, "Hey y'all, hold up! Wait up!"

While Dwayne ran up the street to catch up with schoolmates, Al sat back down in anger at his thirty-year dining room table while his grandson's breakfast sat on

other end of the table, stone cold in the fly buzzing June
humidity.

****

CHAPTER 2

*

The balmy school auditorium was crammed with people on both levels, upstairs and downstairs, all balconies filled. Proud parents, relatives and friends waited anxiously for the junior high school graduating class of 1978. Al made it to the graduation by 10:30, hobbling into the crowded hall with his cane. Luckily for him, the ceremony got off to a late start. The spectators fanned themselves and calmly waited for the children, in spite of the tropical conditions. Al made his way down the ramp looking for a place to sit. A younger gentleman offered his end row seat, sliding over into the next seat.

"Thanks, my man. Thank ya for letting me sit down. They say it's room upstairs, but I already gon' walk up five flights when I get out'chere . . . I'm here to see my grandson graduate," Al stated proudly.

The man nodded and patted him on the back as he fell into the chair. Once seated comfortably, Al looked around for Dwayne. He wouldn't be hard to find, being that most youngsters of the day wore Afros, and Dwayne's makeshift Afro was pretty floppy. Finally, the kids were ready. The children beamed with joy after longing for their big day, while their guests gawked and fussed.

"Here they come now!"

"Those some ugly colors!"

"Why I gotta stand up? So many damn 'fros, can't see anyway!"

The graduating class had arrived, the boys proceeding in blue caps and gowns, and the girls flowing in yellowish-gold caps and gowns. Al was seated on the aisle where the boy graduates were marching. He sat while other relatives stood as the children marched in. Al watched them proudly, getting a tear in his eye.

"I sure do wish Gwenny and Mattie was here to see Baby Al walk 'cross that there stage with his diploma. Oh my Mattie . . . She would'a loved to see Baby Al come in here . . . hmmm . . . Some of these kids are pipsqueaks . . . Oh there go Baby Al's West Indian friend . . ."

Al recognized Dwayne's buddy, Patrick Livingston from 120th Street, who lived close to Seventh Avenue in a comfortable brownstone owned by his family. Patrick was light, brown-skinned, a few inches shorter than Dwayne at 5' 4", and quite a bit chunkier. He was born in Jamaica West Indies, but raised in America. Patrick waved at Al, then grinned and waved towards a bunch of people on the other side of the aisle.

"Must be his family," Al thought. Patrick marched erect while his family snapped pictures. "Damn! I forgot the camera; I am getting old," Al chuckled to himself.

The students happily marched, and bopped on to "Pomp & Circumstance" with the processional band. Al was amazed at how beautifully they played the graduation song.

"Hey, Mister Carter," yelled an ecstatic Arthur Boyd, smiling through buck teeth. Al waved back at Arthur. He lived down the block and across the street from Al and Dwayne closer to Lenox Avenue. People on 117th felt the Boyd's were snobs, and Arthur was considered a nerd. His eyeballs almost looked microscopic beneath his black, horn-rimmed, bottle-like spectacles. Arthur was brown-skinned, had a giant Afro, and he was Dwayne's height.

Someone grabbed Al by the shoulder with a firm grip, startling him. It was Dwayne, staring him eye-to-eye. "Thanks," he said, marching on. Al didn't know whether to smile, or laugh, or to still settle the morning's domestic score. Considering the way his grandchild left the apartment and what was said, Dwayne still needed to be talked to. Did he have breakfast at school? How and what did the boy eat anyway? Was he hungry? Too late now, the ceremony had begun, and it was a beautiful ceremony at that. In between snores and head nods, towards the end of the ceremony while the valedictorian read his speech, Al mentally traveled back to June 1961, Central Commercial High School:

"I'd like to thank my mother Misses Mattie Carter and my father Mister Albert Carter for being there, and here, for me through the good times and the . . ."

Al began to enjoy Gwenny reading her valedictorian speech all over again, stunning, smiling, captivating the audience in front of her, and all around him. Mattie ensured their daughter was to look as if she could grace the cover of "Time" or "Life" magazine. Makeup absolutely flawless, nails polished, matching pearl earrings and necklace, not a strand of hair was awry from her pageboy flip. She read the speech with renewed vigor, and looked directly at Al as she spoke, accepting her many awards emphatically. She pointed to her parents as the crowd looked at Al first, and he turned to look at Mattie, who smiled and waved at her daughter.

"Mattie, tha's our baby girl right there," Al proudly said to his male neighbor about his son. "Uh uh, nah Pops, you talking' bout my son up there my brother."

"Your son," Al asked incredulously. The gentleman nodded and replied, "Yeah, my son. He's the valedictorian .

. . I know it's real hot in here brother . . . Maybe you need some water." Gwenny continued her speech, but it was seventeen years later, two different schools, and two different eras.

By 12:20, the graduating ceremony was over. The graduates marched out of the auditorium, out of the school, to the street. Relatives were happy to leave the humid, sweaty auditorium after fanning themselves forever. Outside, proud families mobbed their loved ones, snapping pictures, hugging and kissing.

Dwayne walked out into the mob with his school chum Eric Martinez. Eric, a tiny light-skinned rough guy with high cheekbones, with a medium sized Afro, lived in the Foster Housing Project on Lenox Avenue and 115th Street. He was responsible for loads of graffiti in the stairways of the projects, the surrounding areas, and in school. Dwayne and Eric met the first day of school in their seventh grade homeroom class, admiring each other's aggression. While Dwayne randomly shot spitballs, and threw erasers at different teachers, Eric "tagged" his nickname E-zo and subsequent graffiti with different colored inks all over the classroom walls, especially when called by his full name. He loathed his extended birth name, Guillermo Eric Martinez-Delacruz to the point of refusal, and after a few courageous confrontations with children and adults alike, he still only answered to Eric for adults only, and E-zo for everyone else.

The boys were called by Shawn Young, a tall, wavy-haired, dark-skinned guy with a wide grin from 120th Street, standing in between two girls. He lived on the same block as Patrick, but at the opposite end towards Lenox Avenue.

"Yo, take this flick with me man," yelled Shawn. He pulled Eric into a pose in front of more girls who were taking pictures of a few guys, who joined them.

"Come on, Dwayne man, you too," yelled hyper Eric,

tugging Dwayne into the crowd. Dwayne, Shawn, Eric, and the rest of the guys and girls yelled, "FREE CHEESE!", as the flashbulbs popped.

"Yo, man, you going to G Dubb uptown," Shawn asked Eric, meaning George Washington High School.

"Hell yeah! Gimme a cigarette! Oh yeah, you know Dwayne from my class, right?"

Shawn recognized Dwayne immediately and said, "What's up cool? I used to see you with Pat from my block." He lit a "Kool" cigarette and passed another to Eric. They slapped hands a second time after Dwayne recognized Shawn. "Yeah! You be on 20th and Lenox too. That's right! I seen you."

Eric looked around at the graduate girls, eyeing some of the more mature breasts. He grabbed his crotch stating, "Yo, y'all, I'm getting me some leg after the prom!" He slapped Dwayne and Shawn five a second time.

"That ain't nothing man! Wait 'til we get up in G Dubb! George Washington, it's gon' be what's happening," Shawn added.

"Y'all going to G Dubb? Me too! We all going," Dwayne cheered.

"We gonna be running the show in that joint, Harlem style in Washington Heights," Eric said. They slapped five again, and then the boys began walking around, looking for more pictures to jump in.

Patrick's face brightened when he noticed his friends Dwayne, Shawn from down the block, and little wild Eric from Foster Projects, as he stood with his family. The Livingston family were waiting for a few more of their relatives to finish restroom duties and exit the school, before travelling to lunch with the honoree of the hour, Patrick the graduate. The second Patrick tried to go and mingle with his friends, his mother grabbed him.

"Pahtrick! No."

"Mum, mi wan' . . ."

"NO!"

"Mum. Mi jus' waan' fa' teke pic . . ."

"Mi don' waan' 'ere nut 'in," Dora stated firmly with lips pursed. Her son stood quietly, upset, but used to his mother's antics. Mrs. Livingston was reluctant to socialize with anyone except West Indians, and she with many of her relatives felt their children shouldn't associate with the American born blacks. Patrick's father, Bradley Livingston, a brown-toned stout, proud brick mason didn't enforce the rule, as much as his robust darker skinned wife. A frown came across Bradley's wide face. Bradley's mother, Mrs. Una Livingston, peered through cat glasses with her salt and pepper colored hair done neatly in a bun; with her stern Jamaican lips pursed, she knew her son and aggressive daughter-in-law were set to argue.

"G'wan," Bradley said to his son, real cool.

"Huh?," asked a confused, but happy Patrick.

"G'wan no'w," his father repeated. Patrick, Bradley and Dora's third son and fourth child had done a fine job in academics, and attendance. It was perfectly normal and okay for Patrick to want to have fun with his friends. The moment his father gave the signal, Patrick dashed off after the guys while his parents argued instantly, and "Mummy Una" shook her head and laughed at them. Her daughter in-law had no problem with making a scene when she felt strongly about an issue. She would start the bout by sucking her teeth Caribbean style, which was more like the kissing of teeth, and she would go for the kill.

"**Brahdley**!!! Dem pickny nuh h 'ear mi tell 'im time and time again 'bout dem yenkee!"

"Dora! Ya nuh worry yuh'self maan! Pahtrick h'im reise up y'ere!"

"Look at mi furst pickny, Bradley, ya unnastand? Eh? Nigel and Frahnklin! Eh, Bradley? Dem turn ah t'ief, dem ah run beh'ind dem raas yenkee pickny dem wid dem blaasted cigarette, no'uw dem gaan ah jail!"

"Pahtrick's a different yout'! H'im nuh Frenklin uh Nigel ya' nuh! H'im nuh go far, be'cauwse de pickny dem waan fill 'im belly!"

Patrick caught up with his friends, Dwayne, Shawn, and Eric, and began participating in the camera fun. He was careful not to stray too far from his family, refusing to miss his lunch treat.

Al exited the school building, looking about to congratulate his grandson at the same moment when Patrick scurried off to catch up with the guys, a few feet away.

"Mister Carter, where's Baby Al," Arthur asked the familiar senior.

"Hey, uh Arthur! I'm looking for him too," Al pondered.

"Wanna take a picture with me, Mister Carter," Arthur asked.

"I don't see why not. Take a picture of an old fella," Al chuckled, wiping more sweat from his brow in a matter of seconds. Mr. Boyd snapped the picture, while Mrs. Boyd stood off to the side feigning amusement.

"Now you can show me off to some young 'uns," Al said.

Mr. Boyd removed the camera from his face, chuckling. "I saw your grandson with a bunch of boys, Mister Carter. As a matter of fact, they're standing by those cars over there almost standing on top of them." He pointed across 114th Street to Dwayne, Shawn, Patrick, and Eric amidst a large group of teenagers leaning on several cars. Some of the guys were taking pictures, posing in the street holding up the one-way street traffic, and some of the hip girls joined in:

"CHEESE!"

"Come on y'all, one more, quick quick!"

"I want a picture with Dwayne."

"Come on love."

"Get down! Yo, can you see now? Don't cut our heads off!"

"Yo it's hot as hell y'all! Let's go! Say cheese already, damn!"

"Get down!"

"Okay, alright! **FREE CHEEEEESE!**"

"Yo, look at that old dude with the big J-5 'fro coming cross the way."

Al waited for a car to pass before limping across the street with his cane. He spotted Dwayne when he stepped onto the sidewalk.

"Hey, Dwayne. That's your grandfather, man."

"I know. Let me talk to him. I'll be back."

Al noticed Dwayne walking towards him. Meeting half way, he extended his hand giving the youngster a firm handshake, turned tight embrace. Dwayne grinned, preparing for another of Al's speeches. Al complemented, continuously ranted, and raved about the accomplishments of young people, speaking with the humored benevolence that kept him a well loved and respected figure in his neighborhood of forty years.

"Hot diggity dog! Man oh man! Baby Al, Lawd have mercy boy I am so proud of you, you just don't KNOW!"

Tears welled in Al's eyes as he continued, "I mean . . . look at me, Baby Al. All I've ever been is a cook, a shoeshine boy, shoeshine man. Man, with the education colored folks is getting today, you can do 'bout anything. Just Anything! Just think! Boy oh boy! My grandboy done graduated from the eighth grade going on to high school. Wait 'til I tell Ain't Lou; she sho' is gone be happy!"

Al often referred to his beloved 86-year-old Aunt Louise Esther often, using the term "ain't", instead of "aunt" or "ant". He couldn't wait to get on the telephone to report on his grandson's promotion to high school level. Dwayne's topsy-turvy arrival into Al's world had truly seemed like yesterday. At the speed of the world's rotations, Dwayne would soon be married and he would make Al a great-grandfather over and over again. Al felt his grandson would contribute to New York City's over-population.

Dwayne started to tune his grandfather out, with other things on his mind, like the prom, that was scheduled for one p.m. in the school's gymnasium. He had never seen his female classmates look so good, so grown up and lady like. Dwayne couldn't wait for his prom to start; he didn't care how hot the gymnasium would be. As his clever grandson remained aloof, the happy senior cheered on just the same, talking fast.

"Nah man, I couldn't get no education like this in my day. Nah buddy, take advantage of the education you get. You got to get this thing called education. It's what you need to do! Oh and sorry 'bout this morning, but you cain't drink out the frigidaire like that. You know that right? Ya' hungry?"

Dwayne shook his head. "So, Pappy, you proud of me huh?"

"Heck yeah! Baby Al, you real smart and I know you gon' make it. You gon'e be JUST LIKE Ya Ma . . ." Al stopped himself immediately before saying the word "mama".

"What?," Dwayne questioned, gazing at Al peculiarly, "Like who, Pappy?"

"Whatcha say?"

Al was hiding something. He usually feigned deafness when he had something up his sleeve.

"Damn," Al thought. "He not ready to know about my baby girl today. Not now. I know he ain't . . . Baby Al just ain't ready!"

Dwayne hissed and said, "C'mon, Pappy. You said I'm real smart like somebody. Like who? I'm real smart like who? Why you play deaf all the time? I'm smart like who, Pappy?"

"Like ya relative boy! Don't question me, ya always questioning!"

"What relative? . . . Who?! . . . You?"

That second, the whole crew surrounded Al and Dwayne. Patrick, Eric, and Shawn stopped to join them while the other guys and girls dispersed, their suits and gowns drenched with sweat.

"Later, Dee!"

"See ya at the prom, Dwayne!"

"Later, E! Later, Pat! Later, Shawn!"

"At the prom, man!"

"I'm dancing wit' you, sweet thang!"

"Uh-huh!"

Dwayne watched Al while Patrick spoke, breaking the ice. "I have to go back to my family. They are taking me to lunch. Hello, Mister Carter."

Al extended his hand, shaking Patrick's. "Hello there.

And uh good luck uh . . . Patrick. Congratulations! I was proud of y'all in there. Where's ya folks? I'd like to meet 'em."

Patrick knew his relatives would decline meeting Al because he was an American born black. And they had all assembled across the street, signaling for Patrick to return to the family.

"PAHTRICK!! COUME!! COUME RIGHT NOUW!!!" Mrs. Livingston was absolutely livid. "You'll get to meet them one day, sir," he replied. "Yo, Dwayne, have a good time at the prom."

Dwayne wouldn't answer as Patrick held out his hand for a soul five. Dwayne stared at Al, desperately wanting to know what his grandfather was hiding.

"Baby Al, Patrick talking to you," Al said, attempting to shift the subject.

"Say what!" Eric and Shawn burst into laughter when they heard the old man call their friend "Baby Al".
Eric teased, "Dag! I heard they used to call you Baby Al back in the days!"

"Coming to the prom, ain't'cha," Shawn asked Dwayne. "Cause Pat can't never hang out, even on our block! They gonna whoop your tail Pat if you don't get back across 14th. Your mama gonna knock you across town!" Shawn and Patrick quickly slap boxed for two seconds. Then Patrick crossed 114th Street back to his family who were heading towards Seventh Avenue.

Shawn repeated, "Dwayne you coming to the prom man, right?"

Al answered Shawn, "Yeah he is! Baby Al, I'm gon' on back round the corner, you go now to the prom. As a matter of fact . . ." Al extended his right arm, "Gimme that jacket and vest. It's going up to ninety today they say, maybe even a hundred. I don't want you to get too hot, and I don't want'cha to lose it. Give it to me."

Dwayne slowly took off his vest and handed the jacket

he had been carrying to his grandfather, staring at Al. He knew Al was covering up something, but what? It was something about him, Dwayne. But what could it be?

"You stay on wit'cha friends and have a good time. Just be on 17th Street 'fore it get dark, Baby Al. Okay?," Al winked proudly at his grandson. "Have fun, Baby Al. I love ya and I'm very proud of ya. All y'all keep up the good work. Hear?"

The other boys nodded while Al gave Dwayne a second tight hug. With his grandson's outer garments on his arm, cane in the other grasp, Al proceeded home.

Suddenly, it was prom time! Musical beats saturated the humid airwaves in front of the school. Rick James' guitar chords meshed with the octaves of his background singers, and the scrumptious intro to "You And I" was heard clear from Seventh to Eighth Avenues, and the last one on the dance floor was a rotten egg! Dwayne entered the school with his two friends Eric Martinez and Shawn Young. He was determined to dance, even though his mind was plagued with Al's secret.

By dusk that evening Al, totally immersed inside of the hypnotic commentating of 1010 WINS, fell into a deep nap on the couch, forgetting about the morning's rocky start; and Dwayne after hanging out at the prom and playing with friends in the park, had totally forgotten about his grandfather's secrecy. The rest of their summer was uneventful, just repetitious routines. There was church on Sunday, with occasional Sunday dinners at church so Al could relax and stay out of the kitchen. Then, Mondays through Fridays getting the numbers in on time, playing checkers in the park on Saint Nicholas, and hoping that Dwayne would tend to new implemented household chores, his own cooking, his own laundry, his own dishes. The nightly menus became less and less flavorful, and more and more bland, as Al visited his private physician Dr.

Wallace, with added therapy sessions. Friday night remained fish night, and restless Dwayne would stay up watching the living room TV later and later, and hang outside all day, claiming to go to the park to play basketball with his friends on weekends.

To curtail the worries of Dwayne's early stages of being a teenager, Arlene took Dwayne to the Bronx for three weeks with strict instructions from Al to keep the past to herself. Once her tenure was over, Jimmy Robinson observed his godson, taking him to The Robinson's carefully structured household in Brooklyn for the latter part of July with three weeks during August, even helping out with new school supplies and clothing for Dwayne the high school freshman. And by autumn, the next season, Dwayne sprouted a few inches. He was doing fairly well as a freshman in George Washington High School with a B average, with added weekly checks and lectures from Jimmy over the phone. Through the holidays into the new year, Dwayne suddenly believed and knew he was a man; and by that next spring, Al knew that Dwayne was becoming a young man, just by the bed sheets needing to be changed nearly four times a week, and with magazines like "Players" and "Playboy" being found in weird places like the dirty clothes hamper, or under the sofa cushions. Dwayne may have felt he was becoming a man, however still through the eyes of Al, Dwayne was still a brand new teenager, under Al's care and guidance, and he still must abide by the rules and regulations of The Carter household, or the loved ones Al trusted him with, either of his godparents.

The days following the transitions of his loved ones had never been easy for Al, but they were long gone in the past; and as the present days, doubled, tripled, with the years flying by, the movement in secret wore on Al's pact beyond prayer, and his dedicated reliance to the memory of Mattie and Gwenny's presence would crystallize the direction of Al's future rotations of time. Storms loomed on the domestic horizon with the clash of veteran machismo versus blooming, crisp masculinity. Like a strong wind giving indication of the imminent, jolting electrical downpour of rain, Al felt his thunderstorm beginning to take place, take shape after being spiritually forewarned.

One summer afternoon, Al was relaxing on the bed listening to gospel music on a new digital clock radio Arlene gave him for a present the previous Christmas. A strong wind swallowed the background routine noise of the streets, and a family of blackened clouds quickly and methodically swamped the skyline. Al turned over and sat on the edge of his bed and buried his face in his hands, when the heavy raindrops suddenly beat against the windowpane and drenched his window screens.

"Heaven done opened up," he thought. He stood and dragged to the left window that was connected to the fire escape, closing that one first after removing the screen. Then he went to the right bedroom window, removed the screen and continued thinking, "Wonder where that boy at in this here storm . . . When I need 'im, he ain't nowhere around . . . he could be here helping me close up all these windows in this house . . . Maybe he at that West Indian boy house I reckon . . . He say he was going to the store wit''im . . . Lawd this place fixin' to be flooded!"

The right window resisted Al as he closed it after he pulled the plug on the gospel broadcast. The warm raindrops wet Al's face and chest until he finally got the window shut, understanding its resistance, after being worn by the test of time, as he was beginning to be. He moved into the bathroom and toweled himself off after closing the resisting bathroom window, while the hovering black cloud outside continued to drench his windows, the entire building, and the rest of the "tri-state area", with classic thundering and lightning effects, raining cats and dogs. He shut off the remaining items of electric in the apartment, recalling the electrical storms of his Arkansas youth.

Once he returned to the bedroom he limped straight to his bedroom closet. Pushing aside the long, exotic beads that hung in the place of a door, Al carefully, tediously, removed a large dark green pine trunk from the bottom on the floor. Catching his breath he thought, "I'm getting old man . . . this thang just getting heavier and heavier . . . But I'm a peek at 'em all . . . Better be quick while Baby Al outdoors . . . hope he got enough sense to stay out that rain, don't need him catching cold . . . Let me get to Mattie and the baby," Al thought. The thunderstorm began to taper off into a drizzle against the washed windowpane, with the evening sun trying its best to shine with the approaching time of dusk.

"I'm coming y'all . . . I know y'all waiting on me . . . I miss y'all so much, I'm coming!"

Excitedly patting his pockets with senility beginning to set in, Al pondered the location of his trunk key. "Now where's that daggone key?," he thought. He checked every bureau drawer until he found a ring of keys inside the bottom. Relieved, he painfully crouched, and unlocked the trunk, pushing its top back, to fully open it. That second, someone started kicking the apartment door. "PAPPY! . . . PAPPY!"

Al stuffed the keys in his front pocket, quickly pushed the trunk back into the closet, closing its top and relocking it.

"Pappy! Pappy," Dwayne yelled, continuing to kick at the apartment door infuriating Al. He moved from his bedroom one drag-limp step to unlock and open the door.

His grandson burst into the apartment with glistening raindrops dripping from his slick cornrowed braids, soaking wet from the afternoon's rain. Dwayne headed straight for his bedroom.

"HEY," Al yelled in the nature of an irate drill sergeant. Dwayne froze, in step, with his back turned. Closing the apartment door and engaging the locks Al spat, "What the devil's the matter with you Baby Al?!"

"Nothing . . . I'm wet."

Dwayne turned around and walked slowly up to Al, staring him face to face, nearly eye to eye. At age 68, Al remained five feet ten inches tall, while Dwayne at 14 stood at five nine and a half. His voice was shuffling up and down as well, caught in the crossroads of puberty and adolescent change.

"If nothing ain't wrong, don't kick on the door, hear? You can knock! Why didn't ya call upstairs from out front and let me throw down the key to ya, like you supposed to do?!"

"The front was open, and I'm old enough to have my own keys."

"When I say you get keys, you get keys boy!"

Al, angry in his own right, refused to take any mess whatsoever from his grandson. Things were changing rapidly, and Dwayne challenged Al's authority left and right as much as possible. The boy was hardheaded and spoiled, thanks to his wife, and Al refused to stand for it. He felt the urge to give the fresh teen the spanking he needed.

"You keep up that squawkin' smart aleck back talk Baby Al, and I'm a tear a hole in yo' behind nobody'll sew up! . . . Where's ya manners Baby Al? Huh?! . . . Where's ya' respect boy?! . . . Me and Grandma Mattie raised you better than that! . . . Baby Al you hear me?!"

Dwayne hissed at the sound of his grandmother's name with tears coming to his eyes. He bolted into his room and slammed the door shut. Apartment # 53 was infinitely reminiscent of Mattie's presence, missed continually by her living husband and grandchild, and Al realized he had mistakenly hit a nerve by blurting her name, a derailed groove for Dwayne, a popped chord for himself.

He ceased his fussing with a somber thought, "I suppose I ain't the only one that thinks uh Mattie 'round here."

Al stood in the darkened hallway in front of Dwayne's door, wanting to knock desperately to remind the teenager that the grandmother who loved him dearly had never left, and that Mattie was always present; yet Al still felt he needed to desperately retain control and authority inside his household, a household inhabited by an inner city teenage boy who needed truth more and more each day.

Overhearing his grandson's crying sniffles through the door started to cut deep, little by little. Al's head bowed lower and lower, with a stubborn sadness as the evening's new storm wore on and on, and into the night.

****

CHAPTER 3

*

A few nights later on a moonlit rooftop behind the chimney, pulling up his shorts, zipping up his zipper, Dwayne hissed, smiling, having victoriously lost his virginity. After attempting sex with different girls who were afraid or simply refused, finally, he got some. Next to him, pulling up her jeans, fastening her bra, and straightening her blouse was a semi-elated 14-year-old girl named Nadine. The fair-skinned girl lived catty-cornered from Dwayne's building across the street. She badly wanted to be with him for close to a year, choosing the rooftop of the tenement next door for their sexual tryst.

"I gotta hurry up back downstairs," Nadine said. "Me and Brina gotta be in before eleven." He walked towards the roof door, ignoring the young girl as she dressed. "Baby Al! Why you ain't talking to me? Didn't you like it?"

"Course," replied a cool Dwayne, winking at her, kneeling to tie his Pro-Keds". He said, "Just walk across to your roof while I climb down here. I'm' a act like I'm coming from Lamont's house so nobody will know. We gon' do it again tomorrow, same time. Bye!"

Dwayne climbed down the ladder and disappeared, leaving her on the roof. She stood and walked slowly over the dividing partition to the roof of her building. She was confused, in love, hurt, and mixed up, all in one emotion. A small gust of wind added cool relief to the humid summer night as young Nadine plunged into deep thought. She would never catch up with her promiscuous 16-year-old sister Sabrina, but her virginity was finally lost. It was lost to her knight in shining armor, her Romeo, her Prince Charming. Nadine thought about having more sex with "Baby Al" all summer, and she was purely happy about it.

Meanwhile downstairs, he emerged from the building, giving evening greetings to the block hangers on, a few dice players, and a few girls sitting on different stoops. Someone had a radio going, blasting Sister Sledge's "HE'S THE GREATEST DANCER." Down the block towards Lenox under the streetlights, nightly card games were going. At the other end near Seventh, Denny and his basketball crew had their game going, shooting baskets with a makeshift hoop made from a milk crate nailed to a streetlamp. Whiting, red snapper, and porgies were frying, beans and neck bones were stirred, and cornbread was baked, swirling with melted butter, from tenement to tenement. Reggie Jackson slammed another of many home runs clear from Yankee Stadium, via a.m. radio. It was just another summer night in the city, in the hood.

Dwayne darted across the street and into his building, running all the way to the fifth floor. He reached the top, banged on the door of the apartment. One minute passed before Al opened the door. Dwayne walked inside and headed straight into the bathroom, closing the door. He pulled down his shorts and underwear to look at his penis. He had heard from some of the older guys that you should wash immediately after having sex, supposedly cutting down the germs. Reaching for a clean washcloth, Dwayne ran the hot water while he stared down at his semi-erect phallus.

"I can't believe it . . . I can't believe it! I finally got some leg, I got me some pussy," he happily thought. He scrubbed himself with the washcloth, checking himself thoroughly, ensuring to get all the excess fluids from his tip.

Al banged on the bathroom door hard, startling him while he happily washed his john.

"WHAT?!!"

"Baby Al! I wanna talk to you!"

"Huh?!"

Al opened the door as Dwayne put his penis away in time.

"Baby Al."

"Can't you wait a minute, Pappy?!"

"Where you been?"

"Outside!"

"No you won't . . . not in front of this building you was not. I told you to stay in front the building right downstairs, OUTSIDE! . . . And I say for ya to stay clear a them fast gals in that there court 'round the corner! When I say sit on the steps downstairs I do mean staying on seventeenth street, like YOU chose not to do!"

"I was on Seventeenth Street!"

"Not in front!"

"So what! I wasn't on the stoop! Send me to the electric chair," Dwayne exclaimed and dropped his used washcloth into the dirty clothes hamper. He proceeded to exit the bathroom and was blocked by Al, standing in the middle of the doorway.

"Excuse me."

"Why can't you obey me, Baby Al?!"

"Excuse me!"

Al refused to move, while the pugnacious teen squeezed his way around his stubborn grandfather.

"Good-night," Dwayne yelled in syllables, hissed and slammed his room door once again.

Later that summer, Dwayne became more curious about his parentage. Who were his parents? Where were they? How are they? Al's not his father, so is he adopted? Are my parents nice people? At age 14, he remained determined for the truth.

Al on the other hand, mentally debated each day in the summer's heat. Should he or shouldn't he tell Baby Al the truth? He was hesitant to tell his grandson the chain of events surrounding his birth for many years. If he told him the story, how should he do it? The truth was something his grandson needed to know. Perhaps knowing the truth would make their relationship better, if Dwayne understood his importance.

Al decided to confide in Jimmy Robinson, his younger cooking protégé. Jimmy took tips from Al for years when the aspiring cook first started his career. Al was there for him and now it was time for Jimmy to return the favor. Jimmy was Dwayne's godfather and who knows, maybe he would know what to do, having an older son and growing children himself. At the age of 43, he surely moved on to bigger and better things in the cooking business. He opened a string of fast food restaurants in the New York metropolitan area called "HAMBURGER HEADQUARTERS" recently, and he moved his wife and four children from a modest brownstone in Brooklyn to a giant nine-room mansion in upstate New York, complete with a built in swimming pool. Still a devoted family man, Jimmy's older children were in the service and college. His younger children were doing well in school. He was the perfect success story from the ghetto, and his mentor Al needed him more than ever.

Al dialed Jimmy's number inside the kitchen. The line started ringing while he chuckled, "Old' Slick . . . Heh! Heh! Heh."

"Slick" was Jimmy's personal nickname for Al because of his grill skills. He even set the trend of calling Al Slick on the job until he was fired on April 4th, 1968, the day Dr. Martin Luther King Jr. was assassinated.

Al reminisced while waiting for Jimmy to answer the line:

"Arlene's my godmother still?"

"Yep."

"She's always talking about that lady Gwenny. You and Grandma Mattie always used to argue over Gwenny. Arlene's always talking about her."

"Baby Al, don't you listen to nobody when they talk about Gwenny. Hear?"

"Pappy, is Gwenny my mother? Is it true that Gwenny might be my mother?"

"It's not true."

"Robinson's residence," answered 7-year-old Edward. Al grinned at the sound of the bright youngster.

"Hey little Eddie . . . This Slick . . . Ya daddy in? Cause if he is I need to talk to him."

"Hold on Mister Slick . . . DADDY!"

Seconds later, Jimmy picked up his line in the basement.

"Yeah?"

"Bruh . . . It's Slick."

"What's jumping, Slick? How you doing man? I ain't hear nothing from ya in a while."

"Hey I'm on even keel. I need to talk to you."

"Shoot! Go right ahead, what's up?"

"It's about my grandson . . . Jimmy, I want to tell Baby Al what happened. I want to come clean. He old enough to know the truth about his mama, but I don't know how to tell him."

Jimmy knew there was trouble once his godson was mentioned. Dwayne was easier to deal with as a pre-teen, but that was changing. Since moving upstate, Jimmy was in less touch with his mentor, especially while handling the growth of "HHQ", his own family, and new life upstate. He would always be close to "Slick & Baby Al", but things were slightly different now with his expansions. Since the change, Al usually called on holidays or occasions, but never with problems. Telling Dwayne the truth about his background had to be troubling him.

He paused and said, "Slick, you should'a been told him. I thought you said something by now; it might kill him. You should'a broke it to him when Miss Mattie passed."

"I know, I know. That's why I called ya man. How can I break it to him," Al asked sadly.

"Slick man, I truly wish I could help you on this one. I say you sleep on it. First ask God to guide you in the right direction, sleep on it and tell the boy the deal."

"He up to something, cause he keep trying to get in my private chest."

"What chest?"

"It's my chest I bring home from the war . . . Been had it since the forties . . . and I keeps it in the bottom of my closet. I keeps everything in it . . . All my daughter's pictures . . . I got pictures of my mama, and my sisters in there . . . my Mattie Mae in there . . . I keeps everything in there . . . I know Baby Al been sneaking around my room at night trying to find the key . . . I keeps it locked up."

Jimmy became concerned, noticing a sudden change in his attitude. No longer was Al the mentor that he knew. He sounded fickle, unsure; afraid of something or someone. He tried to cover up the insecurity in his voice, but Jimmy knew the real Al Carter.

Jimmy said, "Slick man, tell him. Tell Baby Al."

"But how he gon'e handle it, Jimmy? I wanna tell him everything. About the Mucci boy . . . about them riots . . . what they did to my Gewnny in that school . . . about the,

the, murder of my Gwenny . . ."

"Murder?! Slick? What's that all about, for crying out loud? Who's the Mucci boy?"

"Damn man. See, you don't know either," Al stated impatiently.

He explained his domestic skeletons quickly to his protégé, from beginning to end.

He verbally untangled Gwenny's pregnancy, the way Arnold Mucci plotted to have sex with a Negro and once it happened, all of his frat brothers could too. No matter how long the plan would take, maybe years, but it must be carried out. He spoke of warning Gwenny and trying to accept her love for this Italian boy, who claimed he loved her. She wanted to lose her virginity to him. It eventually killed her on many levels.

Jimmy was amazed with the stories, barely recalling the past events linked with his godson's birth. Al also explained the subsequent college race riots in Ohio when the Voting Rights Act Bill was passed and how Arnold Mucci's throat was slashed. In the case of Dwayne's paternal relatives, Al knew of no real way of finding their whereabouts. His grandson had no family, but him, and what was left of Al's disappearing, estranged family in Michigan. Since Mattie was gone, her relatives hardly ever called. Gwenny died giving birth to him. Mattie died when he was nine. His father was dead. Therefore, Dwayne had no real family except for Al.

"How he gon'e handle it Jimmy? I think I'm'a wait 'til the boy is eighteen or twenty-one," Al said. In his mind, he felt his grandson couldn't handle the truth until he was an older teen, better yet a grown man.

"Slick, that's ridiculous. He should know the truth as soon as possible! Look man, I can help. I'm Baby Al's godfather, you want me to tell him?"

"It's my mess man. I think I'll handle it."

"Stop blaming yourself, Slick. It ain't your mess. I hate when you do that! It's not your fault how everything went down."

"I'll handle it. I'll just handle it."

"Slick, man, if you need my help just say it man! You were always there for me man! Always! If you need me let me know!"

Al nodded and hung up his phone line. He dragged through the living room and down the hall to his bedroom. He layed down on his bed, propped up his feet, and hoped that after his nap he would have the answers to his problems.

Meanwhile, one tenement over next door, in a top floor apartment, Dwayne had 15 year-old Annette Wilkinson bent over giving her what she asked for. Dwayne was learning how to give it to girls, nice and hard, just because they asked for sex that way. Coincidentally earlier that afternoon, no one was home at the Wilkinson's, so frisky Annette decided to invite Dwayne upstairs "to get his hair braided". She also wanted her ex-elementary schoolmate for an afternoon romp in the sack.

Annette was on her stomach bent over the side of her mother's bed, with her head squashed into her mother's pillows the first round; and then she was bent over the window sill for the second round, needing it not too hard for three reasons: One, she just had to have more, and it hurt the first time; two, she didn't want to fall five flights head first down below to 117th Street; and three, to keep a lookout for returning relatives.

When Dwayne finished his second doggy style deed about twenty minutes later, he found himself running to the roof to dodge some of Annette's older brothers and sisters who were on their way home, walking up the street.

Pigeons scattered as he blazed through their nest, running straight across the rooftop to his building. Dwayne climbed down the ladder into the hallway, and Barbara Nelson was standing right there, in front of Apt. #51, watching Dwayne's each balancing grab of descent onto the ladder, until he was standing physically level on the fifth floor to deal with her face to face.

Barbara, a tiny brown-skinned woman larger and louder than life, yet only 5'2" at 110 pounds was in her late fifties. She resided in Apt. #52, down the hallway, on the same side as Al and Dwayne, right next door. She was in her position, tapping her foot, lips pursed in usual form. With her eyebrows arched suspiciously, wearing her favorite aqua blue clip-on earrings and platinum blonde curly Afro wig, she awaited her neighbor's grandson to speak another lie, just to let him have a piece of her mind, because she always felt justified to do this. While some of the neighbors described her as the nosiest, living woman dis-gracing planet earth, and the biggest troublemaker on 117th Street, she just happened to know Al and Dwayne's total family history, and claimed to know the history of everyone in Harlem, since the 1940's.

Barbara met Albert Carter the summer of 1941 when Al asked her for an "autograph" and a date after she performed a jazz set in a bar and grill near the Cotton Club in which she turned him down. Not knowing Al was ten years her senior, Barbara refused to date 'a country Negro shoeshine boy with no future 'cept shining them ofay's shoes downtown in Penn Station' she would say. She would eventually have to face Al again, once the shoeshine boy began dating her roommate Mattie Mae Brown the dancer by coincidence, after Al met Mattie one Sunday leaving a church service.

Barbara and Mattie met on their way to New York from South in the Negro car on the railroad; Barbara mistook Mattie for Katherine Dunham. Mattie ironically, was heading to New York City to become a "dancing girl at the Cotton Club" after being told she resembled Katherine Dunham several times; and Barbara wanted to get to Harlem to become a singer. The two women became fast friends, bonding with artistic conversation, and the women eventually became roommates in Harlem, hoping their future would come to fruition in the "Black Mecca", land of opportunity.

"Did you lock the roof properly, Baby Al?"

"Of course," said Dwayne, walking away from her down the hallway towards Apt. # 53.

"Whatcha doing coming in thatta way? One-twenty-eight's got a front door! Only muggers and thieves drop through a roof!"

"Guess I'm a mugger and a thief," he snapped sarcastically, banging on the door.

"Look at me, Baby Al, when I talk to you! Don't you keep yo' back turned to me Baby Al! You ain't got no respect for ya granddaddy but you sho' is gonna have it for Barbara Nelson, honey!"

She usually said her wordy speeches only getting time to breathe when she waited on her opponent's response. While Barbara yelled at Dwayne, Al, awakened by their voices, snatched the door open.

"Barbara Nelson?!! What the hell you harassing my grandboy for?!"

"He ain't got no damn respect, Al Carter, whatsoever! What he doing comin' in through the roof?!"

"Is that any of yo' damn business?"

"You damn right, Al Carter! Everybody's business is my business!"

Dwayne chuckled to himself. "Excuse me, I gotta get to the bathroom," he said trying to get past Al who blocked the doorway.

"Wait a minute," Al stopped him. "Did you just come through the roof?"

He looked at Al, then back to Barbara and grinned. "No, Pappy . . . I was just coming from downstairs in front of the building."

"You damn little red liar!"

"Don't you curse at my grandboy! Hear?!"
"I'll curse at yo' fool behind! ALBERT CARTER!"

Dwayne went to his bedroom, fell on his bed and laughed his head off while Al and Barbara argued in the hallway close to fifteen minutes. Listening to Barbara fuss was familiar to everyone who knew her or lived in the building for the last few decades.

By the time he reached his fifteenth birthday, Dwayne grew past five foot eleven inches, smoked cigarettes, drank beer, and loved having sex. Annette from next door and Nadine from across the street had stopped being friends over a can of hairspray, the perfect news for his ears; he divided his body between the two girls. He had been suspended from school twice, once for fighting a teacher, and once for fighting a student. He spent his days cutting classes, running from the truancy police with his boys Patrick, Eric, and Shawn. They frequented hooky parties everywhere, meeting girls from other high schools, riding the subway all over New York City. Sometimes the guys drank beer in the morning before their first period class, becoming nice and tipsy before 10 a.m., leaving school before the afternoon. Patrick barely passed to the tenth grade, while Dwayne, Shawn, and Eric were held back in the ninth, with major classes to make up.

The summers were spent doing the usual. During the daytime, there were open fire hydrants for many city dwellers who loved running through the spray to escape the heat; there was b-ball, house parties, fistfights, girls, girls and more girls. Stickball and plenty of bike riding in and around Central Park with lots of "pop-o-wheelies" and racing; if you didn't own the hottest bicycle, you stole the hottest bicycle. MFSB's "Love Is The Message" was the melodic message in the air, and a whole lot of sounds of "Funkadelic". Hip-hop music solidified itself in the communities and laid its foundation, spawning great artists as The Sugarhill Gang, Spoonie Gee, Kurtis Blow, with groups like Grandmaster Flash & The Furious Five destined to take the art form to higher levels, and the boys loved every bit of it. Movies here and there, summer youth jobs, Rucker games across from the Polo Grounds, and the Battle Grounds block jams uptown were a must. The four teens did everything in their power to make every block or house party in the area.

Patrick usually missed out because of his very strict family. Hailing from the tropical island of Jamaica, he was the middle child of seven children. His parents, Bradley and Dora Chambers Livingston, migrated to the United States in search of greener pastures in the early 1970's. Upon arrival, Bradley took factory work until he was terminated for challenging his Caucasian boss; and shortly thereafter he found work in the construction business; and he sought his green card, sending for his wife back home. Once Dora arrived in the United States with her visa, she continued her practice of nursing, like in their native country. While Mr. & Mrs. Livingston made money in the U.S., their children remained in Jamaica, parish of Manchester, town of Mandeville.

Eventually, all of the Livingston family would move to the largest and most populated city in America, New York City. Patrick, then seven, was excited by all the strange, tall buildings as opposed to banana trees, sea breeze, and simple, island life. Patrick's older siblings Nigel, Franklin, and Hyacinth fought in school every day. They were often taunted by the American born children because they didn't dress hip, or their colors never matched; and especially, because of their Jamaican accent. They were told by many people of their own skin color to go back to their own country, and they were called "monkeys" or "coconuts".

Mr. & Mrs. Livingston couldn't believe how rude, cruel, and standoffish the black Americans were. With the

West Indian population increasing in New York City, the Livingston family decided to associate with their own kind. They refused to deal with the 'de Yenkee people dem', loathing American born blacks. Practically raised in Manhattan and learning how to fight physically for acceptance and stand up for his rights, Patrick started to enjoy his time with the American kids, who stopped bullying him. His parents were mystified by his behavioral change, scolding him for not being true to his "West Indian heritage". They expected the "Americanized Behavior" from their younger children Andrew, Rose, and Sharon who were born in the United States. Patrick and the older boys were beginning to be known as troublemakers at home.

Al slowly ascended to the top floor, virtually exhausted from the activities of his day. There was the early morning haircut and shave, to making sure "his numbers were in" for the day on time; then there was the doctor's appointment up on Convent Avenue and 145th, complete with routine EKG's, X-ray's, and blood work. Then, it was downtown on the subway to the bank, and, to check on and pay more money to his insurance policies that would take care of his grandson the moment he passed away. Then it was back uptown on the subway to the elementary school down the block to vote Democrat; and then, it was finally time for some food shopping. After coming from the "Associated" supermarket around the corner, and after all of the business of running up, down, and around town, Al was still anxious to get home, even contemplating an evening cup of coffee. It was election night, and he wanted to see if President Carter would make a second term, hoping that his vote would count. The five-floor climb that kept him physically fit during his younger days was becoming harder for the aging man. Al was now 70 years old. Like most aging people, he was experiencing aches and pains all over his body. Still a fighter, yet in subconscious denial, he continued on with bag full of groceries, cane, and all.

"Baby Al should be here to help me, all this stuff is what he likes," he thought passing the fourth floor. "All these daggone Twinkies, and cupcakes, and potato chips, all this foolishness, and I gotta carry it. I damn near cain't walk."

It took him eleven minutes to make it to the fifth floor, a task that used to take two minutes upon his return home from the war, to take care of his wife and one-year old daughter in 1945. He reached the top floor, looking down to the mid-landing, striving to catch his breath with pride. He wished he could run up and down the stairs forever, the impossible.

He came into the apartment, flicking on the hallway light. Turning left, he made his way to the living room. Sitting the bag of groceries on the table, he fell onto the couch back first, relieved to be indoors out of the chill of the November evening, his cane falling to the floor. Staring across the room at the wall unit filled with pictures, his vision blurred. He exhaled, leaned over and picked up his cane, then raised up off the couch. He shuffled across the living room to turn on the tiny TV, removing his autumn jacket. The nebulous black and white picture began to roll, manifesting itself. The broken volume button was turned as high as it went. He picked up the overrun grocery bags one by one and went into the kitchen, barely hearing the poll results.

"Time for a new TV," he thought, putting the groceries away. Once he finished, he returned to watch the elections. Al shook his head watching Independent running John Anderson and President Jimmy Carter get slaughtered by Republican running Ronald Reagan. Fighting sleep, he looked at his watch.

Al thought, "He been coming in late every night . . . I wonder where he be . . . Any second now, he gon' bang on that door."

He peeped at his watch a second time, cognizant of the six p.m. curfew he gave Dwayne.

"Yup . . . Ten after . . . Any second now, he gon' bang on that door."

A minute later, a dead silence then: BAM! BAM! BAM!

Al limped to the apartment door and opened it. Dwayne pushed his way inside, and headed straight for the bathroom and shoved the door. The way Dwayne pushed past Al nearly knocking the senior over, Al knew something was wrong. He dragged in front of the bathroom and peeked inside.

Dwayne's head was buried inside the toilet. He had been out in the Foster Projects staircase tagging graffiti, smoking joints, drinking shots of hard liquor with Eric, and became sick. He looked a mess with half of his head cornrowed and the rest of his hair out and in a frizzy frenzy.

Al entered into the small bathroom to comfort his inebriated grandson.

"Baby Al, what the devil's the matter son? Ya sick?" He touched his shoulder and Dwayne pushed his arm back away without looking, continuing to throw up, face still hidden in the toilet.

Al went to help him again. "Ya sick, Baby Al?"

He shoved his grandfather's arm the second time, turning to look up.

"What the fuck you think?! Huh?! What it look like," Dwayne yelled with fiery, red eyes crossing, proceeding to throw up again. He stuffed his head back into the toilet bowl.

"This boy really gettin' to be too much. We really gon' be fightin' 'round here," Al thought. He decided to try another method.

"Look, Baby Al, I only want to help ya. I love ya son, and you important to me. You okay?"

Dwayne stood up swaying, stumbling from the bathroom leaving vomit all over the outside of the commode. One look at him proved he had drank himself into pure oblivion. He hissed at Al and staggered a few footsteps to his room while bouncing from wall to wall to preserve balance. Feeling for his room door then finding it, Dwayne disappeared inside.

Al creeped to Dwayne's room to look at him. Dwayne was stretched across his bed, snoring within seconds, lying on his stomach.

"Damn," Al thought, "What the hell he doing drinking like that? . . . Smelling like a daggone chimney . . . and a no good polecat . . . I'm'a deal with him in the morning . . . He ain't gon' wan' get up . . . I got a newsflash for 'im; he gettin' out'chere in the morning to get to the school house . . . Drunk or not!"

He returned to the living room and shut off the TV.

"Looks like we got a new president . . . Ol' good ol' Ronald Reagan . . . Seen one of them ol' talkies he played in last week."

He chuckled and hobbled back down the hall. In his hand he had Dwayne's new set of house keys, letting down his guard and hoping that Dwayne was finally ready for the responsibility. He wanted to award his grandson with the keys despite the boy being drunk.

"Besides, the kid is gon' be sixteen."

He crept into Dwayne's room, and slipped the keys onto his homework desk. Al looked down on the grandson he loved. Dwayne dampened his once crispy white pillowcase with a ring of more vomit. Mouth wide open while snoring, he kept his hand in his pants.

Al shook his head, exiting the room quietly. He gently closed Dwayne's bedroom door and resumed his nightly duties.

****

CHAPTER 4

*

One overcast afternoon at 2:30 after school, on the corner of 190th and Audubon, the brawl of the century was going on, and Dwayne, Patrick, Shawn, Eric, and Arthur found themselves smack in the center of the melee. Earlier that week in gym class, Patrick had an argument with a boy, a junior, who ironically was from the same Harlem neighborhood named Marvin Peterson. Marvin and Patrick argued over a basketball call when Marvin called Patrick a "fakin' Jamaican". Patrick then hit Marvin in the face with the basketball, giving him a bloody, swollen lip. Marvin vowed vengeance the moment Patrick returned from his three day suspension.

The scuffle, surrounded by a crowd of "oooohing and aaaahing" teenagers, moved out into the middle of Audubon Avenue blocking the horn blowing traffic. Patrick was getting the best of Marvin, bloodying his nose and unhealed swollen mouth. His ultimate goal was to put Marvin into the nursing home they started fighting in front of. Once Martin Peterson found his identical twin getting beat up, he jumped to his brother's defense. Geeky Arthur Boyd, who was walking with Patrick after their senior meeting in school saw Martin spring from behind a parked car attempting to help his brother. Dropping his books to join in, Arthur's glasses were immediately knocked from his face by Martin. The twins' friend, Omar, also jumped in, kicking Arthur in the stomach, and Arthur was knocked to the ground.

Patrick took on the twins, slamming one to the pavement while capturing the other in a headlock, after he swung at Patrick and missed his connecting punch. Omar jumped on top of Patrick, straddling him, trying to knock wild Patrick off his friend who was choking inside of Patrick's locked bicep, while being punched in the head by Patrick's free fist. Marvin re-entered the scuffle as did Arthur. Marvin punched Arthur in the face before he could get to Omar. After punching Arthur then kicking him in the back, Marvin helped Omar get Patrick off of Martin who was starting to get beat up pretty bad while choking in the headlock.

Suddenly, Omar and Marvin were getting the best of Patrick. Some of the school security officers were out and about trying to restore order; and while Patrick went to quickly check Arthur, Omar dropkicked him while his back was turned. After knocking him to the ground, Martin who had recovered, Marvin, and Omar began to beat on Patrick. Arthur took another swing at one of the twins and missed; Omar snuffed him again.

Coincidentally, after skipping school all day and skillfully ditching the truancy police, Dwayne, Shawn, and Eric were in a Spanish bodega purchasing hero sandwiches near the school when they noticed the crowd.

"Oh shit! That's Pat," Dwayne yelled, running out the store, followed by Shawn cracking his knuckles, with Eric quickly following, going to their best friend's aid.

Dwayne took on Omar, swinging his iron name belt in his opponent's direction. The name buckle was spray painted gold, and Dwayne's name was spelled neatly in the center, until the swinging buckle connected with Omar's left ear. The letters D-W-A-Y-N-E scattered about, and Omar went down to the ground, while Dwayne finished him off. Shawn fought Martin, bobbing and weaving, and punching with connecting left and right hooks, and one swift kick to the kneecaps of his opponent; and Eric finished off Marvin, wrestler style, while stunned Patrick recuperated on the sidewalk in the crowd. Police sirens filled the airwaves as the brawl concluded just in time. Omar and the twins were demolished. A few girls helped Arthur find his broken glasses and wiped his bloody mouth while Dwayne, Shawn, and Eric checked their boon Patrick, ensuring his well-being.

After purchasing a quart of beer, they headed towards the train station laughing about the fight, teasing Arthur because he was beaten up, yet praised his courageous participation while he continued spitting blood. The crew planned the rest of the afternoon.

For some, the afternoon would be filled with babysitting, house chores, tagging graffiti, studying for final exams, and homework. For some, the afternoon would be filled with more quarts of beer, liquor perhaps, and maybe some good ol' smoke. For some, the afternoon would be a combination of both.

They slapped five repeatedly, yelling obscenities to the passing young women and other people. With caps to the back and hats cocked to the side, grinning faces with cuts and bruises, bloodstained hands, ripped clothes, and backpacks filled with schoolbooks, the charismatic boys caught the subway instead of their usual afterschool bus ride and headed for Harlem.

Al stared in the barber shop mirror, admiring his new look. He said to his barber, "Well Bruh Harten, I used to be the Jackson Five grandfather. Guess I'm Mister Clean now."

Billy Harten laughed, "Damn Carter, you still got somethin' crazy to say after all these years."

"Oh yeah!"

Al modified his Afro, going for his cuts and shaves at Billy Harten's Barber Shop on Seventh Avenue and 119th Street. Billy was the oldest barber in his shop, at 62 years old, and he employed a few younger barbers.

"Where the rest of them rascals you got in here man? Daggone whippersnappers!"

"They ain't come in yet."

"Al, you want them young boys on yo' head," Mr. Lewis asked, a bone thin senior from 118th Street.

"Man! You out yo' mind? Those lil' young boys'll have a bunch of stairsteps, doggone staircase in my head. Or some daggone zigzags, a whole bunch of foolishness. Them whippersnapper's ain't gettin' on my head. Nope. No siree, only the old timers like Bruh Harten here."

"Ssshit! Bruh Harten ain't gettin' on my head! And I'm an old timer," Mr. Lewis chuckled. Billy Harten laughed, releasing Al from the barber chair, carefully passing him his cane.

"What I owe ya?"

"Five, my man."

Al passed Billy a five-dollar bill, moving towards the hanging rack for his coat. "Alrighty! Hey men listen up, fixing to be time for the old way at Cadillac Joe's. Don't y'all blow all y'all cash on them numbers y'all."

"Holy moly . . . I got to get my . . . Sssshiitt . . . Let me get to that number joint," Mr. Lewis yelled, standing as quick as his feeble body allowed.

"Ah hell," Al chuckled. "I done got 'im started. Gotta get on round this corner. Bruh Harten, take care of yourself. Hear? Say hey to Rutledge for me. Alright gentlemen."

He waved while exiting the shop. A bunch of young guys heading north on Seventh spoke:

"Hi, Mister Carter!"

"Hey, Mister Carter!"

"Yo tell Baby Al what's up!"

"What's up, Mister Carter!"

"Hello. Hello," he replied, stopping short, removing his brand new glasses, watching their backs and bops as they headed in the opposite direction.

"Now who was them boys . . . Damn I said I'm getting old. I don't know who speaking to me now . . . Must be these new glasses . . . They ain't working too good . . . Gotta tell Doc Wallace . . . Man oh man."

Al walked into his tenement building, grinning immediately. "Barbara Nelson? What the devil you up to?"

His unpredictable neighbor had set up a small table in front of the staircase outside Apt.# 1. She sat behind the desk with her arms folded. He shook his head starting up the stairs. Midway, he stopped to mentally prepare for the long climb.

"Barbara?"

"What!"

"Serious . . . What brought that on? You behind that desk and everything?"

"How could you ask a fool question like that? Al, we been living in this neighborhood and this building more than forty years! You need to be down here with me on my tenant association!"

"Barbara, who and the hell you gon' get to associate with you," Al laughed re-starting his journey.

"Go on! But you gon' wish you helped Barbara, honey! Wit' all these people, including YES INCLUDING, Baby Al coming through roofs all over 17th Street! Y'all ain't taking my stuff! Uh-uh, honey, I'm sorry! Barbara knows cause Barbara's watching!"

Al knew she was still babbling to herself when he reached upstairs. Noticing the phone ringing, he rushed inside his bedroom to answer. By the time he reached the phone extension in his room, the person on the other end hung up. He frowned and exhaled aggravatingly while he looked at the 11-year-old framed portrait of Dwayne, Mattie, and himself. His frown vanished and he grinned at the picture, and started unzipping his coat while watching himself in the dresser mirror. He opened the window, instantly becoming chilly. This particular March felt like December as the sun set. He looked right down 117th towards Lenox, then left towards the corner of 117th and Seventh Ave, and brought his head inside quickly.

"Still cold, gon' be cold, and I'm glad I made it upstairs out the cold," Al thought, closing the window. He went to the closet, pushed aside the beads, hung up his coat, and removed his trunk.

The trunk, cherished since World War II, was filled with memorabilia of the family. After Gwenny's death, Mattie-unable to cope with her passing-had demanded their daughter's pictures be removed and put away; and Al complied with his wife's wishes, storing every photo of their daughter inside the bottom of the trunk. At times like this, when Dwayne wasn't around, Al would dig inside to reclaim his bittersweet memories, the memories of his young life yesteryear, of his good life yesteryear. He would travel back to Pine Bluff Arkansas in his mind's eye. He would take out each picture ID he ever owned and align them along the dresser edge, admiring his good looks during his youth, hating the forthcoming beast of age progression. Time truly waited for no one as the years flew by, glancing from picture to picture.

The trunk also contained crumbling photos of his parents, Frederick & Jessie Bell Carter. There were pictures of Aunt Lou, as well as other ancestors, all sorts of personals important to Al. There were a few salvageable pictures of his sisters who resided in Michigan with their husbands and families after the fleeting separation of the family. The memories were unshakeable, protecting his mother and younger sisters from the KKK, ensuring their boarding of a train headed away from Pine Bluff, rescuing them from a near lynching.

The trunk held his spirit and mental together, after World War ll, his entire being tucked away and perused at meditative leisure. There was Mattie's death certificate to digest painfully, his cooking certificates and awards to read as a victorious chaser in the absence of the two women he truly loved and hoped they were in a place titled heaven; also, there were extra leftover obituaries from the funerals of Mattie and Gwenny.

Unlocking the trunk, he dug inside and bypassed a few of his favorites, from Gwenny's first piano recital, to a couple of birthday parties, the 1961 valedictorian speech, and the college bound Gwendolyn Carter. He removed a couple of pictures, chuckling immediately at the memory. The occasion: Gwenny's first chocolate cake she baked.

Al thought, "Ain't Lou must've taken these."

The black and white photos captured a happy moment in the Carter home. Young Gwenny Carter had listened to her mother's recipe, then she listened to her father's he used from his job; he baked most of his cakes from scratch. She did it her own way eventually, headstrong, self-willed, with a fierce need to be different. The same regal, distinct mannerisms she possessed and that burning need for new horizons led to the turbulent trap of interracial dating in college, and sadly the subsequent gang rape that would send the only child of Albert and Mattie Mae Carter back to 117th Street between Lenox and Seventh, like a boomerang. After she fought and ran for her life on campus that horrifying night, her studious disposition disappeared, and she became a depressed shell of a young woman. Her return to the streets of Harlem and subsequent pregnancy transformed her into a perfidious pariah, ending her studies unceremoniously much to her parents' dismay.

After finding out his daughter's personal plight, Al Carter stood tall and strong for his expanding family, in spite of more Carter devastation:

"My grandson gon' have the world!"

"Daddy, how you know I'm havin' a boy?"

"Cause I know. God is good Gwenny."

"Now daddy, what is THAT supposed to mean?"

*"It means, THAT, the good Lawd ain't gon' send
me no more fool women to deal with."*

"Oh, daddy!"

"And ya still cain't bake a chocolate cake!"

"Daddy!"

He felt an emotional head rush thinking of his daughter. Al dug into the trunk again, removing a generous, unframed 8 x 10 sized picture of Dwayne at 2 months. The description of Dwayne's biological father, Arnold Mucci, stared into Al's soul from the photo; and Al returned the glare holding his grandson's profound two-month old features in the trembling grasp of his right hand.

> *"Baby Al, don't you listen to nobody when
> they talk about Gwenny. Hear?"*

> *"Pappy, is Gwenny my mother? Is it true that
> Gwenny might be my mother?"*

Tossing Dwayne's 8 x 10 back inside and shaking the trunk, he removed his daughter's framed high school graduation portrait. Heart bursting with pride, Al gazed at his favorite picture. And what a beauty she was, high school valedictorian, college bound, psych major, young black woman.

He looked at his watch: 5:30 p.m. Al thought, "I got time." He dumped the other pictures back into the trunk; and moving as quickly as possible, Al limped down the hallway with Gwenny's portrait in hand, wanting to experience it in its original sitting place. He began to fantasize:

"Hey grandson! How's it going?"

"Hey, Pappy! Everything is fine! I got all A's! I'm doing good in school!"

"That a boy! Listen, how are you doing otherwise?"

"Oh, you mean the stuff you told me?"

"Yeah, about . . ."

"Oh about my mama and my dad? . . . I'm okay, man. It hurt at first what you said to me. I ain't believe it, but, ummm, I feel better now Pappy. I really wish my father didn't do what he did to my mother. My mama was SO Strong. My father was a chump, him and his punk boys for doing what they did, being prejudiced and all, raping and hurting her. But my Mama . . . I'm really proud of my mama."

"Are you?"

"Yeah . . . Also, Pappy, I want you to know that I love you. Seriously man, I do! I really appreciate what you've

done for me. How you and Grandma
Mattie raised me. God bless you."

He entered the living room and moved all the pictures on the top shelf of his ornamented unit to the side, making way for Gwenny's portrait. She was stunning, smiling out into the den exactly like she used to, her dad's features intact yet glowing with her mother's complexion. Her hair and nails were done; she grasped her diploma, graduation cap sitting atop an expertly made-up face flanked by a pageboy flip.

The telephone started ringing. Al picked up the kitchen extension, totally forgetting about the open trunk in his bedroom and the picture sitting proudly on the wall unit.

"Slick! It's Jimmy. How's everything? You and Baby Al don't know nobody no more? That ain't hip man," Jimmy Robinson chuckled on the line. Al grinned at the mellow baritone of his cooking protégé.

"Man, you know I ain't cutting it like I used to," Al replied.

"How old you now, Slick?"

"I'll be seventy-one in June man."

"Damn, Slick! Time flying!"

"Time sho' don't wait on nobody, Jimmy. What you about now, forty-four or forty-five?"

"Forty-five."

"See what I mean. I remember when ya couldn't cook a lick! A teenager! Wet behind the ears!"

"Now that's the Slick I know. Check you out! Popping junk and talking mess! You must've told Baby Al everything."

Silence fell upon the phone line.

"Hey, Slick! You still there?"

"Yeah, I'm here."

"You told Baby Al the truth right," asked Jimmy.

Al paused and replied a somber, "No."

"Aw come on, Slick man! You never been the type to fiddle around!"

"Now wait a minute!"

"Why you procrastinating, Slick man? Tell that boy the truth about his background!"

"Excuse me? . . . What the hell's wrong with you, Jimmy? Didn't I tell you befo' it's my mess man? It's my mess! I'll handle it!"

"Slick, you bullshitting man!"

"What?! Watch'ya' mouth!"

"I call it how I see it man! How you gonna keep the truth from the kid like that?"

"I ain't keeping no truth from him! I'm'a tell him!"

"When?! When he's seventy-one too?! Slick man, listen to me, you know I care about you right? You know how much I love you and Baby Al right?"

"And?"

"You're asking for trouble. You and Baby Al never got along. What's gonna happen if he finds out? What's gonna happen if he finds out through the grapevine?"

"He ain't gon'e find out through no grapevine."

"Slick. Everybody knows the deal man! Your block knows. Your nosy neighbor, and even me now. Everybody knows about what happened, everybody except Baby Al. What if he finds out in the street?"

Red-eyed Dwayne stared at Barbara through the plastic glass pane, in the foyer of the tenement.

"Open the door, Miss Nelson," he said. Barbara ignored him, humming while reading her newspaper.

"Miss Nelson!"

"Where's ya keys?!"

"Pappy won't let me have . . ."

"You's a damn liar, Baby Al! Al been gave you keys! You won't get in here! Ya better lend ya body to that little tricking Jezebel next door and go through the roof like you been doing!"

Dwayne chuckled, and used his keys to open the locked second door to the tenement.

"That's alright. You could've opened the door," he said, walking past Barbara's desk, starting his five-floor ascension jog.

"You gonna need me one day, Miss Nelson! You gon' be getting robbed and I'm a know the niggas! I ain't gon' even help you!"

She gazed up the staircase while he disappeared mid-landing. He made it to the fifth floor quickly, huffing and puffing as usual. He heard his grandfather's loud voice yelling at someone.

". . . You heard me! . . . Don't! . . . No! . . . Don't you, tell me what to do! . . . Don't, tell me what to do! I got a mind! . . . T'hell wit'cha then, if ya cain't 'gree with me . . ." It sounded like Al had company, which was rare. Maybe he was yelling on the telephone. Ensuring quietness, Dwayne carefully unlocked the door and entered the apartment.

"Damn. Who and the hell on the phone making Pappy mad?," he wondered, entering his bedroom removing his coat. Dwayne realized Al was yelling at his godfather Jimmy Robinson. He also observed he was the subject of the shouting match.

"I wanna hear this," he thought, sneaking from his room to his grandfather's bedroom. He picked up the phone slowly, being extra careful with his breathing technique, making sure neither party would know he was on the line.

"I don't give a damn what you say! It's my family business!"

"Slick man, I know but . . ."

"But my foot, Jimmy! Baby Al is my grandson! MY grandson! I'll handle our situation! He'll know the truth soon enough! He still been trying to get in my chest! That's why I keeps it locked!"

Dwayne saw the unlocked trunk situated halfway out of the closet.

"Oh snap! It's open! He must've forgot to lock it," he thought, still listening. He knew Al usually kept the trunk locked, refusing to let him go anywhere near it for years. He knew the trunk harbored family secrets, and it was *open*, and at his curious disposal. Maybe some of the many questions he had about his heritage would finally be answered. He continued eavesdropping.

"That boy got feelings too, Slick! Why you think he went off on you at Miss Mattie's funeral? You can't play around with the truth! He need to know that your daughter is his mother!"

Dwayne's piercing eyes widened hearing his godfather's powerful statement.

"Why you so concerned about Baby Al knowing the truth about Gwenny?!"

"Slick! For crying out loud! I've been your friend for seventeen years. I'm Baby Al's godfather! How would you feel knowing your mama died and your people kept it from you purposely?"

Dwayne was in total shock. Gwenny WAS his mother! Up until this point, he was led to believe she was several other people, but not his mother. She, was Al and Mattie's mysterious daughter who died.

Dwayne panicked, thinking, "How did she die? Who's my father?"

Putting the phone receiver down and walking across the room, he crouched in front of the open trunk. He began pushing all the papers around inside, jumbling all the pictures, baby shoes, awards, and other mementos. He slowly removed one of Gwenny's obituaries. The worn program was graced with her beautiful high school graduation photo. He stared at the picture noticing their genetic resemblance. He read her dates of birth and death: September 16, 1943 - April 9, 1965.

"Oh no . . . my birthday, she died on my birthday," he thought, tears falling. He opened the program to gather more information on the mother he never knew. The paper had turned brown, deteriorating in some areas because of its age. He read it thoroughly, becoming enraged. He felt betrayed, cheated, as if he lived a lie. Dwayne needed answers pronto. He began to see blood, the blood of his grandfather, Al Carter.

"Slick, the next time I hear from you, I want you to tell me Baby Al knows the truth. I want things to work out." Jimmy tried to be patient with his mentor, assuming the elder was confused.

"Jimmy, somebody pick up a line in your house? What's all that ruckus going on in the background? All that noise?"

Inside of Al's bedroom, Dwayne dumped the contents of the trunk onto the floor, then kicked the trunk as hard as he could.

"Nobody's here with me man. I'm in the house by myself," Jimmy said.

"I ain't hear Baby Al come in. I'm by myself too."

He went into the living room as far as the telephone would allow. "Hold on, Jimmy. Hey, Baby Al! You here?!"

"I wonder what that noise was, maybe a bad connection Slick."

That second, Dwayne slammed the phone receiver down.

"Slick! Baby Al in there with you?"

Al was frantic instantly, wondering if Dwayne heard

the conversation.

"Hey, Slick! Are you still there man?"

"I'm here," Al replied. He hoped the phone slamming was his imagination. He noticed a silhouette on the hallway wall creep closer, becoming larger. The floor began to creak.

"I think Baby Al's here. He might'a heard me yelling," Al whispered.

"Slick. Don't sweat it. If he did, now's the time to tell him man. Don't delay!"

Dwayne appeared in the corridor. He stared directly at Al, with Gwenny's crumpled obituary in his fist. Al stared back at his grandson, noticing the new darker intensity in his eyes. He knew he overheard everything. This was the moment he feared. It was time to tell his grandson the truth, let the chips fall where they may.

"Jimmy, Baby Al's here. Let me talk to him," said Al.

"Slick, I'm'a call you over the weekend to see how things worked out. Alright?"

"Yeah. You do that. Take care, hear?"

"Alright, Slick. Later."

Jimmy hung up his phone. He layed back on the sofa, propped up his feet, and began praying for his mentor and his godson.

Meanwhile, Al hung up the kitchen extension and limped into the living room.

"I ain't hear ya come in boy. What'cha lookin' like that for," he asked his grandchild nervously.

Dwayne huffed and puffed with his fists clenched. A tear rolled out of his eye while his face contorted with rage.

"Why," he asked, gritting his teeth.

"Why what Baby Al?"

"You love calling me that name don't you?"

Al came towards Dwayne extending his hand, grinning meekly. "Of course I do, Baby Al. That's cause I loves ya."

Suddenly, Dwayne flew into a rage. "Love?! Love Pappy?! What a joke! Your love for me is a dirty joke!" The burning tears streamed down his face.

"Now you wait a minute!"

"You wait a minute!"

"Lower your voice boy!"

"No!"

"Lower your voice, Baby Al!"

"Don't call me that! You couldn't even tell me the truth!"

"Look. Sit down."

"Gwenny my mother! Ain't she?! AIN'T SHE?!!"

The statement spat from his grandson's venomous mouth took Al's breath away, and made his heart skip a beat. Dwayne did hear everything. What would he do now? How could this be fixed?

"So what's up?!"

"Baby Al, listen to me."

"As long as you been calling me that name you could'a told me the truth about Gwenny!"

"Baby Al . . ."

"You gon' keep covering up shit like a fucking cat! You let me go on like a crazy person!"

"You watch that type a language in this house boy! You calm down so we can talk! I . . . I want you to understand son."

"Understand THIS!" He slapped Al across his chest at the speed of sound with the crinkled obituary, and the aged program fell to the floor.

Al turned away from his grandson in shame, and in slight pain from the slap to his chest. Dwayne glared at the back of his grandfather's bowed trembling head.

"You can't face me now can you? Why you keep the truth from me?! Huh?!"

His raging eyes wandered over to a prized new addition to the wall unit. He noticed his mother's framed graduation photo in the center of the top shelf, identical to the obituary's cover. He stormed over to the filled unit and snatched the picture; and Al flipped when Dwayne seized his favorite portrait of his deceased daughter.

"Gimme that picture," he yelled, hobbling over to snatch it back.

"No!"

"Give it to me!"

"How she die, huh?! How?! How?!"

"Gimme that picture! That's my picture!"

"She's my mother! It's my mama's picture!"

"Give it to me!"

"No! How she die huh?!"

Al grabbed hold of the frame while Dwayne clung with tenacious resistance.

"How she die, Pappy?! Did ya kill her too," he teased.

"Give it back!"

"Did you make her have bad headaches too?! Like Grandma Mattie?! Did the headaches kill Gwenny too?! Like Grandma Mattie?!"

"Let go!"

"You ain't stronger than me, Pappy! Get the fuck off Gwenny's picture!"

His grandson's profanity caused Al to grab him by his collar, staring him eye to eye. Dwayne dropped the ageless portrait. The framed glass shattered when it hit the floor.

"See what ya did damn it," Al vehemently whispered, ready to choke Dwayne.

"Get off me, Pappy! Let me go!"

"When I let you go . . . you get a broom . . . and clean up this mess!"

"Let me go, Pappy! I'm not gon' say it no more!"

He wanted to choke him but couldn't, out of love. Dwayne had good reason to be upset but he didn't have to break things.

"Get off me! Get off," Dwayne roared in Al's face. Al

shoved the irate teenager away with every ounce of strength he possessed. Dwayne caught his balance by the kitchen entrance, preparing for his next verbal assault.

"All this time! I'm thinking Gwenny's my cousin! My aunt! She's my fucking mother! I ain't never seen her!"

"Boy! You outta control!

"She died on April 9, 1965! How?! My birthday! How?!"

"We ain't talking 'bout nothing til you calm down and clean up this glass!"

"I always asked you about Gwenny! You and Grandma Mattie! Y'all gave me the slip off!"

"Calm down boy!"

"Why did you say it wasn't true?!"

Al looked down at the glassy floor after Dwayne's last question. He fronted on the truth back in the days once, when the clever youngster inquired about his daughter.

Dwayne stomped from the living room, going to his bedroom for his jacket.

"Baby Al! Dammit! Get back here and sweep up this glass! Now boy! Wait a minute! Come here!"

Al started after him. In a flash, Dwayne's jacket was on and zipped up.

"Where you going?!," Al demanded to know, hobbling into the apartment hallway. Within seconds, Dwayne had the door unlocked, open, with one leg through."You better not leave out this house!" Al grabbed Dwayne by the shoulder.

"Get off meee," he roared, pulling Al from the apartment with him. They stood at the edge of the stairway.

"Baby Al!

"Don't call me that!"

"Get back in the house boy! We need to talk!"

"About what! You dead wrong, Pappy! Dead wrong!"

Pointing and shouting at one another, they were heard clear from the fifth floor to the first floor, which made

Barbara curious.

"I hate you!"

"Well, I love you!"

"And I still hate you! You been lying to me forever! How did my mother die, huh?! You make my mama have headaches?! Huh, Pappy?! Did you drive her crazy like you did Grandma Mattie?! Tell me!! How did Gwenny die?! How?! How my mother die?! Huh?! You got rid of her like you offed my grandmother!!"

Al could take no more of his grandson's malicious taunting. The harsh questions of wounded knowledge, the broken picture frame, with the fervid insinuations about the wife and daughter he missed dearly; it was too much for the disgusted senior citizen to bear for another second, and Al saw the blood of his grandson.

"YOU KILLED HER!! You destroy everything you touch boy! Damn it, Baby Al you killed my daughter!! You killed my baby girl!! You killed my Gwenny when YOU WAS BORN!"

With all the strength he could possess in an angry left hook, Dwayne cuffed Al in the jaw, his spectacles flying from his face. The blow sent the 70-year-old reeling down the stairs. Al airborne, crashed on his back and shoulders then tumbled, ending upside down against the wall mid-landing, between the fourth and fifth floors.

That second, Barbara, moving as fast as she could, was up to the third floor from her first floor position, hustling to get to the top to find out about the commotion.

Dwayne stood dumbfounded at the top of the stairs in front of the apartment, while his grandfather layed steps away, moaning in excruciating pain. He heard someone rushing upstairs. He had to act quickly.

"Pappy! Oh my God," Dwayne yelled rushing down the steps. Barbara and Dwayne met on the landing at the same time. She looked at her upside down neighbor with her mouth wide open.

"Oh God! Lord have mercy Jesus! Al, you alright," she asked, kneeling down, still panting from her climb.

"Miss Nelson. Help me get him up," Dwayne said frantically. "It's gonna be alright, Pappy man! Me and Miss Nelson gonna get you back upstairs."

Barbara eventually grabbed his legs, and Dwayne grabbed Al's torso, placing his arms tightly under the armpits, and they moved him back upstairs. They huffed and puffed, finally sitting him on the top step.

"Thanks, Miss Nelson," Dwayne said, catching his breath.

"The same way you thanked me, is how I'm thanking the cops!," she breathed and snapped.

"What?"

"When they get here to arrest yo' lil' red behind for knocking yo' granddaddy down the steps!" She strutted towards her apartment.

"I ain't knock Pappy down no steps!"

"Oh yes ya did! Barbara heard the two 'a y'all just a yelling and a cussing all the way down to the first floor!"

"Yeah right!"

"And I'm 'a hear the cops when they drag yo' no good behind off to the slammer!"

"Ain't nobody going to no slammer, cause nobody got pushed down no steps!"

He walked over to check his grandfather. "Pappy, you okay?"

Al continued to moan, cupping his forehead with his hand. Dwayne quickly ran down and retrieved Al's glasses from the landing, hoping that Barbara didn't call the police. "Come on. Stand up."

Dwayne helped Al to his feet, guiding him into the apartment. Barbara stood in front of her place down the hall, shook her head, and watched the pitiful sight.

Time passed, and things were touch and go around the apartment. Al's jaw became swollen and bruised, and he was in more pain barely being able to stand from time to time, with black and blue marks all over his body. He awakened each morning to stare in the dresser mirror, sadly rubbing his blemished jaw, with severe back pain nearly unable to move. He was confused and deeply upset about what happened. He knew his grandson would go off the deep end once he found out the information about his mother, but to be assaulted by the teen? He knew the rancorous boy would be upset, but to punch him down the steps?

Tears welled, running intermittently while he re-examined his jaw, flinching because of the discomfort of his touch, and the back pain.

Al said, "Mattie honey, ya wit' me baby? . . . Baby is it true what you told me? . . . Can you give me a sign, baby? I know you with me, talk to me honey . . . I know you and the baby here . . . Is it true what you said about Baby Al before you passed on?"

He hoped for the usual answer. He longed to hear Mattie's rich, buxom voice reassure him. He yearned for relief from spiritual pain, mental turmoil, and now more physical, excruciating pain, all over his body, and especially in his back and face which were heavy laden with the burden of swollen bruises. And he wondered would Mattie's voice be all that he would need right now. He would always love, cherish, and glorify her memory, but after what happened with the grandson they chose to raise because of his parents' absence, was Mattie's reassuring spirit and voice he often heard enough? He wished she would appear in the mirror, like she sometimes would and say, "Yes Albert . . . It's alright . . . Everythang's gon' be alright."

Al questioned himself endlessly, rubbing his big, disfigured jaw and face. The grandson he loved needed severe discipline, but he wondered what his reprimanding tactics would be with the argument and punch embedded repetitiously in his mind.

"How did my mother die? Huh?"

"YOU KILLED HER! *You destroy everything you touch boy! Damn it, Baby Al you killed my daughter!! You killed my baby girl!! You killed my Gwenny when you was born!"*

The spiritual, mental, and physical pain due to choices radiated continuously. It took a week and a half to clean up his destroyed bedroom after the fall. He saw the unlocked trunk while he painfully sat on the bed. There was no more need for a padlock. Dwayne knew the truth about Gwenny.

****

CHAPTER 5

*

George Washington High was scheduled for a half day of classes along with other New York City high schools, so the crew met up together and went to Arthur's for the morning. Arthur was home for the summer, after completing a successful freshman year at college. The Boyd family had moved from another walk up tenement on 117th Street to Paulding Avenue in the Bronx, their own private home. The guys hung out in the basement from late morning until mid-afternoon, watching pornographic movies on the "Sony Betamax"; and they played "Mousetrap" on Arthur's "Colecovision", drinking apple flavored "Malt Duck" and smoking marijuana, rolling the grass in "El Producto" cigar paper after removing the cigar tobacco, creating a stronger effect.

"Yo, pass the cheeba man, stop frontin', you bullshitting," Dwayne yelled at Patrick.

"Word man," added Eric, "Just because you West Indian man, don't mean you gotta smoke up the whole shit "B"! You ain't no real Bob Marley motherfucker!"

Patrick chuckled and said, "Two super-duper seniors with nothing but mouth." He blew three smoke rings, and passed the "blunt" to Dwayne. Eric gave Patrick the finger then passed the half empty quart bottle to thirsty Shawn, and attempted to scribble inside of his new tagging book.

"So what you graduated. That's why YO chick is MY honeydip now," Dwayne said, and took a deep pull from the el. Shawn grinned and added, "I know right. You lucky you live on MY 20th. Impress us rasta mon, and go to school like Art since you graduated. And where's our cheeseburgers WENDY?"

They laughed and Arthur walked over to the stereo unit, turning on the radio, and the sounds of 92 KTU soon filled the Boyd basement. Eric let off a loud five second burp that sounded like antique motor horn, and the guys cracked up with laughter a second time.

"Art! Change that bullshit ass station to Kiss FM man! I can't tag to that. We fuck with the real downtown man! What, you forgot already, moving up here? Change to the new shit!," Eric instructed.

The basement was decorated with wall to wall mirrors, a floor model television, stereo system, and bar. Near the boiler area, they had a washroom equipped with a washer and dryer. The den area had a space for audio and video equipment, and a bar filled to the brim with liquors and wines. This was where all the guys were sitting puffing blunts, one high school graduate, one college sophomore to be, catching a "contact" inhaling second-hand smoke, and three cutting school as usual. Hours later, the crew helped Arthur tidy his basement and air it out so his parents wouldn't be suspicious of company in their absence. They slapped five with their four-eyed friend and headed home, back downtown to Harlem.

After a brief ride, they exited the subway at 116th Street and Lenox, heading for the pool hall. The lively lounge had three pool tables inside, with four video games, one pinball machine, and a jukebox with oldies and the latest in R&B music.

Patrick and Eric shot a game of pool while Dwayne played against an older guy, Mister Gillain from Fifth Avenue, and Shawn took his interest in the video games. He still played the same quarter for nearly a half an hour, while his friends finished their games of pool.

"This nigga love Miss Pac-man! What the FUCK? Shawn be choking his chicken thinking 'bout her," Eric teased, slapping his boys five, blowing smoke in Shawn's face from his lit "Newport", as they laughed. Shawn laughed also, causing his game to mess up on his last turn.

"See what you did, punk!," Shawn exclaimed, playfully pushing Eric, then punching his shoulder. "You always trying to dis man. I'll bust ya' ass in this!"

Shawn began cracking his knuckles. Eric snapped, "Awwww, play me in a real game nigga! Like Centipede, or Missile Command! We can take it to the game room on Eighth and 14th where they got Space Invaders or Defender chump! Those are games for men, and I'll wax yo' ass in all of 'em!"

"OOOOOOOO," a bunch of younger guys said, along with the crew.

"Let's do this! Get a quarter!"

"What time is it," Patrick asked excitedly. They looked at the giant "Budweiser" clock on the wall in unison.

"Damn! It's almost eight o'clock! I have to get home. Later, see you guys tomorrow," and Patrick bolted out the pool hall door.

His boys disgustingly shook their heads. Eric said, "Damn, seventeen years old, got a job, and he still gotta be in the crib before sundown? Nah B!"

"Fuck Pat right now. Yo', y'all wanna play another game of pool," Dwayne asked.

"I wanna play another game of cheeba," Shawn grinned, meaning he wanted to smoke more weed.

"I'm outta cash, wait a minute, let me see," Dwayne said, digging in his pockets, "Shit, all we need is a dollar apiece high, it's three of us. A tray bag'll be cool . . . and . . . I . . . got . . . a buck!"

"Me too," added Shawn, pulling a bill from his pocket.

"Me three," yelled Eric, following suit.

"Let's go," they agreed.

The three teens happily headed to one of their many smoking spots. Bored and with nothing to do afterschool on most days, smoking blunts and drinking quarts became the guys' favorite past time, during the latter days of the spring season. They rotated different spots notoriously on a daily basis.

Al was taken by surprise, opening the apartment door to find Arlene standing with her two children. At 40, she had put on some weight, going from a size 7 to a size 14, still looking well, she was carefully made up. The statuesque dark-skinned beauty was complimented by a pearl necklace, matching bracelet, and earrings. Her navy blue knee length dress was with white polka dots; she wore black high heeled pumps, and she was swirling with "Chanel no. 5." She stood proudly, in between the children, grasping their hands tightly, beaming as she spoke.

"Hiiiiii Mister Carter!! Oh, Mister Carter! I miss you," Arlene exclaimed and squeezed Al tight, while the children stared with blank looks on their tiny faces. Al embraced his daughter's best friend tightly, like he never did before.

"I'm sorry I didn't call first, but me and the kids just came from visiting one of my girlfriends over on 13th Street."

"Do come in, come right in," Al said, backing into the apartment.

"Arlene, I'm so glad to see you after all this time. I know that ain't little Tanasha growing up so nice and pretty. Y'all go on up front." He motioned them towards the living room.

Arlene and the children entered the familiar living room that she left behind years ago. Nothing had changed. Everything was in the same place; the couch, coffee table, dining room table and chairs, old time stereo with eight track tape player, tiny 13-inch black and white TV resting on top, and the wall unit filled with pictures next to the window. She was amazed at the timeless den she played in with Gwenny, babysat Gwenny's son after her tragic passing, partied with others; the place never changed. She walked over to the wall unit.

"Nasha, look at you and me," Arlene said showing off a 3x5 framed photo.

"Oh wow, mommy, they have our picture here too?"

Arlene nodded.

"So where's mine," asked little Dante.

"Because mommy ran out of yours, but we'll get some more," she smiled, kissing him on his forehead.

"What'cha say Arlene, what's cooking? Phone company doing you real good; you looking good, smelling good," Al yelled, hobbling up the hallway.

"Mister Carter, like I said, I had to come by. I haven't seen you in a long time now, how's . . . everything?"

She paused and stared at Al's swollen jaw, which had slowly begun to heal, the bluish tint finally blending in with his caramel complexion. And Al saw her staring at his face, so he instantly focused his attentions to the children.

"Sit down, sit down. Go on kids, y'all want something to eat or drink? Felt like some pig feet and pinto beans in the pot tonight. Y'all wanna watch a little TV?" Entertaining company was a dead issue in his home these days and to have Arlene and the children visiting was a true joy for Al. He became more excited because of company.

She sat on the couch with the kids. "Actually, I hadn't planned on staying too long, but I had to say hi. Where's my godson?"

"Huh?"

"Where's Baby Al?"

"He out running the street," Al began, "You ain't seen him have ya'? Man, oh man me and Baby Al the same height. Matter of fact, Baby Al might be taller than me now, cause I'm shrinking! Let me get y'all some Kool-Aid. This here May is a hot one and I know y'all are thirsty walking up all those steps."

He dragged into the kitchen to get drinks for his company.

"Mommy, we supposed to be home before nine, Michael Jackson coming on TV tonight," Tanasha whined, tapping her mother's thigh.

"Oh my God! That's right! Mister Carter!"

Arlene stood and joined Al inside the kitchen while he was pouring the glasses of Kool-Aid.

"But those kids are thirsty Arlene. They need something to drink and so do you. Hey, what's your boy name?"

"Dante."

"Dondi?"

"Nasha! Dante! Come in here!" Arlene passed them their glasses of Kool-Aid, then sipped from hers.

Al grinned. "See, I knew y'all was thirsty. Y'all not gonna visit with the old man for a while? I can use the company."

"Well I promised to get the kids home by nine, besides I'm still parked over on 13th and I need to get back to my car. I'm not trying to get nobody's ticket. I checked the signs, but Mister Carter we just came downtown to see how you were."

Arlene felt sorry for Al. He had no relatives she knew of except his aunt and Dwayne. The other relatives from Illinois and Michigan remained estranged from his life. His reason for living seemed to diminish like a majority of senior citizens. Walking with a limp, voice becoming feeble, wearing glasses, he wasn't the same stern, loving, funny, man she knew from her childhood on 117th Street.

She sighed, "Mister Carter, me and the kids gonna come by again. We was just shopping downtown, stopped by Howard Johnson's in Times Square, we stopped by a friend's on 13th and we came by here. They gonna drive me crazy if I don't get them home in time to see Michael Jackson on TV tonight."

"He gonna be on TV tonight?"

"Yeah, I think it's some special about Motown Records with Diana Ross, and Michael Jackson supposed to be getting back together with the Jackson Five."

"Well, y'all can look at it here! My TV's work. If y'all get too tired, y'all can stay. Y'all can have any bed and . . ." He rambled on about them staying the night seeming extra lonesome. Arlene wondered if she made the right choice in visiting her godson and his grandfather. Deciding that she did make the right choice and wanting to ease tensions she asked about his relatives, and attempted humor. She asked," Mister Carter, you should be at the show. Don't you have family out in Detroit? And when you gonna get a color TV? That's the same TV you had since I was a teenager."

"Since I say me and Mattie was gon' raise Baby Al and we ain't need no help, seem like they got mad with me . . . and you know none of my sisters ever got along with my wife . . . Nowadays I hear from 'em once in a while, those who left . . . and don't you worry 'bout that TV right there. It still play good enough Arlene. If it ain't broke, don't fix it. You heard that saying before plenty of times, didn't ya', Arlene? Well, me and Mattie had that same TV in that there living room since nineteen sixty-seven. It still play good and until it konk out, I ain't gon'e part with it."

He looked down at Arlene's kids, lovingly. "Lawd, you have some beautiful kids, Arlene. Are y'all two young whippersnappers finished?"

The children gulped down the rest of their drinks, and nodded with young Dante speaking up, "What's a whippersnapper? I don't know what that it is." His young face submerged in confusion.

"What's a whippersnapper? I'll tell ya' what a whippersnapper is. It's a SNAPPA! WHIPPA! HA! HA! HA!," Al yelled, tickling Dante. The youngster giggled while

Arlene and Tanasha both smiled at the sight of the old man tickling their kin.

"Time to tell Mister Carter goodnight. Now, give me those."

Arlene took the empty glasses from the children. Al and his company re-entered the living room, with his guests sinking into the worn couch.

"Now, Arlene, you know how I feel about that Mister Carter jazz. You know you was always like a daughter to me. If you like my daughter, then that makes little Nasha and Donald here my grandkids."

Arlene laughed. "Tell him your name honey."

"It's Dante."

"Who," Al asked, bending down to hear.

"DANTE!"

"Oh! Dan-te. What'd I say?"

"Donald."

"I'm sorry son. My hearing's starting to go. You know, Arlene, see, Arlene, a man is built up like a horse; longer they live, something gon'e give."

"Oh snap, Mommy. Mister Carter raps. You should be on Hot Tracks," said Tanasha.

"What's that sweetheart," Al asked.

Arlene added, "That's this show that shows music videos that comes on after the eleven o'clock news on Friday nights, I think on channel 7. They show all the latest record videos, rap songs and whatnot. I don't like the kids to be up too late but, being the show comes on Friday's I don't mind. I know Baby Al must look at it."

"Please stay a while, Arlene. I can fix y'all something," Al pleaded.

"We ate, I told you that. Is everything alright, Mister Carter?"

She never knew him to beg for visitors, or to ask his guests to stay overnight. Al's disposition was absolutely regal and he begged no one. Something unusual was happening in the apartment and Arlene vowed to investigate when the time was right.

"I promise I'll come by over the weekend if nothing comes up. I promise." She stood and began to rub his back and he jerked away hatefully.

"Oh! You ain't got no time to fool up with old people. Y'all just forget about us old timers and you young'uns just gon'e 'bout ya business."

"Mister Carter, don't think that way. I said I'll be back, I promise. I'll bring the kids back with me. We'll shoot the breeze, who knows, maybe we can go for a ride. Wherever you want."

Al wouldn't bend. Arlene was like everyone else. When you get old nobody wants to be bothered with you; you're just there taking up space, like an old hunk of trash.

"Come on now, Arlene, you know you ain't comin' by to see me."

"I am," she whined. "And I'm bringing Dante and Nasha with me, and we gonna take you wherever you want to go, and stop saying you old. You're not old, Mister Carter!"

"Then what am I then? I'm a be seventy-three next month."

"Thirty seven's more like it, with yo' handsome self. I always said Gwenny father is a handsome man!" Her flattery began to win him over. Al began to soften up, feeling less bitter about his aging.

"Okay, I'll look for y'all this weekend," he said digging in his pockets. "You need gas money?"

"No, thank you anyway. Say goodnight to Mister Carter kids."

"AHT!," yelled Al, stopping the kids short. "Now y'all lookahere, I don't wanna hear the words Mister Carter come out these babies' mouths. They gonna call me Pappy, just like my other grandson."

He proudly gave two dollars apiece to the children.

Arlene was deeply touched by Al's gesture.

"Really, Mister Carter, you didn't have to do that. Really you didn't. Kids give him bac . . ."

"AHT! Don't y'all make one move. Look Arlene, I loves ya' like you my very own, always had, always will. The apples don't fall too far from the tree so, therefore, I loves ya' kids like they was my very own grandkids. They are my grandkids. Right kids?"

Tanasha looked at Arlene, while Dante looked directly at Al, pondering. He looked at the paper money in his hand and nodded his head quickly, with Tanasha following suit.

Al extended his right arm, catching and embracing the jumping children tightly, not wanting to let them go, but knowing he had to. He followed his company to the door, letting them out into the hallway preparing to say goodnight.

"Grandpa, don't forget to watch Michael Jackson on "Motown 25" tonight," Tanasha said.

"If he ain't come on by ten o'clock, I'm a miss him, 'cause I gotta watch my ten o'clock news. But I'll look at some of it. What channel it come on?"

"Four."

"You coming by Saturday, Arlene?"

"I promised you a thousand times. Say bye kids. Thank Mister, I mean, grandpa, for everything."

"Thank you grandpa," the children exclaimed, double teaming Al with kisses. The smooching moment thrust him back to his real grandson's childhood, then, and the only time he received hugs and recognition from Dwayne. He fell in love with Arlene's children immediately, and he wished the youngsters could stay forever. Tanasha and Dante raced for the first floor, while their mother hugged Al as tight as she could.

"Good-night Mister Carter. We'll call when we reach home," Arlene said, making her way down the staircase.

"See y'all," Al said closing the apartment door. He

could hear Arlene chastise the children for running too fast. He chuckled to himself, making his way back to the living room, hobbling over to the wall unit. He stared at the pictures for a few minutes.

"Arlene and the babies just came, did y'all see that," he asked aloud. "They some fine babies too . . . Growing up nice . . . I'm proud of Arlene . . . She gotta come by and see me more often . . . I sho' do miss seeing her face around . . . Not as much as I miss y'all . . . but I miss her."

His speech was cut short by the telephone ringing. Al dragged to the kitchen extension. "Yes . . . hello? Hello?"

"Hello, can I speak to Dwayne," a young female voice asked.

"He ain't here."

"Tell him Iesha called."

"A who?"

"Iesha!"

"Okay, I'll do that! I'll tell him I-eeesha called."

Ten minutes later the phone rang again while Al washed the dishes. "Hello."

"Let me talk to Dwayne!"

"Who is this?"

"Monique!"

"My grandson ain't here."

"Okay. Bye!"

Five minutes passed, the phone rang again. "Hello, may I speak to Dwayne?"

"He's not in."

"Can you tell him that Sabrina called?"

"If I remember. I'll try though."

"Thanks."

"Hot diggity dog! That Baby Al is a Harlem mack already," Al thought, hanging up the phone. Dwayne hardly showed for dinner these days, so he completed the dishwashing task quickly. He made his way back to the sofa to continue watching the "MOTOWN 25" special.

"Man oh man! Oh wow! This show is really saying something! Look at old Smokey Robinson singing with them Miracles like he used to. Man that cat got to be old as me," Al chuckled, during intermittent naps.

Dwayne walked north on Lenox Avenue away from the Foster Projects with an older guy that hung around the Jefferson and Foster Projects named Scheme. They met after a smoking/drinking session, introduced by Eric. Scheme was twenty-three years old, making his living in the streets dealing drugs, having been in jail twice. The rumor had it that it was more drug money to be made in Manhattan, so Scheme left his native Brooklyn far behind for the streets of Harlem with the intent of making big cash.

"Yo, high, me and my boys got shit sewed up on the East Side," he boasted while walking.

Dwayne checked out Scheme from head to toe. Scheme was a true Brooklyn trooper dressed to the nines with a tan mock neck, sharkskin pants, "Cazal" glasses, "Kangol" hat, and black "British Walker" shoes; not to mention his black "doo rag", dangling earring in left ear, and two gold front teeth. "Damn that's some ugly shit Scheme got on, but he's a smooth nigga though," Dwayne thought. At 18 years of age, Dwayne dressed in no name sweat shirt and jogging pants, with black "Pony" sneakers walked at 6'1" while his drug dealing friend to be bopped along at 5'11".

The guys made a turn onto 117th, walking slowly, discussing the drug trade. By the time they reached in front of building 128, Dwayne was fascinated with Scheme. Scheme talked him into selling drugs, starting off small with weed and perhaps moving on to the bigger things like cocaine. They could make a good profit together with the help of Shawn and Eric, plus they would be **big time**. Coke was becoming hot around the way and the money made would be lovely. Speaking of cocaine: "Yo, homeboy, you still look ROASTED," Scheme exclaimed, slapping Dwayne five.

"I just got the crazy munchies man," Dwayne replied, red eyed.

"Yo', man, we can get with some snow right quick man and we could get real nice."

"Snow?"

Scheme became aggressive. "Come on, man, don't play with me! Snow! You know what it is man!" He pinched his nose four times with his fingertips.

"Nah high. I don't fuck around. I mean, I'll try it, but you know it ain't my thing."

Dwayne realized Scheme wanted to sniff cocaine. Plenty of the neighbors and their families indulged but Dwayne didn't want any part of it. Dwayne felt coke seemed to bring about problems in the community. Besides, he was too young, and the snow already took its toll on Scheme's unblemished brown skin. He had dark circles under his eyes and you could drive a tractor-trailer through his nostrils.

"Why it ain't your thing man?"

"Cause I said it ain't."

"Yo', high, come with me man right around Saint Nich man, come on. Five minutes black, let me finish kicking it wit ya' man," Scheme begged.

"Yo', man. Bust it, I'm just meeting you right and you getting on my nerves, man! Why you playing me close?! Go back to Jefferson, high! Step man, damn," hissed an aggravated Dwayne.

"Nah homes, nahhh, don't be disrespecting me, man! I'm trying to put your young silly ass down with some real shit! None of little E-zo's boys be fessin' man! You the first! What you making a big fucking deal for! Why you west side Harlem dudes be acting so scary, and funny?! I GOT DOUGH! I'm trying to school your punk ass! I'll get your ass some grub, nigga, damn! I'll get you another bag of cheeba too! Stop frontin' like a little faggot and come on!"

Dwayne hated a challenge, especially from a cornball new jack so called drug peddler, invading the territory. He knew that doing coke was possibly a bad thing, but he refused to be dared by this uptown newcomer. He could probably sniff Scheme under a table, walk away scot free, and unhooked. He twirled his lips up, glaring at Scheme. Letting out a big hiss, he leaped from the stoop and they continued up the block; and Dwayne walked along impudently and competitively with Scheme, quickly crossing Seventh Avenue then hanging a right on Saint Nicholas.

"Long as we not up in Grampion, you lucky. I want to be upstairs by ten o'clock, high. No ifs, ands, or buts!"

Scheme sucked his teeth, retorting, "Man, stop acting like a little homo, we just stepping on Saint Nich and 18th!"

The telephone rang loudly for what seemed like the millionth time through the apartment. "If that's one more call for Baby Al, I think I'm a jump out the window," Al said standing then dragging to the kitchen extension.

"Hello!"

Arlene was on the other end of the phone, ecstatic, and out of breath.

"Did you see him, Mister Carter?! Did you see Michael Jackson?!"

"Oh yeah. What happened? What's all that screaming going on up there in your house?"

"That's the kids! They're going crazy over Michael Jackson! My silly boy is walking backward trying to dance like him right now!"

"Yeah, I saw him. What the devil done happened to that boy? He still talented and all but what the hell done happened to him? What happened to the boy's nose?"

"I think they say he had a nose job. I don't know."

"Nose job?! He ain't got nothing else better to do with

his money than to fool around with his nose and put all that gook in his head? Lawd Jesus Christ, but he danced his butt off! I thought they needed to put his butt in the crazy house for a minute. Walking backwards and kicking his legs and whatnot! What the devil done happened to them Jackson boys?"

"Baby Al get upstairs yet?"

"No."

"I think I saw him crossing 16th and Lenox when me and the kids were in the car."

"Oh . . . Arlene, I tell ya', sometimes I don't know. That boy don't want to listen to me no more. In fact, he don't period!"

"You told him about Gwenny?"

"I finally got the nerve and told him a while ago."

"How did he take it?"

"Bad. Like he damn near take everything, bad . . . You know, Lawd, forgive me for saying it, but, I don't know if Baby Al loves me anymore, Arlene . . . He's doing so much to hurt me now, and . . . I just wish we got 'long a lil' bit better."

He wanted to tell Arlene about the punch that sent him down the steps; and she desperately wanted to ask about his jaw. Did her godchild punch his grandfather in the face, making his face look horribly swollen? She shook the impossible from her mind, yet curious to know what happened to the face of Gwenny's dad. Arlene decided to firmly get the story from Al at his leisure.

"Look, Mister Carter, I'll be by on Saturday and we'll talk more about this, okay? Don't worry, okay?"

"Okay, I'm watching the news now. I turned away from Motown. That Michael Jackson was enough for me and my old sight."

"I'll call you on Saturday, Mister Carter. Goodnight."

"Goodnight," he responded, hanging up his end.

Al went back to the sofa to finish watching the news,

hearing the apartment door slam. Looking right from the sofa, he watched his grandson come walking quickly up the hall, entering the living room, bypassing him with the speed of a steam engine.

All Dwayne thought of was quenching his thirst, for three reasons. One: he loved the way Al mixed his favorite household drink, grape flavored Kool-Aid. Two: this particular May night was a pretty warm one and he'd been out since the early morning smoking reefer and shooting dice, pretending he was in school as a soon to be a high school graduate, when he wasn't; and the familiar five floor climb didn't help matters much. Last but certainly not the least, three: Dwayne had his premiere dose of cocaine.

Scheme convinced him to do a few one-on-one hits, which led to the purchase of more "snow". They mixed cocaine and reefer together, creating another ill, more addictive effect. Reefer, alone, numbed and soothed his soul troubled with the absence of maternal necessity. But snorting and sniffing the coke added a new heated speed, and aggression to his psyche.

Everything moved slower, while the circumference of life and the living moved away from his body at the same time all around him, at least twenty feet. But he felt faster, and he moved and expedited every move a lot faster. Dwayne soon sniffed up thirty dollars worth of cocaine with Scheme and he smoked two blunts, laced with coke. The high totally blew his mind, making him slightly afraid. Fear was something Dwayne couldn't think about now. The numbing effect of the drug was annoying him. His thirst must be quenched. He disappeared into the kitchen.

Al didn't budge, refusing to move a muscle. By the way his grandson flew into the apartment, he knew some form of trouble was imminent. It could be verbal, such as Dwayne cursing him out for no reason, or physical, like another swollen jaw; something was bound to happen. From day to day, he didn't know what to expect.

Al continued watching the news while Dwayne gulped down the entire remaining quart of grape Kool-Aid from the container. He huffed and puffed, wondering what to do next, unable to control his numbing stupor of speed. Recalling the televised NBC "Motown 25" special, Dwayne zoomed out of the kitchen, hyped, heart pounding, mentally moving at 10,000 miles per hour. He walked up to the television and started changing the channels, anxiously trying to find Motown.

Al took deep breaths, trying not to become upset. Mattie was 100% correct when she gave her husband her deathbed speech. Dwayne was truly bringing sorrow, suffering, and pain, just as she predicted. It was like he was the devil in person. Not only did he enter the apartment without speaking, he just took it upon himself to change the TV to a program of his choice. He didn't even ask Al if he could change the channel, knowing that his grandfather was watching the ten o'clock news. How cruel, how callous!

"What's the fool gonna do next?," Al asked himself. He knew in his heart the best thing to do was let it go. Pay Dwayne no attention, but he couldn't go on like this. Something had to give.

"I was watching the news," Al said calmly to his coked up grandson. Dwayne turned around and stared hatefully at his grandfather, with a formation of sweat beads coming to life in his face, his eyebrows connecting.

"I wanna watch Motown!"

"You coulda asked."

"Asked what?!"

"Asked to change the channel boy! That's rude."

"It ain't rude! I been talking 'bout that Motown shit all week! You know I wanted to watch it! Watch the TV in your room!"

"You think I'm scared of ya' don't'cha?"

"Ain't nobody say that shit, Pappy! Why you always gotta pop shit?"

"You oughta be ashamed of yourself! Nobody treats their granddaddy the way you treat me!"

"Please, Pappy! Nobody do they people like you do me! Always hiding shit from me! You couldn't even tell me the truth about my own mother! You a liar! You a failure!"

"WHAT?! I'm not a failure! Baby Al, I love you!"

"And I hate you! For keeping the truth from me! You lied to me about my mother!"

Al was stunned, his feelings, demolished. Did his grandson truly hate him? Surely his caustic actions were beginning to speak louder than words. Al refused to go down this time.

"You know the truth boy! Pick ya' head up, wipe ya' nose, and stop crying! Like ya' told ya' West Indian friend the other day, put a "H" on ya' back and handle it!"

He removed his glasses and inched his way to the edge of the sofa to make his point, while Dwayne listened in an abnormally warm numbing fury.

"Ya' mama died having ya, but me and ya' grandma loved ya' enough to raise ya'! It ain't the end of the world! Ya grandma had this thing called an aneurysm in her head the doctors say back then, left us on Christmas Eve . . . I wanted ya with me cause you my flesh and blood! Hear?! My flesh and blood . . . Baby Al you got to be stronger boy, n'stead of all dat squawkin' ya do! You made outta Carter blood . . . Them cracker boys run us all outta Pine Bluff that night . . . Said it won't no KKK in town there, and that was a lie cause I had to fight for my life . . . They hung my daddy in the slaughterhouse out back with our pigs! . . . Them cracker boys was in the house beating on my sisters and my mama . . . and I damn near killed 'em all 'fore they killed the rest of us . . . and we got outta Pine Bluff that night . . . Got 'em all on a train heading North 'fore more of them white boys came back to fetch us . . . they tried to find me in that boxcar . . . on that other train headin' up north . . . and when I got to Harlem and ya Aunties got to Detroit they tell me my mama died of pneumonia and all I had was Ain't Lou!"

"Look, that's you and this is me! We're different! You shoulda' told me . . . Everything! And fuck this old ass TV!"

With his last comment, Dwayne pushed the television from the stereo to the floor, the TV falling on its aged side, screen glass cracking with one white streak in its middle, two seconds passing and the television blacking out permanently. Al, the tenderhearted senior was rancorous, filled with venom as he quickly maneuvered his cane to stand. He felt his pressure escalating, hobbling towards Dwayne he raised his cane to strike, thinking the bitter teen would be scared. Dwayne hissed.

"What'cha gonna do with that?! Hit me motherfucker?!," Dwayne hollered.

Al raised his cane a second time, when Dwayne punched him directly in the stomach. Grimacing with pain, Al crouched over, and dropped his cane to the floor. That second, Dwayne slammed Al with a upper cutting blow to the chest that sent his grandfather flying partially across the living room, landing by the sofa, banging his head on the floor.

Dwayne jumped back and forth, fists clenched, beckoning the dizzy, hurt senior to fight him.

"C'mon, Pappy! You so fucking bad! C'mon, nigga, you so fucking bad! Get up! . . . Get up! . . . Get up off the motherfucking floor!"

Dwayne danced on in his glory, demanding that Al join him in a boxing match. Al came to after a few minutes; dazed and unaware of what happened, opening his eyes. Everything around him was a blur, with his crazed coked up grandson dancing around his body, in the style of a boxer preparing to win a title bout.

At the same time of Al and Dwayne's confrontation, hell had broken loose at the home of Dwayne's friend,

Patrick Livingston. Patrick's parents found their elder sons Nigel and Franklin visiting with the family after Dora Livingston had forbid them to set foot in the house, once it was found out they actively participated in selling drugs. She also had barred her younger brother Barrington from the family because he was selling his very own drugs as well.

At the unexpected sight of her sons Nigel and Franklin, Dora flew into a verbally insulting frenzy, demanding that they leave the premises immediately. Her husband Bradley stood in partial, trying to keep his slow to erupt, volcanic temper under wraps. He too was very angry that his brother in-law and sons were selling drugs, and they were wrong for doing so; however, he missed their presence in his home. Bradley soon became angry with his profane wife, after she awakened his mother Una with her screeching voice. The younger Livingston children: 12-year-old Andrew, 8-year-old Rose, and 7-year-old Sharon left their stately, antique decorated living room in tears at the command of their mother. 20-year-old Hyacinth retired to her bedroom, upset with the dissension of her family. The elder Livingston sons exited, angry that they were unable to continue their quick visit, still hoping for reconciliation. The Livingston children were upset, but one decided to stand his ground. Patrick was disgusted with his mother, and he felt she was completely out of control.

"Mummy, wha'da' ya g'wan so," he said to Dora.

All eyes focused on Patrick after he'd spoken out of turn to his mother. All movement in the house stopped, the bedroom procession ceased on the stairway with everyone doing an about face. Sleeping Una awakened because of the commotion. Clad in her nightclothes, scarf and bathrobe, she took her post at the top of the staircase, holding the banister for balance. She started to watch the scene unfold downstairs at the wide open doors of the second floor den. In her vision: her patient son, cantankerous daughter-in-law, and her newly outspoken, out of turn grandson with his scared brothers and sisters lined up on the staircase.

Dora kissed her teeth, placed her hands on her hips, and walked slowly up to her son and said with sarcasm, "Wha' mi Yenkee bwoy talk seh?"

Patrick became angrier with his mother. It wasn't his fault he got shipped to a new country for a supposedly better life, adjusting to forced cultural dissonance. He hated when his Mother referred to him, or his younger brothers and sisters as "yenkee bwoys" or "yenkee pickny". They never messed with Hyacinth because she spoke Jamaican patois fluently at home, and she also despised American born blacks. She had even stopped worshipping at the church on the corner because of too many Americans.

"Heh," repeated Dora, "Wha mi yenkee bwoy ah chat 'bout?"

Patrick could take no more. "Mum! Why ya so prejudiced?"

Dora's eyes almost popped out of her head, jaw nearly dropping to the carpeted floor. She was already angry and shocked that two of her children disobeyed her rules by returning home for a visit, but to have a third child challenge her, raising their voice was totally out of place. She smacked Patrick across his face as hard as she could, the slap making Una gasp upstairs, the other children jump on the stairs, and Bradley angrier. Tears jumped from Patrick's eyes with his own "Americanism" fading with Jamaican temper flaring.

"Ya prejudiced mummy! Why?! Why?! Heh?! Why ya' g'wan so?! Ya teerin' the family apart wit' ya racism! All this American and Jamaican tings! Nonsense maan!," Patrick yelled at Dora.

"Shu'tup!"

"MUMMY! Mi baan in Jamaica! Mi reise up in Spanishtouwn! Kingston, Jamaica! But we're h'ere now! In ah de United Stetes! Mi 'ave mi green caard!"

"Mi sey, **SHU' TUUP Nuh Bwoy! Doan't YOU**

USE dat bloodclaat tone 'a voice, Pahtrick Livingston!
Ya carry on like de Yenkee people dem cause ya nuh 'ave
nuh respect fa' yuh mudder! **Leezy like dem Yenkee!**
Gradyuete 'igh school to not'ing ti' raas! Come owtta mi
yaahrd! Ya dumb ting ya! Ya stupid!"

Patrick cried harder, wanting badly to punch his
mother's lights out but couldn't, out of respect, out of love.
Dora, adamant with her household rules, iron clenched fists
with painted nails, cast her third son out of the home into
the street, bringing extra tears, from Patrick himself, and his
younger brothers and sisters.

Una started down the stairs hoping she could soothe a
darkening situation in her home, shooing the other children
to bed, instructing Hyacinth to assist them, calling out to
her daughter in-law, "Dora! Leave de pickny dem!"

Dora ignored her descending mother in-law, still
chastising Patrick.

"Ya eeeidiot ya nuh! Ya waan chat me like dem?! Ya
cyah be 'ere! Ya wan be like dem?! Coume owtta mi yaad!
Gone ah jail like dem?! Ya eeidiot like dem! Ya waan
smouke dem raasclaat drugs like mi brudders, and sell dem
drugs like mi pickny dem?! Trow yi life h'awey?! Work in de
blasted faas' food ya whole life nuh?! No maan! Mi gaan ah
mi bed no'! . . . Pahtrick Raahbert Livingston, ya cyah **be in
my houwse** . . . coume owtta mi yaad!"

"No Mum," Patrick yelled, defeated, saddened near
devastation with his mother's profanity and demands.
Offended Bradley proceeded to help his hyperventilating
mother from the top step after her one flight arrival as fast
as she could.

"EH BRAHDLEY?"

Bradley turned and looked at his wife; she taunted,
"Un ah stand dere and let dis yenkee bwoy chat me like
dat?!" Patrick and Una looked at Bradley for his response.

"Ya a wort' less sum' in ya' nuh! H'ear mi no'uw,"
Dora fired, belittling her husband.

Bradley darted into the kitchen via the living room with Una following him, knowing any second more, he would pounce on his wife.

Dora looked back at Patrick and said her last command: "Ya wan' g'wan so like dem baambaclaat yenkee people dem? De people dem nasty! Dem pickny dem feisty maan! Ya waan g'wan so?! Carry ya'self owtta mi yaad. Mi ah couwnt ti tree."

Patrick looked down, more tears dropping to the floor.

"G'wan pon ah street maan!"

Inside the kitchen, Una tried to console her son. "Wha hoppen, beby, ya na' worry ya'self maan," she said, rubbing his back.

"Dora! She maad! She's a maad woman ya nuh! Cuss de bwoys dem coume to de howse! Dem mi pickny ya' nuh! She wan' Patrick come owt mi yaad! She wan' all a mi pickny owtta mi yaad!"

"No," Una sadly replied.

"EH HEH! Yeah maan," Bradley roared. "She keep carry on so, I leaving!"

Una shook her head, attempting to soothe her son's forthcoming temper. He threatened to leave his wife once before. One too many brawls would cause Una's son to go over the edge. She felt the current family squabble was ridiculous. The situation could be reasoned out. It was too late to carry on; the neighbors might hear, and the children would soon be trying to sleep. Little did they know, Andrew, Rose, Sharon, and Hyacinth based themselves at Una's old station at the top of the stairs in the dark, with tears in their eyes.

"Mi g'wan out mi yaad! Like mi sons dem! **Make she stey dere!** And tend to de yard and fix de roof and tend to de plumbing! **Meke she stey dere!** And chat foolishness she gaan by 'erself!"

Una understood her son's pain. Having a daughter-in-law like Dora was no easy task. When Dora felt she was right, she stopped at nothing to prove her point.

Bradley pounded the kitchen table and yelled, **"Pahtrick! G'wan fi bed . . . G'WAN TA YA BED**!"

He refused to let his invective wife kick his fourth child out of the house. His home and family was already ruined with intra-racial prejudice and the unnecessary bickering, and the altercations must end. Patrick was a young man standing his ground, stating his own opinion; he didn't have to go anywhere. "Pahtrick! Eh, Pahtrick?!," Bradley repeated. Silence, no answer.

Suddenly, Una and Bradley heard the foyer door slam the second time. They looked at each other, and stepped back into the living room; and before they could make it through into the hallway they noticed Dora. Dora sat on the couch, hands covering her face, crying her eyes out.

Bradley demandingly asked, "Why ya bawl?! H'ih?! Where mi son! H'IH?!"

Dora said nothing, sobbing softly. Bradley ran to his wife sweeping her off the couch to her feet, shaking her violently. "No, Bradley," Una yelled, trying to stop him.

"Why ya bawl nouw?! H'ih?! H'ih?! Where mi son?! H'ih?! Mi pickny?! Where mi bwoy Pahtrick?!"

"H'im gaan," Dora whispered to her husband, face to face, eye to eye. "H'im gaan, Bradley. Mi sorry. H'im gaan 'pon ah street."

Bradley pushed his wife down to the couch to continue her sobbing, and he moved quickly through the foyer and outside the doors of the brownstone, to the top of the stoop to look for his son. He looked towards Seventh Avenue, and he looked towards Lenox Avenue.

"PAHTRICK?! . . . **PAAAHHTRICK**?!," Bradley yelled into the spring night. Far off siren and city sounds quickly returned Bradley Livingston's midnight pleas. Another son was long gone.

Dwayne took a last look at himself in the bathroom mirror. He gargled with the last bit of Listerine, spitting the contents into the toilet, tossing the empty bottle out into the alley. Once he received its shattering response, he returned to his bedroom to shut off the morning hip-hop blasting from his radio he bought on sale from "Crazy Eddie's" with his new drug slinging money. He collected his keys and proceeded to leave the apartment. Before departing, he peeked into his grandfather's bedroom.

Al was lying on his stomach, with the covers hanging from the bed, snoring quite a bit. The windows were open, filled with screens; his dentures were in his glass filled with water, placed on the nightstand to the right with his ticking alarm clock. The other nightstand was equipped with lamp and telephone, Al's glasses, a pencil and pad, a jar of water that he kept for night thirstiness, and his cup to drink.

Dwayne heard Eric calling him from downstairs, giving the new uptown call the teenagers used, sounding like a cross between an owl and a rooster. He walked through Al's bedroom to the right window. Opening it, he looked out over the screen.

"OOOH - OOOOOOH! OOOH - OOOOOOH! OOO - OOOOOOH," Eric yelled, hands cupped around his mouth looking up.

"Yo, yooo . . . E-zooo!!"

"OOOH-OOOOOOH! OOOH-OOOOOOH!"

"Chill, high, I'm coming down!"

"Don't forget the joint! You know I still got stupid beef with them Dyckman heads," Eric yelled, and took a long drag from his cigarette.

"Bet that! I got that!," Dwayne responded, closing the window. He currently carried a .22 caliber pistol in case of "beef", given to him by his new comrade in crime Brooklyn Scheme, shortly after becoming drug selling partners. Al was awakened by his grandson's exchange.

"Where ya going," he asked, mumbling into his pillow.

"Get my report card . . . Oh, by the way, happy birthday," Dwayne replied, leaving the room.

Al was surprised that he even remembered.

"He ain't used to tell me happy birthday . . . He always just want something for his . . . Maybe the boy's changing after all."

"Damn, it's too hot for a jacket," Dwayne thought, looking around his bedroom, gun in hand. He decided to carry the pistol in a little brown leather bag that he used once in a while. It was just the right size for his "joint". He put the pistol inside, zipped the bag up tight, and he was on his way to get his report card.

Al caught a glimpse of his grandson exiting the apartment. He buried his head back into his pillow for an extra ten minutes of sleep.

He thought, "Baby Al remembered . . . Seventy-three years old today, three scores and thirteen . . . Sho' ain't no spring chicken no mo' . . . Lawd . . . Bless Baby Al for remembering the old man . . . Bless his heart Lawd fo' rememberin'."

****

CHAPTER 6

*

The neighborhood fireworks over the Fourth of July weekend with its snap, crackle, and popping sounds was identical to the .22 caliber test shots fired by Dwayne on the roof; and he vowed to change his weapon as soon as possible, for something bigger. For the summer, Dwayne worked with Scheme and made an adequate amount of money. He enjoyed the new sweat suits, and different colors of Lee Jeans that were matching with the Puma and Pony sneakers purchased. The earned income was just enough to manifest the burning desire to make more, and move on to selling other types of drugs that would bring in more revenue. Al noticed the change in his grandson's drive and energy, along with the running in and out of the apartment, round the clock; then again, it was summertime, and Dwayne seemed to change for the better. He began to tend to his own laundry and cleaning as well as fixing his own food. Al hardly cooked any big dinners like the past, but Dwayne took care of himself pretty well for an eighteen year old.

Al came to a new decision:

Reckon Baby Al can know about everything now . . . and it cain't hurt to put my baby's pictures back where they belong . . . cause Mattie Mae sho 'nuff telling me she want to be seen again every night .

. . Bout time Baby Al got acquainted with his mama anyway . . . Sho is gon' be good to see Gwenny back in the living room . . . Got her a nice new frame now, after that fool broke it up carrying on about her.'

The school year at George Washington High School resumed without Dwayne, even though he would leave the apartment each morning, only to meet up with Scheme to handle the business. Al began to mistake Dwayne's brand new hobbies with a sudden form of independence he desperately tried to admire. Soon thereafter, the Carter household became hard to reach, once Dwayne summoned New York Telephone to install his own extension inside his bedroom; so now, there were three telephones in Apt. #53: the kitchen wall rotary, Al's bedroom rotary, and Dwayne's bedroom touch tone designed in the shape of Mickey Mouse, with Mickey holding a yellow receiver and twelve toned push buttons in front of his feet.

Al decided what he didn't know couldn't hurt him any more than how he already had been physically hurt.

After the TV incident, Dwayne had moved Al's bedroom television into his bedroom. He promised that he would eventually get two new televisions for the house in due time. It was a new touch and go, hello/goodbye phase for grandfather and grandson through the winter and spring; and Al hoped for the family conversation and teaching of Carter roots that had been previously violated. Even after returning the few extra pictures to the wall unit, photos that had remained hidden inside the trunk for many decades sparked no basis for conversation. Dwayne was still preoccupied with getting money, money he didn't require from Al anymore. With this income and product, he was able to afford his new habit of smoking and sniffing coke, which became a daily habit, especially after a few glances at the newly framed portraits of the mother he would never ever know. Each added picture of Gwenny colored a different emotion for her son. Partly enjoying the jump rope scene with a very young Arlene underneath another framed glass, what was old to Al, but new to Dwayne was all too painful to bear. He refrained from the living room as much as possible when home, resorting to three main areas in the apartment: his bedroom, equipped with his giant radio with dual cassette deck, Al's TV with other goodies, the bathroom and the kitchen, bypassing the living room. The present new pictures Al added to the unit, including the newly framed graduation picture of Gwendolyn Carter, were gnawing into his angry soul and guilty mind. At times the frames of the good life yesteryear seemed to call him over to be observed, pictures of Grandma Mattie and "Gwenny", and other relatives in black and white photos he wished he knew, but was too high to care anymore. It was about eating, sleeping, getting money on the Eastside, and sexing as much as possible. The new phone extension Dwayne set up in his bedroom from the consistent green became his domestic getaway and gateway to the outside world, and his shield from Al's futile family tree history at this point.

One year and a couple of months passed, and it was Labor Day 1984. Just a few miles north outside of the concrete jungle, the sun shined across the trees in sync with a sudden breeze that made the full bloomed treetops sway back and forth. Aunt Louise Esther sat in her wheelchair, inside a gazebo, staring as far as her eyes would allow. She lived moment to moment inside a retirement home on the grounds of the expanding "Mary Morton Center" miles north outside of New York City, waiting quietly for the day she would be called home by her heavenly father. A day for rejoicing with her younger brothers and sisters that she outlived, a day for rejoicing with all of the people she'd lost in her ninety-three years. The day would come to pass, when she would see and embrace her nieces, nephews, and each of her un-birthed and stillborn children she never was blessed to see; the day would come, a day for rejoicing with her mother, father, and most of all, the day she would get to meet the creator.

Lou Esther's place, a two floor magnificently stout English Tudor remade into a retirement home and rehabilitation center near a hospital being re-built under a financial expansion, proudly stood alone on a hilltop, furnished with lots of rooms, and a staff to accommodate male and female senior citizens who were from well off backgrounds. There was a small patio behind the building, a backyard, gazebo, and acres of beautiful surrounding grasslands equipped with a small pond. The nursing home attendants would push the settled and the ambulatory patients in their wheelchairs out to the patio and gazebo if the weather permitted, or if the patient's strength allowed it.

Like her nephew Al, Louise Esther was swamped with memories, good and bad, hard and easy. Memories of the family second to second became her train of thought, and the caring for her younger siblings during their pre-World War I upbringing marred by Klu Klux Klan terror; reflections of domestic work, prostitution, practical nursing victoriously learned in segregated schools and ghastly miscarriages, two marriages and burying both husbands; memories of Harlem, and of jazz, *'and not being able to attend the "Apollo Theater"* . . .*'ntil Schiffman took it over for colored folks to see some stuff*', and the "Savoy Ballroom: the home of happy feet".

"Ain't Lou" as her nephew Albert lovingly called her, painfully recalled the disappearance of her brothers and sisters, and the execution of her proud parents by the *'mens with them hoods coming always at night on them horses'*; the constant extinction of her race from child eyes, through adolescence and young adulthood, through survival during depression stricken New York City, and the raising of her favorite nephew on the run from the South, after defending the remains of her family going their separate ways; and her nieces and nephews would cultivate their estrangement through the civil rights movement, and through the many changes of the country they lived in, expanding with their own families; and Louise Esther, often decided she would change things if she could turn back the hands of time, up until the very day she sat at age ninety-three inside the gazebo at the home. She was minutes away from her own foreclosed property, lost after the heart attack she suffered shortly after winning a case for a spurious operation she received.

Back when she was eighty-two years old, one evening, Louise Esther was rushed to the hospital complaining of severe gas pains. Months later, the doctors mistakenly removed the elderly woman's large intestine, after insisting it was cancerous. The bogus colostomy case took nine years to settle; and Ain't Lou was ecstatic with the "700,000 dollar outcome", however, due to the heart attack, the happiness was short lived.

She used to wonder what to do with her earnings from the case, and at her age, should she purchase and own a big house? She had never heard from so many people in her whole life at one given time, claiming that they were either kin to Louise Esther or Jessie Bell. After all she had been through, she still would quiz herself endlessly, and after the attack, she decided she really didn't care. She may have one foot through death's door and the other on a banana peel, but one thing was for sure, she loved her nephew Albert Carter-her younger sister Jessie Bell's son-for all eternity. She missed him dearly, not seeing him since her cash settlement, the purchase of her house, or even the heart attack. He was hard to reach by phone with *Baby Al* tying up the line constantly. All Mrs. Louise Esther Davis Reynolds Williams, better known as Mrs. Lou R. Williams, would receive when she called her nephew was a busy signal.

Mrs. Martha Joseph, her companion for the day, reported that she wouldn't have to spend another holiday alone. Her favorite nephew was coming up for a visit with some friends. Martha draped Aunt Lou's favorite pink sweater over her shoulders and exited the gazebo to fix some tea for her profound patient.

"I commin' jus' no'uw Mummy," Martha said in a beautifully rich Trinidadian accent while walking off. Aunt Lou calmly waited for her tea; her white haired wig exactly in place, handsomely perched upon a minimally wrinkled dark face with glasses. Hands clasped together, she waited patiently.

Arlene and the children settled on spending their holiday with Al, driving him to Aunt Lou's and Jimmy Robinson's for visits. She wanted the kids to see Ain't Lou's "huge house" for themselves after hearing so much about it from her excited nephew. From there, their second stop would be north on the interstate for a few exits to Jimmy's barbecue celebration. Business was booming for his "HAMBURGER HEADQUARTERS", with thirty more stores opening in the tri-state area.

Al walked with Tanasha and Dante, holding their hands while Arlene trailed behind, after parking the car. They all were greeted by Martha, at the door.

"It's always a pleasure, Mister Carter, hello. And Arlene, am I right?"

"Hello," Arlene said to Martha, "these are my kids."

"What's jumping baby? Mama you built for speed," Al said, flirting with Martha.

"Mrs. Williams is outside waiting. I bringing she tea, come," she said, leading the way for everyone to follow.

"Woowee, must be jelly, cause jam don't shake like that! Boop-Oop-Ah-Doop, boop-pappah-dop! Lawd sweet baby built for speed," Al said, walking behind the nurse. He liked Martha for some strange reason. She reminded him of Mattie, so buxom and rich, only Martha was darker in complexion. She walked the gazebo path, cup of tea in hand, followed by her patient's company; and she walked like Mattie, tall, proud, weighty, with her hips grooving from east to west in slow motion, like the hips of a Hawaiian hula dancer.

Aunt Lou smiled, noticing people coming toward her. She became more ecstatic when she saw her nephew Albert come into the gazebo, struggling with his cane.

"Ain't Lou, Ain't Lou, Ain't Lou! Boy, am I glad to see you! Couldn't wait to lay my eyes and my helpers on ya'," Al proudly shouted, reaching to embrace her, followed with a three second smooch to her cheek.

Soon the gazebo was crowded after Martha brought extra folding chairs, with Tanasha and Dante hitting at each other, Arlene periodically saying, "STOP!", Al talking to Aunt Lou sitting in the wheelchair with Arlene included in the conversation, and Martha standing behind her. Yelling at times because of her bad hearing, Al enjoyed conversing the late morning and the early afternoon away with his mother's sister.

"Everything'll be fine, long as nobody say or ask nothin' 'bout me and Baby Al," he thought. "I don't know nothing . . .and don't want to know nothing . . . Baby Al just there . . . that's all; don't know 'bout no school, don't know 'bout no job, he just there, at the house still," Al continued thinking. He had it easier at Aunt Lou's, being she hardly asked any questions; she just sat and appreciated how much Al Carter resembled her younger sister Jessie Bell Davis-Carter. At Jimmy Robinson's, it was another story. He began quizzing Al the moment he got him in a corner alone.

"Slick man, tell me, are things okay with Baby Al? I can see it all over your face, you ain't looking good. Send him up here with me. I'll straighten his ass out!"

Jimmy knew Dwayne was an emotionally disturbed teen with an evil streak. To know the truth about Gwenny had to scar his godson's relationship with his mentor. He never saw the senior behave so timidly. There was a definite change after the alarming phone call back when Dwayne slammed the receiver down after eavesdropping.

"I wonder if Slick and Baby Al had a fight. Sure ain't heard nothing from Slick in a while . . . Hmmmm, I wonder," Jimmy thought.

Al's eyes were super-red, practically bloodshot. His face was swollen as if someone had punched him, and he looked as if he'd lost weight.

"Slick man, send Baby Al up like we used to do when he was little. He can hang out with Junior. We can help you man. I know he graduated already. I can give him a job at one of the stores."

Al shook his head listlessly. "Ain't gonna be no use, I need Baby Al with me, Jimmy man. Without my grandson, I ain't got nobody," he said looking straight ahead. "I swear, I ain't got nobody."

Dwayne walked briskly after having his evening dose of cocaine. He crossed Saint Nicholas Avenue, zooming with the overcast autumn evening winds of dusk. Passing some benches inside Al's favorite hangout park, some elderly men stood and stretched, ready to return to their homes before permanent nightfall. He knew if any of the men were friends with Al, they would call him.

"HEY BABY AL!"

Dwayne stopped short and turned around to see the male voice that called him. He noticed chubby Nathan Pope hobbling, with the rest of the men walking behind him. Mister Pope, a chocolate brown version of Oliver Hardy, lived one tenement away on the block closer to

Lenox, having been friends with Al since the late fifties.

"Where's your granddaddy, we ain't seen him in awhile," he asked with concern.

"That's some hairdo ya got there jim," stated another. A few of the men chuckled, eyeing Dwayne's half-done cornrowed hairdo.

"Yeah, Bra' Carter ain't been coming out to play chess," Pope started again.

"Or checkers man! Ain't seen him play no single action or bolitas in the number spot in years," added another.

Dwayne said with fake interest, "Pappy don't like coming down five flights of steps sometime, you know he got heart problems."

One of the men gave a peculiar look. "Why Bra' Carter always got a swolled up face?"

"His heart trouble make his whole body swell up. Later." Dwayne gave a military salute to the men, and then quickly began progressing home. When he was far enough not to hear, the men began their conference: "Ya see?! Ya see?! He done whooped his ass again! Won't let him come out!"

"Never said where bruh' Carter was!"

"That's Baby Al? He done got tall! That cat is mean! See his hair all over his damn head?!"

They went their separate ways with Nathan Pope stating, "Y'all listen to that lying ass Barbara if y'all want. Carter'll break that rascal's neck! He ain't beating on his granddaddy!"

The word was out on 117th Street: "Baby Al Is Beating On Al", and the rumor was spread by none other than Barbara Nelson. She claimed that she heard Dwayne slap Al in the face a few times. Her grandson said he heard and saw it firsthand. While staying with his grandmother a few weekends, the sneaky lad would climb down from the roof on the fire escape and peek in Al's bedroom window. He claimed Dwayne knocked Al to the floor a few times, always filling his grandmother in with a roof report whenever she thought she heard her neighbors argue.

Dwayne ran up the stoop, into the building, and up the steps to the top floor. Entering the apartment, moving quickly into the bathroom, he hook locked the door. He gazed in the mirror. The crown of his head was cornrowed to the center while oodles of thick curly hair draped from the back. His eyebrows connected more with age with his future mustache and sideburns sprouting in place. Signs of Gwenny in his face disappeared with his pace from day to day, and the emergence of young Arnold Mucci's features greeted him more and more. He stretched his lips, examining gums and yellowing teeth; there were signs of imminent decay. He realized the present time wasn't right for his self-examination.

"Just a few more one-on-ones," he thought, removing a folded dollar bill from his pocket. He felt for his sniffing straw, panicking in its absence.

"Where the fuck's my shit?!," he yelled aloud, carefully placing his cocaine filled bill on the sink between the faucets. "Damn! Now I gotta get a straw! Pen top! Something! Shit!" He stormed out of the bathroom, heading for the kitchen. "Pappy better have some straws in here!"

He opened the drawers back and forth. "Where are they when ya' need 'em?!," he yelled, searching the kitchen cabinets. The phone started ringing.

"Man, fuck a phone! I need a straw so I can do my thang," he laughed. Finally noticing an open box of straws by some drinking glasses inside the cabinet, he removed one, running back to the bathroom. Using Al's toenail scissors, he crafted his new device. Within seconds, he was happily snorting cocaine out of his dollar bill. After sniffing all he could and licking the bill, he made his way out of the bathroom.

"Next mission," he thought, flying into the living room. The phone started ringing again. "I'm a buck that phone if that shit rings one more time!" The phone rang a second time. Dwayne left the living room to find his gun, angry with the loud ringing volume of the kitchen's rotary extension.

On the other end of the line was Al. This particular Sunday evening, he decided to attend a late night church revival around the corner. The program was to last until midnight. He had left Dwayne a note, stating he'd be out past twelve. Now he was calling back to let his grandson know that the program would be ending earlier than expected. He hung up the pay phone just in time when on the other end, Dwayne had stormed his way through the living room with a new, brown handle .38 caliber Smith and Wesson special aimed at the telephone. The phone stopped ringing just as he cocked it. Thirsty and panting heavily, he entered the kitchen opening the refrigerator becoming angry, staring at the emptiness.

"Pappy ain't got shit to drink! Medicine! Medicine! Medicine!"

He slammed the door back observing a note that was left on the front. Finally understanding what Al wrote, Dwayne estimated his returning at midnight. His mind began clicking. "I can bring a bittie over," he thought.

After the coke wore off a few hours later, Dwayne summoned an old school favorite, Annette from the next building upstairs. He removed his heavy "boom box" from his bedroom and she finished braiding his hair inside Al's bedroom in no time; Dwayne's intent was his need for a larger bed. The horny teenagers went for their genitals immediately the moment the hip-hop and cornrows finished. And after the insertion of her "slow jam" tape into the cassette deck, and the insertion of his vigorous love into her eager body, the fervent sweetness of dusk lingered into an evening of naïve carnality. "Moments in Love" was her favorite song by Art of Noise, just right for the occasion, and the groove of the music was perfect for the groove Dwayne needed. While the young lovers switched positions, trading their misconceived moans inside Al's king sized bed; Al slowly made his way to the fourth floor. Using his one-two step every five seconds, it took him all of twenty minutes to reach the fifth floor.

He thought, "I'm gon'e tell that super we need to build a elevator. Ya woulda think by now we'd a had one. I ain't gon'e be able to leave the house."

He fished for his keys, removing them from his pocket. Shaking his head at the sound of the blaring music coming from his grandson's bedroom, Al took a deep breath. Unlocking the door quietly, the weary senior entered his apartment worn out from the repetitious climb, yet he was glad to receive the word of Christ after he had neglected church the preceding years. He shut on the hallway light, aghast immediately. The loud music was coming from inside *his* bedroom, and a young woman lay naked across Al's bed, sucking his grandson's penis while he kneeled over her. Dwayne was rubbing her hair; his body sensuously jerking, and then Dwayne yelped during his orgasm. Al thought furiously, "Jimmy can have him! He gonna make me have another stroke! I can't handle him no mo' !"

Al slammed the door shut, stopping Dwayne and his mate in the middle of the oral sex act. The devastated elder glared through his spectacles at the foul teenagers.

Annette shrieked, coughing and spitting, leaping from the bed, scrambling to get her clothes.

"What the devil goin' on?!," Al yelled. "Ain't you . . . ain't you one of Sister Wilkins' gir . . ."

"MOTHERFUCKER!! You *old*
MOTHERFUCKER," Dwayne howled at his grandfather, jumping directly off the bed, going into Al's bedroom closet.

Al entered his room and was hit with a blow to the face, with one of his own shoes, knocking his glasses across the bedroom. Inside temporary, stunned, dizzying, painful blindness, he felt his warm blood trickling from his brow to his eyes, blinding him more as he backed up and grabbed onto the doorknob, to keep from falling. Dwayne threw another one of Al's shoes, this time missing him, hitting the apartment door. Blood continuously seeped through his hands as he tried to cover his horrified, hurt face; the blood dripped onto Annette's broken jar of hair grease Dwayne had also hurled.

"NOOO! . . . PLEASE BABY AL . . . I CAIN'T SEE! . . . H . . . HEL . . .P MEEE," Al yelled, cane falling to the floor, holding his face with more blood spurting through his quivering hands, dripping thick to the floor.

Annette was dressed in a flash, attempting to flee the place. She also heard the rumor that Dwayne was abusing his grandfather. When she witnessed the violent shoe throwing rage, she learned the rumors were true. She managed to move Al out of her way, with some of his blood staining her autumn jacket, bolting from the apartment and down the steps, terrified.

While whisking by the fourth floor, Annette flew past Barbara. She had finished her gossip duties of the evening and was headed home, and seeing *'that Wilkinson tramp'* sprinting from upstairs made her wonder. She knew something terrible was happening with her neighbors, speeding her way up to investigate. When she reached the fifth floor she saw that the Carter door was shut. Pressing her ear to the door, she could hear slaps and knocks inside music. A broken glass after the music stopped! Loud curse words!

'Why the fuck you gotta embarrass me, Pappy?! You a old jealous old motherfucker! Cause you can't get no pussy? You can't get no pussy huh?! You can't get no pussy huh?!! You fucking COCK

BLOCK ME?! You can't get no pussy, you fucking jealous of **meeeeee!'**

There was an awful sounding crash, and Barbara dropped her mouth open wide. Standing up straight, she banged on the door of Apt. 53, determined to put a stop to what she heard and knew.

Dwayne swung the door open, bare-chested, clad in boxer shorts only. He hissed, "What do you want?"

Barbara tried to look inside, asking frantically, "Where's Al? Where's yo' grandfather? Al! . . . Al?! Al?"

Dwayne stared hard at Barbara.

"Yeah," Al answered from inside, trying to quietly breathe, still hyperventilating pretty loud.

"Everything alright?!"

"Yeah! . . . I'm alright! . . . Everythang alright!"

"Bye!," Dwayne yelled in Barbara's face, slamming the door.

Al stood against the wall, wheezing, with blood still dripping from the gash over his right eyebrow, soaking his suit and turning his white shirt maroon. Needing immediate medication, he felt like he would pass out.

"Baby Al . . . Baby Al, listen, listen to me."

Dwayne grabbed Al by his collar, and held him against the wall.

"Shut up! Every time I try to have some fun you find a way to fuck it up!"

Looking around at the mess he made with the shoes, he seemed to get angrier. "See what you made me do! Shit!" He let Al go just as he passed out onto the floor.

"Get up, Pappy! Get up! Stand up! Get ya' black ass up!"

He wanted to pounce on him all night, but for what reason? Was it the concealed truth about his mother still? Was it the return of his mother to her rightful place, frozen in time, perched upon the wall unit in the living room? Was it the need for more drugs?

Looking down on Al, Dwayne realized he had to do something; he couldn't leave Al on the floor unconscious. Besides, Barbara had to have called the cops by now.

"Pappy! Pappy?! Speak to me," Dwayne yelled, aggravated yet fearful. He quickly dialed the operator to be put through to 911 from his bedroom extension.

"Hello, 911 . . . Please . . . My grandfather fell out! He hit his face on the floor . . . Please! Send an ambulance right away . . . One-twenty-eight . . . West 117th Street! Number fifty three top floor! . . . I keep telling him to use his cane and he won't listen to me! . . . Please help us right away! He's bleeding so much!"

Dwayne quickly dressed, swept up the broken jar of hair grease and mopped up Al's blood, while his grandfather slowly regained consciousness in the hallway in front of Dwayne's bedroom, with a twisted up blood stained swollen face, and vernacular lightly above a raspy whisper. The ambulance arrived eventually, and rushed Al to the hospital emergency room. Diagnosed with a moderate stroke, he was admitted into the infirmary for close to a month, with frequent visits from Dwayne, pleading for forgiveness.

He was interrogated by detectives, questioning the domestic abuse he "allegedly" was receiving. Forgiving his grandbaby once again, Al constantly denied mistreatment. He covered it up with any quick lie, saying he fell, or he forgot to use his cane. Arlene, Jimmy & Monica Robinson, and Nathan Pope stopped by for visits. Even Barbara came to visit Al in the hospital, doing her best to find out all she could for gossip purposes. Al was happy everyone thought of him. There were some tough decisions to make. Dwayne had given him a swollen jaw on different occasions, knocked him down a flight of stairs, and broke several things around the house.

Al thought, "He can get his own place . . . I reckon' he 'bout eighteen or nineteen . . . If he stay in the house with me, he gon' have to listen . . . He gon' have to help me . . . I'm sick . . . I'm his Grandpappy . . . He cain't be beatin' on me like I'm his boy."

He was toying with mental ultimatums daily, in the trance of his cardiovascular attack, needing immediate rehabilitation, daydreaming of his deceased wife and daughter, receiving visits from them frequently amidst new trances. Second-guessing his relationship with his grandson, Al drifted off to sleep in and out of stupors, while nurses and doctors hustled Al and his admitted neighbors' diagnoses, some fatal or semi-fatal, simply working about inside the hospital.

While Al recuperated from his second stroke at a snail's pace, outside of the hospital, his grandson and his high school friends were going through their own personal changes.

After graduating from high school more than two years prior and leaving his overprotective, bullying friends in the academic dust, Arthur sailed into his junior year at college miles away north of New York City upstate, in Albany, New York. He would come around the way on his vacations from school in a brand new Jeep Wrangler bought by his parents for successfully making it through school. Donning new contact lenses, destroying his original bubbled spectacles, with new dental work and eliminating his afro, he traded in his former geeky image for a brand new "mack daddy" concept. Arthur had wheels, money, many female admirers and he was feeling complete with his "Jheri curl" and jewels, and he kept the Boyd family happy still maintaining a 3.09 grade point average in school, majoring in business administration.

Patrick, who had messed up in his senior year, owed and obtained three credits, and was awarded his high school diploma in September 1982 after a stint in summer school. He wanted to continue earning money on his job in "Wendy's" that he had during school. He liked bringing his brothers and sisters gifts with the money he earned. College remained a mental option, and Patrick tried to work as much overtime as possible to stay out of the house and out of his parents' way, mainly Dora, who urgently pressed her son about his educational direction.

After the explosion in the Livingston home when Patrick was thrown out of the house, he went to live with his older brothers Nigel and Franklin, and his uncle Barrington, Dora's younger brother who was also cast from the house previously. Patrick's academic aspirations remained in his heart along with his work ethic and loyalty to the fast food business, yet major things were happening to his mind and visual with the current household living arrangement in which he was involved. Right before his nineteen year old eyes, Barrington's drug empire grew bigger and stronger. After another uncle, Dora and Barrington's younger brother Ezra migrated to America because of growing finances, Barrington moved his brother and nephews from 139th Street to a penthouse in Washington Heights. With diligent moneymaking skills and growing clientele, Barrington and his family renovated their penthouse. Patrick stayed excited and wide-eyed through the whole process, even lending a hand to the contractors as they broke walls and ceilings to create a new two-floor penthouse. Once the project was completed, the penthouse became a modern day brothel with numerous women flocking about. The women, the money, and the clout blew Patrick's mind like a hallucinogen. He quit his fast food after-school job after becoming manager at Wendy's, and devoted his life to the drug trade, like his uncles and his older brothers.

After finding out that her son Eric had quit school,

single mom Carmelita Martinez-Delacruz hit him with an ultimatum: **"Busca un trabajo para que me ayudes con los billes o te vas de mi casa!" ("Find a job to help me with the bills or get out of my house!")** Eric soon found himself in the middle of Foster Projects holding dice games for his portion of the rent money. He remained tough and streetwise, but tender enough not to be put out in the street.

Shawn was told by the school he would need eight more credits to graduate, which meant he'd be held over for another year, amounting to seven years of George Washington High School. He abandoned school, but decided to try enlistment with the armed forces after being told by a recruiter that he could obtain his general equivalency diploma during basic training. Upon realizing that he would have to put his new love of "popping" and "breakdancing" on hold, Shawn began to ditch his recruiter at all costs. After a violent confrontation with his aunt and uncle, he ditched their residence as well, settling in with his girlfriend Phetima.

Dwayne never saw school again, deciding it was a true waste of time, when you could make big money instead. He created his very own private arsenal in his bedroom stashing guns, drugs - cocaine and marijuana, in old shoe-boxes, stacking them in semi-neat order. He and Scheme even seized a deserted apartment in the building on the second floor, and because of their green, they were able to manage their names being put on a rental agreement for the apartment. They turned apt. #23 into a weed and coke spot. Patrons flocked to and from the building nicknaming it "seven-eleven", knowing they would cop the good stuff from there, twenty-four hours a day. This made the tenants of 128 West 117th Street go crazy after realizing the building had a drug spot inside. Some tenants chose to move, while others angrily remained afraid for their lives and families.

"Great! Great, Mister Carter! You can do it, you're looking good! Just a couple more steps! One! Two! Three!"

Al received applause from a small circle of physical therapists and nurses. His second stroke left him aphasic, totally slurring his speech, nearly crippling him. A cane wouldn't provide the support he needed to walk; he was instructed to use an aluminum walker. After a week of physical therapy, relying on inner genetic strengths, he was practically running with it.

"See y'all . . . Cain' talk . . . cain' . . . walk . . . bu' . . . ah . . . sho' ih run . . . wid dis beby," he mumbled, attempting to grin.

"One . . . two . . . dree . . . fowur."

He paced himself, taking four steps.

"Great, that's just great," his main therapist said, "You're doing such a great job, Mister Carter, are you sure you're going to need a walker to take home? You move really well."

"Am I . . . gon'e need . . . walker?"

"You move very well with it, I'm questioning it sir."

"Listen beby . . . all de presidents been . . . white?"

"I guess that means yes, then."

"Ya betta . . . bahlieve . . . it."

Al moved around the physical therapy gym, amusing himself with his new toy.

"May I help you, Miss," he heard someone ask out. He looked up and saw Arlene staring directly at him.

"Yes, I came to see Mister Carter. He's doing better, good," she exclaimed, ecstatic.

"Come in, it's okay, they can have visitors down here," a female therapist added.

Arlene entered the gym and looked around at the physical therapy area. She hated going to hospitals because of the infamous smell. As she looked around at the other elderly patients, she felt her happy mood change.

"Ole good . . . ol' . . . Ah . . . lene," Al mumbled with love, "See mah . . . move? . . . Ya' see?" She walked over to him, while he stepped toward her victoriously. "Guess de . . . maker . . . ain't ready . . . fuhr . . . me . . ., Ah . . . lene, I'm still . . . eene . . . Hahlem."

He progressed with another step.

"Who's this, your daughter, Mister Carter?," a female therapist approached.

"She lahk a . . . daughda . . . tuh . . . me," he mumbled. "I watch . . . her . . . grow . . . up, she wa' . . . muh . . . daughda bes' friend."

"Oh! That's really cool! To have a friend for so long, wow . . . Mister Carter here, sure is a ladies' man," the therapist giggled.

Arlene smiled. "He's like a father to me. I feel it's my duty to look out for him."

"Sir, the workout is finished for the day. You can go back to your room anytime you're ready," the female therapist stated.

"Can . . . uh . . . walk . . . back . . . wit' . . . muh . . . walka?"

"With your walker? Mister Carter, the walker belongs to this gym. I don't think I'll be able to let . . ." The therapist paused and thought about the old man's resilience and courage. In her many years of physical therapy, Al Carter was the first patient she saw who recovered from a moderate stroke with such buoyancy. The therapist looked at Arlene, then at Al, and shrugged her shoulders.

"Well, okay Mister Carter, I don't see why not, if your friend wouldn't mind assisting you."

"Sure, I'll help him back upstairs," Arlene said.

"Good! I'll call the floor and tell the nurses to keep an eye out for the two of you," smiled the therapist, walking away.

"You have everything," Arlene asked Al.

"Huh?"

"Where's your stuff!," she repeated louder.

"Oh. I ain't . . . got . . . nuthin'. Just dis ha' . . . robe . . . en . . . pajamas . . . I . . . got on."

"All set," the therapist cheerily announced across the room. "The nurses are waiting on you upstairs, Mister Carter. Take your time."

Al and Arlene advanced slowly from the gym, down a long corridor, past encouraging smiles to the elevator bank. While waiting, Arlene took a hard look at Al. The tall, hardworking, handsome cook with the no nonsense attitude was long gone. His handsomely rich caramel skin had turned wrinkled, ashy, and blotchy; his skin had dark bruises, and blemishes all over. He even had a brand new stitched up cut, equipped with a darkening swelling over his eyebrow. His hair was unkempt, growing into a nappy, white forest. The bellowing voice flavored with southern scars and northern delusions was absent, replaced with a dull, low, raspy, mechanical, mumbling rhetoric. And she was amazed that she still understood Al. Arlene exhaled uneasily, still mystified by the wrath of the aging process.

They reached the appropriate floor with Arlene leading the way. Al came slowly, yet triumphantly, managing his walker with ease. Al mumbled, "Yuh kno', Doc . . . Wuhllis . . . suppose . . . come . . . bah here. Wha's day?"

"It's Saturday, Mister Carter. You still go to Doctor Wallace up on Convent Avenue? He still living?"

She opened his room door, allowing him to enter.

"Ol' man Wuhllis . . . been . . . dead. Heah . . . son . . . duhn . . . took ovva . . . de pra'tice."

"Oh. Cause I know you and Miss Mattie was going to Doctor Wallace since I was young."

Noticing the late hour, Arlene carefully helped Al to bed. She said, "Listen, I'm going to leave now. I need to do some food shopping for the kids."

She kissed the overwrought elderly man on his

forehead, bidding farewell while he prepared himself to lie down.

Minutes after Arlene left, Doctor Wallace peeked inside and approached Al's bedside. The doctor tapped his patient a couple of times, noticing the drastic change in the senior's disposition. He too, like Arlene, was bothered by Al's hideous, new look. His father had always spoken highly of the Carter family, often referring to Al and Mattie Carter as "hardworking Negro folks". Something was definitely astray with his patient.

"Mister Carter, Mister Carter, it's Doc Wallace," the middle-aged man said tenderly. Al opened his eyes slowly.

"Hey . . . doc," Al mumbled.

"Mister Carter, you're going to be discharged on Monday. Will your grandson be coming to pick you up?"

"Guess . . . so . . . Recka . . . so."

"You sure? I can arrange transportation for you."

"Uh huvve uh way home," Al said sluggishly, drifting back to sleep.

Doctor Wallace shook his head, staring down at one of his favorite elderly clients. He knew in his heart that Al Carter was the victim of domestic elderly abuse. He couldn't tell how long, but he displayed all the signs. The unexplained face marks, bruises, strokes, lethargic confusion, the secretiveness; and there were the lies about the falls, the over-protection he showed towards his grandson, the deep-rooted guilt, and ugliness of it.

The following Monday morning, Dwayne snatched up the ringing phone extension in his bedroom, before leaving the apartment to shop for Al's coming home present.

"Yo, yo," he yelled into the receiver.

"Yo, high, what up?!," Patrick exclaimed on the other end.

"Yo, who this? Pat! That's you man?!"

"Yeah black, what's up Dee?!"

"Cool, money!"

"How ya keeping homeboy? How's your grandpops, Dee? Shit is cool with Mister Carter?"

"Yo, high, Pappy in the hospital. He about to get out though man."

"So what's up, high?"

"Pat man! How you been?!"

"You know I'm uptown high, with my Uncle Ezra and my Uncle Barry. I can't talk too long right now, but my people giving me a three-day party! You know my birthday's Sunday."

"A WHAT?! Get the fuck outta here Pat. A three-day party?! That shit is fly!"

"Bust the move, the party starts at eight on Friday the twelfth, and it goes straight through to my birthday. Bring Shawn and E-zo. We got stupid catching up to do! Remember, your code is Baby Al."

"Yo . . . Hold up! Gimme another code."

"Umm, nope! See ya at the party. Later high!"

Patrick hung up, while Dwayne on the other end was overwhelmed by the conversation. "Patrick chilling stupid hard," he thought, "I'm a get with that nigga, a three-day party, this I gotta see."

He lit a cigarette at the stove, and then went back into his wreck of a bedroom to continue dressing. From his black hoodie, to his black denim Levi jeans, to his laced black & yellow high topped Nike sneakers, Dwayne now was ready to shop. He dug into one of his stacked shoeboxes in the closet and removed a wad of money. Set on buying a present to make amends, he jetted from the apartment.

He began his familiar five-floor descent, passing the second floor and chuckling to himself noticing his customers holding court in front of seven-eleven.

Dwayne thought, "Shawn or the nigga Scheme probably inside."

He left the tenement looking towards the sky then checking his watch. The Harlem morning was mild as the weatherman predicted. Rich chunks of white clouds sat still amidst a pastel blue sky. Down inside the concrete jungle, the hungered addicts pestered Dwayne before he could reach Seventh Avenue, the routine of a pseudo-celebrity hustler.

"Welll!"

Al cringed at the sound of the all too familiar, high pitched voice, greeting him and Jimmy at the top of the staircase. Barbara had perfect timing, bumping into them after Al's release from the hospital. Jimmy had struggled with Al's folded walker in one hand and he practically carried his mentor upstairs with his other shoulder and was exhausted.

"So nice to have you back in one piece, Al Carter," Barbara said, looking Jimmy up and down, "Who are you? You look familiar?"

"Awww Bawbah! You start yo' noseniss uhredddy," Al mumbled.

"I'm Jimmy Robinson," Jimmy replied, catching his breath.

"Oh yeah! The cook that worked with Al for years, got fired and opened up a business and now you rich and fancy huh? Yeah honey I remember you! Yeah! Looking for ya godson?"

Jimmy looked at Al, confused. Barbara returned an attentive glare.

"Al Carter, tell him!"

"Jummy, Bawbah knows . . ."

"Everything," she cut him off.

" 'Bou' . . . evah . . .body," Al added.

"Well, nobody answered my question? Don't y'all want to know where Baby Al **IS**?"

Jimmy spoke up to get rid of the insane, troublesome

woman. "Okay, where is Baby Al?"

"Did ya check the second flo', huh?"

"No, we didn't check, why?"

"Huh! You think Barbara gonna tell it honey?! Huh, you're sadly mistaken! Just come on down to seven eleven," she rambled, starting down the stairs. Her nagging voice became faint as she descended lower in the building.

"That's right! Y'all ain't gettin' Barbara to tell it! Naw honey! Come on and go on to seven-eleven! You'll see him, honey! Seven-Eleven! Seven! Come on!"

"Aw, she ohwayze go' . . . 'ne 'bout nuthin'," Al mumbled. In a split second, Dwayne snatched open the apartment door.

"SURPRISE! Welcome, home," he said, slowing down when he saw Jimmy, "Oh wow! Hi Jimmy."

Dwayne shook his godfather's hand, noticing he held a walker. "Dag, Pappy, y'all ruined my surprise! I got a walker for you too." He moved behind the door so Al and Jimmy could enter the apartment.

"Why, didn't you get your granddaddy from the hospital," Jimmy asked, placing Al's walker in front of him.

"I been busy looking for his present," Dwayne answered, closing the door.

"See Jummy, how dut fool dahn da' hall stah 'bout Bebah Al," Al mumbled.

"Who, Miss Nelson right?," Dwayne threw a hiss, "Miss Nelson always starting with me and the whole building. Now she says she's the president of the tenant association of this building."

Dwayne helped remove Al's coat, then tossed it over his shoulder into Al's bedroom on top of the freshly made bed. Jimmy started toward the living room, examining his mentor's place. Al followed him, pleased with the scent of his home. It smelled of air freshener instead of the permanent perspiration, hominy grits, and dead mice. He glanced at his grandson's usual messy bedroom while moving, still ecstatic with the rosy aroma and the apartment's mysterious cleanliness in his absence. It seemed to be a brand new residence.

"What's the deal on seven eleven Baby Al," Jimmy asked.

"I don't know," Dwayne answered, walking behind Al.

They entered the living room and Jimmy helped Al sit on the couch.

"How y'all know about seven eleven," asked Dwayne.

"Thought you ain't know nothing!," Jimmy snapped.

"I don't know nothing!," Dwayne fired back, staring at Jimmy.

Jimmy returned Dwayne's gaze; he thought, *'You might have your grandfather scared of you sucker but I'll bust that ass!'*

"See what I got ya Pappy," Dwayne said, breaking the escalating tension. He placed the walker he purchased next to the stereo. On top of the closed stereo sat a new 13-inch colored television. "See, got a new TV for us, and this walker's got wheels, so you can speed around the house." Dwayne turned on the TV looking back at Jimmy, and Jimmy kept his piercing eyes glued on Dwayne.

"See Pappy, now you can see your man Dave Winfield working that outfield in his white and blue striped suit, instead of his black and white suit," he announced with affection.

Al grinned. "Mann . . . ih dat ding . . . ah beauty. Ain't dat . . . uh . . . nize TV . . . Jummy?," he mumbled, while Jimmy stared continuously at Dwayne.

"Yeah, Mister Slick, it's a nice TV," he replied softly.

Dwayne looked away several times, and again to Jimmy, and Jimmy still glared at him. "Pappy, you feeling better? You look better than when you left."

"Uh-huhm . . . I betta . . . Mah' fine uh ya tuh keep da place clean . . . Bebah Al."

"Yeah, well I know you was extra sick."

"Thought you don't like ya granddaddy to call ya Baby

Al anymore, what's the deal?"

"Well, I ain't no baby no more, you know the half," Dwayne began, "I don't want him to call me Baby Al but sometimes, Pappy slips up. It's cool though. Long as he don't do it when the bitties call," he chuckled. Dwayne noticed Jimmy frowning this time.

'*This black ugly motherfucker gonna be trouble,*' he thought, gazing back at Jimmy.

"Pappy, you want something from the store?"

"Naw . . . I . . . fihe . . . thank ya'."

"Okay. Once again, Pappy! Welcome home!"

He walked over to Al and kissed him quickly on the forehead. Jimmy noticed Al wince and shake when his grandson came near him.

"Okay, nice seeing you, Jimmy." Dwayne went to hug his godfather when he stopped him.

"Hold on, hold on, Baby Al. Don't be in such a rush man. You ain't got no time to chat with your godfather?"

"I got to be somewhere, but if you'll be here when I get back, we'll talk."

Jimmy shook his head. "No, I need to talk to you now, right now," he stated.

"Pappy, see you later. I'll try to be in before it's too late." Dwayne walked from the living room.

"In the hallway, outside," Jimmy yelled, trailing behind Dwayne. Dwayne opened the apartment door and walked into the hallway, with Jimmy quickly following.

Jimmy was shorter at five-feet-ten while Dwayne at 19 years was six-foot-one. Jimmy closed the door and he verbally tore into his godson immediately:

"Spill it! Spill it right now! Goddamn it! Spill it!"

"Spill what?"

"What the fuck's wrong with Mister Slick?! Huh?"

"I don't know. What you think? He just got out the hospital!"

"How in the hell did he get there?"

"He had a stroke! Why you yelling Jimmy?"

"You gave it to him! A second goddamn stroke!"

"What?"

"Look, Baby Al, don't fuck with me! I got two sons that I raised up! I'll jack yo' ass up like I jack they asses up! Don't play with me! I'm from Bed-Stuy! Do or Die! Where I come from we eat little Harlem pussy motherfuckers like you for BREAKFAST!"

"What the hell is wrong with him?," Dwayne thought, becoming amused with Jimmy's antics. He resembled a coal black animated Budda symbol, operated by marionette strings.

"So what's your point?! Godfather!"

"I don't know what the fuck you done did to Mister Slick in there, but let me tell you something. The bullshit will stop! Right here! Right now!"

"What you mean?! Yo, why you riffin' Jimmy?!"

"If you touch him again, your high-yellow ass is going behind bars! You old enough now damn it! And Miss Mattie ain't here to protect you! And they raised you the best they could! You're a sick piece of work IF YOU BEAT ON HIM!"

Al opened the door just in time to see his protégé and grandson glare at each other, for the kill.

"Wha's carryah onne, out'chere," he mumbled.

Dwayne ran down the stairway, crazed with anger and filled with guilt, while Jimmy caught his breath. "It's okay . . . it's okay . . . Slick. It's okay."

"Oh . . . Uh heah . . . y'all . . . wa' back . . . eene de . . . livin'ruhm," Al mumbled, backing into the apartment. Jimmy followed his mentor, desperately wanting to quiz him on what was really happening. He knew Al would protect Dwayne so it was really no use. He helped him sit on the sofa a second time.

Al grinned sheepishly and mumbled, "Duh t.v. Bebah Al bow mah's sumthin' nice. You . . . like't . . . it?"

Jimmy sadly shook his head while Al admired the "gifts" from his grandson.

A few days later:

"How many times I gotta tell you about calling me Baby Al?! That's not my motherfucking name! It's Dwayne!"

Dwayne leaped from the couch and stormed over to Al, and snatched the kitchen phone receiver out of Al's hands.

"What!! . . . Hello?! . . . Yeah! . . . Yeah!! . . . Tell that nigga I'm coming!"

He slammed the phone down, and stared hatefully at Al who returned the glare with tears in his eyes, shaking while standing halfway in the kitchen and halfway in the living room.

"What the fuck you looking at? You got a eye problem?! You a fucking faggot now or something," Dwayne yelled. He stormed away from Al, down the hall into his bedroom. He removed his stash of coke from one of his shoe-boxes inside the closet. Hungrily sniffing, Dwayne overheard his phone ringing. Deeply submerged into his habit, he looked at the innocent Mickey Mouse figurine deciding to ignore the telephone.

"Pappy! Let me know if the phone's for me!," he shouted, engrossed in snorting a few more one-on-ones.

Silence, then: "Bebah Al . . . Hu-hey! . . . Bebah Uhll!"

Al raised his voice as loud as he could. Dwayne burst from his room, heart palpitating with fury. He entered the living room full speed, snatched the receiver out of Al's hand and covered the mouthpiece. With his face contorted with rage, he roared, "Are you hard headed or are you a stupid Jack ass?! My name ain't no motherfucking Baby Al! It's Dwayne! Albert! Carter! Now say it again, so I can beat the living shit out you!"

Al stood petrified. This was no way to live. "How can

I go on?," he thought, while Dwayne secretly conversed on the kitchen extension. Suddenly, he spun around with his eyebrows connecting.

"Pappy! Did Shawn call me today?!"

Al was terrified. What would he say? He couldn't remember everyone that called the house. People for him, people for Dwayne; there were endless female voices and countless male voices.

"Ah . . . Ah! . . . Ah . . . duh . . . know," Al mumbled upset, "Ah nah sh . . . shu' . . . shuo . . . sho'! Ah nah sho', uh duh know!"

He backed away slowly with his grandson's savage eyes piercing his timid soul. Dwayne hissed twice. "I'm not in the mood, Pappy! Yes or no!!"

Al questionably replied, "No?"

With the back of the telephone receiver, Dwayne smashed Al repetitiously with blows to the top of Al's shoulder and collarbone; every word and breath constituted another slam.

"**What!** . . . **If!** . . . *The fucking* **call was important?!** . . . **Huh!** . . . ***Huh!*** . . . ***Huh!*** . . . Shawn's on the phone now! . . . And he **fucking!** . . . **CALLED!!!**"

The receiver hit the floor, and Al used his walker as quick as he could to get away from his beating, stopping short in front of the wall unit, in front of his daughter. Gwenny the graduate valedictorian, smiled directly through her sobbing father's reflection inside her wall unit position, while her son cursed repeatedly into the phone receiver after picking it up from the floor, eventually to slam it back down on its hook.

With his hurt back still turned, Al heard Dwayne's infuriated footsteps stomp closer. He bawled on, closed his eyes, and hunched his stinging shoulders, terrified but prepared. He opened his eyes when he heard noises coming from the direction of the bedrooms.

"See you old fuck-up," Dwayne yelled. There were

crashes and thuds, mixed with loud, blaring music. "These motherfuckers 'bout to pick me up to go to Pat's and I ain't ready!"

Al thought he heard the toilet flush with some jingling keys, the lock turned, a door opened. He moved to the corridor and caught a glimpse of his grandson exiting the apartment.

"P . . . PUH . . . PUHLEAS' . . . WUH YA GOIN'?" Al asked.

Dwayne looked nonchalantly at him, hissing.

"Party uptown in a penthouse! What's it to you? Ain't no old folk's party! You can't come! Ain't no fucking checkerboards allowed! All you'd do is have another fucking stroke! Probably on the dance floor!" He hissed again, and slammed the door.

Al stood frozen with heartbreaking pain. Suddenly, he let off a yell that could be spiritually heard for miles. He cried hysterically; tears of fear, tears of loneliness, tears of mental and physical pain, tears for his deprivation of love, and tears for his abuse.

Patrick's three-day birthday party was a huge success. His uncles, Barrington and Ezra along with his brothers Nigel and Franklin took extreme measures with women, food, drugs, and artillery. Dwayne and Shawn arrived red-eyed during the Saturday night portion, after smoking a few blunts beforehand, anxious to see their childhood friend. Neither of the guys had seen Patrick since his mother threw him out and his uncles gave him shelter. He had slimmed down and was super fit, and had grown a few inches to five foot nine, yet still a bit shorter than Dwayne and Shawn. Rumor had it that his uncles and brothers made big time money, light years away from the "pennies" made in seven eleven. Patrick's crew was well on their way to locking down the drug world uptown. Dwayne and Shawn's eyes popped out of their heads as they followed Patrick through the festive event at his uncles' two-floor penthouse.

Reggae and calypso music boomed through the rooms out the windows, filling up the clear starry sky with the sounds of a true Jamaican/American party. West Indian cuisine was the delight of the night with the spicy aroma and taste of the finger foods and entrees, tickling the partygoers' palates. The aroma of certain other refreshments stroked others' nostrils. People sniffed cocaine in one room, while others smoked marijuana in another.

"So what's up, Shawn man," Patrick asked, hugging Shawn.

"I want some ass, high. I can't front," Shawn replied.

"Word? Hold on . . . Yo' Shayla! Come here," Patrick yelled to an exotic, dark-skinned female with teased up hair, wearing a leopard suit draped in costume jewelry. The girl joined the guys, giving them a sexy once over.

"My man here, he wanna get with you," Patrick said, pointing to Shawn.

"Cool," Shayla replied, continuing to look Shawn up and down.

"Get another female for my man Dee here," Patrick said, pointing at Dwayne. She nodded, walking off.

"Damn, high! What's up with the gottas? I'm ready to smoke, stay zooted! It's your birthday party high, I know you got shit sewed up," Dwayne laughed, and slapped Patrick five.

"Yo', who that," Shawn asked Patrick, referring to another beautiful brown-skinned woman with a tight, white, one piece, see through mini skirt set; with her thick tanned legs crossed, while laid back on a lounge chair, she stroked and patted the head of a light brown colored pit bull.

"Oooh! She look dumb good! I'm a slide up in that before the night is through," Dwayne said.

"Nah, high, that's me! You take her dog, while I get that cat," laughed Shawn.

"I'll take the dog alright," Dwayne mumbled, developing a fondness for the young lady's canine.

"Yo what kind of dog that honey dip sporting? Yo that's a pit bull right," Shawn asked Patrick.

"Yeah it's a pitbull. They're no joke man. They trained to kill, some of them. Hers is pregnant. See the belly there so," asked Patrick.

"I see a whole lotta dog titties," Shawn replied.

"You're a mad man," Patrick chuckled.

"Pregnant, eh," Dwayne mumbled.

Dwayne watched the pregnant dog, and his mind began clicking, putting two and two together for a future plan.

They stood in their tiny kitchen, with the window closed because of the forthcoming snow.

"Whah hih numme? . . . Wha's ya gone . . . cawl 'im . . . Dd . . . Dwiynne," Al asked, peeking at the package in his grandson's palms.

"General . . . General, that's his name. He look like one, don't he, Pappy," Dwayne stated proudly.

The male newborn pit bull slept in his master's hands peacefully during the Christmas serenity, soon to be trained deadly, for new years to come.

****

CHAPTER 7

*

Hanging out at Barrington's penthouse once in a while convinced the crew that they were missing out on a good thing. The chump change being earned inside apt#23's seven eleven would never measure up to the net proceeds Patrick's uncles raked in. Little by little, each of the guys, especially Dwayne, wanted out of their current drug dealing arrangement. Peddling from apartment # 23, exactly four floors below the Carters, was dated and the job soon became dry, corny, and troublesome. After a few thrilling apartment searches from the NYPD, as far as they were concerned, it was in with Barrington, out with Scheme, particularly with Dwayne who always craved more in any situation. He was tired of Scheme insisting he was the boss of operations, and he needed a change.

Eric was the most hesitant, feeling some sort of loyalty to Scheme. Scheme was his friend in the first place, and Eric felt that Scheme was responsible for their financial gains. Eric felt that if they join forces with Patrick's uncles, Scheme should be included in the mix. He had become family.

Shawn didn't care, as long as he made his money, had time to hang around other buddies in the Zulu Nation, and pursue his loves of hip hop, the breakdance, and the electric boogie. He could rock uptown in Washington Heights with the Livingston crew or stay downtown in Harlem, long as they kept a slew of women on deck, and kept the bread coming in, with or without Scheme, it didn't matter.

Dwayne remained determined. Patrick didn't know Scheme-Dwayne continued to think-so why would he and why should he go all out to accommodate "the next man", someone he didn't know, especially this Brooklyn cat that appeared out of nowhere like a genie? Patrick would want his old crew down, which meant no Scheme.

Pretty soon, the seven eleven crew ran into problems, their entire vibe thrown off. Dwayne and Scheme started to hate each other, wanting to kill one another. Shawn and Eric tried to remain neutral but, as each day passed, that became harder to do. Dwayne knew his friends like the back of his hand, and it took nothing to agitate Eric's temper. Shawn also was quick tempered, and could be easily fooled. A couple of lies wouldn't hurt. In fact, lying would help! Besides, Scheme seemed to beat them out of their money on a regular basis. He would take the biggest chunks of money claiming "the bills" needed to be paid in seven eleven, and he needed to keep the cops off their backs. At least with Patrick's relatives they would surely make more money; with their childhood buddy, they were less prone to get beat. Patrick would never let his boys down, especially if he knew of their interest in joining his uncles' crew. He would put in a good word with his family for them. Dwayne decided he would turn Shawn and Eric against Scheme and at the same time, get out of the apartment lease he shared with Scheme which would definitely cut him loose; lying was the way. The atmosphere was strained enough for an explosion; and the battle stations in the spot began overheating.

"Count the bags right! You fucking up," Scheme shouted at Dwayne one evening. Eric was handling the door, and Shawn stepped away to the bathroom down the hall. Dwayne stopped counting, hissed, lit his cocaine laced Newport, and continued counting. Scheme said again, "Yo what the fuck! You retarded? You need to leave that shit alone if you can't handle it! You don't count bags of wee . . ."

"Man FUCK YOU! What! What!! . . . You a crab ass nigga anyway," Dwayne yelled, flicking his lit cigarette across the room at Scheme. Scheme stormed over to Dwayne. "What I told you 'bout disrespecting me?! Huh?!," Scheme roared, arms outstretched and revved for a fight.

Dwayne jumped up out of his seat and into Scheme's face. Eric shot from his post at the door into the living room and squeezed in between them.

"Chill y'all! What y'all doing man?! I'm tired of y'all shit B! Word up," Eric yelled, managing to contain Scheme.

"Yo what's up," asked oblivious Shawn returning to the illegal den from the bathroom. "Damn I just went to take a leak, how y'all just started going at it like that? Chill D! Come back on this side of the room," Shawn chuckled, moving Dwayne away from Scheme and Eric.

"Nah man, fuck that!! FUCK THAT! E-zo! Shawn! You don't even know the half on this nigga! Yo man E-zo?! This nigga Scheme ain't really down! Don't you know E-zo?! Don't you know what this nigga did?!! He told stupid heads in Jefferson and Taft that we suckers and he gettin' us set up," Dwayne shouted over Shawn's shoulder.

Scheme threw up his hands in disgust and began to grit his teeth. He yelled, "Man, get outta here, man you crazy! Dee man! You lying!"

"I know the half! You ain't setting up nobody! Yo, E Man! This nigga Scheme running around talking stupid yang; this sucker nigga been popping crazy shit, even in fucking Mitchell uptown, and around here! Think I don't know muthafucka?! I got connects!"

Eric and Shawn started looking at Scheme, peculiarly. They began to get angry with each of Dwayne's new lies. Shawn believed Dwayne, more than Eric did. Eric was upset, but not as much as Shawn who backed off to the side while Scheme and Dwayne continued bickering, until finally

Dwayne shouted: "I'll BUCK YOU!"

"Yeah?! You all that?!! Go 'head and pull out! You gon' buck me?! Buck me then motherfucker!"

Dwayne pulled out his thirty-eight and aimed toward Scheme.

"Nahhhh!!! **WHAT YOU DOING**," Eric screamed, quickly pushing the weapon back. "Go 'head up, Dee man! You ain't no sucker! Don't go out like that!"

Dwayne pushed Eric against the wall. "Stupid ass! This nigga trying to set us up! E! Man, fuck is up wit'choo?! Man fuck this, I'm getting' with Pat! Our REAL peoples! This nigga here said he gettin' other niggas uptown to buck us down! You wanna keep fucking with him, in this bullshit ass seven eleven?! This SHIT ain't the MOVE no more!"

Scheme became vehemently frantic. "E! Don't listen to him! That nigga lying! How I'm a set you up when I'm cool with your people from Milbrook! Me and Paco dumb tight man!"

Noticing Shawn ready to pounce on Scheme after his trademark move of cracking his knuckles, Dwayne added, "I told y'all! I told y'all not to be trusting those Brooklyn niggas, man! They fucking wack! They always trying to take shit, trying to get niggas! Always want what niggas got! Trying to set up motherfuc . . . "

"Man fuck you!," Scheme interjected, "Duck ass nigga! I put you on! I gave you what you got! And I'm a Brooklyn nigga! What!! I made you what you are! You lucky you E-zo man, coke sniffing punk motherfucker!"

Dwayne and Shawn paced closer, while Scheme spoke, looking them in their eyes: "You ain't shit! You ain't never been shit! And you'll never be shit! I made you! Pussies! Them Jamaicans y'all wanna get down with, they ain't gon'e give a fuck about your Yankee American asses! Fuck you! You's a punk, and you's a uptown pussy! If you was so fucking bad, you would'a bucked me already with that tray eight I got you! Bitch!"

On the "B" note, Scheme went in his vest for his gun and was slammed to the floor by Shawn. Dwayne and Shawn jumped on Scheme, beating him like crazy, and they took his gun.

Astonished Eric stepped back in slow motion while Dwayne beat Scheme in the face with the butt of his own thirty-eight.

"Chill out, Dee man! Chill, high," Eric screamed, at the top of his lungs, angry with his partners for the unnecessary clash.

Dwayne caught his breath, and hissed, "Fuck that! Fuck that! Don't no niggas come uptown trying to play me close and run shit, I don't care where they from! Yo, get his ass outta here, and get that nigga coat! You know he a wack ass Brooklyn nigga, sporting sheepskins in eighty-five!"

The crew hauled blood faced Scheme out of the building, down the stoop, and into the bitterly cold January evening. Once finished, they ran back up to seven eleven. Dwayne went into the bathroom to clean Scheme's blood from his hands. Shawn carefully took apart and cleaned Scheme's weapon, and Eric sat in a troubled, angry daze, attempting to scribble in his tag book to calm down, to no avail. A few minutes after Dwayne entered the room and they had resumed their duties, uncomfortable Eric stood and went for his coat.

"Fuck this shit, I'm jettin'," he stated storming through the apartment.

Dwayne stopped counting bags of smoke to glare at him.

"What's up with you?"

"What you think?! Shit is fucked up!"

"What? We just bussed somebody's ass, that's all! We did it before."

"That nigga got crazy juice high! You know he down by law! Why you flipped on him like that?!"

"Man that motherfucker planned on robbing us! I'm supposed to stand there and let that happen? Nah high, I don't think so!"

"You coulda went head up with him Dee. You ain't have to pistol whip him! You ain't have to go out like that!"

"Well I went out like that," Dwayne snapped, "So fucking what! If I know a nigga trying to set me and my boys up, I'm going all out for mine," Dwayne said, re-starting the bag count.

"Dee, you my man and the whole shit," Eric began, "If you go down then I go down too. We all got beef high, I'm telling you! Scheme and them Brooklyn cats never fess! They ain't nothing to fuck with!"

Eric went to exit the spot. A wide smirk spread across Dwayne's face while he watched Eric prepare to leave the apartment. He said, "Oh I'm scared! I'm petro! My heart don't pump no motherfucking kool aid, and you know that E! That nigga ain't got no real juice uptown, I'm not sweatin' the nigga! . . . Yo . . .Ya' leaving your book . . . Yo leave me a cigarette, high!"

Eric slammed the door to the spot without looking back. Dwayne looked at Shawn, then back towards the door, then back to Shawn again and shrugged his shoulders. "Fuck 'im," he announced.

After selling a few bags of reefer and some packs of coke to their faithful nightly customers, Dwayne and Shawn slapped each other five for the evening, exhausted by the day's turn of events. Going their separate ways, Shawn left the building, and Dwayne conveniently headed upstairs. While coatless Scheme staggered the chilly streets of Harlem vowing vengeance, Dwayne retired for the night in his dimly lit, tepid bedroom in apartment # 53. He enjoyed wrestling and playing with General, his three-month old pit bull.

Dwayne stayed on General's back for the remaining

winter months; he trained the dog to be the best, smartest, and deadliest pit bull alive. General grew fast, and was more obedient of his master each day. He was a handsome dog, light goldenrod with a patch of white across his chest, his wagging tail joined a set of golden eyes filled with love for his master; and he learned to jump at Dwayne's every single command. Dwayne taught General to sit, stand, or attack when he wanted, dutifully walking him in the early mornings and evenings. The pit happily sat chained, while his master entered stores, or hung out with his friends. Whether hanging inside Foster Projects playing b-ball, or hot dice games in the hallways of the Johnson and Wagner Projects; whenever it was time to go check out the females in Drew Hamilton or the Lincoln Houses, or frequenting his favorite "coke" spots after devouring his own product, Dwayne and General had become an inseparable team. There was no stopping man and his best friend.

"I fine . . . ehthang ih fihe . . . yeah, I'm sho'," Al mumbled into his bedroom telephone receiving extension, while lying down on top of his bed. Jimmy Robinson on the other end questioned with concernment, knowing his mentor was still behaving timidly. He was pleased that Al was regaining most of his speech due to his determined strength and stamina. But with his enigmatic godson Dwayne still lurking in the apartment, he wondered if Al was receiving the attention and care that he desperately needed, but was too stubborn to receive.

"Where's Baby Al?"

"Hiz name ih Dawayne . . . He don't like tuh be called Bebah Al no' mo', Jummy."

"Where and the hell is Dwayne then? How's he treating you Slick?"

"Fine. I already told ya dat."

"The truth Slick! I want the truth! He ain't been hitting on you no more, has he?"

"He nevva hit me in da fuhst place Jummy. Things fine 'round here."

Dwayne entered the apartment, letting General run free.

"I'm back," he called out. He walked down the hall, tossing General's leash inside his room. There was no movement in the living room so Dwayne did an about face and walked towards Al's room.

"Pappy, did Patrick call?!"

"I say it . . . ain't . . . no beating goin' on . . . I swuhr . . . t'ain't no beatin'," Al murmured into the telephone.

Dwayne pounded Al's bedroom door, making the old man jump.

"WHO IS THAT?!" He stormed over to the bedside and snatched the phone receiver from Al's grasp.

"Why don't you worry about yo' own ass getting whipped at home, and leave us the fuck alone," he obliviously yelled into the receiver, slamming it down.

"Pappy, who you told I been hitting you?!"

Al shook his head, "No . . . body." He slid his entire body beneath the bedcovers exposing only his face.

"Did Patrick call?!"

Al shook his head again.

"Are you sure?!" The phone started to ring.

"Let me get it," Dwayne snapped, snatching up the receiver.

"Yeah," Dwayne spoke into the receiver, listening to the angry exhalations of the person on the other end.

"I'm coming down there right now goddamn it! No one talks to me like that and gets away with it," Jimmy shouted.

"So come on down! Who cares! Who gives a shit!"

You little high yellow fucker! Ya just like those damn crackers! The white man! The white man! Always wanna do in black people!"

Dwayne's piercing eyes widened, softening his frown

and separating his connecting eyebrow, with a curiosity for his ancestral background once again.

"Oh, so I'm white now, huh?"

Jimmy breathed hard and angry. "Ya damn skippy! Your father Arnold Mucci was a white fucking devil like you are!"

Dwayne eyed Al, while the senior citizen trembled. Al felt like his heart would stop any second, staring into his grandson's magnetic gaze. Frantic, he thought, *'That big mouth Jimmy! Now Baby Al REALLY knows everything!'*

Jimmy said, "That's right! I said it! And if you touch your grandfather you white devil, I'm a kick yo' ass! Matter of fact, I'm coming down there to bust yo' ass right now!"

Jimmy slammed down his receiver, briskly storming through his ostentatious living room and ran to the upper level of his home. Monica sat on the couch braiding their granddaughter's hair, while 13-year-old Edward entered the house. He entered the room and kissed his mother on the cheek, then gently touched his niece's face. "Mom, where's Dad," he asked.

"He's upstairs. He got into it with Baby Al again, screaming and cursing on the telephone."

They watched fuming Jimmy descend into the living room. "Just where do you think you're going?," Monica exclaimed.

"Monica! I been wanting to put my foot up Baby Al's ass forever and a day! Plus he beating Slick!"

"How do you know that honey?"

"Slick say it ain't happenin', but I know better! . . . We used to cook together! . . . I know my teacher!"

Monica watched the tears rise in her husband's eyes.

"Dad, let me come with you," Edward piped in. The loyal teen was an inch taller than his father and in his spitting image, prepared for a squabble at any time.

"No, stay with ya mama! No way in hell that cocksucker's gonna get away with talking to me like that!

NO WAY!" Jimmy stormed out of his mansion, destination: 117th Street.

Dwayne slowly put the receiver on the hook. He looked down at his grandfather who lay frozen, in his anticipated attack position.

"So, I'm white now huhm," Dwayne asked calmly, swallowing saliva, air, and taking a deep breath. Al nodded quickly, mumbling, "Uh huh! . . . Italian!" Now the bed sheets fully covered his face so only his eyes were exposed.

"Italian?! . . . I don't believe that . . . Is it true Pappy? Am I really half white, half black? Arnold Mucci is my father's name? I'm Italian?"

Al remained terrified under the covers recalling the outcome when Dwayne learned the truth about Gwenny. To learn about Arnold Mucci, and his wicked frat buddies, what happens now? What would happen now after learning the deal that he was born of rape? Another swollen jaw? Would he beat out his remaining teeth? He was relieved once Dwayne hissed and walked from the room. He heard him whistle for his pet pit.

"I don't believe that garbage. Italians is black anyway. Hey, General! C'mere General boy! You hear that boy? Master Dee's Italian," he laughed, entering his bedroom. Al let out a deep, tension-releasing sigh. He thought, "Thank you Jesus. I can't take another black eye. Thank you Lord, for making that easy."

Al immediately prayed to the Almighty for easier times once again. He knew things had to get better for him and the nearest relative he loved. They would deal with each other better as the spring bloomed, he hoped. The season rolled around and sweetened things, and Al was getting stronger and even less aphasic. Prayer made that happen and Al knew the heavenly father was the only one that could repair his and Dwayne's relationship, physically, emotionally, and therapeutically. "We'll get by," he thought after prayer. He wished he could fix something to eat, but his tired old bones knocked him out. He was pooped, having cooked and cleaned the whole day, using his walker every step of the way. The laundry was even completed; he had hung the laundry out to dry, folded his and Dwayne's clothes, dusted the living room, and cleaned their rooms. Suddenly, he noticed a thunderous crash come from Dwayne's bedroom.

"PAPPY!!!"

Al heard his grandson's door swing open and hit the wall; footsteps, a few floor creaks, past the bathroom, and there he stood in the doorway, livid eyebrows connecting.

"Where's my shit Pappy?!!"

"What's wron . . . wr . . . wro . . . wrong Bebah Al? I . . . m . . . mean . . . Duh . . . D . . . Dw . . . Dwa . . . Dwayne?"

The phone started ringing again. Al reached for the receiver, jumping back startled when Dwayne ferociously swung, connecting only with the mattress.

"Don't fucking touch it!! Let it ring!! Where are my shoe boxes with my pieces in them?!"

Al forever trembled under his bed sheets. He thought the attacks from his grandchild were over. Were they?

"You took your nosy ass in my room, fucking with my shit! Where are they?! Huh!! Answer me!"

Al heard a low-guttural rustle coming from the floor. He glanced at General, who stared from the doorway growling, letting off an evil bark while the phone continued to ring louder.

"Back in the room General boy! It's okay, I'll handle it," Dwayne instructed.

"It migh' be Patrick callin'," Al interjected, eyeing his grandson.

Dwayne paused, hissed, and snatched up the telephone

receiver: "**WHAT**!!!"

"Damn high, you answer the phone like that?! Damn," Patrick incredulously said on the line.

"Yo high! My grandfather done threw away my shit!! All my shoeboxes is gone!"

"Word?!"

"Word is fucking born! I could kill him!!"

Dwayne shot Al his "you're a dead man" look, while Patrick reassured him. It had been a few years since he saw his younger siblings from the old house on 120th Street. Even though he enjoyed the good life with his older brothers and uncles, he longed for the old times with his family. He missed his relatives dearly and he didn't want Dwayne to make the same mistake.

"Go easy on him Dee man, he didn't mean it. You know he old high! Before you go off on him some more, come uptown and check me."

"Yeah?"

"Yeah high. Come outta seventeenth street man. You can crash up here. I got some cuties wit' some big booties for ya. They stupid fresh!"

"Word?"

"Come on Dee. You know, all the girls I clock is crush high! It's just me and Frankie here. Everybody else outta town. Bring General. It's cool, if you want to."

"Yo high, I'm there!"

"Cool. See you in a few. Tell Mister Carter I said what's up."

"Bet. Later."

"Later."

Dwayne put the receiver on the hook. He grabbed Al up by his pajama collar, staring him face to face, eye to eye.

"Where's my stuff," he violently whispered, smelling horribly of cigarettes and liquor.

"I . . . I . . . I cleaned ya room, this m . . .m . . . morn . . . . morning . . . I thought de stuff wa' junk . . . I'm . . . s . . . ss

. . . s . . . sorry."

"Everything that you don't know about ain't junk, nosy ass! Do not FUCK AROUND in my room no more, unless I say so. Understand?!"

Al nodded.

"Good. I knew you'd see it my way. I'm a chill at Patrick's 'til tomorrow. Take my messages." Al nodded. "And one more thing Pappy, because I will not say this again; stay out my room. When I tell you to clean up in there, then you go. Other than that, stay out of there, got it?"

Al could barely breathe.

"GOT IT?!"

Al nodded quickly. Dwayne shoved Al back down on his bed with all of his might, nearly snapping his neck, leaving him in tears.

"Got it," Al mumbled beginning to cry, as he wet his bed for the very first time as an adult.

Later on at the penthouse, Barrington's thumping music system was adjusted to a medium volume for the carnally charged young folks occupying the place. In the living room atop the piano, Franklin received a blowjob. Upstairs in the tub room, Dwayne and Patrick filled the jacuzzi along with three more young women, happily pouring glasses of "Canei" white wine for one another.

"Yo! This is fresh! You know I'm blasted high! Word 'em up! This is! The life," Dwayne said to Patrick. Patrick was busy in between two young women; one brown-skinned girl, and a Puerto Rican girl, and he tongue-kissed them both. The girls' friend, also brown-skinned, wrapped her arms around Dwayne, kissing his body all over, down to the bubbling water. The five young adults were enjoying the midnight hour in Uncle Barrington's jacuzzi.

While a hot, steamy, penthouse semi-orgy took place, back on 117th, Jimmy pounded on the Carter's apartment door over General's incessant barking. "Slick!! It's me Jimmy!! It's okay . . . you can open the door!!" He paused, taking a deep breath. If he could just make his mentor admit to his abuse, he could have nasty Dwayne put behind bars. The senior citizen could get the help he needed.

"Who's that making noise in my hallway?!"

Jimmy turned in Barbara's direction, with her snooping head hyper-extended from her apartment. She said, "Oh. It's you. Don't you know folks 'round here's relaxing?! Can't you see nobody's home?! Al probably sleeping!" Her head shook continuously as she spoke. Even the wrapped transparent peach scarf she wore couldn't keep her awry wig in place.

"Have you seen Mister Slick lately? Is he okay," Jimmy asked.

"Far as I know. You need to come 'round at a decent hour, with all this carrying on."

"You seen Baby Al? How he doing?"

"Gettin' on my last nerves with that monster! Ya hear him barking?! Shut up! Shut up that noise! Shut yo damn mouth," she shouted in the direction of the Carter apartment. "Ain't no dogs supposed to be here, and I already told that dumb super of ours! I done told Al and Baby Al that I'm reporting it! Let 'em keep on ignoring Barbara honey! The ASPCA gone be here, or, I'm a pay the Chinamen to put his ass in some **beef and broccoli!**"

"Well, when you see Slick, tell him Jimmy came by please."

"Uh-huhm," she mumbled, closing her door.

"Wait! Just a minute! Miss?!" Jimmy walked in front of Barbara's apartment. She re-opened the door with the chain lock on.

"Listen, sorry to bother you. I wanna ask you a question." Barbara looked at the middle-aged dark man, strangely.

"What's going on with Slick? Baby Al taking care of him?"

"Go on from 'round here asking questions! Go on! Barbara ain't telling it, honey! Get Al to tell it! If he ain't telling, then Barbara ain't telling it honey! I know Mattie Mae and Gwenny just a spinning in they graves, if they watching!" She slammed the door in Jimmy's face.

He shook his head thinking, "Damn that woman's crazy." He walked back to Al's apartment, raised his fist to pound on the dilapidated door, and stopped suddenly. He looked at the aged stickers and decals pasted all over by Dwayne as a child. General was growling, whining, then the angry pit bull gave off a few more barks. Letting out a deep sigh, Jimmy put his head down and descended the stairway. He wanted Al to reach out to him for help. He wanted Al to treat him like the son he never had, like he used to; it was too late. Al was receding like an ailing tortoise into its decaying shell as an elderly man, with no turning back. Jimmy, as much as it hurt, decided to mind his own family and their problems.

He exited the tenement, trotted down the stoop, and did an about face, looking up. Al's bedroom lights were out. Jimmy shook his head, saying, "Slick gotta face up to the problem. He gotta deal wit' it. Poor ol' soul. I gotta let it go . . . I just have to. I don't want to . . . but I got to."

Jimmy jumped in his car and headed back upstate, to his home and family. He made the vow to continually pray for his mentor and his godson.

Dwayne finally convinced Shawn and Eric that working for Patrick's uncles was the thing to do. After the confrontation with Scheme, the crew found themselves flat broke with no clientele, no incoming weight, and no product. Scheme had been in charge of everything and he was gone. Dwayne broke the lease for apartment 23, and seven eleven was no more. Within days, the guys joined Barrington's clique, becoming bigger and more active participants in the drug game. The guys' world was transformed under their new management, quicker than ever.

Shawn and Eric were given "tools" and tasks immediately. They were instructed to stay aware of all drug rivals, and if they knew of any forthcoming beef, they were required to murder anyone. Dwayne and Patrick stuck closer to home, monitoring shipments, the cooking, the bagging, and the cutting up of the drugs.

Nigel and Franklin continued their security jobs: cognizant of traffic at the penthouse. Barrington and Ezra as head guys continued overseeing the whole project, giving it their all.

Ezra loved handling foreign shipments and dealings, especially in Jamaica. Barrington remained laid back, just don't upset him. He kept green eyes, the color of money. He felt, the less big time drug lords, the more money and respect for him, and if you had to murder anyone, just get the job done, even if you pulled homicides for fun.

One Saturday night, the guys decided to hang at "Saturn" instead of playing "The Fever" in the Bronx. "Saturn", the hippest roller dome in Manhattan, played the latest in hip-hop and R&B music. Guys were usually outnumbered by the girls; Friday nights were jumping, and Saturdays, anything went down.

The rink was jam-packed this particular Saturday night as the disc jockeys battled back and forth. Packs of guys and girls skated around the rink floor and off to the sides, people danced, chatted, smoked weed, etc. The jamming crowd skated around and around as the deejay spun hit after hit. From an elevated angle, the roller dome actually resembled the sixth planet, with orange colored mist periodically rising from the center of the rink floor. The center was guarded by a short wall that was average waist height; in this area, patrons sat and smoked in lounge recliners, they danced, or they mentally geared themselves to roller skate. Outside the skating track there were wall lockers, the restrooms, and the walls were decorated with glowing plastic moons and stars symbolizing outer space, and the action was identical to the center of the floor. The skaters zoomed around on top of the yellowish, glowing rink tile, and the glowing floor changed colors from blue, to yellow to green, every fifteen minutes. The skaters were oblivious to the outside jamming, totally submerged inside the banging hip-hop beats in outer space; this was a weekend teen ritual, uptown Saturday night.

Dwayne and the new crew stepped into the jam, in which they were already cool with the security checking patrons at the door. The adage "money talks & bullshit walks" was in effect as the team entered Saturn unchecked. Dwayne was strapped with his thirty-eight, snug in his brand new shoulder holster, while Patrick carried his .357 Magnum; Shawn walked with his own thirty-eight, while Eric carried a forty-five. Nigel and Franklin both carried nine-millimeter semi-automatics. They were strapped, cool, checked in, and ready for all beef.

Eric bumped into Debra, one of his ex-girls from high school who frequented Saturn with her posse of girls.

"Whatever happened to that other corny guy y'all used to be with?"

"Who," Eric asked, shrugging his shoulders.

"The one who got beat up back in the days, remember, when the twins from 19th jumped Patrick."

"Oh! You mean that nigga Art! He upstate!"

Her braided extensions flew as she did a double take. "Jail," she asked in disbelief.

"Nah, school!"

Two of her friends crowded around Shawn, who

leaned against the wall while dancing, and Dwayne was put into a quick "sandwich" by two other girls. Patrick prepared to skate.

"Yo Dee! You not skating?!," Patrick asked Dwayne.

"You know what time it is high!"

Patrick moved up to the rubbing threesome, slapped Dwayne five, took a few steps, and whisked away into the skating crowd. He saw a girl he wanted to take back to the penthouse, so he skated after her.

An hour and a half later, while UTFO's "Roxanne, Roxanne" mixed with Billy Squier's "Big Beat" blasted from the speakers, Scheme and five of his Brooklyn boys appeared, checking out the familiar uptown club scene. Scheme spotted Dwayne nudging up on a girl in a corner and whispered to one of his boys. Scheme's boys shoved security out of their way and quickly moved towards Dwayne and the girl he was with. Scheme and his partner were five feet away when his man pulled out a shiny instrument. Patrick checked the entire episode and skated off the roller rink floor in a flash, tackling Scheme's partner down. Scheme pulled out his "iron" and was shot in the head immediately by Franklin who emerged from the shadows.

Bedlam! Improperly laced roller skates flew from the overturned ankles of terrified, trampled patrons. Two more of Scheme's boys opened fire catching a few emerging guards, while more people panicked, injuring each other.

Frenzied Eruption! Patrick banged his opponent's face into the floor. Dwayne snatched him up just in time before he got stampeded.

Broken Arms, Legs! Scheme's buddy on the ground flipped himself over and was shot in the arm immediately by Dwayne. Shawn and Eric smoked two more of Scheme's henchmen while the screaming patrons ran for their lives. Nigel led the guys to an emergency exit and they escaped with some of the crowd to the avenue above.

NYPD and paramedics rushed the area of the club; streets were blocked off. The incident left five casualties, including Scheme. The crew amazingly escaped before the authorities arrived. And because of bad press, the Saturn roller rink would eventually close its doors, never to open again.

When Barrington received the news about the shootout, he was concerned with one thing: "Dem a die?"

"Yea maan! Mi a smoouke dem poosyclaat," Franklin exclaimed, while the rest of the crew laughed their heads off.

"Word up! Sucker niggas don't want none of this," Dwayne added.

Business was back to normal in no time. Barrington and Ezra held it down, while their nephews and crew carried out their missions. Eric and Shawn happily shot rival lords when necessary, and as long as they were backed by Barrington and Ezra, they felt they could "buck niggas" forever.

Barrington's posse became the biggest hustler's around, with the crew's cash flow nearing the six-figure range. Each member did different things with their earnings.

Barrington made investments, participating in the stock exchange, finding more ways to bring in cash. He purchased a brand new Mercedes Benz from the showroom floor, and a home on the north shore of Long Island for himself and Ezra. He gave the penthouse to his nephews as a gift and for future operations.

Ezra commuted to England, and then back and forth to Jamaica for drugs and vacation. More family oriented than his brother, Ezra always thought of relatives back home and overseas, dearly missing his older sister Dora Chambers Livingston, and the rest of the family on 120th

Street.

Nigel and Franklin wined and dined fine women all over town, both buying their own cars. Nigel purchased a 1985 BMW 735i sedan, and Franklin acquired a black Corvette with gray interior.

Patrick liked to send his other siblings money. Their requests seemed endless, but he didn't mind. Andrew always asked him for the latest footwear, jewelry, and music equipment; Hyacinth moved into her own place away from Harlem in Brooklyn, needing household knick-knacks, and assistance with college fees while pursuing her nursing degree; while Rose and Sharon satisfyingly received the monetary gifts he sent them.

Shawn and Eric made the least amount of money, but they were still content with their earnings. Shawn shared his money with his family emulating Patrick, and he was the first one from the crew to start a bank account. The days of his first love for breakdancing and popping were totally extinct. His "Ellesse" sneakers and "Lee" suits became snakeskin shoes and silk suits; and he even contemplated donations for USA for Africa. His live-in girlfriend popped up pregnant, so to stay loyal to his pockets, crew, and expanding family, he continued pulling stick-ups on a regular ensuring that all rival drug lords were cut down.

Eric bought himself a motor bike, dividing his time between robberies with Shawn, tagging, and his main girl Twanika. Whatever she wanted, she got it: nails, weave, clothes, jewelry, earrings, the sky was the limit for her.

Dwayne divided his time between the penthouse and 117th Street. At home, General had grown into a strong, deadly pit bull that destroyed everything under his master's instruction. This excited Dwayne to the fullest. He allowed

General to participate in dog fights, and when frightening the neighbors, he even instructed his pit to chase and eat off the heads of alley cats. With the new, fresh money being made, competing with Eric Martinez and Arthur Boyd, Dwayne bought his own motor bike, and a black 1985 Jeep Wrangler. And to celebrate Al's 75th birthday, he arranged for their entire apartment to be remodeled. Hiring movers and fix-it men, he demanded everything old be replaced with new, up-to-date, appliances, audio, and video systems.

Gone, was the antique closed-top turntable equipped with eight-track tape player, with makeshift 13-inch colored TV sitting on top. A brand new 25-inch remote control floor model television was wheeled in; and Dwayne even added one of his past hobbies to the newest TV, attaching an advanced Atari 7800 video game system, with endless games. A Sony rack stereo system, equipped with dual cassette deck, turntable, and five feet high speakers replaced the old stereo. Gone was the old time washing machine, replaced with a brand new washer and dryer; and the refrigerator was replaced with one that dispensed ice cubes, crushed ice, and ice water in the front. The stove was replaced with a new one, and Dwayne also added a microwave oven and blender to the kitchen. The furniture vanished, replaced with a plush set including a new dining room table with chairs. Gone was Dwayne's tiny, cot-like bed, and Al's ancient bedroom set. In came two new bedroom suites; both with 19-inch remote control colored TV's that sat on stands with wheels.

It took one full day for the deliverymen to execute the mission. Dwayne paid cash, top dollar; a huge four figured total for labor, furniture, etc. He told Al that they would spend the entire day together for old times' sake. Al sat with his grandson and General on some benches across Seventh Avenue from the morning, spoke to familiar neighborhood faces, even played a couple of games of checkers together. He was totally unaware of what was happening in his apartment. Once he became restless, Dwayne decided to take his grandfather downtown, so he wouldn't suspect. He loaded Al and General into the jeep and they left the neighborhood.

By the time they returned from riding all over the city, the apartment was remodeled to the fullest. The head man in charge of the operation left the key to the apartment under a brand new white carpeted doormat that read in embroidered red lettering, "HAPPY BIRTHDAY, PAPPY".

Dwayne helped Al up the stairs while General ran playfully up to the fifth floor, then back downstairs, then back again. "One step, two step, three step, four," Al steadily repeated, climbing upstairs.

The men climbed forever with thirteen added rest stops, and gawking neighbors that bypassed to and fro; it took them thirty minutes to reach the top floor. General barked happily, wagging his tail, watching his master and his grandfather finally approaching.

"Yo Gen man, shhhh! Don't tell Pappy about the surprise high." Al gave his grandson a strange look. "Me . . .What did I do tuh get a surprise?"

"It's your birthday man! You're seventy-five today. Gotta surprise ya sometime. Starting with this!" Dwayne pointed to the new doormat, bending down to retrieve the apartment key.

"What does that say," Al asked.

"Go on and read it."

"Ih loo' like it say 'happy birthday, Pappy'."

"It does. You like it?"

"Dunno wha . . . tuh . . . say. I, I . . . love it. Cain't thank ya enough. Dunno . . . how to thank ya, Baby Al."

"You can start by not calling me Baby Al."

"You right. You ain't Baby Al no mo'. Thank ya, Dwayne. Please, I . . . getting so . . . so weak, standing up on mah feet."

Dwayne opened the door, and General darted into the darkened apartment. He shut on the hallway light while Al grabbed his walker, heading straight for the bathroom. "All that hangin' out today make me wanna pee," he mumbled, pushing into the bathroom.

Dwayne did a quick scan of the apartment making sure everything was in place. He shut the lights off, and waited by the bathroom. Al ignorantly finished his duty wetting the entire bowl and seat, staining his trousers with urine.

"Did you enjoy riding in my jeep Pappy?"

"Oh, very much," he replied, leaving the bathroom with sleep on his mind. Zooming around in Dwayne's jeep with barking General had worn him out.

"You liked eating at the old restaurant you cooked at downtown, right?"

"Man, that place is the same. It was never no colored folk around, and it still ain't. Thank ya, and God bless ya for everythang Dwayne. I'm a make mah way tuh bed nah, thanks for the surprise too."

Dwayne laughed at his grandfather's simpleness. He couldn't have thought the doormat was his only surprise birthday present. Al surely would respect the brand new apartment created for him while they were out.

"It's more to the surprise Pappy, damn!" Dwayne walked into Al's room and turned on both of his new lamps and television. Dismayed, Al crept into his lavish bedroom, mouth dropping in amazement and confusion while Dwayne grinned, checking his watch. Al trembled, looking around at his new furnishings.

The room was changed completely, too much for his seventy-five year old mind. He would never get used to his room. The new furniture lacked his family's past, and it was completely absent of dear Mattie's presence.

"Dwayne . . . how? What, what happened," he mumbled.

"Oh it's more, much more, Pappy man. Come on!"

The restless young man beckoned his amazed grandfather towards the living room. Al with his vision blurring, aghast, crept towards his brand new den.

"How do you like the house? Pappy, happy birthday! Happy seventy-fifth birthday, Pappy man!"

Al entered the living room, a room fresh from another time, another place, chock full of advanced technology, filled with glass, blaring glitter, and piercing glamour. How could his grandchild produce all of the new furnishings, and a brand new jeep? Dwayne was just twenty years old, no high school graduation, no college, and how did he make all of this happen Al pondered. He felt himself heaving.

"What's all this foolishness?"

"What," Dwayne answered, mood changing.

"All this glass, all this stuff, how did it get'chere? Where did it come from?"

Dwayne hissed, looked at the ceiling, and became totally disgusted. All of his cash blown on accessories and furniture for a shabby apartment he hardly stayed in. He could have spent his hard earned dollars elsewhere. After staying away from the penthouse for such a long day, his pockets were taking a definite loss. If Al knew what was good for him, he'd better enjoy his new gifts and accessories. If not, then major capital would be down the tubes.

"Where's all my other stuff? I don't know how to use this stuff."

Al dragged himself over to the floor model TV, watching the Atari 7800 demonstration of Pac-man. Suddenly, the TV blacked out by itself. Startled, Al turned around and saw Dwayne with the remote control in his hand. He knew his grandson was angry with him but, what could he do? The new styled apartment was too much for his heart to bear. He wouldn't know where to begin.

"Where's de other stuff?"

"Where you think? In the garbage!"

"Why ya raisin' ya voice?"

"I'm not raising my voice!"

"So why ya yellin'?"

"I'm not yelling!"

Al's heart raced faster, knowing his wicked grandson couldn't have changed much since maturing; the evil had returned.

"See what I mean! You make me yell and shit! All that FUCKING CASH I SPENT, and all you can think about is, where is the other stuff!"

"If he hits me tonight, he going straight to the jailhouse," Al thought as Dwayne came towards him.

"Where'd ya get all dis munney from boy?"

"What's it to you!"

"I wanna know. I'm yo' gran'pappy!"

"None of your fucking business!"

Al clung to his walker, trembling as his impetuous grandson continuously came closer.

"What the hell you shaking for Pappy?!"

"Where'dya get all dis munney for all this fanciness?"

Al thought of Barbara's youngest son Floyd. Floyd had been a ferocious, drug selling menace to society in the late sixties and early seventies, still spoiled by his conniving mother. In and out of prisons all of his life, he was a helpless, homeless, drug addict by age 37. He didn't want the same life for his grandson. Dwayne's everlasting rage mistakenly clashed once again with his grandfather's memories and suspicions. Al made up his mind. Not only was his grandson peddling drugs in the building, but he must have been indulging!

"Yah on drugs? Or ya sellin' 'em?"

"None of your business!"

"Jus' lihke Floyd."

"That's all you think of me Pappy? A fucking dirty bum? Huh?"

"Bawrbara was righ'. You selling dat stuff in twennythree."

"You listen to that big mouth bitch?!"

"Yah killin'off colored folks."

General entered the living room and started growling at Al when his master's eyes reddened with fury. "I'm white remember? What the fuck do I care about colored folks!"

"You using 'em too!"

Dwayne seized Al by the throat, attempting to choke the old man to death. Al, shook by Dwayne, was unbalanced, quivering, glasses ajar. General barked loudly, siding with his master. Dwayne snapped to reality the moment Al's walker crashed to the floor. Once freed with his glasses hanging from his face, Al sat atop the new floor model TV, leaning back, his sweaty fingertips pressed to the wall as another anchor, struggling to catch his breath.

Dwayne growled, "Let me cold break north before I kill your old black ass! It was like Anderson's in here! A fucking funeral home! You think Grandma Mattie coming back by keeping all that old time shit?! I'll never do shit for you again! I should let General fuck you up!"

He jetted from the living room whistling for his pit. "Come on General boy! He ain't worth barking at!"

Dwayne put General in his room and closed the door. He opened the door of the apartment, stopping to look down the hallway at his grandfather who gathered enough strength to hold on at the edge of the corridor, gazing directly at his grandson. Dwayne sucked his teeth and walked out, still able to throw a classic tantrum at twenty years old, leaving Al at home with the final gift of strangulation for his birthday.

With the intake of enough room oxygen, Al picked up the walker eventually, and made it down the hall to his bedroom. Still taken aback, Al's refurnished bedroom was different from what he was totally accustomed; he almost was afraid to even enter it. He had a brand new oak bedroom set with a lighted headboard and mirrors, with two crystal lamps, a 19-inch colored television that sat on a stand with wheels, and wall to wall carpeting.

"Lord have mercy, Jesus . . . The fool done went and put a rug in here . . .Why he got the windows closed . . . It's June 27th . . . Now I know my grandboy's on that stuff," he frighteningly thought, creeping up to his windows.

"Where de screens fo' di windas . . . wait a minni' . . . hmmmm . . . a general electra air condition . . . No wonda ih ain' no mo' screens."

Al let out a deep sigh, and figured out how to use his new presents.

Saturday, August 3. One Hundred Twentieth Street was swarming with screaming, happy children playing in the fire hydrant spray; girls were jumping double-dutch, guys were playing stickball and tag. In the middle of the street other kids raced with their bicycles, tricycles, "go-karts", and skateboards; it was all in good fun during their block party.

Barbecue posts were set up everywhere. If the grill person in charge knew you, you could eat anywhere on the block. Some families were selling lemonade, other beverages, and snacks. Other families were sharing food, drinks, and everything they had. You could hear the thumping hip-hop, you could smell the hot dogs and burgers in the air; you could feel the blissful party vibe from miles around. Traffic was scheduled to resume after 11 o'clock, and the children dreaded the forthcoming hour when the sun would go down. They played on, while the adults cooked on, enjoying themselves on this sweltering summer day.

Shawn left Barrington's early and dropped in for some good ol' hamburgers and franks his aunt fixed. The rest of his family along with his girlfriend Phetima, barbecued under a tree in front of their building, while enjoying the festivities.

The Livingston family even set out a barbecue grill, deciding to participate. They also celebrated Dora giving up her prejudice towards American born blacks. Bradley had threatened to leave her once she found out he was socializing with a few Americans after work hours. After a brand new domestic situation happened that was identical to the extrusion of his sons and brother in-law, Bradley disciplined his wife after she verbally embarrassed the family in front of his American guests. He then set forth some new rules and regulations in the house, ending the intercultural racism that tore his family apart. Within days, the Livingston home was required to change their views, changing their outlook on black Americans. Black was black; no matter if you were American born black, Virgin Island black, Jamaican black, Guyanese black, Haitian black, Puerto Rican black, Trinidadian black, African black, Dominican black, Panamanian black, or any person of color; you were all descendants of Africa, dropped many different places at many different times via the slave trade. It was time to end the divisions in black. Bradley refused to allow Dora, or the rest of the family to speak nonsense about American blacks any more.

Dora changed her entire attitude even wanting to make amends with her older sons and her younger brothers. A message was sent to the penthouse informing Barrington and Ezra of their older sister's change of heart. The rest of the family hoped they would show up at the block party. Andrew was ecstatic about the "family reunion", especially since he set up his DJ equipment that Patrick bought him outside of the house. He and some friends planned on jamming after sundown.

Time passed on and the hot sun descended, making way for a full moon that masked itself with thicker, still humidity. The smaller children turned in with some of the parents, giving way to the hip-hop loving teenagers. Crews of other teenage guys and girls came from surrounding areas to "jam" on the block.

Down the street closer to Lenox Avenue, Kenny Blankenship brought out his turntables and music causing an admiring crowd. Up the block little Andrew Livingston had a larger crowd, spinning the hits like Kurtis Blow's "A.J. Scratch", Doug E. Fresh & Slick Rick's "La-Di-Da-Di/The Show", Whodini's "Five Minutes Of Funk", and many others. Whatever the current hit, Andrew and his boys had it. They cut it, mixed it, scratched it, "transformed" it like there was no tomorrow. Andrew's crowd got so big that he stole most of Kenny Blankenship's crowd. Packs of teens danced with and against each other in front of the Livingston house.

Una sat at the top of the stoop, while Dora, Bradley, and Hyacinth sat nearer to the bottom, amazed at Andrew's skills on the turntables. Rose and Sharon, complete with their pigtails, matching pink and white sundresses with their feet covered with sandals, played jump rope in the yard; they danced every now and then, amusing the rest of the family. The loud music soon permeated Una's elderly eardrums forcing her to retire early. She entered the house while the family and crowd still watched Andrew on "the wheels of steel".

While Andrew spun on 120th, uptown on 155th and Edgecombe, Eric's head was slammed to the pavement by the police, after being fingered by a few witnesses to a crime he did commit. He had shot some guys who allegedly robbed his girl of her jewelry. Once she realized her own uncertainty about the crime and the guys Eric shot, he choked his girlfriend and tried to flee the scene on his motor bike. Barely making it across the 155th Street Bridge, he was spotted by NYPD and by 9 p.m. midway into the 120th Street jam, Eric found himself in central booking.

After closing down business and sexual pleasure for the evening, Barrington, Ezra, Nigel, Franklin, and Patrick, cruised Harlem in Barrington's air-conditioned van. Little did they know, they were being tailed by a hazy moon, and another, smaller van equipped with tinted windows. The followers tailed Patrick and his relatives quietly, clocking Barrington's every stop and turn with dexterous sight. The trailers were morbidly concealed with dark masks and shades, some dripping sweat drops of apprehension. Their prey was in sight and they drove along complacently waiting for the right time to pounce.

While Barrington, Ezra, and their nephews were being followed, Dwayne rode the streets of the Bronx, looking for more cocaine to sniff up. He already sniffed up to $50 dollars and was combing the streets for more; he felt he wasn't high enough. He became such a valued crew member that he practically moved into the penthouse. In his absence from 117th, he paid thirteen year old Malik Ballard from apt #31 to walk General twice a day. Young Malik was very content with his earnings, doing his duty well; General was tended to, Al happily was given some space, and Dwayne was pleased.

10:13 P.M.: A cool gusting surge of wind stirred soiled napkins, paper cups, plastic soda empties, and rolled empty Calvin Cooler bottles into a whirlpool of garbage; and Shawn and pregnant Phetima were in the crowd at the same time dancing to Run D.M.C.'s "King of Rock". Blunts and quarts of Old English were passed about as Andrew cut in "Rock the Bells" by L.L. Cool J.

Shawn, popping & locking, was pulling on two blunts stuffed in his mouth once some of Phetima's friends finally coaxed her away from "watching" Shawn's antics, convincing her to join them in a walk to the corner store, while Andrew cut in The Treacherous Three's "Turn It Up" followed by "Gotta Rock". Shawn was impressed by

Andrew's skills. It reminded him of the good old days at the "battleground" uptown, hearing great hip-hop music and *'shooting the gift to crazy bitties before Tima got knocked up'*. The moment the Boogie Boys' "Fly Girl" began to spin, the youngster "transformed" like mad.

After checking on her mother in-law inside the house, Dora returned to the top of the stoop to yell over the music. "Cindy?! Frahnkie dem nuh come," Dora asked her daughter anxiously. Hyacinth couldn't believe her ears. Her mother actually referred to her as Cindy? She actually called her older brother Frankie? At one time, those names were too American sounding. There truly was a God, or maybe the world was coming to an end.

"Mummy! Mi tink Frenkie dem soon coume!"

"Eh heh, de party soon finish nuh maan! Mi wan' mi brudders see de pickny dem pley de muzik." Dora was truly proud of her baby son's ability to command a crowd of people dancing to the music that he played. Time moved on.

10:48: The block association head ordered Andrew to stop the music. Teens began to leave the block after having a ball, having danced all night. Some of the brothers and sisters courted; dice games started up on the corner of Lenox, and some families continued their night barbecues. Shawn returned to his girl, and he, Phetima and her friends sat in front of his relatives building, while their neighbors stood around snapping, ranking, and playing the dozens on each other.

"I thought for sure Pat and his uncles was coming through. And I ain't hear nothin' from E-zo all day. He said he was gonna slide through after he checked his girl," Shawn said. Phetima looked at her watch and said, "It's almost eleven. They still might come."

10:58: Dwayne pulled over on the corner of Lenox and 120th, jumping out of his jeep, slapping five to a few block teens who were in awe of him. He crossed the street and walked over to Shawn and Phetima. "What's up, cool," Shawn said, giving Dwayne a five-turned hug, introducing him to a few adults that sat with his family.

"Ezra and them get here yet?"

"I ain't seen 'em. Heard from E-zo?"

"Saw the brother earlier. He still uptown probably."

The block barricades were lifted, allowing traffic to resume through. "Yo man, look like the van coming through down the block," Dwayne noticed.

Barrington's van pulled up in front of the Livingston house. Shadows and silhouettes were running and jumping in front of the headlights; the Livingston family happily embraced Barrington and crew while they exited the van.

"I wanna find out the game plan for later man, I'll be back," Dwayne said, slapping Shawn more "five".

"I'm a chill with my girl for a minute; I'll be down there. Yo, they family making up with each other?"

"Think so."

Dwayne stepped up the block towards Patrick's house, while the speed of the wind escalated, blowing dirt and dust into his eyes, giving him temporary blindness. The humidified moon disappeared giving way to roving, darkened clouds. Up the street, the Livingston family wouldn't let the weather spoil their mood after the wonderful block party and their long awaited family reunion.

Dora hugged her brothers and sons like never before, ensuring they knew how much she truly loved them. Bradley exited the house, walked down the brownstone steps to the sidewalk and repeated his wife's gesture, beckoning his third son Patrick for some good old family treatment. After he embraced his parents and siblings, making amends with his family, Patrick saw his best friend and partner in crime bopping up the block.

"Dee man, come! Mummy, remember Dwayne? Mi gaan ah school wit'! Elementary, junior high and high school," Patrick explained, beckoning Dwayne ecstatically.

Dora whispered into her son's ear, "Mi caan t'ink no'w, h'im baan 'ere? Eh Pahtrick?" Patrick gave his mother a dirty look.

"No maan. h'im h'allrite maan. It's okey," she smiled, hugging him tightly. Dwayne shook hands with Bradley and Dora, a move Patrick never thought he would see. He exhaled a sigh of relief, glad to witness his mother's change for the better. There was no need for anyone to be prejudiced, especially within their own race.

Ezra called his nephew Andrew over for a quick hug, interrupting the diligent teen and his friends who were carrying the music equipment into the house. "Tell de friend dem g'wan 'bout dem business maan, de faamily'll help," Ezra instructed.

"Yo yo, it's cool; my uncles and my brothers'll help me with the rest, thanks." Andrew slapped his crew five and they were on their way. Ezra, Franklin, and Nigel assisted young Andrew with the rest of his stuff. Bradley went into the family cooler and popped open the last cans of beer for his brothers-in-law.

11:12: "Yo Dee, where's ya wheels man," Patrick asked Dwayne, as they stood on the curb.

"Huh?" His mind was on more cocaine.

"Where's ya jeep, high?"

"Oh, at the corner. Lenox and 20th."

"Why don't you bring it on the block man? We breaking out soon. It's some shit going on in Queens, out in the Bridge. Behind Queensbridge Projects high, it's a fly ass jam out there in the park we checking out in a few!"

Two tiny, munchkin sounding voices yelled out, "PATRICK! PATRICK!" Everyone paused to look at the baby members of the family, Rose and Sharon. "Come," Hyacinth called up to her sisters. The pajama clad youngsters wouldn't budge from the top of the stoop, continuing to giggle, laugh and point down at their relatives.

"Wha' hoppen," Patrick announced to his little sisters.

Before she went to sleep in her queen-sized bed, Una observed her family from her third floor bedroom window, enviously wanting to participate in the fun. She relayed a stern message to the family via Rose and Sharon, and the girls found the message funny.

11:13: "Wha' ya' laughin'," Bradley yelled to his daughters. Sharon spoke up, "Cause! Mummy Una said if Frankie and Patrick and everybody don't come in the house, you gonna be a stiffy!" Dwayne looked at Patrick confused. Rose added, "Everyone gonna be a stiffy ready for a duppy box!"

The whole family laughed including Dwayne. He shook his head, chuckling. "Yo Barry, what they said? Dump the box?"

"Nah high. Duppy box," Patrick answered. Dwayne gave another confused look, came closer to Patrick and asked, "What is a duppy box?"

Patrick laughed. "H'im nuh k'no' 'bout dat," Dora added, smiling.

"It's a casket high."

"So, a duppy is a dead person?"

"Nah maan, it's like a ghost," Bradley said.

"A spirit like," Nigel added.

"Yo y'all, I'm going to get my jeep. Y'all bugging out!" Dwayne walked off shaking his head, chuckling. Hyacinth giggled, "Mummy, wi skeered Pahtrick's friend."

"De Yenkee bwoy 'freid fih us no'uw," Dora replied, laughing.

Patrick ran to the top of the stoop to hug his sisters. "I missed you so much. I don't ever want to be apart from you ever again. I love you two like mad. Ya miss me?"

"Yeahhhh . . . Uhm-huhm," they nodded. He embraced the girls until their perspiration was one, and he held them for dear life, as tight as he could. He inhaled the aroma of their innocent scalps while his tears welled and further conditioned their hair. He wanted them to be cognizant and sure of their older brother's love. He wanted them to feel his infinite affection for them.

Dwayne caught a sniffling attack midway through the block before he reached the corner of Lenox. "Damn I need some blow! These niggas need to hurry up!," he thought. He approached Shawn's family as they were disassembling their barbecue party due to the weather change. The wind gusts suddenly were up to 30 miles per hour intermittently and heavy raindrops slowly began to fall.

11:18: "Where Shawn go," Dwayne asked.

"He's at the corner," Shawn's uncle replied.

At the corner of Lenox and 120th, Shawn kissed his girlfriend and put her in a taxi, then he walked back onto the block.

11:19: Shawn and Dwayne met up on the corner. Dwayne said, "Yo high, Pat and his family bugging up there, talking about ghosts and shit. They called it duppy, or guppy, or some shit. Jamaicans is crazy. That's why it's a storm." He gave Shawn "dap" and attempted a cigarette.

Shawn asked, "So what the crew gettin' into later? You going back to the penthouse?"

"Something going down in Queensbridge Projects . . . Niggas talking about riding out there, I'm driving; you can ride with me," said Dwayne.

11:20: "I'm a see what they talking about right quick before it really starts coming down." Shawn slapped five with Dwayne and started walking in the direction of Seventh Avenue.

"Bet! I'm a bring the jeep around."

Dwayne walked to his jeep and sped off.

"I'm going up the street, I'll be back; Tima caught a cab," Shawn said to his aunt and uncle, continuing past.

11:21: Shawn walked up the block towards Seventh Avenue, slapping five to everyone that passed him.

11:22: "I want you to go downstairs and give your other big brothers Nigel and Frankie a hug. It's starting to rain, and I don't want you to become sick," Patrick said to Rose and Sharon. He released his sisters to let them walk down the stoop.

11:22:32: A black van screeched to a halt in front of the Livingston house. Six masked men jumped out the back and front, armed with semi-automatic and automatic weapons. The gunmen were relatives of Scheme, fresh out of East New York & Brownsville, Brooklyn. Two of them survived being trampled in the shoot-out at Saturn in Harlem, and they remembered Nigel, Franklin, and Patrick, after several weeks of uptown investigation. The van was the same mysterious van that tailed Barrington's for hours. Scheme's people were out for blood and finally, they captured their prey.

From the top of the stoop, with the lamppost as a spotlight, Patrick saw the heavily armed men open fire on his family. The echoing sound of bullets rang out and Patrick reached for Andrew, who tried to carry little Sharon out of the gunfire. Andrew was shot six times in the back carrying Sharon up the steps, dropping her as he fell dead; she was shot in the face twice, dead. Little Rose, frozen in fright, was shot twice in the chest, dead. Ezra reached for his silver nine-millimeter and was shot several times in the stomach and chest. Hyacinth was shot in the head and neck while Nigel, successfully shooting one of the gunmen, was shot in his abdomen and his private parts. Franklin was shot in the head reaching for his pistol, while Barrington got his back blown out.

Bradley screamed, "NOOO!" His brains were blown against the brownstone. The gunmen waiting by the van laughed at the terrified people running amok in the rain, amidst a deadly lightshow with booming sounds and ricocheting bullets; and the last gunman emptied his rounds into Dora's skull. The pleased bandits ran back to their van for the getaway, job of revenge well done for the most part.

"**Motherfucker**," Patrick yelled tearfully, shooting down the last gunman with his tool, a courageous, concealed move from the top of the stoop, trailed by a wave of karma. The driver clapped fire at the top of the stoop from his seat, and the intended round struck Patrick in the calf. Another gunman, wanting to finish the job, jumped back out of the van to cut Patrick down. The gunman aimed at Patrick with his tech-nine and got shot in his temple long distance by Shawn; he saw the whole shooting episode while bystanders continued scrambling for cover from the forthcoming thunder and bullet storm.

The van pulled off, full speed ahead with the driver busting off rounds from his .44 Bulldog revolver, his other hand on the steering wheel. Shawn let off two more shots from his thirty-eight, running out of the way of the speeding, swaying van. He brandished his weapon in the middle of the street, preparing to smoke a few of the gunmen before they could get away. The van gained control of its direction and sped past him with the back doors opening; two of the gunmen let off several shots. Shawn fell in the middle of the street.

Dwayne made a right turn from Seventh Avenue onto 120th Street, completely oblivious to the massacre, pulling up in front of Patrick's house. He jumped out of his jeep, and his eyes followed the light of the streetlamp nearly sending him into shock. "What the fu . . ." he stammered aloud observing the dead bodies, then he vomited after observing Bradley's opened scalp and his brains sliding against the house with streaks of rainwater as a conductor, in the spotlight.

There they were: Bradley, Dora, Barrington, Franklin, Hyacinth, Andrew, Rose, Sharon, with three opposing gunmen; they were all bloody corpses in summer and nighttime casual attire, their blood and brains, oozing all over the pavement. Dwayne threw up again, after looking at the three survivors of the blood bath. Swollen Ezra laid over the curb with his face squished into the gutter, trembling, blood saturating the inside of his tank top, spilling from his chest.

"... Faddah! ... Faddah Almighty!," he spat out; while Nigel screamed in pain, shaking with head against the brownstone steps. And at the top of the steps in front of his house on the second floor, Patrick, .357 in hand, trembled in shock, unaware of his hot wounded calf. Slowly, he put his gun to his head and proceeded to pull the trigger.

'Patrick!!!'

Dwayne stepped quickly over the bodies to the top of the Livingston steps.

"NOOO! PATRICK! CHILL MONEY!" He grabbed his best friend's shaking arm. "Listen ... Give me the gun high ... Give it to me Pat man, it's okay!"

Patrick blindly stared at nothing while his childhood buddy coaxed his gun away from him, practically crying in his ear.

"Give me the gun, Pat ... Gimme the fucking gun! **IT AIN'T WORTH IT BLACK!**"

He slowly removed the gun from Patrick's grasp, throwing the iron clear into the middle of the street. Patrick grabbed Dwayne's shoulder with a talon grip of iron, looking down at his family members, from his parents, to his uncles, to all of his brothers and sisters. Everyone was dead; all except Mummy Una, who lay dead to the world asleep in her bed, Nigel who was rapidly spilling blood onto the wet pavement, and Ezra, who was slowly but surely fading away in the gutter.

Police cars roared through, screeching to a stop in front of the massacre scene. Overcome with grief, Patrick punched his fist through one of the glass foyer doors, falling on the top step, screaming, bawling.

"AAAAAAAAH HAAAAAAAAH! AAAAAAAH! MI FAAAAAMILY! NO FAMILYYYYYY! MI 'AVE NO BRUDDER! NO SISTAAAHH! NO FADDAH! AAAAAH HAAAAH! GODDDD! NO ONE IN AH DE WUHLD! AAAAAH! MI SISTAAAAAAHHSS! HAAAAH! HAAAH! HAAH! AAAAAAAAAAAAAH HAAAAAH! HAAAH! HAAAAAH!"

He swung blindly at nothing while Dwayne tried to console him during his bereavement, carefully ducking so he wouldn't get punched in the face. The blood from Patrick's cut fist splashed on Dwayne's silk suit leaving the effect of living graffiti.

Down the block in the middle of the street, block inhabitants, passerby, paramedics, and bereaved Mr. & Mrs. Young crowded around their nephew Shawn's dead body; and up the block Patrick sunk down over the bodies of his younger siblings. His bloody hands swam in their blood, and they were one for the last time, while he screamed out for God's mercy.

"Yah understan' where I'm coming fra' Arlene," Al asked his company from his brand new rocking chair Dwayne purchased. Arlene impatiently sat, nudging her son Dante to wake up. She had come by to see the remodeled apartment. She was also summoned down from the Bronx to go over Al and Mattie's insurance policies.

She conversed patiently with Al as much as she could.

"I understand, Mister Carter. In spite of all that's happened, you still want the best for Baby Al."

He nodded. "Um-huhm. If anything happen to me, I want you and Jummy . . . make sho . . . my grandbaby get his money."

General began barking from inside Dwayne's room. Suddenly, Dwayne burst into the apartment, the silk shirt bloodily plastered to his physique. He ran straight for the living room, stopping short. Al and Arlene stood scared, noticing his bloody shirt and trousers.

"Baby Al, what's wrong," Arlene asked.

Dwayne, lethargic, looked around the room at Dante, at his godmother Arlene, and at his grandfather Al, and then he collapsed on the living room floor.

****

CHAPTER 8

*

Jimmy sat on the side of the Robinson family swimming pool mumbling to himself, his legs and feet dangling in the water. Twiddling his thumbs with worry, he kicked his heels against the pool tile, troubled after a failed attempt at calling 117th Street, encountering a changed phone line. Monica managed to scrap their children and grandchildren for the weekend, hoping to spend a couple of romantic, sequestered evenings with her love of twenty-five years, and attend church Sunday morning. Instead, she encountered a hypertensive, upset man. She returned to her husband's side from the kitchen with a bowl in her hand.

"Try some of this honey, here, take some," she said, offering a forkful of some new potato salad she made.

"Bring me the phone, there's got to be some mistake, gotta be," Jimmy replied sternly. She paused, eyeing the back of his head. He spun around impatiently. "Go! Bring me the phone woman!"

"Oh you make me sick!," Monica snapped, walking away, sucking her teeth. It hurt her to watch the man she loved fret over someone who appeared unappreciative. Her family often extended their love to Al and Dwayne and suddenly it was if they gave less than a damn about the Robinsons and their devotion. Seconds later, she returned to the patio with the phone, playing the obedient wife's role.

Jimmy dialed Al's number again: "One . . . two . . . one . . . two . . . six . . . six . . . three . . . nine . . . two . . . uhm . . . uhm." The phone company message replied, "THE NUMBER YOU HAVE REACHED . . . SIX, SIX, THREE, NINE" . . . Monica watched her husband in silence, anticipating an outburst.

"DAMN IT," he yelled, slamming the phone down. He angrily jumped to his feet, wetting his wife in her flowing sundress, and began pacing back and forth. She sucked her teeth and said, "Honey, why are you getting yourself worked up over Mister Slick, he can take care of himself. Come sit back down, come on. Please honey!"

Monica led her husband to one of the poolside lounge chairs and sat beside him on the edge; she began massaging his shoulders. "Honey, listen to me," she said. "I love you baby . . . and I can't stand to watch you run yourself raggedy over Mister Slick and Baby Al . . . I know you care, honey, and he stuck by us when the kids were little . . . Mister Slick was there for us, I know."

Jimmy put a fingertip on his wife's lips and said, "Shhh! Be quiet baby. I already know where you headed. I know what you're about to say, and you're right."

Monica couldn't believe what she was hearing. Jimmy never backed down easy when it came to his mentor. He embraced his wife and gave her a huge kiss on her lips. They lovingly gazed in each other's eyes.

"So you understand me then? You're going to stop letting Mister Slick and Baby Al worry you so much?"

He nodded.

"I mean, you keep worrying like you been doing, and you're gonna have the same strokes he's had. Mister Slick knows you're here for him; our family is always here for him when and if he needs us. I can't watch my husband run himself raggedy for nobody . . . Except me," she added, returning a kiss.

"Is it still some Bud in the fridge? If it is, bring one sweetheart," Jimmy asked. Monica winked her eye and walked off to get a can of beer for her husband. Jimmy adjusted his chair to lay back, to catch a few more hours of tree shaded sun. He thought of his father like genial mentor, wanting desperately to reach out to Al, but he couldn't. Al and Dwayne's phone number had been changed without notification. Jimmy assumed that Dwayne secretly changed the number, as he cursed his godson in his mind. What he didn't know was that his mentor changed the number, because of what happened.

The harassment from the press and the authorities made Al want to protect his grandson from the outside world. Harlem used to be an easier place to live. Juke joints, fashion, and good meals were on every corner, back in the days when Al first hit New York City's Harlem. Wars and hard labor separated the men from the boys; life was, oh so different now. Tenements that were full of life and overrun with loving families were ghosts of yesteryear all over the place. Not many stood tall and proud, only dilapidated and bricked in every window frame, each sill with stories to tell. Harlem was visually familiar yet different for the worst; and the tragedy of 120th Street added to the neighborhood misery.

News of the Livingston Family execution hit the tri-state wire services like a ton of bricks. A whole family slaughtered by bloodthirsty, vengeful, relatives of a slain, misunderstood, drug seller. A family torn apart by the ugliest racism of all, intercultural racism: racism within their own race. After spending many years with their self-inflicted division, they would make amends only a few hours before meeting death in cold blood. The Livingston tragedy shocked everyone who knew the family, from Dora's co-workers to Bradley's construction team, to schoolmates of the children, with each faculty staff of the children mourning the tragedy. From Andrew & Hyacinth's principal at Brandeis High School, to the ex-nursery instructors of Rose and Sharon, to Hyacinth's nursing school partners from Brooklyn's City Technical College; their newly arrived cousins from both sides of the family-Chambers and Livingston-residing in Brooklyn were devastated, including relatives abroad in England and Jamaica. All of Harlem, New York City, and the neighbors from the streets of all involved were also affected.

Four of the surviving henchmen, including the driver, didn't make it out of Harlem that fateful night without being apprehended by the police. Scheme's people never saw the FDR Drive, and back out in their Brownsville & East New York Brooklyn neighborhoods, as more funeral arrangements were handled, the young men were the talk of their environment. The press, news media, and police detectives consistently harassed Patrick and his grandmother Una, who went into shock over her family's massacre. Some of Una's well off relatives from England joined the family, to provide spiritual and mental support, agreeing to handle various responsibilities through the funerals; and for the burial arrangements, as the bodies of the deceased were shipped to Manchester Jamaica, Una, Nigel, and Patrick were whisked off to the countryside, deep in the hills of their native country, until they were ready to return to the United States. Sadly back in America the Livingston kinfolk from the five boroughs with the family hailing from England, would experience further sadness. Ezra, who stubbornly clung to life on a life support respirator in Harlem Hospital, finally let down his life resistant guard; he was "called home" by his heavenly father. Ezra Chambers quickly joined the rest of his deceased family in Jamaica, with no funeral in New York.

Shawn's aunt and uncle, Mr. & Mrs. Young, and the

rest of his family cried incessantly for their gentle, but young, aggressive kin. His wake and funeral at Anderson's Funeral Home was jam packed with screaming young women, many ex-girlfriends, their friends, his friends from his early days of breakdancing, popping, and trying to remain part of the Zulu Nation with their families. Even though Shawn had spent most of his latter time with Barrington and crew, during his last days, he still found time to spend with his family. His earthy ways were succumbed by the streets at the tender age of 19. His girl Phetima gave birth six months later, and their baby girl was like millions around the world, an infant without a father.

After receiving the news from reliable sources inside and outside, in "C-74" on Rikers Island, incarcerated Eric Martinez cried his eyes out for his now deceased schoolmate Shawn Young. He flew into a razor cutting frenzy, slashing up a few inmates during his blind rage of grief. Not only did he add more time to his sentence, he also found himself in an isolation cell.

Once sleep ensued after the cocaine finally wore off, Al was able to nurse Dwayne for two straight weeks; and the first week was rough. As the senior citizen strived to rehabilitate himself, he pushed hard to provide his grandson with three meals a day, soup, tea, and other beverages given while in bed. While Dwayne was recuperating, Al ensured peace and quiet for his grandson, waiting on him hand and foot, and he did his absolute best in fending off the authorities. He was at Dwayne's beck and call every moment he could be, as much as his old deteriorating body would allow. Malik Ballard continued walking General twice a day. Al couldn't pay Malik like Dwayne used to, but nevertheless young Malik remained happy. Dwayne stayed in bed, only leaving his room to use the bathroom. During Dwayne's bathroom treks, Al watched his grandchild with concernment. His heart suddenly filled with guilt, blaming himself for Dwayne's misfortune. If he had only told Dwayne the truth about Gwenny sooner, maybe their lives wouldn't have taken these terrible turns. Their lives would be much more tranquil instead of luridly violent. His grandbaby wouldn't have turned to the street life; his grandbaby wouldn't be sick, and most of all, his grandbaby wouldn't have beat him. Along with his personal medication schedule and household duties, Al successfully played the evil cards life dealt him, managing to work on his distraught grandson and keep house.

At the same time, all Dwayne thought of was his best friend, wading in his brother's blood; and, he had seen the brains of Patrick's sister, plus witnessed Uncle Barrington's actual kidneys on the sidewalk, oozing blood into the rainy sewage of New York City on a horrific, hot summer night. The second week, Dwayne felt a little better, actually wanting to go downstairs. A few more days came to pass, and he mustered up enough strength and courage to walk General. Things began running pretty smooth inside the apartment between Dwayne and Al. Al's speech changed for the better, hardly ever mumbling, and sounding much clearer. Dwayne started running errands for the household and did the food shopping. He provided the remaining dividends that he earned at Barrington's. They enjoyed themselves in their new, styled apartment throughout the fall and into the winter. Each of the holidays were spent with Aunt Lou, with an occasional visit from Arlene and the children. Things were on an upswing, until the spring.

The dewy scent of Harlem filled Dwayne's nostrils while he walked General on a misty April morning, after the canine unusually awakened him hours earlier. It had stormed cats and dogs the night before ending at dawn, adding a mystical aura to the overcast, glistening New York City streets. General moved ahead, while Dwayne tugged along behind his trusty one and a half year old pit, trooping north on Seventh Avenue. They passed an occasional drunkard, here and there, dutifully walking while the constant traffic avoided collisions the best way the drivers could. They passed an occasional man or woman of the working class, briskly walking to their subway or bus route of choice, or flagging a taxi to anywhere. General turned right on 120th Street with determination, forging ahead with all his might. Dwayne followed his dog onto the brownstone-lined street responsible for his seclusion.

Suddenly, he realized where he and General were walking. They were on Patrick and Shawn's block, and he hadn't been on the block since the murders. Luckily, Dwayne and General walked the opposite sidewalk yet, the closer they came to the murder site, the sicker Dwayne became. The telepathic situation worsened the moment General stopped walking. He growled, with his ears raised in place, starting to viciously bark in the direction of Patrick's house across the street.

"Come on Gen man! Why you bring me deep in 20th anyway? Chill, General! . . . General! What's the matter man, huh?," Dwayne anxiously asked his pet, pulling on General's leash. He refused to look at the cursed brownstone once inhabited by the entire Livingston family. He felt a magnetic field draw his pupils towards the house. General continued to bark stubbornly, paws welded to the pavement while his master feared looking across the street. His eyes of fear eventually traveled too much, causing him to look directly at the house. He had to remove this doubt, remove his fear; he had nothing to be afraid of because he was alive. What was there to be afraid of? He was cool for a moment, and even let off a hiss of relief, until he noticed movement going on inside of the house. Dwayne saw some lights flash on and off, with people moving around.

"Oh shit General! I thought all them niggas was dead. Maybe they was really into that Jamaican ghost shit after all!"

He waited for a car to pass, and they crossed the street. Dwayne looked up at Patrick's house while General became more vicious. "What's wrong man," Dwayne asked, with worry.

"I wonder what's in that house that's making you go off like that."

"GIMME THE FUCKING GUN! IT AIN'T WORTH IT, BLACK!"

"MI FAAAAAAMILY! NO FAMILY! MI 'AVE NO BRUDDER! NO SISTA! NO FADDAH! GOD! NO ONE IN DE WUHLD! AAAAAAAAHHH!"

Patrick's screaming voice echoed in Dwayne's mind. He painfully recalled his distraught, overwrought friend and what they saw. Little Sharon with half her face shot off, Andrew sprawled over the steps, the brains dripping down the side of the house; Mrs. Livingston, with half of her head; Ezra, with his bloody hands cuffing Dwayne's ankle as he reached out from the curb. Then there were the others, and Shawn: "C'mon, General! C'mon boy! We gotta get outta here man!"

"What is a duppy box?"

"H'im nuh k'no' 'bout dat."

"It's a casket high."

"So, a duppy is a dead person?"

"Nah maan, it's like a ghost."

"A spirit like."

"C'mon, General, shit! Let's get outta here! Let's go," yelled Dwayne. General refused to move. "Fuck it then! I'm leaving you! General! Come on! It's ghosts in that house! Them niggas is all dead!" Dwayne looked up at Patrick's house.

"Nah maan. It's like a ghost."

"It's like a ghost!"

"It's like a ghost!"

"It's like a ghost!"

A sudden gust of wind blew, mixing with a light new drizzle. General hatefully growled while his master pulled at him.

"It's like a ghost!"

"It's like a ghost!"

The second floor entrance doors-that were boarded up because of Patrick punching his fist through the glass-shook wildly back and forth.

"Come on General, SHIT!"
"It's like a ghost!"

The door swung open! Dwayne ran down 120th Street, with General trailing behind him, running non stop until he reached the corner of Lenox. He huffed and puffed, out of breath, leaning against a lamppost waiting for obedient General. The pit finally caught up with his master and they headed home.

Dwayne thought of his dead friend Shawn, who lay in the middle of the street that dreadful night. He thought of Shawn's aunt and uncle, who were still grieving since the tragedy. It took all he had not to break down again, after thinking of Patrick's pretty older sister Hyacinth, a promising young nurse to be, with a bullet hole in her neck. So many bloody red taped silhouettes and sheet covered bodies of people he came to know plagued his mind. This Harlem morning equaled the painful recollection of a ghastly, rainy, summer night filled with victims of a grimy chain reaction of lies started by Dwayne himself, from his early days of drug slinging with Scheme. He began sniffling, using the back of his hand to wipe away tears of remorse, when General stopped walking to defecate. The morning was slowly becoming brighter, with the sun trying to shine. The streetlights went out, as the day continued its bleak wetness.

General barked, informing his master it was time to finish the rest of their morning walk. Dwayne stepped quickly with his dog, thinking of Patrick's eerie house standing alone in his mind's eye of guilt, looking like a murderous castle.

They turned the corner of 117th and Lenox, passing by a crew of old customers from the seven eleven days sitting like wet looking zombies on an abandoned stoop. General trotted on happily, and with each of his footsteps, Dwayne became more eager to get rid of his pet, so he could sniff some morning blow. Some coke would ease the tension of his mind, as he sadly thought of his old crew one by one. Eric: locked up on Riker's Island; Patrick: crying himself to sleep every night underneath the beautiful Jamaican moon, with one surviving older brother Nigel, paralyzed, but by his side; Shawn: dead, never seeing his beautiful daughter, Shanté take her first steps. Their friendship began as early elementary, via middle school through high school, big time soon after in the drug world. Within a few years, with the exception of Arthur, everyone separately went their tragic routes. "Thanks to me, it's all over," thought Dwayne, footsteps from his building.

They came into the apartment with the usual force. Dwayne released his pit, peeking into Al's bedroom to see if his grandfather was still asleep. The windows were slightly elevated, with brand new air-conditioner in the right window still unused. The urinary stench inside the room had gradually become stronger as the months whizzed by. Al was watching "Good Morning America," sitting straight up in bed, fully dressed. Without looking from the TV, he asked, "Ya' hungry?"

Dwayne sat on the edge of Al's bed, shrugging his shoulders, staring into the television. Still upset from being on 120th Street, his guilt gnawed continuously at his soul, like a hungry termite with a corroded log. General entered Al's bedroom and licked at his depressed master's hand, and Dwayne ignored his pet, staring into space.

"Wha's uh matter," Al asked.

"They gone, Pappy."

"Who?"

"All of 'em . . . Patrick's whole family dead . . . It was bloody murder Pappy."

"I know son . . . I know."

"Patrick was laid out in his brother and sister's blood."

"Lord have mercy!"

Dwayne turned to look at Al, tears welling in his reddening eyes, then dropping as he spoke, "But, Pappy . . . All I did was drive the jeep around the corner . . . I had just met all of 'em . . . I just chilled with all of 'em. And I went around the corner, and . . . they . . . they was all dead. Shawn too . . . my homeboy Shawn . . . in the middle of the street. All of 'em dead . . . I ain't never . . . seen it before . .

. dead . . . all of 'em . . . that many . . . people."

"But you living," Al began, "You be a grown man soon, you gon'e be twenty-one in a coupla days. God fixed it for you to keep on living boy. You still here for a reason."

"You think God left me here for a reason, Pappy?"

"Um-hum," he nodded.

"What?"

"Dunno? Get on ya knees eene ask 'im."

"You believe in ghosts?"

Al squinted at Dwayne. What was the peculiar young man getting at? What made him come up with such a strange question, and why? He was back to walking the dog regularly, morning, noon, and night; things had been running smooth. He seemed to be doing fine the last couple of months after the tragedy. Al thought that maybe Dwayne was holding things in after being traumatized. Then, after a simple dog walk, out of the clear blue he comes up with a kooky question about ghosts. Al wondered what role did his grandson play in the Livingston massacre, and was he really telling the truth. Perhaps Dwayne was coming clean this morning.

"Well, do you?," Dwayne repeated.

"Do I what?"

"Believe in spirits? Ghosts?"

"You bein' haunted?"

"Can't you answer the question, Pappy?"

"Naw . . . I don't believe in no ghosts . . . I know there is life after death, ah reckon . . . Say it is . . . I believe ya' do unntah others as they do unntah you . . . ya' reap what'cha sow . . . wha' goes around comes around I guess; why, we got ghosts 'roun' here?"

"On twentieth-street, General sniffed 'em out."

Al chuckled and said, "Oh he sniffed 'em out alright . . . you had something to do wid' dem murders boy?"

"What?"

"You goin' on 'bout some ghosts on twentieth street.

Boy, you guilty about something?"

Dwayne smacked Al hard across the face.

"FUCK YOU," he yelled, jumping off the bed, bolting from the apartment. The door closed with General scratching, standing, and whining for his master on his hind legs, and Al's face burned from the slap, while his teardrops cooled his scorched skin.

Dwayne climbed to the roof, coming into the brightening morning. With all the strength he had, he punched the deteriorating roof door, fighting off more tears of guilt. He stood and slowly walked towards the roof's edge.

"Trying to jump nigga?," a raspy, familiar voice startled him.

Dwayne spun around to see down and out Floyd Nelson, Barbara's son, laid against the chimney. Compared to the clothes he wore in his heyday, Floyd looked a mess in his faded dirty jeans he constantly wore, dingy white shirt, and his unlaced shell toed Adidas sneakers. With missing front teeth, and unkempt graying hair, the once black stud of 117th Street was a sight for sore eyes at age 38. Dwayne had heard that Floyd lived on the roof after returning back to the block to live after being evicted from his place in Queens; his mother had re-kicked him out for stealing and selling her wigs. Dwayne checked his ex-customer from head to toe.

"Baby Al, gimme a cigarette."

"I was going to ask you for one."

Observing Floyd's sneakers, Dwayne chuckled and said, "You must think you Run DMC."

"I need those muthafuckas' money," Floyd replied.

"Don't scare me like that no more man! I coulda' fell off!"

He came closer to Floyd while he looked up at Dwayne, scratching his neck like a dog that had fleas.

"Nigga, you wasn't falling nowhere . . . Shiiiiiiittt, then again I don't know; you might wanna meet up wit' ya boy from twentieth-street, Miss Young nephew."

At the sound of Shawn's description, Dwayne turned away from Floyd.

"Yo, who that?"

"Oooh! She look dumb good!
I'm a slide up in that!"

"Nah high, that's me! You take
her dog, while I get that cat!"

Dwayne reminisced back to one of the many conversations he had with his buddy Shawn at Patrick's birthday party. The women had packed Barrington's and they were wild about Shawn's magnetic personality. His newly purchased gold teeth would gleam, offsetting a smooth, dark complexion with his low cut hair full of "waves", stocked frame covered in a Christian Dior sweatsuit with a Kangol derby, with Nikes to match; and he would flirt with every woman that approached him. Shawn slept with nearly all of the girls that he met the Saturday night portion of the party he attended with Dwayne. Now, two years later, there were no parties, no women, and no friends.

Dwayne looked around at the hazy Harlem skyline. In the northern distance he could see Saint Nicholas Projects, and the State Office building on 125th Street. To the east there were more tenements and projects; to the west, more tenements, giant Graham Court, blooming trees in the distance surrounding Columbia University, perched upon hilltops. Behind him, the trees and wooded areas of Central Park rose high above tenements and more tenements.

He felt lonely and guilty. Maybe if he wouldn't have

pistol whipped and lied on Scheme everyone would be alive. He knew Scheme's people must have pulled that hit on Patrick's family. Eric surely spoke the truth. Now, thanks to his pranks, he had his conscience to deal with, and it was getting beside him, real bad. Some coke would do him just fine right now. A few one on one's wouldn't hurt, or maybe about five or six lines; maybe a few blunts laced with some nice blow from 118th Street.

He started "foaming at the mouth", and became mentally thirsty. "I can get nice . . . Yeah . . . That's what I'll do . . . Cause I can't take it no more . . . I got dumb cash downstairs," Dwayne thought, remembering the last of the dwindling stash of cash left over from the penthouse. The earnings had decreased quite a bit during his "recuperation"; luckily, he still managed to have close to 5,000 dollars saved. His jeep and motorbike were still parked at a nearby garage with the rising cost of his parking spaces ticking away into the thousands. He needed to get back into hustling, or find a real job, but his guilt and need for drugs possessed his soul and clouded his aspirations.

Dwayne turned around, staring at Floyd in amazement. He asked, "Yo, what's that man?"

"Fuckin' crack! That's what it is. And the muthafucka sho' is good."

Floyd sat with his legs crossed in a meditating position holding a pencil sized glass pipe, equipped with a small bowl on its end. He reached into his pocket and removed a tiny cylinder like plastic vial, stuffed with an orange colored top, with two miniature white rocks squished inside.

"When ya had ya back turned and shit, I already smoked one of the muthafuckas up! Damn this shit is good, see, watch me."

He proceeded with his crack smoking demonstration, dumping the rocks into the tiny bulb on the blackened edge of the glass pipe, taking his lighter and lighting the edge of it. The rocks dissolved into smoke, and Floyd inhaled hungrily; his parched lips glued to the glass while his eyes rolled upward in their sockets, as his brain swam in pure ecstasy from the drug.

Dwayne watched thinking furiously, "Damn . . . that's that new ill shit called crack . . . I think it's crack . . . I heard dumb people is getting strung out on that . . . I wonder if I'll get hooked?"

"Floyd! Hey, Floyd!," he yelled trying to capture Floyd's attention. The derelict was totally out of it, close to three minutes into his "high". "Yo, Floyd! Get up man, damn!"

Dwayne shook and kicked at Floyd until he knocked off one of the hobo's sneakers. Watching his reaction to crack reminded Dwayne of a time when Floyd almost lost his life to heroin. A lowdown pusher had given him a "hot shot" inside a bar on Manhattan Avenue, and he was rescued by a few junkee friends from 122nd Street; they walked him back to life, then they rushed him to Sydenham Hospital. Dwayne and his friends had seen the whole episode-the slapping, the kicking, the walking-and he wondered if this new drug was as powerful as heroin. Floyd finally came to, and he instantly read Dwayne's pondering mind.

"Boy ain't never make me feel like this. It's only three dollars too," he said, already preparing for his next "high."

"Damn, high! You lightin' up another one?"

"Hell motherfucking yeah!," Floyd laughed, putting together his materials, "Wanna try?"

"Nigga like me might get strung."

"No you won't. The high is only for three minutes man. That's a buck a minute. Ya can't go wrong, come on, check it out."

"Three minutes?"

"Yeah."

"Fuck it. What I got to lose, I might like it."

Dwayne crouched next to Floyd, eventually sitting in

the same position.

"Take a few hits, I don't mind, you know that. I wouldn't've said take some if I did," Floyd explained carefully.

Floyd guided Al Carter's grandson through the motions. Dwayne inhaled deeply from the glass pipe.

Ten a.m., the next morning. With his walker carefully placed in front of him, Al stood over the new stove, stirring his morning oatmeal. Out of nowhere, his grandson's morbid behavior returned, leaving the frightened senior citizen with more doubts and tough decisions to face. If the violence should escalate from a basic slap in the face, should he seek help this time? Should he clue the police-or maybe his doctor-or even the neighbors; should they all be involved in his personal business? He was grateful to God for restoring his strength and ambidexterity, however with each stir of the cereal, his scared heart pounded harder.

The apartment door slammed, making him jump. His face still stung from the early morning smack laid on him the day before, and subconsciously, he knew more was coming.

Dwayne stepped up the hall while General barked happily at his master, running behind him. Al turned around in the nick of time. Dwayne gave him a juicy kiss on the cheek, in the same spot where he had smacked him the day before, knocking Al unbalanced, and his glasses off. Ecstatic, and high off crack, Dwayne caught his bewildered grandfather, stood him up straight, and replaced his spectacles. He embraced Al, yelling, "What's up, Pappy? My main man!"

"I smell a rat," Al thought.

"Yo man, gotta go, gotta go! COME ON, GENERAL!"

Dwayne ran from the kitchen, through the living room and into his room. He snatched the top drawer from his oak dresser out and dumped the contents on the floor. Realizing he pulled the wrong drawer, he tossed the first drawer, then snatched the second drawer from its bureau track. The green shower of crisp Ulysses S. Grants, Benjamin Franklins, and Andrew Jacksons floated in the air, easing and dropping to the floor; and Dwayne caught the bills in mid air, grabbing and scooping up what he could, acting like he had won a lottery jackpot. He gathered $250 dollars, grabbed General's leash, and was out of the apartment at the speed of sound, leaving his bedroom in a chaotic mess. General bolted down the staircase as well, while the door creaked slowly to its destination.

In the kitchen, Al's oatmeal began to boil and he turned off the gas. The apartment suddenly was still; there was no scratching or barking from General, and no Dwayne. He exited the kitchen, went past the blaring floor model television and into the hallway. He noticed the apartment door was ajar. Al thought, "Reckon he left it wide open . . . Lawd, wha' mah grandboy gone get eentah now?"

He pushed the door shut, locked it, and turned himself around to return to his cereal. He stopped short the moment he observed his grandson's bedroom. Broken bottles of cologne, clothes, and piles of money were left in a heaping mound of garbage in the room's center. The overturned dresser drawers were smack in the middle of the human tornado aftermath. Al even thought he saw a gun in the middle of the mess. He returned to the living room. Once he sat down ready for breakfast, while stirring his oatmeal, Al shook his head thinking, "Stay up to no good . . . Um-um-um . . . that fool never ceases to amaze me."

Dwayne walked at top speed with General in tow, dealing with his new found "high". His yearning haze felt good to him, and he needed more. The zone he was currently in wasn't like blunts, or blow; it was another level of feeling. It was a three-minute high, but it was the best high he had in his entire life. All the joints and blunts smoked, with all of the cocaine sniffed in the world couldn't measure up to this new stuff.

From 10:30 that morning, until eleven that night-for twelve and a half hours-Dwayne and Floyd smoked crack on the roof, with both their eyes rolling up in the sockets, and their bodies trembling. They faithfully sailed back and forth to the crack spot until Dwayne's money ran out. Loving the new high, the two new friends smoked crack for the rest of the week; they did it every day, every night, non-stop, to the wee hours of the morning. After a while, Floyd couldn't hang with his partner's smoke habits; Dwayne even obtained his own pipe, so he could ritually smoke day and night. He started piping as much as his lungs allowed, keeping General with him at all times. The neighbors from the block thought he was just dutifully walking his dog in the beginning. Everyday he would sleep until five in the afternoon until time to walk General. After that, Dwayne remained wired through the night until dawn, General's morning dog walk. Then he would retire and repeat the dog walk-eventually becoming crack walk-routine all over again. Dwayne was well on his way to being addicted, with diminishing funds, and a sudden wardrobe reduction. The "Fila" suits, "Coca-Cola", and "Gap" wear soon vanished; the jewels, neck chains, rings, and medallions began to evaporate. Dwayne's weight started to decrease along with many leather & sweat suits trimmed in Louis Vuitton, Gucci, and Fendi purchased from his beloved Dapper Dan's, and his behavior became more bizarre.

Al started feeling guilty for the umpteenth time. He felt as if he had provoked his grandson's latest mood swing. He knew Dwayne had never recovered from witnessing the catastrophic outcome of the massacre on his best friend's family. If only he hadn't questioned his grandson about the murders.

Approaching age seventy-six, Al Carter realized the worst had happened. He had become a battered senior citizen, and he felt alienated more than ever. He couldn't afford to be left alone by his only able relative in New York. Dwayne was suddenly staying outdoors for days and nights at a time, and Al knew it was because of his unnecessary quizzing of the Livingston murders, and he wanted to make amends, in case domestic savagery was imminent.

To pay his grandson back for furnishing the apartment, on Dwayne's 21st birthday, he planned a big surprise for him. Al gathered enough energy, pushing himself to bake two cakes. He baked Dwayne's favorite, a two-layer devil's food cake with chocolate icing, and he baked a rum cake. He felt since his grandson was legal drinking age, a rum cake with plenty of rum in it was sufficient. Pushing himself, Al fixed Dwayne his favorite meal: pot roast and gravy, homemade stuffing, mashed potatoes, collard greens, yams, with a big bowl of zucchini to mix in; last but not least, to wash down the meal, grape flavored "Kool Aid" was chilling in the refrigerator. He invited his extended family: Arlene and her children, over for dinner. Pushing himself, Al worked non-stop from morning; he even tasked Malik and his buddy Terrence from downstairs, to do the food shopping.

He mixed the cake batter by hand; the gravy for the roast was homemade; and the rum was picked up after he sent a note-via the boys-to his old partner Joe Rutledge who owned a liquor store/numbers establishment on Lenox and 123rd. Al gave the boys a big tip after they promised not to tell their parents about the liquor store errand.

By four that afternoon, he nearly completed his plans causing him to reminisce to the glory days when he was a sturdy, young cook. Back then, he could flip burgers, bake cakes, fry eggs, and scrub pots and pans at the same time-as if he were a kitchen octopus. Forty years later, all he had left was his initiative to work, and memories.

The surprise birthday dinner was set for six p.m. only the surprise was on Al instead. He was unable to wake the birthday boy. Al put General inside his bedroom and pulled his door shut so he wouldn't antagonize the company once Arlene and the children arrived. The guests tried and couldn't wake Dwayne. Al called out his name, Arlene tapped him, and the children shoved at him and still, no Dwayne. He snored, sprawled out over his bed, dead to the world. They decided to eat dinner and to let him rest, hoping he would awaken to enjoy the birthday celebration that was prepared for him. Dwayne usually jumped up the moment he smelled food cooking-always claiming to be hungry-but things were different this time. He had been up all night smoking crack on 115th Street, spending up the last of the money he earned with Patrick's uncles. Within a few weeks Dwayne had spent close to $700 dollars and counting, smoking crack.

Arlene helped her best friend's father set the table. She was impressed with his strength once again, and she knew he loved Dwayne unconditionally, and would go to extreme lengths to do anything for him. She wondered if her godson felt the same about Al, and if he was staying out of trouble. She also wondered what Dwayne could have done to deserve such fine treatment; a re-furnished apartment surely wasn't enough. When Dwayne was a child, Al often complained of his wife spoiling him, she recalled. Had he taken on his wife's characteristics out of fear? Was it due to his aging and loneliness?

After the table was set, and grace was said, Arlene and the children sat down and ate, while Al turned on the television for the evening news. Suddenly, General gave off continuous roaring barks from Al's bedroom. The intelligent pit bull knew it was time to smoke crack.

"Why General barking like that," asked Dante.

Al, in his rocking chair replied, "I don't know why dat

dawg is barking. If he know like I know he better hush up that carryin' on. Wheel of Fortune fixin' tuh come on. I gotta solve them puzzles!"

"Ol' Baby Al too tired to get up and participate in his own birthday dinner," Arlene asked, in between delicious bites.

"You know these young boys, Arlene. Run the streets all night, sleep all day, cain't tell 'em nothing."

General barked louder, beckoning his master to awaken, Dwayne's canine clock. "Hush up back there, General," Al yelled. General growled, then whined and proceeded to bark again.

Dwayne's bedroom door flew open. He walked into the hallway stopping short. Facing the wall, with both palms against it, Dwayne yelled, "PAPPY!"

Everyone stopped eating. Al stopped rocking.

"PAPPY! WHERE AND THE FUCK IS MY DOG?! WHERE AND THE FUCK IS GENERAL?!"

Al looked at Arlene, while she looked at her kids, and they all returned puzzled stares. "Baby Al, bring your butt in this living room and get something to eat," Arlene said playfully.

The second General heard his master's voice, he barked happily, hoping to be rescued. Dwayne waited impatiently for an answer from his grandfather.

"COME HERE, PAPPY! NOW!"

"I know he ain't gon' hit me in front of Arlene and the kids; he ain't that bad, he ain't that crazy," Al thought, frightened. He stated nervously, "Man, I done fix yo' favorite meal and two big birthday cakes! Get yo' 'hind parts in here! We all wanna tell ya' happy birthday!"

Dwayne sucked his teeth and went back into his bedroom. He came out of the room with General's leash in hand. He walked to Al's bedroom and opened the door.

"C'mon, boy," Dwayne instructed his pet pit. He attached the leash to General and walked to the living room.

"It's about time you woke up," Arlene said, smiling while Dwayne stepped straight to Al.

"What the fuck you put General in your room for, huh?! You always! Always! Always! Is fucking with something you ain't got no business fucking with! General stays in MY ROOM! HE'S MY FUCKING DOG! NOT YOURS PAPPY! NOT YOURS! MINE!"

Dwayne and General glared at their company. The malevolence in his face and voice made Arlene's children shake with fear. General gave a killer growl at the children while his master continued his persecution.

"WHY PAPPY?!"

"Well, Baby Al . . . it's ya' birthday . . . we all . . . I ain't . . . we . . . I . . . see . . . ," Al's words fluttered, as he nervously fought back his tears.

"Fuck my fucking birthday! I'm a fucking murderer! All y'all know all about it too! Fuck my birthday," Dwayne yelled, fighting back his own tears thinking of the tragic young woman named Gwenny, who passed away giving birth to him.

"Why you put my dog in your room?! He belong in my room!"

"The kids, Arlene and me wanted to tell ya' happy bir . . ."

"So what!!"

" . . . Happy birthday, and they . . . they, they couldn't . . . help me wake ya up. If General was wit' ya, he might bite somebody."

"Who?!"

"One of da' kids."

Dwayne let out a sinister laugh. Watching Al, and knowing General wanted to bite Dante, he released his grip on General's leash, dropping it to the floor. The hungry pit bull hated Dante at first sight, eyeing the nine-year old wickedly, growling towards him. He regarded the young boy as a tasty morsel, wishing he could eat him whole. General came closer to the dining room table, which was neatly arranged with the beautiful birthday cakes, the roast, gravy, and the rest of Dwayne's birthday meal.

Dwayne changed his voice to an evil, coarse, commandeering voice. **"Ssssic 'em**! **Ssssic 'em**," he instructed his pit bull.

General barked and jumped onto the dining room table, immediately going for Dante's throat, sewer rat style. Before the venomous pit could do damage, his master hypnotically stopped him.

"Halt! General! Halt! **Halt**," clapped Dwayne. Dante ran to the aid of his mother who stood from the table, wrapping her arms around him for protection. Tanasha froze in her seat, watching her mother and brother cower in horror, backing away from the table. General walked over the pot roast and mashed potatoes, knocking plates, glasses, and silverware to the floor. He kicked the rum cake with his hind legs, tail thumping through the demolished feast, and he squashed the chocolate cake looking for the quickest way down to the floor. He jumped from the table, and left Al's birthday dinner in a complete, dog pawed disarray. He obediently walked to his master's side, tracking food through the entire living room.

Dwayne squatted, never taking his eyes off of Al. He grasped General's leash, stood then roared, "Don't ever put my fucking dog in your room! I wouldn't give a fuck if President Reagan was in this motherfucker! **Fuck** company!"

Dwayne and General left the room, tracking the rest of the mashed potatoes and cake icing down the hallway. Dante sobbed, face buried in Arlene's side; and she stood angry, brushing her terrified son's hair with the back of her hand. She beckoned her daughter Tanasha from the table, extending her other arm. Petrified and scared to eat another bite, Tanasha jetted from the table to the strong safe arms of her mother. Arlene held her children for dear life while in the rocking chair, Al sat hyperventilating, fighting his tears. They heard the toilet flush, and out the door went Dwayne and his best buddy, General.

Al could hold back no longer. First, the sniffles started, then he fought for air, eventually breaking down into loud sobs. He flung his glasses across the room, covered his face, and cried out loud and hard. The second Al started crying, he drowned out Dante's minimal yelps.

Arlene looked at her children with love. "You okay," she asked. They nodded.

"Sit down, go on," she instructed them to sit on the sofa, and then she walked over to Al who was overcome with fear, embarrassment, and sadness.

Arlene was angry at what she saw. The terrible scene with General jumping onto the table, getting his paws in the food and dessert. She glanced at the gravy running from the overturned saucer like a tranquil brown waterfall, now dripping off the table's edge. The chocolate iced, mashed potatoed paw prints through the apartment disgusted her. The ageless plates that Mattie had purchased were demolished on the floor, with pieces of her children's disrupted dinner. She rubbed Al's back, doing her best to comfort the old man in his terrible situation. When her best friend Gwenny went into labor inside her bedroom, who would've thought that the child would grow into a spiteful, vindictive beast? Arlene recalled the day Dwayne was brought home from the hospital. He was a totally different Dwayne then, so tiny, innocent, and harmless. Al was a different Al, strong, tall and handsome, with salt and pepper hair; he was stern, humorous and overprotective. He would give his life for his newborn grandson, Dwayne Albert Carter. Twenty-one years later it was another story. The tall, stern, humorous man had become a battered, elderly coward afraid of his own shadow, thanks to his once innocent, harmless grandson who had become a moody, maniacal, crack addict. She recalled the sudden change in Al's behavior over the years, his previous hospital stays, the bloodshot and hideous looking black eyes, and his mottled skin. She knew Mattie and Gwenny would never forgive her if she allowed the abuse to continue; she couldn't let Al suffer anymore. Arlene walked over to the kitchen telephone wall extension, picked up the receiver, and dialed furiously. Al sat shaking his head, continuously crying, face still covered with his once strong hands.

"Can I have the 25th Precinct, please," Arlene said into the receiver. "Thank you."

"No . . . Arlene . . . Please . . . please don't call them cops . . . wait, baby . . . please don't call no cops," Al pleaded in between sniffles. He reached for his walker, putting it in front of him.

"You need help grandpa," Tanasha asked.

"No, sweetheart," he replied, rising to his feet with walker in place. Al refused to have the police involved in what was going on. He dragged over to Arlene.

"Hello, twenty-five," the officer said on the line.

Arlene looked at Al questionably, wondering if she should protect her godson because Al was afraid of him, or follow her heart and involve the police.

More tears spilled from Al's eyes. "Don't . . . Please . . . hang it up. Please hang up the phone, Arlene."

She exhaled disgustingly and put the receiver on the hook. Dante tapped Al on the forearm to give him his glasses after picking them up.

"Thank you, son," he said, replacing his glasses. He said to Arlene, "Go on . . . say it, why I want ya' to do that right? Why I want'cha to hang the phone up. I know that's what you gon'e ask me."

"Mister Carter, I can't let him treat you like that! He's got to be stopped!"

"He's just been sick, he's sick. My grandboy is sick, he'll get better."

Arlene was totally shocked at Al's fright. Things were really bad on 117th Street.

"Sick?! Mister Carter, you're not safe in this house anymore, you have to get out of here!"

She thought of her children, the scene of violence they just saw and experienced. Arlene was very protective of her children, and of the things they saw and did. The verbal abuse Al sustained in front of them was too much. General jumping onto the kitchen table, biting at her son's face at the command of the merciless Dwayne was the last straw.

"I think it's time for us to go now, I'm going to call Donnell and have . . ." Arlene's statement was cut short by Al, beginning to cry once more. "Nasha and Dante, get ready, I'm calling for Daddy," she instructed the kids.

"Please . . . No . . . Please! . . . don't leave me . . . you can't go," Al begged his company. He broke down once again, bursting into tears, shaking while he clung to his walker. "Y'all cain't just leave an old fella! . . . Y'all cain't do that to me! . . . Y'all cain't leave me here alone! . . . Please!"

Tears came to Arlene's eyes, while Tanasha and Dante both went to rub Al's sagging back. They all cried together.

By June, Dwayne was totally out of money. By July, he was staying out of apt #53 for three days at a time. His weight had dropped from 175 to 150. Appliances were missing in the house, like the toaster, and the microwave oven. By August, everything bought from his drug-slinging heyday was sold. Gone, was the "Atari 7800" game system for the TV, Al's pots and pans, and the blender. Gone, was Al's TV in his bedroom, Dwayne's TV set, the new living room lamps, his Mickey Mouse telephone, and disassembled pieces of the "Sony" rack stereo system. As he passionately smoked crack day in and day out, Dwayne's motor bike disappeared, along with his "Wrangler" jeep. He sold his possessions for cheap prices, for no more than $100 at times, anything to keep his habit going. Though he loved piping in the beginning, Dwayne often became sick behind the usage. He found himself throwing up, or having diarrhea, because of his poor eating habits. In spite of his changing physical state-no matter what-Dwayne made sure General was fed, and General stood strong during his master's crack binges. They were inseparable, master and pet, spending their days and nights running back and forth to the crack spot. While brothers and sisters traded "The Snake" for the latest dance called "The Wop" all over town, Dwayne snaked in and out of crack houses doing the wop with new smoked out friends, freebasing to his heart's content.

One night, Dwayne and Gerald Ballard had a curse out match in front of the building. Mr. Ballard had found out about his son Malik's many store errands for Al; he even found out about the liquor store deed from the previous spring. He forbade Malik to do any more favors, and Dwayne *'had better start taking care of his grandfather, or else there'd be trouble'.*

Mr. Ballard was chased into the building by snapping General while a few of the block teenagers watched the scene and laughed at it. Malik's mother Florence, on the other hand, felt it was nice for Malik to help out the troubled old man. After gossiping with nosy Barbara Nelson from the fifth floor and Mary Wilson from the first floor about the issue, Florence became concerned about "Baby Al being a crackhead with his grandpa in the house". Eventually, Malik continued to help Al whenever he needed assistance.

One evening after the temperature cooled, a few of the building tenants and some neighbors from the block came together into a discussion about Al and Dwayne, spearheaded by the original busybody of 117th Street, Barbara Nelson. Barbara created her own forum of spectators out of Nathan Pope, Gerald & Florence Ballard,

Chuck & Mary Wilson and a habitually drunk woman called "Miss Edna", claiming Dwayne was beating Al every day.

"Damn it, y'all gon' wait 'til poor Al get killed by that fool! Then y'all gonna be satisfied! I can't wait to see the looks on everybody's face when he pushing up daisies like Mattie and Gwenny! Then I'm a say I told ya so," Barbara said, in her usual one breath. The Wilsons didn't believe her accusations, neither did Miss Edna.

"Oh there you go again Barbara! Always stirring up some gossip," Edna retaliated, "How you know Baby Al is beating on Al? I heard he spent a cool mill on him, did the house over and everything. You always got something going!" She waved her hands and sucked her teeth.

"It's so typical of a drunk hussy to catch the tail end of everything! Barbara hears the punches! You live in that firetrap across the street! You don't know what goes on over here in one-twenty-eight!"

"The bottom line is," interrupted Gerald, "If there is some beating going on, we have to get Mister Carter to confess. He has to speak up." Everyone nodded, adding in their "Yups" and "That's rights".

"I know he beating 'im! I pressed my ear to the door! Sometime I ain't even gotta do that! You can hear that fool yelling for the heavens to hear," Barbara interjected.

The crew debated on about the problems of Al and Dwayne, finally deciding to pay Al a visit. "I think I saw Baby Al leave out with the dog close to an hour ago," Nathan Pope said.

"He on fifteenth-street smoking that damn crack, finnah to come home and bust Al's ass! Oh it's something goin' ON, on my floor, honey," Barbara threw up her hands.

Miss Edna looked around. "I got to get to Joe's, I have to get my last in." She staggered off in the direction of Lenox Avenue. Barbara rolled her eyes and waved her hands in Edna's direction. She stated, "I don't know why that drunk heifer came over here trying to be nosy. She getting her last number in alright, the last goddamn suck on a dick of Smirnoff! Last damn trick!"

Florence gasped and laughed until Gerald gave a "don't pay Mrs. Nelson no mind" look. His wife slowed to a giggle and gave him a peck on the cheek, playfully brushing off his suit and straightening his tie.

"Well, I'm going upstairs to see what the deal is. Ya' with me," asked Mr. Wilson. Immediately forgetting the run in with Dwayne and being chased by General, becoming courageous, Mr. Ballard said, "Hell, yeah! No way in hell our son Malik should be doing Mister Carter's food shopping, when his nasty grandson is laying upstairs, coming in and out of the building with his dog. He could do the shopping for his grandfather!"

Reluctant to climb to the fifth floor in case the mission would be done in vain, Mary kissed her husband and wished him well, overflowing with pride because of his neighborly concern.

"Me and Bruh' Carter go way back . . . To the fifties damn near . . . He's a good man . . . Look out for 'im," Mr. Pope added. Tipping the scales at 300 pounds, he knew without an elevator he couldn't make it upstairs to help his friend, but he wished the "good samaritan" team well.

"Don't you worry, we're gonna find out the truth, right now," said Mr. Ballard. They entered the tenement.

Barbara blurted, "How and the hell you gon' stand there and tell that damn lie when you know Baby Al just a whipping yo ass for breakfast, lunch, and dinner Al Carter!"

While Barbara, Mr. Wilson, and the Ballards interrogated Al to the fullest, Dwayne stood behind the opened apartment door, ready for another crack binge with General. Al hoped his grandson would ignore their neighbors' accusations.

He vehemently denied his abuse: "Damn it, Barbara!

For close to fifty years . . . you been nosyin' . . . lyin' on people . . . and mindin' niggas' business! . . . Take yo trouble makin' ass down duh hall and stop lyin' on my grandson! . . . Babah Al ain't do a thang to you!"

"Oh! I'm lying! Call him Baby Al and let him knock ya dentures out! I knew Baby Al's mama! Yo daughter before you and Mattie Mae had her! Poor Gwenny and Mattie spinning in they graves like tornadoes! You raised that high yellow pain in the ass as best ya could! What the hell he beating, cussin' and stealin' from ya for?! Tell me please! I gotta know!"

Barbara's irritating voice sparked anger in General, causing him to bark continuously. Dwayne tried to calm his pit so he could hear more information. He shook him, and rubbed his shoulders.

"Shhh Gen man, it's okay. Be quiet so I can see what they gon' do," he whispered in his ears. General whined and growled, wishing they could attack.

Mr. Wilson tried to ease the questioning by speaking up, "Everything okay up here?"

"Sure, fine. Everything is just fine," replied Al.

"Well that's a fine lie," Barbara started again.

Mr. Wilson and the Ballards shook their heads wishing they had never brought Barbara. They knew she would've butted in just the same, hyper-extending her head from her apartment the moment their entourage came to the top floor.

Al looked at the spectators and said, "I don't know where this woman get these crazy lies. Jus' cause she thank she know muh . . . Go on, Barbara! Just go' ne nah! Ain't nobody listenin' to ya' lies, woman! I don't know why you hate my grandboy so much! Babah Al ain't nevvah did nothin' bad to ya! Ya always hated my boy!"

"On the contrary, Mister Big Stuff wanna cover everybody and they mama's ass, yo grandson is the one who hates! He hates you! And everybody else around! Why?!

Why? Barbara can't take it no mo' chil'! I got to tell it! Lawdy, lawdy, lawdy!! Barbara got to spill the beans," she said, jumping up and down.

"Cut it out," Mr. Ballard shouted; he could take no more of Barbara Nelson.

"Barbara, calm down," soothed Mrs. Ballard; their vile neighbor was ruining their focus. Mr. Wilson put his head down shaking it with sadness; he suspected he knew.

"Cause ya just a lil' too **black**! Ain'tcha, Al Carter?! Huh?! Like my grandbaby say, y'all know what time it is! You just a little too black for his taste! We all are! That Baby Al take after them honkys! He the white man child!"

All of Al's neighbors' jaws dropped, mouths opened wide, while Barbara screamed out the Carter family skeletons. Al was extra furious: "Shut up, Barbara Nelson! Shut up I say!" Deep down he was devastated; how could Barbara turn his life into an open book? She unfairly took advantage of her own history with Al and Mattie by causing this ruckus. The neighbors didn't need to know his personal business, or did they? Could they really help?

"Uh-huh! Whatcha got to sat to that, Al Carter," Barbara further taunted; and he was flushed with anger and embarrassment.

Unknown power pulsated through Al's veins as he partially lifted his walker up and banged it on the floor. He desperately wanted to throw the walker in his neighbors' direction with the strength he suddenly possessed; it was unknown strength, camouflaged aggression, diluted courage. The neighbors suddenly knew the truth, and he was fighting a losing battle, the battle of the cover-up. Al stared Barbara eye to eye, and he knew she saw through his transparency. As far as she was concerned, he needed to come clean and seek help. Al knew Barbara meant well in spite of her shenanigans, however this wasn't the way to go about things, with the world in your business.

General started barking again after his moment of

silence. "Well," Barbara started again.

"Shut up," Al shouted at her.

"Don't you tell me to shut up! You tell that mutt to shut up! Shut up ya damn mutt!! Baby Al beating you 'cause he hates ya skin! Just like them white folks! You a nigga to him!"

Dwayne stepped from behind the door while General kept barking.

"What's up? What's going on? Hold up . . . ain't y'all a little too old to be selling candy? Why you bothering my grandfather? Why he trembling, Miss Nelson?"

"You know why he trembling! 'Cause you gonna beat the shit out him, that's why he trembling!! Barbara knows honey and it's gonna come to a stop! Right now damn it!"

Al and Dwayne looked at each other with choreographed confusion.

"**SHUT UP GENERAL**," his master firmly instructed. Dwayne rubbed Al's back and softly said, "Pappy, go inside man, I'll take care of it. I'll speak to them."

Al backed into the apartment slowly, and General obediently stopped barking.

Once Al entered the apartment, Dwayne closed the door to face his nosy enemies head on. The Ballards and Mr. Wilson had become angry like Barbara. Al's denial of his abuse and his protection of Dwayne made the concerned neighbors extra upset; and the senior looked worse than ever with a puffed up face, and urine stains all over his pajamas.

"What's the fucking problem," Dwayne shouted.

"Whoa! Hold up! You watch your language," snapped Mr. Ballard.

"Yeah man, watch ya language," added Mr. Wilson.

"I ain't gotta do shit but stay black, die, and take care of my grandfather!"

"Yeah, well you don't do a good job of it! Malik does

what you're supposed to be doing! My son shouldn't have to do your work," Mr. Ballard announced.

"I been taking care of Pappy and I always will!"

Barbara spoke up: "How?! By sending him to the grave?! Ain't nobody deaf, dumb, or blind! Yo granddaddy might be scared of ya, but Barbara ain't! Next time ya touch 'im, the cops gon' be here to arrest ya! They gon' throw yo high yellow crack smoking behind away, then the good Lord gon' kick yo' UN-ORIGINAL ASS!"

Gerald Ballard added: "And stay away from my son. I'm not going to say it anymore! Malik has his own chores, he doesn't need to do your chores! And walk your own mutt!"

"Your wife's a fucking mutt," Dwayne yelled. Flabbergasted, Florence placed her hands on her hips, and sucked her teeth.

"I don't need ya pussy ass son to walk my dog! I walk my own shit okay! And you! You," Dwayne looked at Barbara, directing his verbal line of fire, "You wig wearing, troublemaking big mouth! Floyd's the crackhead! He steal everybody's shit! His shit! Her shit! Yo shit! My shit! He stole from us! Took everything from me and Pappy! Mind ya business and leave me and my grandfather alone!"

He backed inside the apartment and slammed the door with all his strength, making everyone jump. Al stood in his bedroom with his back turned, clinging to his walker, afraid for life. Dwayne eased into the room behind him.

"Hey, Pappy, can you believe that dog breath bitch from down the hall, and her pussy posse? Talking 'bout I'm beating on you and shit. Can you believe that mess man?" he chuckled, patting Al hard on the back.

Fighting the tears unsuccessfully, Al gave his walker an iron grip and replied, "I . . . I . . . I told 'em nothing . . . was going on."

His tears dripped to the soiled, grimy carpet.

One night, weeks later, Dwayne hadn't eaten in four days so he decided to join Al at the table for dinner. There were only a few pieces of silverware, one pot, one frying pan, three plates, and four glasses left in the apartment thanks to Dwayne selling everything for crack. Al was practically down to one meal a day, only oatmeal in the mornings. This particular evening, he desired a change of routine. He put together one of the meals Aunt Lou had raised him with. He thought he would have dinner all to himself until Dwayne unexpectedly showed up. Al had become accustomed to his "house prisoner" role, and he could usually predict when Dwayne and General would arrive home. He ordinarily feigned sleep when his grandson came into the apartment to rest up from his crack missions.

"I know that's pot roast, right? I want some," Dwayne said.

Al quietly consumed his meal of liver and okra, a meal Dwayne abhorred since childhood. He watched his barbaric grandson walk toward him while he sat at the table. Dwayne's horrifying aroma filled his elderly nostrils with each approaching footstep. He tried not to look up at him, but he caught a shocking glimpse of the loved one he swore he knew.

"You save some of that pot roast for me, Pappy?"

He walked into the kitchen, to search for extra food. His hair, usually kept in neat cornrows before he started using drugs, was out and raging about. The white Coca-Cola tank top he wore was a dingy goldenrod, smudged with dirt and bloodstains. The Levi jeans were filthy, and his untied construction boot soles were run over.

"You ain't got no more pot roast, Pappy?"

"Listen, it ain't pot . . ."

"You greedy man! Why you ain't save me none?"

"But it's not . . ."

Dwayne returned to the living room, and yanked Al's fork out of his hand. Before Al could react, his body was trembling all over from fear. How could the grandchild you loved and raised from infancy torture you so? Al knew, beyond the shadow of a doubt, Dwayne was really hooked on something. This deadly drug was no marijuana, when after using you came down; you could function and dress normally with subsequent amnesia. This stuff was no cocaine, making you aggressive and prone to strokes and heart attacks; you may lose loved ones, life, or a job with escalated usage. This was no heroin, which would make his grandson nod all over the place, and possibly steal some of his goods. This drug was something entirely new, making him steal all of his goods; it was current, and it was a killer of all communities.

"Damn, Pappy! Don't hide, shit provide! I'm starvin' like Marvin out here," Dwayne said, stabbing the liver with the fork, "Why you cook okra with the pot roast, man? That's not you."

He put a morsel of liver into his mouth, and Al stared straight ahead, expecting an outburst. Dwayne spit the piece of liver on Al's head, mortified.

"WHAT'S THAT?!!," he screamed.

"Huh?"

"Don't play deaf! What did I just TASTE?! *What the fuck* **IS IT**?!"

"Liver."

In one sweeping motion, Dwayne yanked the entire tablecloth off the table with Al's dinner. With his other hand, he turned the table over, making it separate to halves once it crashed, and everything came smashing to the floor; the plates, the glasses, and the remaining silverware which was usually set in place for two to dine.

Dwayne grabbed Al by his neck, and shoved him against the wall banging his head against it, violently shaking him back and forth. Al's head smashed to the wall with each statement from the deranged young man.

"LIVER! . . . LIVER! . . . LIIIVERRR! . . .

LIVER! . . . WHY?!! . . . WHY?!!"

General came into the room, growling at the scene. Al's spectacles fell to the floor during the attack, and with one foot stomp, Dwayne crushed them by grinding his boot into the floor. General barked loudly, trying to get his master's attention. Sensing that his pet wanted to participate, Dwayne let go of Al's neck right before the elderly man turned blue.

Falling to the floor, Al fought for his breath, partially blacking out because of the head pain and air loss. He thought he heard his maniac grandson tell his pet pit bull to bite him. The room intermittently faded to black, and he thought he saw Baby Al pointing at him from across the living room; the room was spinning suddenly and coming to light, and fading to black, then light; and the pain, his head swam in excruciating, horrific pain.

General moved closer, barking at abused Al while Dwayne stood back in a hyper, cracked out stupor, watching with glee.

"Ya hungry, Gen? Ya got beef with him, Gen? Ya want some of that?," he laughed, then commanded: "Grrrr sic 'im! Sic 'im boy! Grrrr sic 'im boy! Get 'im! Get 'im, Gen!"

General pounced on Al, and violently bit into the old man's leg; and Al screamed out in pain with his flesh tearing, blood squirting. The wild pit was seconds away from breaking his leg with its powerful jaws, when Dwayne yelled, HALT! He gave a solid handclap, stopping his pet instantly.

General freed himself from the old man's bloody thigh at his master's command. The living room looked like a cyclone blew through, a major catastrophe. Al was left in the center of it all, in tears, in shock, and wet with blood that saturated his pants from General's dog bite.

Dwayne's crack abuse took on a new level when he

and General started mugging people. The first robbery took place by Morningside Park, late at night. A couple was walking together enjoying the breezy pre-autumn weather. General burst from between two parked cars, attacking the couple, distracting them from the additional evil that lurked in the shadows.

While the frightened couple fought the wild dog, Dwayne emerged from behind a tree. He tackled the man to the ground and beat him bloody, and the woman screamed in terror as General bloodied her legs, jaw gripping them to the bone. Dwayne dumped the contents of her pocketbook, then gave her boyfriend two hard kicks to the rib cage because of no wallet. He sprinted with General, his trusty partner in crime, through the moonlit woodlands of the park making off with sixty dollars.

He pulled off subsequent robberies in the same fashion, every other day. He kept a low profile, fearful of being picked up by the police because of a neighborhood rumor that "a young man was robbing people with a dog". Dwayne concealed himself most of the time, until his basing funds disappeared; he even bought more time by selling the air-conditioner he purchased for Al, which had only been used twice. Whenever the crack money ran short, more robberies with General were done.

One sunny morning, they robbed a Spanish woman by a school on Amsterdam Avenue. As she walked through the schoolyard, Dwayne and General lunged for the attack, only making off with fifteen dollars worth of food stamps.

On an overcast night before dawn while eyeing a well-dressed businessman, Dwayne decided that this "nerd" was the next victim. Within three minutes, the educated young businessman was out of $200 dollars worth of cash and jewelry. He was beaten up with a kicked in bloody mouth, several dog bites all over his handsome gray suit, left in a daze.

A few weeks later, one afternoon before Dwayne left

for his binge, someone began banging on the apartment door.

"WHO IS IT," he angrily asked.

"Open the door, high," the familiar voice answered.

Dwayne opened the door. "Oh shit, what you doing here?"

"I'm back, high. I'm better," Patrick said, dressed in a three-piece suit with necktie. The two friends hugged one another for old and new times' sake, bursting into laughter.

****

CHAPTER 9

*

Dwayne and Patrick walked north on the downtown side of Lenox Avenue. Patrick dropped the bomb news that while he was in Jamaica recuperating from the murders, he had repented his sins and became a saved, religious man. Dwayne laughed and teased him, calling him names like "Preach" and "Reverend Ike", and Patrick was prepared for his friend's outburst and jokes. Things really had changed since the summer of '85, and their lives were bound to remain on separate paths due to circumstance. Once the euphoria of meeting up dissolved, while they were walking, Patrick became concerned about his friend's appearance. Dwayne had lost lots of weight, and he didn't look himself at all; his crispness and neatness were totally gone.

Patrick suspected drugs, maybe even the new one on the streets titled "crack", then again, Dwayne would never lower himself to that level, especially after hustling. It had to be the stress of the block party shootout, even a year later. The impact of his family's slaughter continued to touch the neighborhood, his friends, and everyone around. Patrick felt he was lucky to have given himself to Jesus, and that God was responsible for his strength, and his subsequent surgery and skin graft for the removal of the bullet from his calf. The power of God left him totally blind to what really happened during his Jamaican seclusion. People around the way saw Dwayne's deterioration first hand. While Patrick was out of the country turning his life over to Christ, his main man Dwayne had turned his life over to the pipe; and Patrick was oblivious to the many stares he received while walking the streets with Dwayne.

They turned the corner of Lenox and 120th, slapping five with a few teenaged guys who were leaving the block.

"Damn man, I can't believe Shawn is dead man, I'm still bugging off that," Dwayne said, while they walked past Shawn's building.

Patrick replied with pain and anguish, "It was terrible man, but the good Lord knew best. My family might have been alive today if we would've praised the Lord together. You don't know, man . . . sometimes I can't believe myself, what actually happened . . . I miss my family . . . I really miss them, man, all of them . . . Scrambling, hustling, slinging, and getting money really wasn't all that important . . . Even though I have cousins uptown and downtown, I don't have any immediate family here now except for Mummy, but we have the Lord . . . I have to speak the word. Nigel stayed back home, but Mummy wanted to come back with me . . . and I prayed about it, and God told me it was okay, and everything would be alright."

The closer they came to the Livingston house, and the more Patrick preached about God sounding as if he would bawl any second, Dwayne's need for a hit of crack increased. Amidst the subconscious screams from his soul, he still tried to concentrate on catching up with his friend and the good times that they shared. Dwayne needed to talk about the actual good times: busloads of women, young and old, the money earned and spent, the sex; Dwayne missed the jeeps, motor bikes, and cars; Dwayne needed to recall the cutting of classes, stealing bus and train passes and selling them, the smoking of blunts, and the drinking of "quarts and forties"; Dwayne hoped that Patrick was where he was mentally, missing the cutting of drugs, and the making of money, money, money; it was always good times, and good food, and good friends.

He trooped on with Patrick's redundant God speeches in one ear and the voice of the pipe in the other. With his head down, he watched every boot step hit the ground, and all the bad times plagued his crack needing mind: the fights with Scheme and the lies told, the fights with Al, the shootout at Saturn roller rink, the coke, *'no Gwenny-no mommy! I killed my mother by being born!',* the shootout on '20th', **the corpses!**

"Yo, Pat man, I can't go no further," Dwayne said, stopping.

"What's wrong man, you okay?"

"No man . . . I'm just . . . I'm just . . ."

Patrick eyed his childhood friend, still ignorant to Dwayne's crack habit, but noticing a far off look that he never had.

"I'm just so hungry, high. I'm starving Pat! I'm starving like Marvin high! . . . Please, can you help me get some grub? Can you help me man?" He tried not to seem obvious.

"Why didn't you eat before you left the house? You didn't cook?"

"Yeah right man. Pat I don't cook. Pappy do that, but he been sick, and we ain't got no food right now. Yo, I'm stupid hungry right now high."

"Yo man, you want to borrow a coupla dollars? I can spare a few."

Patrick dug into his pockets, and Dwayne was elated.

"Damn, high, you saved me man, I woulda starved to death!" He couldn't wait to get to the crackhouse. Patrick was a true blue homeboy after all, a definite friend to the end. He handed Dwayne a crisp, ten-dollar bill.

"Thanks, high," Dwayne said, slapping Patrick five

then, hugging him. "Good to have you back Pat man! Word up, high!"

"I couldn'tve did it without Jesus Christ, our Lord. I'm saying, Dee man, God is real. Trust me on it man, God is . . . dope!"

Dwayne laughed at the new updated version of Patrick, trying to carry himself grown up and religious as possible. They started walking again with brownstones sailing through their peripheral vision, coming closer to the Livingston house.

"When you got back again?," Dwayne asked.

"Two days ago. My grandmother just came back from Jamaica last night. We couldn't catch the same flight. She had a few things to take care of anyway. And God said he would provide and take care of everything."

"Yo, high! I think it's some guppies in your house!"

"What? What do you mean by that? I don't understand?"

Stopping in front of the Livingston house, Dwayne whispered his question, "Yo man, what's that Jamaican shit like a ghost? Guppy, duppy, what is it?"

"Duppy?"

"Is it some in your house man?"

"No, I hope not," laughed Patrick.

Dwayne let out a sigh of relief. "Oh, cause me and General went by your crib right, we was walking the other morning right, and General wanted to come on twentieth right; I didn't know if anybody was in there right; and it looked like all I saw was ghosts and shadows flying around in there! Pat man, when I saw that shit, high, I ran like hell!" Patrick laughed at his impossible friend once again.

"The shadows that you saw were my cousins from England. They have been here for a while now. Some of them are so excited about the World Series. They even went to the parade."

"Yo I was downtown yesterday at that shit," said

Dwayne. "The Mets finally came off. Kicked the Red Sox ass. Boston still dope though. I got crazy hats, t-shirts, buttons, and shit. Gotta get that bread Pat, word up! Still got a few hats at the crib to sell. Yo, your family was downtown too? That shit was packed homeboy!"

"A lot of family is here now to support my grandmother and I, you know, to help us out, after, what happened."

That second Dwayne felt bad for Patrick, even though he looked remarkable, dressed in a suit and tie like a businessman. He had always struggled with weight since they were teenagers. In their drug-slinging heyday, Patrick shed his pounds and developed a buffed physique that drove women wild. Now, his complexion was shades darker because of the stay in Jamaica and his weight had increased to tremendous proportions in his mid-section, though his muscular constitution was still there.

"While we're here on God's green earth, we have to love each other and praise his holy name. My whole family was murdered right here, murder D! Cold blood in front of my eyes. I couldn't go on man, life wasn't worth living. I even wanted to die. Jesus Christ showed me the way; I've never felt better! I didn't know that the Lord could make me feel so strong, and turn my life around so good, praise God! Halleujah!!," Patrick cheered.

All the God talk began making Dwayne sick to his stomach, because his savior called him loud and clear too. With his ten dollar award he received, he needed to ditch Patrick; to hell with God, they could chat about Jesus later. The most important thing now was crack!

The door at the top of the stoop swung open and out emerged a chunky, pretty brown-skinned woman with an orange head wrap; she placed her hands on her hips.

"T'cha! . . . T'cha! Pahtrick! In de howse right no'uw. T'cha! In de howse nuh maan," the woman scolded, re-entering the house.

"Who and the hell was that," Dwayne asked, letting off a hiss.

"No problem, that's my cousin Ivy. I don't take them on. They worry about me, cause of what happened, and all. They don't want me to, lose it."

"Well, I'm'a step off kid, I gotta walk General. I'll check you later, now I know you back, I'll come through."

They gave each other "dap", and hugged tightly once again. Patrick walked up two steps and stopped. He said, "Come inside and say hello. My grandmother hasn't seen you in the longest while man. Come, quick for five minutes."

When they were children, Patrick's family wanted absolutely nothing to do with Americans; what was the big deal all of a sudden? Trying not to blow his cover, or lose his temper, Dwayne took a deep breath.

"Yo high, can't it wait?! Damn, gimme time, I'll see ya grandmoms. She not going back to Jamaica right?!"

"No."

"Aiight then!"

"Aw, come on man, stop fronting and come inside chump!"

Dwayne furiously thought, "Damn, I need my shit! I need to smoke! Man, fuck this nigga grandmother! Damn Pat!" Feeling trapped, he started up the steps.

"To be a saved nigga, you sure pop a lotta shit! Pat man, word to **God**, five minutes high!"

They skipped up the stoop and entered the Livingston home. Dwayne winced at the pungent, spicy scent inside the house.

"Damn high, what in the hell is that smell," he whispered.

"They're making curry goat in the kitchen, that's what that is."

"Oh, damn high! Sometimes I forget you West Indian man."

"The rest of the family is probably upstairs or in the dining room. I'm going to let Mummy know you're here."

Patrick led Dwayne into the spacious living room. The ceilings were high and painted peach like the wall above the mantle and mock fireplace that faced you the moment you entered. The mantle-which was once overrun with photos of the Livingston family-now held framed pictures of the living only, with their cousins and in-laws, along with odds & ends, and vases of fake flowers. The walls on both sides of the fireplace were covered with mirrors, while the floor was covered with wall to wall burgundy carpeting. There was a glass coffee table placed in front of an extended couch that fit snug into the corner by the windows. The hallway corridor that led to the kitchen was closed off by double doors, and a 25-inch floor model color television stood catty cornered on four legs next to a grandfather clock to its left, next to the blocked partition that led to the dining room and kitchen. There was a stereo system to the left and other soft cushiony couches to snuggle in comfortably.

They spotted a woman's handbag on one of the loveseats near a tall lamp. Being a neat freak, Patrick shook his head disgustingly and said, "I hate when Mummy leaves her things around. She loves leaving her bag around with her important things inside, and if you touch her stuff, she likes to get mad. She's lucky there are no thieves in this house."

The ten dollars Patrick "lent" Dwayne was burning a hole in his pocket, and he needed more. Una Livingston's bag looked tasty. She was bound to have more than a few dollars in her pocketbook after flying back and forth to the Caribbean. Dwayne slyly licked his lips, wishing for the handbag.

"Word to mutha, she lucky y'all ain't no thieves."

"PAHTRICK, COUME," a male voice shouted from the kitchen.

"PAHTRICK! COUME," female voices yelled from upstairs.

"Damn, high. Ya' family trying to split you in two."

Patrick chuckled and headed in direction of the kitchen.

"Bet! Now I can get that fucking bag," Dwayne thought, creeping towards the purse.

Patrick quickly returned, startling Dwayne.

"Yo, you scared me man!"

"What? Did you think I was a duppy man," laughed Patrick.

"Don't play like that high."

"Would you like something to drink, something to eat? You said you were hungry."

"Nah man! Look man, where's your grandmother? I told you I gotta step off!"

"I'll get her now, make yourself at home, brother."

Dwayne watched Patrick jog up the stairs from inside the living room.

"You ain't gotta worry about that black, I'm'a make myself at home," he chuckled, eyeing Una's handbag.

At the speed of sound, Dwayne opened the purse, stealing thirty-two dollars and Una's house keys from inside. He replaced the bag like nothing happened.

Seconds later, Patrick and some family members descended downstairs.

First, a tall man, then second, another woman then third, the lady with the head wrap. Patrick and his grandmother Una-slowly but surely-brought up the rear. Patrick introduced each member of the family, saving his grandmother for last.

"Mummy, remember Dwayne?"

She nodded, "Eih hih, yea maan; h'im teke off weight?"

"Just a little," Dwayne answered before Patrick could. "Pat man, I'm out! I gotta walk General, see y'all."

He walked into the hallway, trying to unlock the doors.

He didn't want to seem obvious that he needed drugs, but the longer Patrick took, the more aggressive he became. A few seconds seemed like hours when he heard Patrick tell his relatives that he was letting his company out. Patrick entered the foyer.

"Damn, high! Why you had to take so long, I gotta go," Dwayne exclaimed, trying not to shout.

"Calm down," Patrick responded, unlocking the doors.

"I told you man, I had to go, I told you that! General probably shitted up the house already!"

Patrick let Dwayne out, slapping him a quick five. Dwayne trotted down the steps, briskly heading towards Lenox Avenue.

"Yo, Dee! Why you going the long way?! What about General?!"

Dwayne forged ahead, with the crack spot as his destination; General's evening walk had to wait.

Back on 117th, General barked endlessly, pawing frantically at the apartment door. The pit bull was no fool, giving verbal indication that he needed walking, and fast. Minutes passed, and after running about in the apartment up and down the hallway, he defecated by the apartment door in front of Al's bedroom.

Inside his room, Al was finishing a brief, sore nap, awakened by General's earlier antics. He woke up face down, dentures popping out of his mouth. Using decaying strength, he managed to sit up on the bed's edge, feeling like he was nearing the end of life's winding roads. The room was dark and blurry, even after he painfully turned on the remaining crystal lamp; Dwayne sold the other lamp for crack.

Al put his dentures inside an empty denture cup-given to him during his last hospital stay-he kept on the nightstand. The familiar, incessant feeling came, and he needed to get to the bathroom unable to locate the walker.

Squinting, he spotted his urine can, knocked over near the closet. He stood, using the nightstand for balance, wetting his pants instantly. He exhaled heavily, embarrassingly, while the urine escaped gushingly from him with no control.

He was hungry, lonely, abused, old, and sick, in need of medical attention. The bruised bite General left him with became infected, rotting, leaving Al with a soon to be gangrenous limb. His arms and legs were covered with the same unchanged outfit; the unwashed plaid-brown flannel shirt, and the ripped, urine smelling, blood stained gray trousers he had worn for close to a month. With radiating sharp pains inside and outside of his body, looking around, Al questioned himself endlessly; he also gave himself some mental ultimatums while the tears ran from his eyes, subconsciously accepting imminent death.

'Where General?'

When he woke up earlier, General was barking up a storm' and now the apartment was quiet. The tired pit might have fallen asleep, being that he was beginning to suffer the same amount of torture from Dwayne as Al was; with all the instructed attacks, robberies, and the all night, ongoing, crack strolls, even the relationship between 'man and his best friend' had become strained.

'Where Baby A . . . Dwayne?'

He didn't hear the maniac run in and out of the apartment for the last few days.

Al wanted to use the phone. His bedroom telephone had disappeared-Dwayne sold it for five dollars-so he had to muster enough power to get to his kitchen wall extension. It was time to reach out and touch someone, to get help, but on his own terms. He had to reach out for help before it was too late; his life was in danger now more than ever. Luckily, the phone line was still in service, thanks to Arlene occasionally paying the bill through her many job connections, behind her boyfriend's back; and how long could that possibly last?

Taking small steps, he used his right hand and sweaty fingertips to grab different items for balance, the dresser, the doorknobs, the walls. He slowly came out of his bedroom stepping barefoot into a fresh pile of General's manure. Thinking the feces was food left on the floor, Al pressed on with the kitchen as his destination.

Al thought, "Where's mah walker? I cain't make it 'round here without mah walker . . . I ain't gon'e make it without mah walker . . . I hope that fool ain't steal it for that stuff . . . I sho' hope he didn't . . . the good lawd knows I ain't gon'e live much longer."

The elderly man shivered with dizzying fright as the living room spun around and around. He fell onto the sofa face first, to quickly recuperate from his lightheadedness. He immediately dozed off to sleep, worn out from his journey to the living room with dog manure smeared on the bottom of his feet.

Dusk and many hours had passed, and the autumn night had begun. The apartment was cold, pitch black, with minimal light shining through the window that led to the side alley. Al repetitively recited the Lord's Prayer, knowing that God was the only one who could free him of his current moment of desperation. The apartment was still, with no movement, except for some scratching noises that came from the kitchen.

Suddenly, the telephone came to life ringing and echoing its arrival in the darkness. Al didn't have outside contact in weeks, and the ringing phone continued crying for attention which snapped him out of his current daze. He had to complete his mission of reaching out for help.

Arlene was the only one he wanted to talk to. She was the only one compassionate enough to understand his worsening domestic situation.

He wanted to reach out to Jimmy Robinson for old times' sake also, but his protégé seemed to have a deep-rooted hatred for his grandson. Outside animosity and hostility was the last thing Al and Dwayne Carter needed; they needed inside love, devotion, attachment, repairing. Arlene was Gwenny's best friend, and the absence of Al's daughter fueled the problems in apt #53 in the first place. Arlene always came to his aid, just like a real daughter. It was imperative that he reach her.

Al crawled from the couch, around the dining table to the area where the overhead light switch was located. He grabbed the doorway of the kitchen partition to help him stand, then he shut on the lights in the dimly lit kitchen and living room. A humongous black rat with a two-foot tail jumped from the top of the washing machine, thumping itself between the dryer and the sink. Different sized cockroaches ran for their lives while the flies happily buzzed about, fortunate for life because of existing filth. He ignored the vermin in his beloved apartment with one thing still on his mind, his phone call to Arlene. Inhaling deeply, Al looked at the living room from inside the kitchen he knew since 1938.

The once, well-furnished, futuristic apartment now looked desolate and drab, with practically nothing in it. The mess remained on the floor from Dwayne's last attack, the table in halves, corroded food, broken dishes, etc. His rocking chair was gone, along with pieces of the stereo. The only two working items left of importance were his overturned walker without wheels-Dwayne had reclaimed the other one equipped with wheels-and the telephone on the kitchen wall. The only things that remained of some value were the floor model television, the dirty living room set, the disassembled dining room table remaining in halves, and the wall unit filled with knocked over pictures. There were no clocks or watches around, thanks to Dwayne selling them, so he didn't know what the actual time was. He knew one thing though; he had to leave his place of residence after nearly fifty years, and Arlene had to help him.

Al staggered to the phone and picked up the receiver from the hook, glad to hear its dial tone. He dialed Arlene's number.

"Hello," an unfamiliar, scratchy voice answered.

"Is Arlene there?" The person on the other end hung up.

"Huh?" He heard the loud dial tone as a response.

Frustrated, he tried again, "Damn . . . I know her number been the same since she moved up eene de Bronx . . . Wait now . . . nine . . . eight . . . three . . . four . . . seven . . . five . . . this should be it."

A sleepy woman with a Spanish accent answered."Arlene there?"

"No, wrong number." Al pushed the receiver button down.

"Dammit . . . what's Arlene's number . . . Damn . . . I cain't even remember . . . I cain't see . . . I cain't hear . . . Still cain't speak clear 'nuff . . . I wants help and cain't get it . . . Why me, Lord?! Tell me why?! It ain't fair!"

He nervously patted his foot with more tears welling, frantically pondering.

"You see daddy, we warned you. I told mama to tell ya'."

"Chil' I told him! But you and I both know that ya' daddy's head made outta stone and brick!"

Al vividly heard his deceased wife and daughter

discussing him, like they were actually watching over him. He felt their dear presence much closer than he had in years. Al felt their aura inside the room like he used to, their complete vibe returning.

"Sho' did . . . My Mattie told me to get rid' uh' 'im, she did, she really did . . . I ain't wanna believe her," he thought, continuing to hear the voices he missed for many years gradually come closer:

> *"Mama, you sure did say Daddy*
> *was hardheaded."*

> *"Just like you! Y'all two peas in a*
> *pod honey. I told you not to mess*
> *with that white boy and yo'*
> *hardhead behind went on and did*
> *it anyway. Now look what's*
> *happened!"*

> *"I know."*

> *"I told ya' daddy get rid of that*
> *boy! Same daggone thing!"*

Al tried to dial Arlene again.

> *"Mama, daddy needs help!"*

> *"Gwenny, please! I can see!*
> *He wants Arlene number. I*
> *can't remember that child's*
> *number! I do know one thang,*
> *he better try and hurry up."*

> *"Daddy! Listen to me, it's*
> *eight, nine, three, four,*

seven . . . five . . . "

"Got it!" Al dialed the last digit; and the line rang until a husky male voice answered, the voice of Donnell Smithson, the father of Tanasha and Dante, Arlene's children.

"Hello . . . I . . . I . . . put Arlene on the phone," Al tried not to stutter.

"Huh . . . Who and the hell is this, this time of morning," Donnell asked, with sleepy hate. With no way to tell time in the apartment, Al was totally ignorant of the fact it was hours after midnight. Donnell & Arlene would have to understand. He needed them now more than ever, in his time of despondence.

"It's Al . . . uh, I'm sorry . . . I need to talk to Arlene."

"We sleeping man! You know what time it is?!"

"No . . . I'm sorr . . ."

"Damn near three in the morning! Call some other time!"

Donnell slammed his phone end down. The line went dead.

"Oh no . . . Oh no," Al began to sniffle, "I . . . Oh . . . I . . . oh . . . oh . . . oh Jesus! Oh no! Oh no!"

He dropped the receiver to the floor and stumbled towards his walker, moving like a giant toddler learning to take steps. He fell chest first to the floor, next to his aluminum helper.

"She . . . she . . . I need Arlene, Lawd . . . please . . . please God . . . Oh no! I need her . . . Baby Al's trust fund . . . Somebody help me," Al cried out in his dilapidated living room. He turned over on his back, limp with grief, faint with physically and mentally confused pain, crying out to God above.

"Baby Al's in'shu'ance . . . Arlene . . . Lawd please . . . I gotta get to Arlene . . . please . . . he twenty-one . . . he twenty-one now . . . he need his money . . . God . . . get

239

mah tuh Arlene . . . so he . . . he . . . stop . . . beating on me
. . . Lawd I cain't take no mo'! Lawd! Please! Please! Please
don't let him beat me no mo' . . . Please . . . Baby Al . . .
please . . . he gon'e kill me . . . I'm gon'e die . . . hi'
inshu'ance ready . . . Arlene can straighten it fo' me . . . I
showed her de papers . . . she can fix it fo' muh . . . he gon'e
beat me again!"

He cried himself back to sleep face down on the living
room floor.

Time moved on, and the glaring overhead den light
left stains from his evaporated teardrops, drying the heap of
mucous stuffed in his nostrils. He awakened minutes later
next to his walker. He managed to stand with it, and return
slowly to his bedroom, spirit still overrun with a fierce need
for privacy, with his plans still intact.

An hour after Al retired, Dwayne and General burst
into the apartment. General dutifully entered his master's
room, and his master staggered up front and fell to the
living room floor, in crack ecstasy, oblivious to the
scattering rats and their litter who were enjoying the fossil
morsels of liver on the floor. He had smoked up every
coppered cent of the money he'd stolen from Una
Livingston's pocket book, right on the roof, even carrying
General to and from the roof on his back.

With eyes rolling upward in their sockets, for the first
time in apt.#53 Dwayne lit his blackened glass pipe. He
deeply inhaled the smoke of the dissolving tiny powdered
rock trapped inside its glass house of wrapped heat,
writhing in pure crackstasy, next to the overturned table
halves. Eventually when finished, on his hands and knees,
he started crawling from the living room towards Al's
bedroom, feeling as if he were a jaguar in the wilds of the
jungle, soiling himself even more with the grime of the
nasty floors. Inside Dwayne's opened bedroom General's
ears raised, and his eyes opened. Seeing Dwayne crawl past

the doorway, the pit re-closed his eyes, having been used to his cracked out master's many antics.

Dwayne slid into Al's bedroom, coming to a final stop at the window. Opening the window, still on his hands and knees, he looked down on the block where he was born, raised, and had lived his entire life. He saw a few friends fiending on their nightly crack and alcohol strolls. He noticed Floyd Nelson, walking briskly down the other side of the street, merging with the shadows of other base-heads.

"Damn you Floyd . . . damn you motherfucker," Dwayne hissed, gritting his teeth. He brought his head back inside the bedroom, when suddenly, the room started spinning in a horrific whirlwind causing him to stand and fall down. His fall to the floor made snoozing Al open his eyes. The room was dark and quiet, but there was breathing, loud, heavy breathing. He became scared as usual, anticipating another attack from his grandson.

"AAAAH! LEAVE ME ALONE! NOOOOOO! LEAVE ME ALONE," Dwayne yelled, from under Al's bed.

The hallucinating base-head saw a pregnant image of his mother Gwenny. Her face was sliced up, blood streaming from the wounds, eyes bulging from her head, with a bloody fetus hanging from her vagina, laughing at him. The face of the fetus was his face, smiling, laughing; the gums and teeth in his mirrored dream were dripping with blood.

Loud booming laughter started, taking him to newfound terror, with the volume escalating, echoing.

"Leave me alone! I'll kill your ass! Nooo! Please!," Dwayne screamed at nothing, rolling around the floor.

The hideous laughter went non-stop in Dwayne's cracked out mind. "I'll kill that motherfucker! I'll kill 'im! AAAH!" He stood up, and frightened Al cowered under his bed sheets thinking, "I'm dead."

With the combining assistance of the first lit hues of sunlight and streetlights, Dwayne wickedly scanned the room for the laughing culprit, noticing Al's dentures in his clear denture cup. The teeth started chattering in a chuckling fashion; and Dwayne found his guffawing enemy, and it was snickering away at him, right from the nightstand.

"I'll kill that motherfucker!"

Dwayne ran from the room. Al buried himself under the last of his sheets, that hadn't been sold, with tears streaming. He knew his demise was near, while his dentures sat perfectly normal in its resting place, ready for wear in the morning. He felt himself becoming short of breath under the covers, needing a little air. Al inhaled quickly, and peeked above the sheets just in time. That second, Dwayne returned with a wooden baseball bat he didn't sell.

"I'm gonna kill you! I'm gonna kill ya ass!," he yelled. Dwayne swung at his laughing enemy, crushing the denture cup, smashing Al's dentures into four pieces. He swung again at his giggling enemy and missed, breaking the remaining crystal lamp. The laughter became even more intensifying, while Dwayne went to war with his invisible opponent, beating his grandfather's false teeth with unperceivable indignation. Dwayne missed Al by two centimeters, swinging wildly at nothing as Al cringed terrified beneath the bedcovers. He knocked at the walker, pounded on Al's dresser, swinging and swinging, bashing out the dresser mirrors, when finally the mental laughter began to subside, replaced with a telephone ringing, and an unknown voice with instructions:

'Kill that fucking phone and come and smoke me . . . you know it feels so good when you smoke me . . . you have to kill that phone so you can smoke me . . .'

Dwayne bolted from Al's bedroom, running down the hallway to the kitchen wall extension. The phone continued to ring until Dwayne, standing in a homerun batter's position with the intent of knocking the ball out of the park, swung and smashed the telephone into pieces from off the wall.

"Ya dead! Motherfucker! Dead bitch! Dead!," he yelled as the laughter and ringing stopped, leaving Dwayne in a mental state of shock.

He needed more crack right away after this last experience. Seeing the mother he never knew and his face on a laughing bloody fetus hanging by its umbilical cord from her sanguineous vagina was too much for him to bear. The laughter of malevolence with sudden hallucinatory instructions added to his crack needing mania. He needed to soothe his broken heart over his mind's eye. Just the thought of his deceased mother, being just a memory, hurt. The recollection of a woman whom he never saw, felt, touched, or even professed his juvenile love to, hurt. She brought him into the world, dying seconds later, and he only knew her through nostalgic photos.

Through his crack hungered haze, Dwayne observed the annoying, raspy sounding sobs of Al, and rabid Dwayne dropped the bat in the center of the messy living room. With the subliminal laughter returning at a deafening volume, Dwayne ran to Al's opened bedroom, and noticed his frightened grandfather under the bed sheets in sheer cowardice, unsuccessfully trying to not move or breathe.

Dwayne sprang onto Al's bed and yanked the covers from over Al's crying face, grabbing him by the collar. Al's head nearly snapped from his neck while Dwayne obnoxiously shook him back and forth, his head and shoulders crashing to the mattress repetitiously, grandson glaring at grandfather eye to eye in narcotic desperation, between shakes, screaming, "Please, I need some money . . . Pappy man, this fucking . . . Please, this fucking crack got me . . . IT GOT ME! **IT GOT MEEEEE**!"

He wished to shoot his grandfather dead for the money, but couldn't because he sold his gun, so he would shake the money out of him with his bare hands. Al tenaciously held the mattress; and Dwayne continued shaking him while the abominable drug hungry laughter was unbearable, with only rocks of crack to feed it, satisfy it.

"**GENERAL!**," Dwayne bellowed, darting from Al's bedroom, and out of the apartment.

Like clockwork, General ran out of the room at his master's command, carrying his own leash in his mouth, knowing his smoked out boss had forgotten it; and down the steps he went, desperately trying to catch up with him, while the apartment door closed by itself.

At the same time uptown in the Bronx on Randall Avenue in the Soundview Projects, Arlene cursed out her fiancé inside their bedroom. Once she had realized that it was Al who called the house at three, possibly needing help, she verbally tore into her man for not waking her during the night. Receiving a busy signal, she slammed the phone down and re-dialed Al and Dwayne's hoping that the telephone company didn't shut down the line. She waited angrily for Al's phone to ring.

"See, it's still busy! Nigga, if something happens to Mister Carter, your big black ass is gonna pay for it! Me and Jimmy Robinson are the only ones that care about him!," she yelled, dialing again. "You could'a woke me up! Mister Carter can call here twenty-four hours a day if he needs to! Don't you ever do that again!"

Donnell relaxed in bed with his arms folded behind his head, while his woman fussed on; it would be minutes before the usual bedside alarm awakened them both. With a blank facial expression, he turned over in bed and said nothing.

Al finally mustered enough strength and courage to sit on the edge of his bed, grateful to be alive after his last attack. His mind was made up, a definite, firm decision. It was time to go. He still loved Dwayne, and always would, but he had to leave before the crazed drug addict killed him. The first minute off of 117th, he would check into a hospital; he didn't know what he would tell the doctors or the authorities, but he would think of something.

The last crystal lamp, given to him as a birthday present was smashed, turned off permanently. He could barely see the silhouette of the wrecked dresser mirror. He knew it was demolished, and so were his dentures.

"Mattie warned me, she warned me," he thought sadly, looking at his destroyed bedroom.

Someone began banging on the apartment door.

"I wonder who dat is? Ah cain't even see where de walker is," Al pondered, "Yeah? . . . Who there?"

"POLICE! OPEN UP!"

Outside in the hallway, Barbara stood with two Caucasian male police officers, patting her slipper-covered foot. "Um-hum! I know he dead mister police officer, cause Baby Al really kicked his you know what this morning. Honey! I couldn't sleep a wink! That yelling and a screaming and a banging kept me up all night! Lock his RED ASS UP!"

"What's taking this guy so long," one of the policemen asked.

Al clinging to his walker, finally opened the door, routinely staring dumbfounded, asked, "Yes, what can ah do for ya?"

"We got a call about a disturbance. Everything okay, sir," asked the other officer.

"Well, suhh," Al began, "Me and my grandboy had an argument. He not in de house righ' now, gon'e out to let off lil' steam. I know everythang gon'e be fine in a coupl'a hours."

Barbara's mouth dropped, and she yelled, "No, Al

Carter! No you didn't! You ain't just lie to them cops! Ask him 'bout the marks on his face! And that damn black eye of his!"

One of the officers stared peculiarly at Al, remembering him from a call he and his ex-partner received years ago, the alarming buzz about an old man being battered by his grandson. He stared at the current, unhealed, horrifying bruises Al had to offer; he saw knots and gashes all over the old man's forehead, a swollen jaw with a black eye. There were dark stains and rips to his pants with a meaty gash to his thigh, a soiled musty shirt; and the elderly gentleman barely stood with his walker. The stench radiating from the apartment also was horrible. The policeman remembered everything, and he wished he could lock his grandson up and throw away the key this time. If only he could get the damaged senior to press charges. He touched Al's bruised, blotchy skin with sympathy. "Did your grandson do this to you, sir," the policeman asked gently.

Al flinched at the policeman's gentle touch, and then he looked past his broad blue shoulder at Barbara with hate and disdain in his eyes, and replied, "No."

Defeat for both parties. Barbara returned to her apartment, sad for once, mumbling to herself as she too wondered if Mattie Mae-her old roommate-and her daughter were watching the tragic events that was hurting everyone who knew what was happening. The police knew the old man was lying about his problem, having seen many cases of elderly abuse all over town, especially after crack hit the streets. They angrily returned to the 25th Precinct, knowing they couldn't take any action as long as Al covered up his abuse, and covered for his abuser.

"EH-YO . . . EH-YO . . . EH-YO," Dwayne yelled at Patrick's window. A curtain moved back, a fourth floor window opened, and Patrick brought his head out, squinting.

"Dee, you know what time it is? It's six in the morning. You're lucky some of my family's up cooking man!"

"Pat man, I need a favor! Come downstairs, I need ya man."

Patrick kissed his teeth Caribbean style and shut his window.

Excited, Dwayne led General up the stoop to the second floor of the brownstone; he knew his "ace boon coon" would never let him down. Moments later, Patrick led Dwayne into his doorway because of the temperature of the autumn morning.

"Stay boy! Don't move! Sit! Look sit your ass still," Dwayne instructed General, while Patrick pulled the glass paned door shut.

"Shhhhh! No cursing. What you want man, I need some more sleep. The whole family's going out today, we're going to Brooklyn."

"Word?"

"Yeah, but I might just jet to my girl's house later while I'm out there man. I have plenty of time to be with more family. What you doing out this early? Walking General huh?"

"Yeah . . . Me and Pappy had another argument this morning."

"Word?"

"Word up. He said he want me to get the fuck out."

"Yo, no curse words!"

"Sorry high! I just don't know what to do."

"Serious?"

"Word is born. I'm dumb hungry. You got five dollars?"

"Nah. Hey, Mummy's cooking some saltfish and dumpling, and there's some porridge. If you want there's even some callaloo and dumpling left from yesterday."

"Calla who?"

"Callaloo. I'm saying, would you like some breakfast, because I have no money."

Dwayne was crushed; what would he do now? Patrick having no money meant he would have to catch a new "vic"-and that meant hurting another innocent person-but he had to do something. Crack was calling him loud and clear, and the yells were becoming unstoppable.

"Yo, I need dough man! Look, I gotta do something about my grandfather. He crazy senile, I think he gon' die soon."

"You have insurance man? You better get some, so if he dies you can survive."

With Patrick's last statement, Dwayne's brain started clicking. The only way of survival in the land of the free was to have money, and lots of it.

"You get money with insurance?"

Patrick gave his friend a look of amazement. "Yeah man, Dee why you bugging? Like you don't know that; you didn't know that? How do you think me and Mummy survived what happened? You gotta have insurance in life, some kind of way. That's how we took care of the funerals, and my relatives came from England and handled the arrangements, and this is the last time I want to talk about that man." Patrick's voice raised an octave; he still grieved internally for his family, his younger brother and sisters especially.

"So if someone dies, you get money then," Dwayne repeated mysteriously, the best news he had heard all year.

"Yeah homeboy, you deaf? Look man, I'm going back upstairs and catch some more Z's. My family's breaking out in a few hours. I'm not trying to see no more relatives, man. And Mummy's scared to leave me alone, as a matter of fact, they're all afraid to leave me home alone."

"Word?"

"The only way they'll leave me is if my girl Michelle

comes over and keeps me company. I told them that I would go to see her instead while we're out. I refuse to stay in this house alone."

"Damn. Where's the Patrick I used to know? You sound dumb white man," Dwayne laughed.

"Look, Dee. I'm saved. I don't care if I sound white or black anymore. The Lord doesn't care either."

Dwayne slapped Patrick five, and exited the foyer, snapping his fingers for General to join him. He descended the stairs to the sidewalk of 120th Street. The eerie feeling remained deep within his heart, knowing that Patrick's younger siblings were murdered in cold blood barely one year ago, on the same steps where he had just walked.

"Yo, where y'all got your insurance from," Dwayne asked, holding General by his collar.

"I don't know man. My moms and pops had lots of insurance from way back, from when we first came here to this country. They were into things like that, real important things. Man, what's up, General looks big and crazy. You have him out there killing people?," Patrick chuckled.

"Yeah, yeah! But yo, what I'm 'a do about my grandfather's insurance?"

"Yo, it's one place across from Saint Nich projects that pays big, like about a hundred g's."

Dwayne did a double take. "A hundred g's black?!"

"Yup. I believe they do. Walk there and see."

"If my grandfather dies, I get a hundred g's?"

Patrick's statement was hard to believe. Then again, there was no way he would lie claiming to be a "saved" man.

Patrick said, "Far as I know. Go check it out. I think it's on Seventh and twenty-eighth, or twenty-seventh across from the projects."

Dwayne was ecstatic, overjoyed with the information Patrick provided him with. If he killed Al then he would have $100,000 dollars! He could smoke as much crack as he wanted, and still look good. Al had to die immediately. Excited by the news, Dwayne forgot about the money Patrick had refused; he was set on getting some "insurance" for his grandfather.

"Yo, high, I'm jetting! If you come across some dope Brooklyn bitches, or wherever your honey from let me know! Bring 'em by the crib!"

"I'll see what I can do," Patrick replied, shaking his head.

Dwayne and General stepped off speedily, as if an imaginary starter let off a shot, and they were racing competitors. The quicker they could get the insurance policy initiated, the sooner they could have oodles of money.

Patrick watched the image of his vulgar buddy and his pet pit get smaller as they crossed the street near the corner. He closed the foyer door with his bed on his mind, anxious to catch some extra hours of sleep.

****

CHAPTER 10

*

The lingering flies in Al's bedroom created a homemade alarm clock for him. He opened his eyes after a fly romped inside his ear twice, with his body remaining painfully numb, and his stench permeating his stuffed nostrils. He would never stop wondering what he did to deserve his current way of living, and he wondered would he make it to Orange County alive. The Mary Morton Center was his destination, a place where he should have fled to a long time ago. He was a senior citizen too, for more than ten years. His eleventh year would be spent in the grave, if he didn't escape his grave domestic situation. The powers that be at the home would accept him in his current condition. He had absolutely nothing to lose and he would have an extension added to his diminishing life. To be around Aunt Lou again on a consistent basis was a family reunion long overdue. At age 95, Mrs. Lou R. Williams was alive, cared for, and in much better shape than her nephew. As far as Al was concerned, if they lived together in the 1930's, they could live together in the 1980's. As logically as possible, he carefully planned his escape route.

Knowing the social security check was due and in the mailbox, he needed to get a message to Malik or Terrence to break open the mailbox and obtain the check for him. Since Dwayne knew when the checks came, the boys would need to act quickly. One could run the check to Joe Rutledge's liquor joint, and the other could help him down the stairs. Joe always cashed checks for neighborhood buddies, even when the store wasn't open. Upon returning, the boys would flag a taxi. If any of the neighbors questioned his atrocious appearance, he would think of a quick story. As long as the youngsters returned with the money so he could pay them for their services, pay the cab driver, and flee for his life. For the first time in years, he didn't have time to cry.

Practically with zero strength, he made his way from the bedroom, down the hall, and back to the kitchen phone extension, to no avail. In the center of the chaotic mess, the phone lay demolished with its broken shell, separated rotary disc, wired insides, and ringing bell exposed on the floor. Clinging to his walker shaking with sickened fear, Al looked about the room with blurred vision. He wondered would the den that held so many positive memories opposed to the negative, suck the life from him; could the room swallow him whole as he felt the barren, filthy walls closing in?

Should he attempt to make it down the staircase because time was running out? Should he open the bathroom or the alley windows and scream for help?

Should he bang on the apartment doors of the neighbors that he had lied to, yelling and pleading, "Help . . . Help me please! I lied! I was wrong! I lied! I lied to you all! My grandson is beating me! Help me please! He's going to kill me! My grandbaby gon'e kill me!" Should he reach out after concerned people attempted to help him, and he shafted them? Should he try and hide next to the wall unit and when his grandson entered the room, use the same baseball bat on him that lay amongst the debris of broken glass, table, telephone, rotten food, dried blood, dried urine, buzzing flies, dust, dust and more dust?

Feeling faint again, he staggered back to the sofa to plot a next move of coherence. The wrought iron wall unit stood sturdy in place, with its dead plants and overturned portraits inside frames with no glass, filled with stories to tell, all watching and debating his fate. Infinity crept closer.

Meanwhile, "man and his best friend"-Dwayne and General-were practically sprinting down Seventh Avenue. His insurance plot fell through for the time being, after finding the office closed. This made him double hungry for a hit of crack. With no money, and no means to get any, he recalled the house keys of Una Livingston he'd stolen. Feeling in his pockets, Dwayne kissed the ring of keys, heading quickly for 120th Street, with aggravated, hungry General following behind him. His unannounced visit this time was with the intent of cleaning out all of the valuables he could possibly hand carry.

"Shhh! Don't you say nothing," he whispered to the pit. He quietly unlocked and closed the first glass door of the foyer, giving his dog a stern look, covering his lips with his index finger like an early childhood teacher does their class. General growled at Dwayne, semi-rebellious out of hunger. "You better cool out General boy, what the fuck's wrong with you?! I'm getting loot now so you can eat and I can get my shit. Do what I tell you! Sit! I'll be back! Don't start barking neither!"

He quietly unlocked the second door leaving General in the foyer, and crept into the house, hiding behind each door, moving quickly as possible. The second floor of the brownstone was quiet as a church mouse in Dwayne's mind, drowned out by the loud, rapid thumping of his anticipated heartbeat. The lingering scent of curry was calm; and Dwayne was elated, believing the Livingstons had expensive things worth a pretty penny. He peeked into the living room, checking the time on the grandfather clock.

"Eleven-thirty . . . good! Ain't nobody home, I don't hear nothing. I hope them coconuts stay out the house!," he thought, moving swiftly up the staircase.

Inside the second floor kitchen, Patrick's cousin Ivy was cleaning the breakfast pots, pans, and dishes, engaged in conversation with two newly arrived male cousins from England, Carlton and Grant. Muscular Carlton removed some ackee and codfish from the microwave oven, and tall, slim Grant smoked a cigarette. Laughing and reminiscing about the good times the entire family had in their native Manchester, Jamaica, they felt living in the United States and life in the London ghettos were the same; they both were a bit tedious. Monetarily, they were grateful that "Jah" blessed them with "green cards". Each time they returned to the Caribbean, life felt better.

Grant noticed the sound of footsteps moving quickly

up the stairs. "Ya 'ear dat," he asked, with a strong, baritone Jamaican accent, mixed with a bit of British. Younger Carlton added, "Ya always 'ear somet'ing. Ya imahginetion crehzy nuh maan." They all laughed, continuing their conversation.

Grant stated, "Look ah de gal dem sheke dem body." Carlton turned up the television on top of the counter, gawking at the "Soul Train" broadcast. Ivy stopped her duty and put down her dishtowel to look at the girls shake their hips on the television. She kissed her teeth, and waved her hand, knowing she could do better if she was at least ten years younger with the right reggae beat. Carlton quickly finished his leftovers, tossing his plate in the sink so he could concentrate on the "tellie". Ivy finished off the dishes and sat down at the table with them to watch Melba Moore & Freddie Jackson perform their #1 smash "A Little Bit More". Grant looked peculiarly at the ceiling, hearing more strange creaks and noises over the blaring television. It sounded to him like someone was on the third floor of the house. Perhaps *Mummy Una* and the rest of the family had returned.

Upstairs, within a ten-minute time frame, Dwayne had gone through all of the bedrooms and the bathrooms, searching wildly for money or anything of value. He practically inspected every article of clothing, all bureau drawers, closets, and he found nothing, aggravating him more, contemplating a climb to the fourth floor.

"These cheap banana boat motherfuckers ain't got shit in here! Damn! Where the fuck do Patrick grandmother stay in this house?! Her old ass keep fresh money! That's right, she probably took everything when she jetted! Let me get the fuck outta here, shit! I'm sorry I came!"

He finally spotted a ring on a dresser inside the last bedroom, a diamond studded gold wedding band. The yellow colored metal was worth something!

"Cool! Yeah, yeah!" Dwayne ran to the dresser and slipped the ring into his pocket. "Now, I can mo-ti-vate," he said happily, tiptoeing from the room towards the staircase, when he heard the steps creaking. He peeked over the banister and saw Ivy, head bowed, primly ascending the stairs.

"**Shit!**," he thought, heart racing. At the speed of light he was back into the bedroom looking around for a hiding place. "What the fuck she doing here? She supposed to be out of the house! Is she the only motherfucker here?! Shit!," he thought. Scooting breathlessly underneath the king-sized canopy bed would be the ideal hiding place, but the mattresses were too close to the floor. Where could he go?

'*The closet!*'

The opened closet across the room was filled with women's hats, shoes, gowns, dresses, and other garments in a mass abundance; and it was there he decided to bury himself. Dwayne darted inside the closet, concealing himself behind some dresses, unaware of Ivy's sleeping Siamese cat. The aggressive feline, who liked to curl up and sleep inside the closet because of its cluttered warmth, was suspicious of the stranger who inched his way closer. With her sharp claws extended, the cat was ready for attack after having her afternoon nap interrupted.

Dwayne thought his eardrums would explode because

of the deafening volume of his heartbeat while he held his breath, relieved in the closet with his back against the wall. He eased himself down on top of the irritated cat by mistake.

"*Rrr*MEOWrrr," the cat screeched, leaping and scratching furiously at Dwayne's face, claws stuck in his hair knocking him off balance. "Ow! Shit! What the fuck," Dwayne yelled loud enough for Ivy to hear. "Pahtrick," Ivy spoke out with question at the top of the landing.

"OW! OW! OW! GET THE FUCK OFF ME!"

The cat clung to Dwayne's trouser thigh until he kicked and smashed it against the closet wall, pulling dresses off their hangers. He tumbled out into the opened bedroom.

"*WHAT DA RAAS*," yelled Ivy, recognizing Patrick's American friend immediately. How did he get into the house without permission, and why was *he* falling from inside *her* bedroom closet? She started screaming, "AAAAAAH! AAAAAAAH! HELP! STOP DE BLAASTED T'IEF! AAAAAH!! STOP T'IE . . .!"

"Shut up bitch!," Dwayne yelled, snatching the frightened woman's head wrap off, dashing down the steps for his quick getaway. He could hear his trusty pit giving the alarm from his post in the foyer, warning his master of forthcoming trouble, but it was too late.

Grant appeared at the bottom of the steps to see what the strange barking and mysterious interior commotion was about, a target in the direct line of fire. Dwayne leaped from the stairs, leg extended in kick position, and knocked Grant to the floor. Collecting themselves after a few elbows, punches, and kicks, Dwayne and General were out the door, down the cement steps, and running for their lives while the block inhabitants and passerby all wondered what was going on.

Carlton, still engrossed with the shaking hips inside the television, heard the ruckus too late. Ensuring that his relative was okay first, Carlton then ran out of the brownstone after the thief and his canine accomplice. By the time Carlton reached Seventh Avenue, Dwayne and General were streets ahead, too far ahead to be captured.

Pondering, Carlton became infuriated while thinking, "Grant . . . H'im 'ear right . . . H'im 'ear de t'ief coume inna de howse . . . H'im de one t'ief Mummy's keys . . . and de money in h'ar bag yesterdey . . . Wi mus' know 'im . . . or meybe dat was Pahtrick's friend . . . De Yenkee bwoy h'im coume by de h'owse laast night . . . When h'im leave de howse an' gaan 'pon ah street, de t'ings dem gaan . . . "

Carlton walked back to the house past the chuckling onlookers, amid the neighborly tip offs to who Dwayne really was. Carlton was blinded by embarrassment, and avenging anger. He joined his hurt and distraught cousins in the living room.

"CAAAL DE POLICE, MAAN," Ivy shouted, placing a cool towel on Grant's forehead.

"Ivy, it was Pahtrick's friend. Wasn't it?," Carlton asked.

"Yea' maan! H'im coume owt mi bedruum like a mad maan! H'im t'ief mi 'eaddress, give Graahnt a flying kick, maan! T'cha! Mi waan give de yenkee bwoy a kick in h'im baackside, ya' nuh!"

"We'll 'andle it. We'll teke cere ah it!," Carlton

exclaimed. Ivy kissed her teeth, Caribbean style while Grant muttered, "Ih-hih! We'll do jus' dat. Teke cere a dem bloodclaat t'ief!"

Grant and Carlton slapped hands, and shook firm.

Dwayne sold the ring and Ivy's head wrap for ten dollars, just enough to get a couple of quick hits. There were still a few hats left from the 1986 World Series Champs, the New York Mets that could be sold if needed. The insurance money became an emergency, because his highs were shorter, and his base pipe needed its vitamins. Deep down, he hoped that Patrick's relatives didn't recognize him. It would break Patrick's heart to know that his best friend stole from his house.

Offended General dutifully followed his master, wishing that Dwayne would feed him. In the beginning, Dwayne worshipped General like the pit was an actual human child, like he was his very own son. Now, General went for days without food, was in dire need of vet care, and the dog was extremely vexed with his master.

An icy breeze with swirling multi-colored leaves swift and quick gave the indication of an express change between the seasons. The holidays would be just around the corner, and the forthcoming year would be spent for the first time without Al. The pipe was beginning to talk him into killing his own grandfather, and this gave the weather a more chilling effect; and he would remain with a wintery heart, combing the streets until he came to a final decision on how to dispose of Al for the insurance money.

Back in apt#53, Al managed to stand the walker up

and used it to move back into the hallway. He used the upper right side of his body to move, with no feeling to his left side after General's attack on his left leg. It took so much air and strength to move, and the pain was hot like fire, with his month old trousers acting as a bandage, being stuck on the outside and the inside of his fleshy dog bite wound. "It's only a matter of time now," Al thought, while grasping at his right walker handle, slouched, hunched over its top rail. Each step was an inch and a minute long as he moved closer, and closer, and closer to the apartment door. Dwayne's bedroom finally inched into existence on the left, and the bathroom was next at last, which meant God answered his prayers. The apartment door was a few minutes away to his right. Tired, Al took some deep breaths for more strength before his exit, again reciting the Lord's Prayer:

"Our Father who art in heaven

Hallowed be thy name

Thy kingdom come, Thy will be done

on earth as it is in heaven.

Give us this day

Our daily bread. . ."

"Where ya goin'?," the evil, familiar voice startled Al, as it burst through the door. Seeing a blurred version of Dwayne and the once beloved General was one thing, but hearing his grandson's venomous tone, along with the pit's horrific growl, kept the senior terrified.

Al thought, "Barbara, where ya nosy tail at when I needs ya!"

Dwayne slammed the apartment door shut, engaging the chain, seeing blood once again, his strongest crack stupor ever.

"Got somewhere to be?"

General gave off small barks as Dwayne stepped up to Al; and he clutched his walker with an iron grip, shaking, not knowing what to expect.

"What's up? Where ya' going? Stand up straight and look at me when I'm talking to you! Remember you used to tell me that? You gonna answer me, Pappy? . . . Huh? You gonna answer Baby Al? . . . Where ya' going? . . . Taking a fucking TRIP?!!" On the word "trip" Dwayne double punched Al's hands making him fall forward, and Dwayne caught him in an embrace, face to face.

"See, now why you crying like a little bitch Pappy? I should be crying. You leaving right? Ain't cha'? Ain't cha', Pap!" He stood his grandfather up replacing his hands on the walker handles, covering them with his fists.

"Where the fuck you going, man?"

General began barking ferociously, growling then repeating. For Dwayne's intensifying high, General's barks seemed to get louder, aggravating him to the extreme.

"Damn, General, you hungry or something? Shit! Tear his old ass up then! Get 'im! *Get 'im boy! Grrrr sic 'im! Grrrr sic 'im!* Get this old black motherfucker boy! *Grrrr sic 'im! Get 'im,"* Dwayne commanded. General refrained, continuing to bark and growl, buying time for Al before another dog biting attack.

"Why you doing this to me, Baby Al, why?!," Al cried out. "I've done all I could for you . . . Please don' hurt me no mo' . . . I love you . . . That's why I raised you . . . I love you . . . You my grandson . . . I . . . I . . . cain't go on like this!"

Dwayne was nauseous in between crack waves, while his conscience played with him. With Al copping pleas in between sniffles and with General's loud, garbled barks, he became confused. *Should* he kill Al? Should he kill the one surviving family member that loved him with all of his heart, raised him from an infant, raising him as a son? Staring into Al's reddened eyes with infinite tears, Dwayne's heart told him no, but crack and his body said yes. It was matter over mind, once again. He needed more crack, especially with General's deafening barks.

"General! I told you what to do already! If you ain't gonna do it then shut up! Shut the fuck up! Shut the fuck up right now!"

"Oh my Lord! Mama, you see this."

"Gwenny, honey, I warned him but he would not listen to me. My baby fixing to get called home! He need to be. He don't need to keep suffering cause he stubborn. He just would not listen to me!"

"Ooh, mama! You better get ready to close your eyes! You ain't gon' wanna see this!"

General growled at his master, viciously directing his angry barks and growls toward Dwayne.

"I said shut ya' ass up! You gettin' on my nerves Gen man! Shut the fuck up!"

After his master's profanity, impetuous General ran at Dwayne full speed ahead, jumping on his master, knocking him to the floor. This time Dwayne's leg was on his menu as the pit locked onto his master's thigh with all of his teeth.

"AAAAAAH! GENERAAAAAAALLLLL," Dwayne screamed. *"AAAAH! GET OFFFFF!! HELP!!! Pappy!"*

Dwayne punched General in the head, knocking the crazed animal off of his leg. Knowing Dwayne was angry for doing the wrong thing, General ran down the hall into Al's bedroom, hiding underneath the bed. He always remembered Al being sympathetic during times like this when he was disobedient. Dwayne lay hurt on the floor, with a rip in the thigh area of his jeans, wound exposed, oozing blood. Al was shocked, yet relieved, with the act of violence he saw.

"I'm 'a get out'chere while that maniac on the flo'," he triumphantly thought, moving towards the door of the apartment.

"Chil' why I got to watch this on my birthday of all days Gwenny? Oh my God, Albert! Albert hurry baby! Hurry up! Get to that chain! Get that chain off de door honey! Hurry up!"

"It ain't gon' help him mama."

Al fumbled with the chain on the apartment door, dropping his hand just in time when Dwayne swung his trusty bat full force, knocking the corroded metal off the door.

"Where the fuck ya' going Pappy?! You turned my own fucking dog against me! You made General bite me! He bit meeee," Dwayne screamed at Al face-to-face.

Al knew his death had finally arrived, but he wouldn't go down scared. He wasn't afraid anymore, and he had served his life's purpose; he refused to bite his tongue from this point on.

"You brought it on yo'self Bebah Al," he yelled back at Dwayne, a gesture he hadn't done in five years.

Dwayne let out a spine-chilling roar and snatched Al's walker from the old man's grips riding the wavecrest of his cracked stupor. Al fell to the floor landing with a sharp thud, yelping, whimpering, and crying out like a hoarse newborn. Dwayne pulled Al by his shirt collar with one hand, and took Al's walker with the other, dragging him back into the living room; and then, wildly brandishing the bat, he knocked the pictures from the wall unit including Gwenny's. He tossed Al with walker in front of the couch. With the bat still in hand, Dwayne scanned the living room.

"General . . . Oh General! C'mere boy, here boy! C'mere now . . . Gen! Come on Gen."

Al heard General exit his bedroom, obedient paw steps trotting toward his master's voice. Tears welled in his terrified eyes, listening to his crazed grandson's rapid breaths as the drug addict raised his bat to strike, concealing himself behind the wall. Dwayne waited dutifully for his pet to enter the living room, with drops of his own blood pelting the floor.

Once General entered the room Dwayne, standing in a homerun batter's position, swung the bat at General, breaking the dog's spine and rib cage with one bash. He hit General's body three more times, breaking the dog's legs, severing his torso all over. With the fifth and last blow, he viciously swung the bat at the head, splitting the skull open, sending brains and blood all over his face and chest.

General was gone, bludgeoned to death by the master who raised him from a puppy, and trained him to follow each wicked command, just before his second birthday. The dead dog leaked from each orifice and skin break while Dwayne chuckled at the sight, spitting out bits of brain that landed in his mouth. Wiping blood with the back of his sleeve, remembering the insurance office on Seventh Avenue, Dwayne limped over and looked down at tortured Al, wondering if he should really go through with killing him. Al swallowed gulps of air while his murderous grandchild pondered his denouement.

Dwayne thought, "I gotta kill this nigga . . . I just gotta . . . Cause I need that money . . . I need it . . . show me the money . . . Oh . . . Damn . . . Oh Pappy."

He reminisced back to his childhood, overtaken with guilt. The old man had always been there for him, through thick and thin. When he was burning with fever during a chicken pox attack at age five, Al was there. Who taught him to ride his "Apollo" five-speed bicycle at the Milbank Center, then chased off teen hooligans with his cane when they threatened to take the bike?: Al; who was at his every beck and call in his grandmother's absence?: her husband, Albert Carter; would killing him be worth it? Could they make it? Could they let go of the past and truly love each other?

Dwayne kneeled over his grandfather, sending the existing flies away from Al's tearstained face to feast on General's body and the other permanent filth. Al sobbed continuously, wishing he were totally blind, instead of having just enough vision to see. He never saw the devil, but he was absolutely sure that his grandson was the upside down spitting image of Satan. Dwayne's fair-skinned face was reddened in blotches, decorated with several scratches. His thick, curly hair was matted and nappy for life; his shirt was partially ripped off. General's blood dripped from his brow with his connecting eyebrows acting as a dam, while he grinned. This had to be hell. This had to be eternal damnation, right in Harlem.

"Ya love me Pappy," Dwayne asked.

Al didn't answer. He shut his eyes super tight, continually reciting the Lord's Prayer, hoping that the maker would hear and accept him, body and soul.

Dwayne stated, "You know what . . . You need to stay here 'til I figure out what to do with you and General . . . Yup . . . That's what ya need to do."

Al knew Dwayne was going to kill him. And finally, he was ready to rejoice with so many loved ones who had passed on and that he never saw. Although this was not the way he envisioned his homegoing, he refused to die without speaking his mind. He had to have his final say, and the grandchild that he would always love unconditionally must listen to him, for the last time. His incessant prayers to The Almighty were halted abruptly, and he mustered courage to speak.

Al spoke: "Baby Al, I've raised you to be a strong black man . . . You're my grandson and I love you . . . I'll always love you, no matter what you say or do . . ."

The bloody look of fury softened; and Dwayne looked at Al confused, wondering what he would say next. Dwayne came around Al's body, and then he lay down next to his grandfather, while in pain from his own torn flesh, he and Al sharing identical dog bite wounds. He swatted at an occasional returning fly, while listening to Al continue his tearful, breathy, victorious speech.

"I raised ya' best I could . . . Me and Grandma Mattie gave ya da world . . . And ya cheated us . . . I know ya hate me 'cause uh mah dark-skin . . . darker than you . . . I'm sorry but, I cain't . . . help that . . . I'm 'a still love ya 'cause you muh grandson . . . You Gwenny son . . . Gwenny was my baby girl . . . mah daughter, and you's a product of her . . . Remember that . . . my baby los' her life fo' ya . . . Remember the things I tell 'ya, Baby Al, and also remember this . . .

You abused me, ya cursed me . . . Ya' beat me . . . Ya stole from me . . . Ya knocked me downsturs . . . All them bad thangs . . . Sho' ya' bought new stuff for de house, but . . . Ya stole evathang fuh dat stuff . . . All my pots and pans . . . Broke mah glasses . . . I cain't see . . . I cain't hear . . . I cain't eat . . . While ya did all that . . . Did ya' ever stop to say . . . Once . . . That . . . I love ya' . . . Pappy? . . .

Ya' reap what'cha sow boy . . . What goes around . . . Comes around . . . Ya do unto others as ya' want done to yo'self, Baby Al . . . Cause yo' conscience can kill ya', Baby Al . . . Do unto others as they do unto you . . . cause yo' conscience can kill ya Baby Al . . . yo conscience will kill ya

Baby Al . . ."

"I'M DWAYNE MOTHERFUCKER!," Dwayne
hollered rising on his hands and elbows, mechanically ready
for a traditional backhand, then he froze. During the
moment of silence, the raspy voice started again and this
time it was not the voice of Al, Floyd, or his very own; it
was the voice of the pipe. The pipe conversed immediately,
with new sets of instructions for Dwayne.

He used the edge of the couch to stand over his
grandfather's body, took the walker and grabbed Al by his
collar again, pulling him from the living room, down the
hallway through the apartment by his neck. He tossed the
walker into his bedroom for space to drag his dying
grandfather to the bedrooms and back to the den, twice.
Upon their second arrival into the living room, Dwayne
turned him over and dumped Al's body on top of General's
broken corpse, face first and chest down. He walked
around Al and looked down on him. Al stared into
General's body, with labored breathing.

'Guess Pappy'll be dead when I get back.'

Dwayne exhaled an infamous hiss, picked up his bat,
retrieved the walker from his bedroom hoping for some
money, and limped his way out of the apartment. He was
running late for an unbreakable date with his love of all
loves, torn between smoking crack and needing emergency
medical attention for the dog bite.

And inside his vermin infested living room, the end
was near more than ever for Al. He would weather the
ordeal because safety, solace, Mattie, and Gwenny were

guaranteed, but he would die angry. He was livid for every welt and each bruise his grandson put on his body over the years, in time. What started as gibberish soon became a coherent chant, opposite of the previous repetition of the Lord's Prayer, but a call for universal retribution; and the abused senior citizen's lips moved back and forth against General's bloody fur.

Al mumbled and grumbled repetitively, "Ya reap what'cha sow . . . Ya reap what'cha sow . . . *Ya reap what'cha sow* . . . **You reap what you sow!**"

****

CHAPTER 11

*

He stood on the edge of an abandoned loading point alongside the Harlem River Drive. After smoking the afternoon away, a few hours had passed since he cashed his grandfather's check, and sold the senior's walker for crack. Behind him, cars raced in the night sounding like the Indianapolis 500, while sewer rats ran around fighting like alley cats nearby.

"It's gettin' kinda' cold out here, damn, shit! It's like January or February more than October, November," Dwayne thought, shivering, staring at the lit skyline of the Bronx across the river. Wishing for at least a cigarette, he covered his head with the hood on his sweatshirt, concealing a matted forest of hair that hadn't been braided for months. He wore a pair of corroded military trousers, with an old pair of "Spot-built" sneakers, which were the last of his clothes; everything had been sold for his girlfriend crack. The cargo pockets of his trousers were filled with some of the memoirs his grandfather had once kept hidden. He gazed into the murky, yet tranquil currents of the Harlem River, keeping balance with the bloody bat he used to kill his once beloved General.

He moved to a more lighted area and opened his pockets, and in seconds his heart beat faster, seeing new pictures of Gwenny. The pain of an absent mother he would never see arose again, while he removed some baby shoes labeled with his name, sniffing their nostalgic scent.

He pulled out Mattie's obituary and started to read, reminiscing automatically:

"Grandma Mattie, whas' de matta?"

"Baby Al, promise me you ain't gon' fight and get in trouble. Promise Grandma you ain't gon' cut up in school."

"I promise."

"I gotta get to a spot over here . . . It's a spot over here . . . Gotta get to it . . . Where's that spot over here . . . Eastside . . . Eastside . . . " Dwayne wondered, eyes burning with tears, yearning for fresh crack. He looked at Mattie for the last time and dropped her obituary. The paper twirled and tumbled with the wind along the dock, eventually landing in the river. One last document to look at; he fiddled inside his pocket and came out with Gwenny's obituary, reading it thoroughly. He read it twice more, hanging on to every tragic word.

"She leaves to mourn, one son . . . One son . . . One son . . . one son," Dwayne repeated, seething. He flung the bat into the river.

"One fucking crackhead son! One goddamned crackhead son . . . A fucking crackhead son who killed her," he yelled, clutching his mother's obituary. He felt inside his pockets for cash, the routine. The money had been decent, but the checks would soon end. The social service agency had been trying to contact Al for months, so he would have to finish his mission immediately. Remaining emotional, Dwayne kicked empty beer cans and bottles, dodging dog manure, heading towards the closest available crackspot.

"She . . . She . . . She leave to mourn . . . her death . . . one . . . fucking crackhead . . . a fucking crackhead son who

killed her . . . I killed my moms . . . I . . . Shit . . . I ain't shit .
. . I ain't nothing but a fucking crackhead," Dwayne cried.

*"That doggone Mayor Koch need to do something child! These
homeless bums is on the rise, and they gettin' younger and younger
too!"*

Two women dressed in church attire walked past
Dwayne while he lay in front of a dilapidated building the
next morning, sunlight and their critical female voices
awakening him.

"I wonder what time it is," he thought standing up,
urinating in the doorway. "I gotta get back to the crib . . .
shit, I got business to take care of . . . I gotta get that
insurance on Pappy so I can get my loot . . . Damn, I can't
wait!"

He headed home, sneezing incessantly.

The neighborhood was the same as usual on a Sunday.
Churchgoers passing through the streets, while its
inhabitants held court, up and down the various blocks.

"Hey, Baby Al! C'mere man, I gotta talk to ya'
brother," Floyd yelled to Dwayne while he crossed Lenox
Avenue. Floyd held post these days on the corner of Lenox
and 117th begging for money and cigarettes.

"Baby Al! Yo-yo! Hold up, come here!"

"Suck my dick! Get a life! I ain't got shit to give ya'!
I'm a head, just like you now nigga," Dwayne responded
without turning back.

"I NEED A STOAG MAN! Aw . . . aw . . . you know
what, FUCK YOU TOO Baby Al . . . say . . . say . . . bruh'
can ya' spare some change?," Floyd began asking the Lenox
Avenue passersby.

Dwayne was a few footsteps away from his building,
when he quickly dodged in front of a parked van, after

noticing Patrick and his cousin Carlton. The guys quickly emerged from his building on the opposite side of the street and were looking upset, like they were bickering. Carlton was the angrier of the two, screaming at the top of his lungs. They stormed towards Lenox Avenue. When the coast was clear after they walked past, Dwayne came out from behind the van and watched the guys cross the street and turn the corner at Lenox.

"Damn . . . Damn! Patrick knows! Shit! His cousins must've dropped dime that I was up in the crib! Shit! That nigga Patrick knows! Damn!"

Dwayne was deeply saddened knowing that his best friend knew the truth about him stealing from his house. After the pipe gave its reminding yelp, he didn't have time to think about Patrick, his cousins, grandmother, or any of the Livingston family that he hurt. Off, he headed for the apartment, needing to smoke.

The next morning after sucking the glass pipe all night, Dwayne dressed himself in one of Al's church suits that had been salvaged. Today was the day he needed to be presentable to apply for his insurance policy. He stared at his reflection in the bathroom mirror.

"I need a cut bad," he said, trying to run a comb through his hair. Shaking his head, he exited the bathroom and limped up the hallway, talking to himself while checking his pockets. "Damn . . . I'm broke already . . . I couldn't've smoked that much . . . I gotta hurry up and get that insurance . . . If I start robbin' niggas again I might get caught this time . . . I'll be on the island just like that nigga E-zo."

Al lay on his back next to General, his lifeless forearm across the dead dog. Dwayne limped over and kicked him in the thigh. He bounced back, still hanging on.

"Hey! How you turn back over like that? Why you not dead yet?"

No answer from Al as he only returned a stare.

"Oh shit! Maybe he IS dead! Now I can get that bread even quicker!"

The feasting flies buzzing about and the pungent stench from General's body put Dwayne in the mood for some breakfast crack, while Al still parted his dry mouth to speak. Dwayne stopped moving about to read his dying grandfather's lips.

Al repeated with no voice: "Ya reap what'cha sow . . . you reap, what you sow."

Dwayne exhaled a hiss, and left the living room.

The overcast afternoon was on the edge of a light drizzle with scattered showers in the forecast. At the barber shop around the corner and a few blocks up, Billy Harten yelled at one of his barbers the moment he reported for work. He pointed to a sperm-filled condom on the floor of his office, while his employee Michael Mertz tried not to grin. The bell sounded, followed by the buzzer, indicating a new customer.

"Look, go to work Mike! Y'all got one more time for me to come in here and find mess like this! Yeah! I found it this morning damn it! You young cats too damn sloppy when it come to a piece of ass! Clean up ya mess! One more time and somebody out the door! The word is discreet when ya gotta have it, like that chick in that new movie! Now get outta here!"

Michael exited the back area of the shop, laughing to himself. "Damn! That stupid nigga Tay-Tay always leave his trojans around," he thought, recalling the onsite tryst of the previous evening.

Dwayne was about to sit down, when he noticed Michael enter the room.

"Oh dip! Dee! What up! What up, high?," Michael said, holding out his hand for a five.

"Yo, Mike, it's been a while man," replied Dwayne,

hugging Michael quickly. "I ain't think you was cutting. Where Tay Tay?"

"School. Yo, get in the chair man, you definitely need a cut right about now."

Michael had heard a rumor that Dwayne and his dog were crackheads, and he had lost everything he owned by being simply greedy. After seeing him, he knew the rumors were true. Dwayne looked a sight, wearing a giant rusty brown suit with stains, with a light blue tie, soiled dingy white shirt and construction boots. This was a far cry from the brassy brother he knew who "co-ruled Harlem with the Jamaicans from 120th Street", dealing with loads of women, eating, doing, and wearing the finest of everything. He even smelled like a base-head.

"Can't believe this nigga wants a cut," Michael thought sarcastically. He said, "Alright homeboy, what'cha need?"

The two young men gazed in the long barber shop mirror, greeted with the reflections of themselves and other men being groomed by two middle aged barbers, and an elder barber exiting his office into the five chair salon, equipped with a television and music.

"Ummm . . . Gimme a baldie, high . . . Fuck it, that's what I want . . . A baldie," Dwayne stated happily.

"What? How you want it," Michael asked incredulously. "It's gettin' cold now, you sure?"

"Just cut it off, black, I ain't got all day. I'm already running late, I got business to take care of man."

Minutes hummed and buzzed by, and piles of Dwayne's unkempt, thick hair fell to the floor while the young men talked, with occasional glances to the Seventh Avenue traffic and passerby.

"Yo, you seen E-zo, man," Michael asked.

"Nah," answered Dwayne.

"Word? I heard he got out. When he get out? He shot some dudes drinking Cisco uptown in the Boogie Down right, in Forest Projects right?"

"I don't know high."

"Yo, that's what I heard. Heard they be messing with that liquid crack. Eric is back home in Foster, that's what I heard. Hey, I seen Arthur kid!"

"Where?"

"At Grant's Tomb. He got a dope ride man! He came through fourteenth over the summer."

"Yeah?"

"I heard he doing music now! He rhyming! I heard he be hanging with Whodini and stupid Brooklyn heads, the Disco Three, you know they changed they name to the Fat Boys now, Divine Sounds, all them niggas. He even opening up shows for The Treacherous Three."

"From uptown, Dead Man Hill? Arthur be up there? I heard they not together no more."

"Oh word up! Kool Moe Dee is dropping joints for self now, since last year I heard . . . Arthur said he know all them older uptown cats too, Sugarhill, Caz & Cold Crush, Kurtis Blow and crazy other MC's. He be with them new dudes Ultra Magnetic too! Man, I remember Arthur used to be softer than baby shit. Remember? Said he's about to be signed to a deal with Tommy Boy, and his name is Boogie Art. This I gotta see!"

Half of Dwayne's head was shaved totally bald, while at the same time Patrick and his two angry cousins, Grant and Carlton stormed down the uptown side of Seventh Avenue. Their destination: 117th Street again, mission: to kill Dwayne, reason: for stealing their grandmother's keys and money; also, for stealing Ivy's wedding band given from her deceased husband. Grant and Carlton preyed on Dwayne's blood, and the misty light rain made them angrier.

Patrick was really frustrated. After hearing about what Dwayne did at the house, he also was annoyed, like the rest of the family. At himself first, for not realizing sooner that

Dwayne was a crack abuser. Second, at Dwayne for pulling the crazy stunts he did. He understood his cousins' pain and anguish. To steal from someone was uncalled for and Patrick hated thieves. To steal from his grandmother Una was definitely the last straw, but the frustrating part, Dwayne was still a childhood friend. Dwayne prevented Patrick from blowing his own brains out after the Livingston massacre. With his forgiving heart, Patrick stressing to be a man of God, felt Dwayne deserved another chance.

The aggressive threesome crossed 119th Street, coming closer to Billy Harten's establishment. They trooped on, not knowing that their stealing foe was nearby. Grant was strapped with a .380 semi-automatic pistol in his belt. Carlton carried a nickel-plated 9 millimeter. Patrick had to act quickly, wanting to offer everyone an alternative.

He immediately thought of his girlfriend, Michelle. She mentioned to him once that she had a cousin, who worked as a drug counselor in the South Bronx. She described her cousin as a "big shot" in the program, recently graduating from Grambling State University in Louisiana and Hunter College in New York City with high degrees. Patrick hoped that Michelle's cousin could possibly hook Dwayne up into a crack program that could cure him; more murder was not the answer.

"Yo, wait I have an idea man! You don't have to kill him! Wait! Wait nuh," Patrick yelled, stopping by a pay phone.

"Come nuh preacher maan! Coume! Coume nuh," yelled Carlton, while Grant had stopped walking, kissing his teeth.

"Look, let me call my girl's cousin!"

Carlton and Grant looked at each other, throwing up their hands in disgust while Patrick pleaded.

"COUME NUH MAAN," yelled Grant. After Dwayne had kicked him in the ribs, his intent was to slaughter.

"Wait," screamed Patrick. He quickly dialed Michelle's job number. He knew if he didn't get to her in time, his childhood friend would be a dead man.

"Shell . . . It's me! Gimme your cousin number quick . . . Hurry up! I need it! Quick!"

Patrick wrote the number on his palm. "Thanks sweetheart! Call you tonight!"

Carlton was livid. How could Patrick help a crackhead thief that stole from his house and hurt his family? So what if they were childhood friends! Carlton shoved Patrick.

"Why you push me," Patrick shouted, trying to maintain his religious cool.

"Wha' hoppem?!," Carlton yelled in his face.

"Come on! Give him a chance! Thou shalt not kill! It's in the bible!"

"Maan, FUCK de Bible! We went true this yesterdey, Pahtrick! H'anyone that t'iefs should be dead and we burnin' 'im! Dead maan! We burnin' 'im! We nuh cyere de boodclaat yenkee bwoy ye friend dem. Wid' dem type ah friend, ya nuh need h'enemy; ya call de people dem friendemy, ti' raatid!"

"No! But he's not in his right mind, he needs help, he didn't mean to do it! He didn't mean it! Let him beat the crack!"

"What da baambaclaat ya a chat 'bout de raasclaat! H'im coume a mi yaard! H'im t'ief Mummy bag 'n keys to de howse nuh maan! Mi kil' 'im dead de baamberaasclaat! Coume nuh maan! De fuckers dem! Fuck de blaasted preacher maan!"

Patrick knew there was definite trouble and blood after being cursed by his cousin, as they continued their pilgrimage to find Dwayne and murder him.

Dwayne's head was shaved three fourths bald when Carlton, Grant, and Patrick walked past the shop spotting him getting his hair cut.

"GRANT! Look 'ere nouw," Carlton shouted, pointing.

They burst into the shop without ringing the bell, with a shot from the .380 to the door, and a blast to the ceiling; and Carlton extended his "nine", pointed in Dwayne's direction.

Billy raised his hands in fright, and the rest of the other men scrambled for cover, frightened for their lives, frightened of the armed men. The culprit was in sight, sitting defenseless, trapped in the first barber's chair. Carlton and Grant put their weapons to Dwayne's temples.

"Noooo! Noooo," Patrick yelled at his two cousins, "Carlton, listen! Thou shall not kill! No!"

"Mi kill de t'ief! Mi muhhrrder de raasclaat t'ief," screamed Grant, cocking his weapon.

One by one, the barber shop patrons ran out of the shop. To them, it seemed like the gunmen found their prey. Dwayne trembled.

"I'm sorry! I'm fucking sorry man!"

"See! H'im sorry! Chill! Give him a chance! H'im seh h'im sorry," Patrick yelled, pushing Grant's arm back. Grant pushed Patrick back out of the way, repositioning his gun at Dwayne's temple.

"Y'all niggas wanna kill me man?! I said sorry man! I ain't mean it y'all!"

"Dee man! My cousins gonna kill you man! Tell 'em you'll get help! Tell 'em you'll pay 'em back! Tell them! Tell mi couzins dem wha' ya 'ah DO!"

Dwayne snarled and hissed at Grant. Grant backhanded Dwayne with the butt of the weapon to the temple, then smacked Dwayne against the forehead and in his mouth with the gun.

"Okay! Okay! What the fuck y'all want from me?! Pat! I'll do it! I don't wanna die man! I'm sorry!" Dwayne fought tears dizzy, spitting blood on the barber apron while his mouth bled, and his forehead swelled. If he could just smoke his crack now, everything would be okay. He felt like his world was coming to an end.

The almond colored young woman let out a deep, annoying sigh of uneasiness. "Paperwork, paperwork, paperwork. Is there no end, to paperwork," she exhaled, clasping her hands together with fresh painted red nail polish. Twenty-four-year-old Nicole Ryerson looked around her office with brief admiration, but back to her desk with disgust. After a long weekend, the desk remained in disarray with unfiled papers and folders of past and current clients. She held her own, being a top worker at the "ROBERTO CLEMENTE CENTER FOR NARCOTIC REHABILITATION."

She was the top counselor-everyone's favorite-having been aboard for close to six months. Her goal: to give back to communities plagued by drugs, came to fruition weeks after graduating from Hunter College with a Master's degree. The drug program took its turn for the better since she joined, with addicts kicking their habits and finding jobs with places to live at a higher rate. Her work was so outstanding that she was facing a promotion to be coordinator of affairs at the center. The clientele and staff found themselves mesmerized with the innate beauty Nicole possessed from the inside out, to the outside within.

All heads turned when her stacked 38-25-38 shape moved with regal purpose around the company, standing at five foot eight inches tall. The word spread around the center about the gorgeous afro-centric beauty, smart yet caring, sensuously earthy, and extremely approachable.

She checked her watch, frowning. "Time flies every other day when I'm not hungry. I'm starving to death, and it's not even eleven-thirty," she thought. She picked up her desk phone, dialing.

"Andre . . . Will it be Chinese food today . . . If so, let me know honey, okay . . . I know . . . Me too . . . I must have a tapeworm . . ."

The buzzer on the telephone rang, indicating an outside call.

"Andre I gotta go, I have another call, don't order without me okay . . . Bye hon."

She pressed the phone extension where the call light flashed. "Ryerson."

Her face took on a look of confusion. "Yes, this is Nicole Ryerson, who's this . . . Patrick, hi . . . Of course I know you, Michelle's new friend from Manhattan . . .Why you sound so out of breath? . . . You okay?"

On the other end of a pay phone line, while Patrick begged Nicole to set Dwayne up for treatment, behind him Carlton and Grant held Dwayne by his arms, with their weapons cemented in his ribs and back. He still was covered with the hairy, bloodstained customer apron, after being snatched from his seat and dragged from the shop. Patrick quickly passed the phone to Dwayne to get directions to the center after being given the violent ultimatum: "get cured or get killed". He was instructed to get treatment for his crack addiction, supervised by Nicole, eventually pay Ivy back for her stolen ring, and pay Una for the stolen money. If he didn't comply with their instructions, Carlton and/or Grant would murder him, and there was absolutely nothing Patrick could do about it.

Hurting because of no crack, guns drawn, the dog bite, and being treated like a punk, Dwayne made the arrangement to meet Nicole the next day at the center, bright and early.

"You betta go, o' ya dead maan," Carlton said in Dwayne's other ear.

"Let's step off! The cops," Patrick announced, noticing two cop cars cruising their way in the distance. Grant nonchalantly stashed his piece back inside his waist and prepared to cross Seventh Avenue, heading towards 118th Street. Carlton quickly put his piece away, and kicked

Dwayne in the back knocking him to the ground, while the dangling phone receiver swayed back and forth. Patrick headed home, north on Seventh, and Carlton quickly hooked a right on 119th, while Dwayne angrily stood from the ground. He heard a few people call him a "crackhead" while passing. He ripped the cape from around his neck, while the other barbers, onlookers, and passersby laughed and gawked at him. The strange looking guy had a bloody mouth, with most of his head shaved bald, with one piece of hair extending from his face to his neck. He looked down at the clothes he wore, and limped from the forming crowd, moving fast as he could until he could find a place to hide, and heal. He found a small, glass-paved alleyway.

"Damn, what's happening . . . What the fuck's happening . . . Damn you, Floyd . . . Damn you, Floyd," he thought. He stood against a brick wall, rubbing his hands against his smooth, bald scalp, and the large bump on his forehead. He grabbed the mass of hair that Michael didn't get to cut, yanking, and pulling at it until it hurt. Dwayne pulled and pulled, getting a handful of hair in his hand.

"Damn this fucking crack! I don't know what the fuck to do! I don't know," he screamed, extracting more strands of hair from the follicles. Then he beat his fists against the wall until he saw blood, to match his mouth, and the small cut on his head.

"Yo, what's that man?"

"Fuckin' crack. That's what
it is. And the muthafucka
sho' is good."

Dwayne covered his ears with his hurt, throbbing, bloody hands:

"Nigga like me might

get strung!"

"No you won't. The high
is only for three minutes
man. That's a buck a minute.
Ya can't go wrong, come
on, check it out."

"Three minutes?"

"Yeah."

He ran off in pain, with a long piece of hair flying in the wind.

Al was near the point of being semi-comatose. With the last bits of gumption from the glory days of yesteryear, strength and oxygen in his battered body, he low crawled World War II soldier-styled through the night, away from the carcass of General into the hallway. He was determined to make it from the apartment before Dwayne returned this time. Perhaps someone, anyone, even Barbara could get him to safety. The light of dawn revealed his position from his overnight tactical move; he now lay in front of the bathroom and the apartment door, near to his bedroom.

There were voices he began to hear, in the hallway outside the apartment door. Other neighbors from across the hall in apartment # 50; or could it be Barbara from next door in 52? Was it the young girl, single mom with four small children about to give birth to her fifth in 51? Maybe it was the gas man or the super? Al, with extremely blurred vision, looked up at the door, and attempted to reach for the knob. The voices became clear, male voices. Al reached for the doorknob, with hand falling back to the floor; he was simply too weak.

He traveled back to his past youth via his mind's eye

and heart, when the strength and purpose for his survival was prevalent. Inhaling as much air as he could, he hit the door with his hand. The men continued their conversation in the hallway, oblivious to any gentle knock that could come from inside any of the four apartments on the fifth floor. Al hit the door a second time, and the voices came closer. Another door opened, and there she was, fussing and rambling with the men outside. Barbara joined the conversation. Al hit the door a third time.

"Barbara . . . Bawbah . . . rah! . . . Bar . . . Bruh," Al tried to yell to no avail. Al heard a creaking noise and the shutting of her door, and the voices of the men came closer with their chat. Al hit the door for a fourth time. He could hear the men walking down the stairs and the hallway was quiet again.

Al thought, "What I'm gon' do? . . . Cain't die here . . . Gotta be seen by somebody . . . I ain't gon' lie no mo' . . . they cain't hear me . . . gotta get help . . . cain't feel my legs no more . . . Lawd why me . . . why me Lawd . . . He . . . .he . . . he smash the dog head in . . . oh my Lawd . . . Gen'rah . . . . Gen'rah! . . . Baby Al smash his head in . . . oh my God in heaven . . . he gon' kill me . . . ain't nobody gon' help me . . . ain't nobody gon' see me . . . but I'm gon' on tuh that fire 'scape . . . sho' hope they see me now . . . I'm gon' on tuh that fire 'scape . . . I gotta make it to muh winduh . . . OH MY LEGS IS BROKEN!! THEY GON'E!!"

Al burst into a new set of weakening tears when all of a sudden there was a click of a lock, and the apartment door swung in, hitting his groin and lower body.

"What the fuck," said Dwayne, unable to enter the apartment because of something blocking the entrance. He pushed then shoved the door, peeking inside and noticing Al's limp body. He squeezed inside and shut the door. After locking the door, Dwayne looked down on Al who lay on his stomach with labored breathing.

"What you doing up here Pappy? How you got up

here?! I left you in the living room with General! I left y'all in the back, cause you and General fucked up. Goddamn! You ain't dead yet? Maybe he still alive too!"

Dwayne stormed off down the hallway towards the kitchen, talking to himself very loud, and answering his own questions. Al faintly heard his grandson's incoherent voice rambling from the kitchen, and the deliciously clear voices of his wife and daughter fussing over him:

"Now what you crying for mama?"

"Cause I can't believe my eyes!"

"I told you stop looking. Mama
we can't change what's happening
to Daddy!"

"Why?"

"We can't!"

"Please Gwenny!"

"You warned him
already, Mama! Just
like I warned you."

Inside the kitchen, leaning against the washing machine that had not been used in months, and testing a pencil with a dull point, Dwayne announced, "They just gon' have to kill me! Word up! But I ain't never getting off crack! Never! Fuck that! And fuck counseling! And when I get these papers and this loot, I'm a be aiight!"

After he had cut the rest of his leftover hair, Dwayne wrote two phony letters, both allegedly from Al. One, he would show to the insurance company while begging for the policy. The other would be for Al's buddy, Nathan Pope. Dwayne wouldn't have to worry about people questioning Al's whereabouts once he killed him, the quicker Mister Pope could spread the word to his "gossip roosters" that "Al left for Detroit". He finished scribbling the notes and signed them sloppily like Al would. After folding the letters, Dwayne left the kitchen walking quickly as he stepped over Al's body into the bathroom, checking his look in the mirror. Dwayne's head was bald, with a dark line of cut hair near the right side of his neck. Straightening Al's tie and brushing off Al's suit for the final time, Dwayne was ready to initiate his money plan. Turning to exit the bathroom he stopped short.

"Pappy, you can't be just lying there and blocking the door. You gotta move out the way! I left you in the back with General in the first place. Who the fuck told you to come up here? Die already shit! I need my money!"

He flipped Al onto his back with his left foot to stare at him, eye to eye. "This time, I'm a make sure you stay up front with General for good!"

Dwayne painfully crouched to grab Al again by his collar when Al stated breathlessly:

"Ahlene got'cha money."

"What?"

"Ah . . . Ah . . . Ah . . . lene . . . got . . . cha money . . ."

Dwayne paused. "Arlene?"

"Have . . . ya ins' . . . ins' . . . ins'hu'ance . . . money . . . I don' . . . wan . . . wanna die."

"Word Pappy?! Arlene got bread for me?! How you know I need insurance for when I kill you? Oh shit!"

"Y . . . Ya . . . Ins . . . ins'huance . . . Ahl . . . lene . . . got . . . cha . . . mon . . . money."

"Bust it. I hope you telling the truth. I need this dough right now, word to mutha! I don't have time to fuck around. Cause if I find out you lying Pappy, you already know what's up!"

Dwayne used the apartment door knob to stand with one hand and then pulled Al by his collar into the master bedroom, dumping his grandfather in front of the dusty dresser near the window.

"Stay there until I get back. And I mean it Pappy, word up!"

Dwayne left Al's bedroom, unlocked the door, and exited the apartment. He did an about face to lock the door when suddenly, Barbara's door flew open. She rushed over to Dwayne, interrogating him immediately.

"Alright damn it! Baby Al, where is he," Barbara snapped.

"Where is who Miss Nelson," Dwayne aggravatingly replied.

She placed her hands on her hips: "Don't you even try it, Baby Al! Barbara ain't stupid!"

"You sure about that?"

"You ain't getting away with this one, honey! Na-uhh!"

"What do you want, Miss Nelson? Damn!"

"Where is your grandfather and that damn dog, Baby Al?! What have you done to them?!"

"Look! Pappy went to Detroit and General ran away in Central Park, which is something I wish you'd do."

"You lying little red, crack smoking nigga! You was just talking to ya granddaddy just now out'chere! Barbara heard ya!"

"Pappy went to Detroit!"

"Where is my Al Carter you lying crackhead?! And what have you done to that mutt?!"

"Yo go home Miss Nelson! I told you the deal already! Trying to dis me all the time! You should know all about the crackheads with chump ass Floyd taking your shit he can't get a dollar for, and them other dumb ass niggas you can't keep outta jail! I don't owe your horse face no explanation!"

Dwayne trotted down the steps. "Bitch," he snarled, loud enough for Barbara to hear.

"Come back here, Baby Al! Come here! Who you callin' a bitch?! You get yo' red stinking ass back up here," Barbara screamed.

She rushed into her apartment, rambling, with her own mission in mind. "Na-uhh! I'll be damned! I'll be damned! I got yo' bitch! I got yo' bitch alright! Na-uhh! I got yo' bitch!"

Barbara stormed about in her empty apartment.

A few tenements away, on the first floor inside of 120 West 117th apt#2, Dwayne paid Nathan Pope a visit. Approaching his eighties, Nathan stayed home all the time with his wife Marie, usually entertaining their large family. He responded well to the letter, saddened that Al left town without a goodbye, still wishing him the best. He gave Dwayne their telephone number to give to Al in case his grandfather ever called or wrote again.

After his smoothly ran move, Dwayne returned to the autumn morning. Malik and his mother Florence were leaving the building when Dwayne walked up the stoop to the tenement. "What's up, Dee?" Malik said, while his mother rolled her eyes in Dwayne's direction. "What up," answered Dwayne, continuing into the building. He wouldn't see Florence pinch Malik while walking in the direction of Seventh Avenue. "What's your problem fool, you like associating with crackheads," Florence snapped.

Barbara anxiously waited for Dwayne to enter the

building, standing on the first step of the staircase. Dwayne shut the second door of the building, turned around, and was startled by a violent, babbling Barbara.

"BITCH?!! I'm a bitch huh?! I'm a bitch huh?! You back mighty quick from smoking that damn crack! Call me a bitch now!!"

She hopped from the step, and began pacing toward Dwayne in the manner of a gunslinger. Dwayne saw the gleaming butcher's knife in his neighbor's fist.

"Yo chill Miss Nelson. You bugging! Stay away from me . . . What the fuck you gonna do with that! Cut me?!"

"Call me a bitch again! Go on! So I can slice and dice ya' lil' red half-breed, high-yellow crackhead zebra motherfucker!!"

Inside their apartment while eating a late breakfast, The Wilsons shook their heads, hearing Barbara's voice as clear as a bell.

"I wonder who Nelson arguing with now, Mary," Chuck asked his wife.

"I don't know honey, but I ain't never hear Barbara yell like that. Sounds serious," Mary replied.

Meanwhile in the hallway: "Why you always trying to fucking violate, Miss Nelson?!"

"Try Barbara, motherfucker!! Why you call me a bitch, Baby Al?!!"

"Step off 'fore I dis you again!"

"You know what a bitch is you high-yellow bastard?! Huh?!! Why you call me a bitch, nigga?"

"Cause you keep fucking with me and Pappy! You ain't nothing but a nosy troublemaking big mouth bitch, bitch!"

"Ya mama's a bitch!!"

She moved closer and kept cursing at Dwayne while his temper unfolded. The moment Gwenny's name was mentioned, he saw blood.

"You deaf now huh? The bitch is dead honey! I'll show ya' a real bitch! Honey, Barbara knows all the bitches! The

Bitch! Couldn't have a baby by a colored boy on 17th Street! The Bitch! Couldn't get an abortion when the white man ain't want her Harlem nigga ass and raped her Harlem nigga ass at that damn school outta state! **The Bitch** is **Gwenny! The nasty, cracker loving bitch is dead!"**

In a flash, Dwayne cuffed Barbara's neck, slamming her head to the wall, the knife falling to the floor.

The Wilson's door flew open the moment they heard the human flesh "boom" against their wall, which made Dwayne jump back as Barbara slid to the floor next to her knife. Some other first and second floor tenants came out into the hallway to spectate. A few of the women attended to Barbara, who was a little dizzy, while Chuck wanted a piece of Dwayne.

"You's a real man now, huh?! Picking on a woman ya' faggot! Pick on me! Slam me! Damn it! Slam me," Chuck yelled at Dwayne, face to face.

"She was gonna fucking cut me! Then what?! She called my . . . my . . . ma," he stopped before he spoke the word he was totally of touch with: "mama". The crowd looked at Dwayne while new tears of frustration raced down his unwashed face.

"Oh ya gonna cry now! Barbara need to call her sons to come over and tear ya butt up if I don't!"

"Honey, don't," Mary restrained.

"I know you beat yo' granddaddy! I know it! You gonna get what's coming to you! You just can't hurt up people and get away with it! You could'a killed her man!"

Mary stood in front of her enraged husband, while Dwayne backed off to the side, huffing and puffing.

"Fuck that! She was going to shank me! Fuck that . . . It ain't fair . . . She talked about . . . Gwenny . . . I . . . I wouldn't . . . I wouldn't've did it . . . I swear . . . She called my . . . my . . . ma . . . my . . . ma . . . Gwen . . . Gwenny a bitch."

Badly in need of his stem with heated favorite

medicine, Dwayne watched the women monitor Barbara, returning stares of hate towards him.

"But . . . she called my mama a bitch . . . My mama . . . Gwenny . . . she . . . she . . . my mama dead . . . she ain't do nothing . . . to her . . . she's dead . . . My mama's dead."

He ran from the first floor as fast as his legs could carry him. All he needed was a hit, nice and quick. It wouldn't hurt. It would ease his decaying mind. Barbara's words about Gwenny punctured his soul, and demolished his mental:

> *"Ya mama's a bitch!*
> *The bitch is dead!*
> *Ya mama's a bitch!*
> *The bitch is dead!"*

Barbara's words combined with Mr. Wilson's words during the ascent between the third and fourth floors, embedded completely in Dwayne's thoughts:

> *"You gonna get what's coming to you!*
> *'I know you beat yo' granddaddy!*
> *You gonna get what's coming to you!"*
> *"Ya' mama's a bitch!"*
> *"You gonna get what's coming to you!"*
> *"The bitch is dead!"*
> *"I know you beat yo' granddaddy!"*
> *"Ya mama's a bitch!"*
> *"You gonna get what's coming to you!"*

Dwayne charged into the apartment that reeked of imminent death, straight into the living room that was just a barren shell of hip yesterdays. The dining room table on the floor in halves, broken dishes with rotted food, floor model TV, the wall unit with no pictures, and the corroded couches with loveseats remained, with the other added fixture: the mangled body of a pit bull, its head split open in two pieces, one eyeball protruding with brains exposed, surrounded by flies, flies, and more flies. Dwayne searched frantically for his pipe through the apartment, while Al's ultimatum joined in with the repetitious mental words of Barbara and Mr. Wilson. He had to find his pipe; anything to kill the cacophony of voices:

> *"The Bitch is dead!"*
> *"You gonna get what's coming to you!"*
> *"Ya mama's a bitch!"*
> *"Ya reap what'cha sow boy!"*
> *"You gonna get what's coming to you!"*
> *"The bitch is dead!"*
> *"What goes around . . . comes around!"*
> *"Ya mama's a bitch!"*
> *"I know you beat yo' granddaddy!"*

"Leave me alone," he screamed, spinning around, covering his ears.

> *"The bitch is dead!"*
> *"I know you beat yo' granddaddy!"*

"No! No . . . it ain't true! It ain't true!"

> *"I know you beat yo' granddaddy!"*

He yelled at nothing, "It ain't fucking true! It ain't fucking true! Pappy! You still here right? You still with us right?"

He quickly skipped to Al's bedroom with concern, kneeling face to face over Al while the senior lay on his back in front of the right bedroom window.

"Pappy . . . You wit' me right . . . I . . . I . . . I want you to say . . . say something!"

"I know you beat yo' granddaddy!"
"Ya reap what'cha sow boy!"
"The bitch is dead!"
"Ya' mama's a bitch!"
"The bitch is dead!"
"Ya mama's a bitch!"
"The bitch is dead!"

The other voices began to subside while Barbara's remained, saturating the crack fiending caverns of Dwayne's brain. There was no response from Al, and it was time to base, but still no pipe in sight.

"Shit! Where the fuck is it?!"

He bolted, hopping into his bedroom, swinging his box spring with no mattress or head-board, away from the wall.

"IT AIN'T HERE!"

He fished in his pockets and removed two vials of crack. Opening the tops, he sprinkled and mashed the rocks into his mouth hoping for a possible, quick high; anything to stop Barbara in his head. While eating the bitter crack, Dwayne noticed Gwenny's graduation picture inside his closet on the floor. Barbara's voice stopped once Dwayne seized hold of his young mother's beauty, inside the broken picture frame; and tears streamed from his eyes while he thought of her. The need for crack worsened, making him feel weak, feverish, with a dull, agonizing pain that radiated through his whole body. His bedroom became slanted, turning sideways.

"Oh shit . . . Oh shit . . . What's up, what's going on," he asked himself, startled. Dwayne staggered from his bedroom into the hallway, trying to get back to the living room muttering, "Pap . . . Pappy . . . Papp . . ."

The living room continued turning until it stopped upside down. Lightheaded Dwayne fell to the floor instantly, sending flies everywhere. Once he came to, squinting his eyes painfully, Dwayne noticed his pipe across the room next to the dining table.

'THERE IT IS!'

Dwayne crawled towards the pipe, saved, happy, and victorious! Now that he found his best friend, he could smoke some crack to ease the physical pain from his fall to the living room floor, the dog bite that was well on its way to becoming infected, and he could ease the mental pain from his self-inflicted torture.

Dwayne crawled around the table, grabbed the pipe, and moved into the center of the room, right next to General. He sat up like a big baby, with his toys of unknown and present love, holding Gwenny's picture in one hand, and his base-pipe in the other. He happily put the portrait down, licking his cracked lips, kissing the pipe, like a lover does their spouse. He frantically patted his pockets.

"Oh no! Damn, I ate the shit! **NO! I ate it!**"

He gazed at the stunning glass in his palm, the key to all of his current problems. It began talking to him again, instructing him to do things. It made Dwayne want more; to smoke crack until kingdom come was his purpose in life, and now he must commit murder.

"Did you kill him yet," it asked.

"Huh?"

"Did you kill him yet? For the dough? You can't have that insurance money without killing him first. Kill him now, for the loot . . . Kill Pappy . . . Do something high, cause he gotta die . . . Turn on the gas . . . Do something nigga . . . But kill him now!"

"What?"

"Don't you want that dough . . . You want that insurance money don'tcha," the new voice asked.

"Yeah, but . . ."

"Yeah but my ass! Kill that old senile nigga . . . He's almost dead anyway! Kill him . . . And smoke more of our friend."

"Nah."

"Do it brother man!"

"I don't have to kill him . . . my godmother got some loot for me he said."

Dwayne trembled as his glass dictator continued barking commands.

"Crush his skull and go! . . . He's lying! . . . Kill him and smoke! . . . You know them bitches downstairs already calling the cops! . . . You gotta go! Hurry . . . Kill him and smoke! . . . Get our friend," the stem insisted. *"Smoke our friend . . . Get our friend, and smoke it . . . Smoke it . . . SMOKE it . . . SMOKE IT! . . . KILL PAPPY MOTHERFUCKER! . . . SMOKE IT! . . . SMOKE IT! . . . **SMOKE IT! . . . SMOKE . . . IT!**"*

Dwayne ran from the sinister voice inside the apartment. Nearly falling down the five flights of stairs, he was out the door of the tenement as fast as his dizzy legs could move; running, he ran, and ran, and ran; he ran for his life, and his grandfather's life; he ran non-stop, destination: Anywhere.

Mania, fear, and exhaustion changed his course in a matter of minutes, and Dwayne ended up at the rehab center, flying past security into Nicole's office, nearly collapsing at her feet. Once he relaxed, she allowed him to get more comfortable. She arranged for a chaise longue to be brought to the room, and he layed in front of her desk and poured his fiending heart out. He filled her in on certain things, listlessly spitting his skeletons to the ceiling, and Al wasn't mentioned once during the conversation. After taking notes at stenographic speed, Nicole decided to do lunch. Dwayne was ready to go back to Harlem, as crack desperately called his name, but something had happened during this particular meeting of the minds. This attractive heroine began to interest him, little by little.

Why did she welcome him, a murderous, low-life thief into her office so willingly without budging, or screaming? Why did she promise to buy him two packs of cigarettes? How did she easily find the words of encouragement she used towards him, and why was she working hard at patching his spirit immediately? Could this attractive stranger care this much? She even offered lunch. It couldn't have been because of the Livingston family ultimatum. She even provided him with a jacket to wear.

He softened up, grinning ear to ear, walking off with his newfound friend and counselor.

She exited her office and the center with her "special case", a code the staff used when a family member was in crisis. She occasionally checked her watch, while her hair blew in the wind; she was different than most of the women he had ever dealt with, ever. She reminded him of Arlene, only she was younger, close to his age, highly intelligent and very down to earth. She moved with style, class, grace, and most of all, she believed in him. Nicole strongly encouraged Dwayne to beat his addiction, and she promised to get him affiliated with the right people to be around. It would be a long hike back, but with confidence, dedication, a change of social circles and environments, with the drive to say no to drugs, things would have to work out.

While getting to know her newest addition to her extensive roster of addicts, Nicole Ryerson was reluctant to mention her cousin Michelle, his now ex-partner in crime Patrick, the Livingston family, or their subsequent threats of murder. According to Michelle, Dwayne prevented Patrick from committing suicide after his entire family was murdered right before both their eyes in broad night light. Anyone could turn to hard drugs after such major traumas; there was no time for moral judgment. It was time for her client to heal, and to fight the horrible plaguing disease that possessed his soul and was destroying beloved communities across the United States.

They strolled along, exchanging ideas, talking personal problems, getting to know one another. Finally, Dwayne and Nicole agreed that he would stay off crack, come closer to God, and let his evil ways come to an end. She assured him that God would extend a helping hand, if he helped himself. He was desperate to trust.

They sat down in a Spanish restaurant on East 138th & Saint Anns, for a two for one lunch advertising special. The beauty and attentive kindness of this young woman progressively nourished Dwayne's hunger, while he steadily fed his stomach at the same time. The delicious food brought Al to his mind, suddenly.

Across the table, Nicole spoke regally about the strengths of her Argentinean mother coming of age during the Juan & Evita Peron regime, yet securing a Ph.D. with no knowledge of how to speak English, still becoming an English professor. Nicole beamed as she talked about her African-American father, a retired Air Force physician originally born and raised in the Jim Crow plagued South, who also spent time in the Black Panthers and flew choppers during Vietnam. She laughed about being a middle "black sheep" of three girls, one older married sister still spoiled by her parents, and one rebellious younger sister. Her conversation encouraged Dwayne's mental to remain embedded in the past.

Was it too late for a fresh start, or for change? Was it too late to tell Al that he had always loved him? The old man had stuck with him since birth, and Al was the only father he ever knew. He had to make amends, there had to be a chance; someone believed in him, so he had to believe. With only 1/4th of the food digested from his plate, Dwayne stood from the table.

"Yo! I gotta go! Yo, I gotta get home," Dwayne said,

pushing his chair under the table.

"But you haven't finished eating," Nicole replied, puzzled. "Listen why don't you come back to the center with me? I'll get the waiter to wrap our plates, and you can spend the rest of the day with me. I'll cancel my other sessions. How about it? I know you have more things to tell me."

She knew her client wanted more crack which worried her. Patrick and her cousin painted the picture of Dwayne's situation as a grave one, and Nicole would hate for the guy to be killed, like many others, just because of the wrong choices made due to drug usage.

"Good looking out, um, um Miss um, Miss . . ."

"You forgot already? Ryerson, but call me Nicole."

"Yeah, yeah, Miss Nicole Ryerson. We gon' build later. We'll blend later. We'll blend! I gotta go! I'll call you later!"

She added, "Listen now, we have more work to do . . . Wait! Wait a minute. Wait a minute!"

Nicole searched inside her Gucci purse for carfare. First she decided on taxi money, then instantly changing her mind to a couple of subway tokens she could spare. This way it would be a bit more tedious for her client to cash the tokens for a hit. By the time she dug through her pocketbook and looked up, Dwayne had run out of the restaurant. Nicole sucked her teeth, slid from the booth, paid the bill and walked out onto the street. Her client had vanished into thin air and was long gone.

Back on 117th, like a feline with nine lives, Al still was determined to escape.

> *"Go 'head, baby! You can do it!*
> *That's the Al I know! The man I*
> *love! The man I married!"*

> *"Daddy **IS** a strong man!"*

*"That's why I love him. In spite of
everything, he still wants to crawl
his way out. Albert Carter, you
something else!"*

Al heard Mattie and Gwenny again, and they were
closer. He also heard Barbara outside in the hallway,
arguing with a male voice.

"Ba . . . Bar . . . Barb . . . BARBARA," he cried above a
whisper; and no one heard him, only God, his wife, and
daughter. He lethargically convinced himself that if he
possessed enough strength to make it out onto the fire
escape, he could signal for help. Al inhaled, turned his
body around, pushed up the window enough, until both his
arms stretched through the windowsill.

"This is where I turn my head again?"

"I think you should, Mama."

Tenaciously gasping for more air, Al closed his eyes
with the determination of the soldier who lived within him;
and the trooper was anticipating more strength to land on
the fire escape, that was just his shattered illusion. With
every movement, his vision went from blurry to total
darkness, and then it would lighten up again. With all of the
stamina in his upper body and arms, Al accomplished the
feat of kneeling straight up on weakened kneecaps,
recounting his ultimate race against the clock.

At the same time, after walking the South Bronx and
ignoring the piping pleas of his existence to smoke more
crack, Dwayne jumped the turnstile after finding the
Seventh Avenue-Bronx #2 train to get home as soon as
possible. Five stops downtown from Jackson, anxious

Dwayne bolted from the subway station to get to the block, run-skipping to save his grandfather's life.

On the block, recalling the drive of a young man deep within himself, a quick witted serviceman who rescued his family after the murder of his father, Al breathed and pushed up with the legs he thought were destroyed. Managing to push and pull his battered torso over the windowsill, Al was half outside and half inside his bedroom. Mouth dry as the sands of a desert, he inhaled the aromatic, elevated breeze of Harlem, with its blaring car horns, rumbling trucks, and sirens of ongoing life that would continue inside New York City.

With the sounds of the hood, he heard the fighting voices of Mattie, Gwenny, and other familiar sounding ancestors like Frederick & Jessie Bell Carter; however, he refused to deal with the sentimental energies that would avert his urge for safety. Breathing still strained, Al's feeble fingers touched the building's bricks.

With futile aspiration, he pushed himself blindly for the rescue he needed from his right bedroom window. The right window was the wrong window, due to the left bedroom window being connected to the fire escape he had known for almost forty-eight years of his life. The last push with the expected immediate landing proved to be his last fatal step towards the painful unknown. Al fell from his bedroom window.

The fall to the sidewalk in front of 128 West 117th Street killed Al instantly. The senior citizen landed directly on his back; his elderly blood spilling immediately in an expansion pool under a body tattered for years, with bones crushed inside a formless mass of flesh, the back of his head chopped open plastered to the ground, with eyeballs popped from the cranium.

Dwayne screamed himself hoarse falling over Al's body after witnessing his grandfather's final flight and landing to the hardcore streets below.

"Pappyyyyyyyyyyy! Oh noooo! Oh NOOO!! NOOOOO! PLEASSSEE! Help HIMMM! HELPPP SOMEBODYYYYY!!! PAPPYYYYY!!!! NOOOOO!!!! Oh Nooo, NOOOO!! PAPPYYY!!! OHHHH NOOOOO!!!," Dwayne yelled to the horrified onlookers assembling to the gory sight.

All who could bear to view gathered near to their bodies, and watched calamity in an eerie silence.

****

CHAPTER 12

*

Dwayne wept, sobbed, and cried incessantly. His hospitalization was of no justice, whatsoever. Even the new amount of supportive friends couldn't help this newfound grief he was experiencing. Patrick and Nicole chose to help him out, and stick by him but encouraged him to remain strong and read the word of God. The peaks and valleys of their friendship usually panned towards the negative, but this time the positive won out, and Patrick refused to let down his childhood partner in crime. Patrick found the word of God-and the praising of God to be a magnificent tool-and felt with proper ministering, Dwayne would be on the road to recovery. Patrick's family felt the opposite about the situation, and his new girlfriend Michelle also reluctantly walked with him every step of the way.

First cousins Michelle and Nicole Ryerson were close in age and relation but also contrary in some ways. They were reared in similar fashion with their fathers Charles and Craig Ryerson, two southern brothers from Pensacola, Florida spoiling their wives and daughters with the sky being the limit. The girls were raised with high standards, education, and etiquette; however, Michelle was an only child raised in a three floor Brooklyn brownstone on Jefferson, and Nicole was one of three sisters raised in a one floor ranch style home in Jefferson, but Jefferson Township, New Jersey.

Nicole was nearly five years older than Michelle, while Michelle regarded herself as more mature, because she was saved, and she felt Nicole was "worldly" in many ways. She still looked up to her three first cousins as older sisters; and Nadia, Nicole, and Nefertiti saw their cousin as their spoiled, tattle-tale, bratty sister also.

All of the Ryerson women began college immediately after high school with Nicole landing a scholarship that whisked her south to Louisiana, and Michelle immediately started taking college summer prep courses, still maintaining her secretary job from her work study program in high school. Their likeness, subtle competition between family, yet detached differences spread to communication on certain levels, especially on the subject of Dwayne. Michelle abhorred Nicole's over-counseling of her new client which also led to lukewarm quarrels with her man Patrick as well.

Patrick, Michelle, and Nicole waited patiently outside of Dwayne's hospital room a few hours later after he was rushed there for shock. After the incident on the brisk November afternoon when his grandfather fell to his death, Dwayne attempted to cradle Al's pulverized head, but the notion hit that it was too late. Much too late to even strike a conversation with one whose body was broken smeared history, with battered heart, mind, soul, and body turned stagnant. Witnesses and neighbors watched Dwayne scream until the oxygen was exhausted from his lungs, more irrational as the authorities pronounced his grandfather dead at the scene.

"He'll be okay. Dwayne's always been strong, since we were younger," Patrick said, hugging Michelle, staring into her eyes with love. "You know, I'm the luckiest man in the world. The good Lord sent you to me, I love you so much. God wants us together."

"I know, honey." Michelle smiled, and kissed Patrick on the cheek.

She was taller than Nicole with her "Jheri-Curl" occasionally pushed back into a bun or ponytail, a few shades darker, and weightier, taking the stockier, paternal side of the Ryersons. Patrick instantly thought of his grandmother once he met Michelle, meeting the Brooklynite when she and his sister Hyacinth were studying together to be nurses. After Michelle lent a helping hand to the funeral services with floral arrangements, cards, on spot verbal prayers, and food, plus the frequent correspondence to Jamaica, Patrick knew that Michelle would be the woman for him. The strength, stamina, and comparison of sole surviving Una (Livingston, plus the memories of his brothers and sisters, especially Hyacinth was all he could think of at times; he needed to continue dealing with this thick, statuesque, young child of God. She had to be his Eve.

Three doctors exited the room, after completing their rounds. "Come," Patrick said, entering, followed by the two young women. The stench inside the room was atrocious, thanks to Dwayne's elderly roommate who reeked of feces and urine. Bearing a startling resemblance to Al, Dwayne's roommate was in a coma, kept alive on a noisy life support machine, with nasogastric tubing tangled with the intravenous lines going into his body.

On the other side of the room's dividing curtain, in a bed next to a window facing Mount Morris Park, Dwayne stared at the ceiling. He tossed and turned occasionally, with his cracked out conscience coaching him for the imminent flight necessary to go on. There were plenty of spots near North General where he could quickly cop, and many of his friends were right across Madison waiting on him for contact. He heard some female voices entering, one of the speakers stating: "Yuck."

A familiar almond brown hand with red painted nails pulled his curtain back slightly, and there she appeared, joined by Patrick and a young woman holding Patrick's hand.

"How are you friend? Are you okay," Nicole asked, embracing him.

"I don't know . . . I guess I'm chilling, but not really. Yo high . . . "

Patrick hugged Dwayne, as the fecal smell became stronger in the room. Losing her ethical poise, Michelle blurted, "ILLLLL, it stinks in here! Nah-uhh honey, where IS the staff to clean up that man?"

Nicole giggled, covering her mouth and nose, when one of the nurses walked into the room. She bypassed the first man's bed, and came over to Dwayne's, placing some pills on his bedside table; then she poured Dwayne a cup of water from the pitcher on his bedside table.

"Mister Carter, you have a visitor downstairs who'd like to come up. One of you need to go downstairs," the nurse stated, proceeding to exit the room.

"You can do us a favor and clean up that man," said Michelle.

"He's not my patient," the nurse retaliated.

"Well in the name of Jesus, send somebody in here to do it, honey," Michelle spat while the nurse exited the room. "The nerve! We all wanna breathe you know, the nerve of her."

"O-kayy," Nicole added.

"She didn't even give him his medicine. I would never ever be that kind of worldly nurse! I need to go downstairs before I backslide. She must not know what time it is. I'm from Brooklyn."

"Wait, Shell, I'll join ya'," Nicole exclaimed, wincing and fanning her face.

Dwayne became concerned. "You jettin' so soon," he asked, looking directly at his counselor.

"I'll come by after I leave the center tomorrow."

"But, ain't tomorrow Saturday?"

"I still go in on Saturdays, you know, once in a while, to tighten up a little on my paperwork. It's so busy during the week; I hardly get the chance, so I go in on Saturdays, sometime." Walking sensuously to his bedside, Nicole touched Dwayne's face; dropping the key in her voice, she gently said, "I'll be by to see you, you sure you don't need anything? I'll promise I'll get it."

Dwayne asked, "You coming through tomorrow then,"he asked looking up into her eyes. She nodded.

"I need to say a few things to him anyway. The two of you can wait for me downstairs," Patrick announced.

"Mañana, and remember to take your medicine," Nicole stated, and Michelle waved, following her from the room. Patrick sat in a chair and moved close to Dwayne's bedside.

"So what's up man," Dwayne said pulling up the bedcovers, then popping his pills, drinking his water; he threw the empty cups across the room.

"I don't know, you tell me," said Patrick.

Dwayne shrugged his shoulders, tears welling in his eyes.

"Ya' ready to repent?"

He shrugged again and turned his back to his friend, staring off into space outside the window, with new droplets of guilt, travelling his face and saturating the linen. All Dwayne thought of was the frozen glance of reflection, attempting to save the life of the grandfather he tortured, limping onto the block. Out of nowhere, a body hit the sidewalk in front of the building as he approached, landing on its back. Dwayne, oblivious to the consistent pain of General's infecting bite, quickly gained momentum to see who fell in front of the building. In the thick of the blood curdling screams, in between the random "**OH MY GOD's**" & terrified "**OH SHIT**'s", he imagined he heard at least one 'Oh no that's Mister Carter'; **stop! Baby Al no don't look!!!**'

The bloody mass of flesh and bones that was Al, mashed in front of his beloved tenement was downright bizarre and confusing, because hours before, the desire was to kill him for barrel loads of proposed "insurance money", or so he thought. The weekend prior to Al's death, Dwayne stole merchandise and money from the home of the very friend who now sat at his bedside out of merciful concern, and love. Two more tears rolled down each side of Dwayne's face. One tear was for Patrick, and his forgiving heart of friendship, and the other was for Al, for the only relative Dwayne truly ever had, and severely mistreated until the death he inflicted upon himself, to finally escape the mistreatment.

"Dwayne, you have to talk about it. If not with me then at least with the Lord," Patrick stated with concernment. "John, fifteenth chapter-fifteenth verse, Jesus said 'but I have called you friends'. The Lord is here for us, and you have to get right with God my brother, to get through this."

"They all hate me, Pat! They all hate me. You seen 'em! You was there!"

"What do you mean? Who are you talking about? What do you mean they hate you? Who are they?"

Dwayne aggressively flipped himself over to glare at Patrick. "You know who! You was there, black! You was with them!"

"Who?"

"17th Street!"

"17th Street?"

Patrick was alarmed, misunderstanding what Dwayne meant. He wondered if these statements were the first signs of a nervous breakdown. The message Patrick received was that Dwayne left Nicole in a restaurant on 138th Street; next thing he heard Dwayne was in a hospital, and that "Mister Carter" had fallen to his death from their window on the block, and no one understood how.

Dwayne, tears running continuous now, said, "All I wanted to do, Pat . . . was . . . tell 'im I loved 'im . . . That's it . . . That's all, high . . . I only wanted to tell Pappy I loved him . . . I never told him I loved him . . . I never told 'im I loved 'im . . . I never told him I loved him! I never told him I loved him! AAAH! AAAAAH-HAAAAAH!"

Patrick jumped to his feet, using all of his strength to console his mourning friend, putting him in a bear hug. He cried heavily as well, while trying to smother out his buddy's bereaved screams. Dwayne continued his grief struck warpath, kicking his mattress, bawling like he did during childhood; and Patrick was glued to him, until his medication kicked in, causing him to drift off to sleep.

Arlene arrived and stood one full minute outside of Dwayne's room, overhearing the commotion between the young men. Dwayne's yells and screams got to her, reminding her of the love she had for Al, after knowing the Carter family for over thirty years. She wiped her face quickly before her makeup smeared, dabbed her eyes, and then entered the room. She vaguely recognized Dwayne with his shaved head or Patrick from the neighborhood, but recalled the news reports from the previous summer pertaining to the Livingston family. She watched the two friends hugging each other tightly, and once Patrick noticed her, Arlene gave him the signal that she would return to see Dwayne at a later time. She would update Dwayne on his trust fund, Al's will, and the news that he was on the verge of getting the cash he wanted so desperately for Al's death.

Later that night, Dwayne tossed and turned in bed, unable to sleep. He tried his luck at counting sheep, and he was constantly awakened by the alarming of his roommate's respirator, with the counted sheep transforming into crack vials, and strange female voices.

"Look at him Mama. You see him right?"

"Yeah honey. Baby Al suffering."

One of the voices was familiar, an older, experienced woman, with lots of wisdom. The second voice was unfamiliar, close to his age or younger, a very sexy sounding young sound. His roommate's respirator started up again, causing him to awaken in a cold sweat.

"Shit," he hissed. "I can't sleep man! If that man ain't shitting up the place, stinking up the fucking room, this nigga machine is beeping like crazy!"

Dwayne raised the head part of his bed, moving himself to its edge. Standing, he went to look on the other side of the dividing curtain.

"I wonder why that machine keeps . . . OH SHIT!"

Dwayne froze in terror watching his elderly roommate choke, gag, and regurgitate dark blood inside the respirator tube attached to his mouth. His eyes bulged out of his head, fishlike, red, and fiery, and he was Al! Albert Carter fought for his life on the ventilator, gazing through pus ridden eyes at the grandson who plotted to kill him dead for crack money.

'PAPPY!'

Dwayne backed away, confusing his present sight with the horrible memories, blazing with narcotic need while his roommate shook violently, kicking the mattress. Dwayne yelled into the hallway, "Nurse! Yo, nurse! NURSE!" He limped to his bedside phone and dialed with guilty fright while the doctors and nurses eventually entered the room, handling their business. The cardiac arrest of Dwayne's roommate was paged throughout the hospital as more staff, equipment, and lifesaving noise entered the room. A couple of the nurses pulled the dividing curtain while Dwayne stood petrified, in mental agony against the wall by his bed, suddenly flipping out.

"Pappy! . . . I'm sorry man! . . . I'm so, so sorry . . . Jesus knows I'm ever so sorry," he yelled at the medical staff on the other side of the curtain, while they attempted life preservation.

"Somebody save him! Save my grandfather! Get an ambulance! Do something!"

Still holding the phone receiver like a bullhorn, his pleas of sorrow became incoherent demands: "It's my Pappy! Don't fucking stand there! Do something! Y'all motherfuckers gonna let Pappy die! Do something! Help us!"

On the other end of the phone connection, Nicole wiped the crust from her sleepy eyes, lethargically turning on her lamp. Finally eyeing her alarm clock, she noticed the time: 2:30 A.M.

"What, huh? . . . Who? . . . Dwayne, is that you?"

"Y'all ain't shit! None a y'all! My grandpops dying! He's dying! HELP US!"

Nicole inhaled and screamed, "DWAYNE!," and she yelled his name four times before he realized he wasn't on 117th Street, struggling with his tragic fantasy.

"Dwayne! Calm down, it's Nikki! It's Nikki!! Look, relax! RELAX!"

"I need a fucking hit! Shit! . . . Nikki! . . . I need . . . I need . . . I just need some shit! . . . PAPPY! . . . I need some . . . SOMEBODY! Get me outta here. I gotta get the fuck outta here!"

"No! You will not leave! Talk to me! Tell me what's wrong!"

"He dying! See, he . . . He . . . He look like my grandpops! I gotta get outta here!"

She took a second deep sigh, and she said soothingly, "Look, I'll be by the first thing in the morning, soon as visiting hours begin. As a matter of fact, I won't even go by the center. I'll come stay with you okay?"

"No! I want out of here!"

"For what?! To go out in the street, right! And do what?! Get more crack?! Smoke more crack! Continue to throw your life away and never get better right? Oh, no you don't," she spoke firm, "Dwayne. Relax and pray. Remember what we talked about honey, remember? Nikki's gonna make it alright for you. Relax and pray. I'm here for you honey!"

"You don't understand love," Dwayne cried. "This nigga looks like my . . . my grandpops . . . when . . . my . . . he . . . I . . . when . . . he was broke up in front the building."

Nicole sat silent for a second, understanding her client's pain. Dwayne's life must have become even more nightmarish once he left her at the restaurant, everything happened so fast.

"Honey, remember I'm not like Shell and Patrick right? I believe in the Lord, and you know he knows what's best. Relax, then pray," she repeated. "Relax, and pray," she eventually sounded hypnotic. "Relax, and pray, repeat after me, come on honey. Relax, and pray. Relax, and pray. Relax, and pray. C'mon sweetheart, relax, and pray."

"Relax, and pray. Relax, and pray," Dwayne finally repeated after his counselor and friend.

"Listen to me honey, I'll be by the hospital in the morning. Dwayne, we have to work together. Promise me you'll be there."

"Aiight, bet . . . Bet . . . Okay."

"Promise me!"

"I said bet!"

"Promise!"

"Promise."

"I'll be there, Dwayne. I promise you! Remember relax and pray. Goodnight, honey."

The line went dead, along with the pandemonium

inside the room on the other side of the curtain. The doctors attempted, but could do nothing to revive the elderly patient. Dwayne later found out from one of the nurses that the gentleman had been mugged and beaten to a pulp by a group of young thugs for his social security check. At the sound of his roommate's tragic history, Dwayne demanded his room be switched.

Once settling into his new room, he was still plagued with insomnia. The unknown, familiar voices of the women who conversed about him, and the prevalent, ever-loving voice of his base-pipe, pleading for a hit to ease current tensions drilled him.

Before he could spell c-r-a-c-k, he had run from the hospital to roam the streets for a new victim, to satisfy the infinite need. And as the sun gave light to the streets of East Harlem and the South Bronx, he allowed the gnawing freebasing need to transform itself into rational thoughts of cognizance. Nicole greeted her client sitting on the steps of the closed center, and she held him for the duration of the taxi ride back to North General to check back into the hospital.

At the conclusion of the cab ride, Nicole had fully encouraged Dwayne to trust her thoroughly, and to get much needed thigh surgery for General's bite before the weekend passed. She also advised him to get additional psychiatric counseling for the duration of his hospital stay, to ease the painful trauma of what he witnessed in front of his building on 117th Street.

Wednesday November 12th, 1986: 9:45 AM. Arlene showed love to Jimmy Robinson, his wife Monica, and two of their children while funeral-goers gathered inside and outside the "Anderson Funeral Home" to pay their last respects to Albert Carter: June 27th 1910-November 4th, 1986. Jimmy embraced Arlene and said, "You're a better person than me, I tell ya. God will bless you for what you've done for Mister Slick, taking on the arrangements and all, making sure his aunt came down from the nursing home too; man, sister, you are beautiful."

"Well I promised Gwenny when we were girls that if anything ever happened to her, I'd look out for the family best way I could, and she always said she would do the same for me. This service is for her, Miss Mattie, Ain't Lou, and Baby Al of course."

Arlene felt the icy chill of the Robinsons' aloofness at the sound of Dwayne's timeless nickname. The change in their disposition wasn't to be confused with the coolness of the autumn weather. Arlene felt the need to look past their mood swing. There were many other important issues concerning the Carter family in which she was involved, and she knew her girlfriend would rest in peace if she applied the identical family love they all once shared on 117th Street. Arlene was well prepared for Al's death, having discussed policies and procedures with the old man in the previous year, when he thought his grandson would actually kill him with his bare hands.

During the early seventies, Al set up a trust fund for Dwayne which was worth 15,000 dollars. He also had a policy with Mattie stating that in the event of their deaths, their grandson would be awarded a large sum of money. At the time of Mattie's death, the policy was still void, mentioning that her spouse must also be deceased in order for any beneficiaries to claim money. The policy had practically tripled its value by the mid-eighties. Now, Al and Mattie Carter's sole beneficiary was awarded 87,263.14, ready to be claimed. Al's will stated that another sum of money, equivalent to 16,000 dollars, be split four ways between Arlene, Aunt Louise, Dwayne, and Jimmy Robinson.

The news struck the neighborhood, the tragedy of Al Carter falling over fifty feet to his death, elderly body smashed in the front of the entrance to his building. The neighbors mourned, and some were still confused on how it really happened. A few heard he went to Detroit, some thought he left for South, others heard he was out of state. Some of the tenants claimed to be the victims of repetitive building thefts, believing that thieves broke into the apartment, killed General, robbed Al, and pushed him from his bedroom window. General's cracked skull and lifeless body was later found inside the apartment, practically in the same condition as Al's body after landing in front of the building. Many saw and attested to Dwayne limping up the block before the fall, so no one suspected, or even cared if he had anything to do with Al's death. If he did, sadly, "by-gones were by-gones" as far as they were concerned.

Arlene knew her godson was on drugs and abusing his grandfather all the while, but what could she, or anyone who knew, truly do about the situation? Al continually denied his abuse, always protecting Dwayne from the authorities, out of fear and love. Al's denial of his abuse suffered at the hands of his grandson disgusted most that saw. It was all over now.

By 11 A.M., the filled chapel was mourning the earthly absence of the stern, loving, humorous, gentleman from 117th Street. The neighbors' eyesight beheld a mini photographic collage of Albert Carter, placed next to the head of his gold colored closed casket. The assortment of photos Arlene collected painted the total picture of a man who stood and braved the tests of time, the peaks and valleys of life. He remained in his cooking glory amongst the cold, hard stares from the Caucasian patrons in one timeless portrait circa 1947, many years prior to the senior's fateful rollercoaster ride of life. Another picture showed a healthy, robust, soldier fresh out of World War II with his women on his mind; his aspiring dancing wife Mattie, and their four year old Gwendolyn were at home waiting for him, and thirty-nine years later, his respect paying friends were left behind with these particular memories.

The flowers were at the foot of the casket, different types, neatly arranged. Floral arrangements were sent by everyone from Harten's Barber Shop on Seventh Avenue, to Rutledge's Liquor Store on Lenox, to a sector of relatives from Chicago contacted by Arlene, with cards from the Carter's of Detroit, to a few nurses from the Mary Morton Center, a place of mortal peace Al never got the opportunity to escape to. During the service, different friends and neighbors approached the tiny podium in the chapel to give their fondest memories of Al, and people sang church hymns.

The Robinson family sat in the first pew, with Jimmy grieving heavily for the man that he'd known since his early twenties. Monica rubbed her husband's back while he bawled like a baby. "Slick! Slick, Slick, Slick," Jimmy cried. The moment the funeral attendants opened the casket to view the body, the aura became more tragic. While Al eternally slept, his head appeared much larger in his stilled coldness, and he frowned. One by one the funeral goers viewed their neighbor for the last time; and the chapel slowly but surely became hysterical with the pipes of the organ. There was someone in each pew crying a river of tears for Al. Mary cradled Barbara's head, shaking the woman gently like a mother does their child.

"It's okay baby, it's alright," Mary soothed. Barbara ignored her neighbor, bawling on: "Oh my Al! . . . My neighbor! . . . Been my neighbor since I came to New York! . . . AAAH! HAAAAH!"

Chuck lent a hand to his wife to help with Barbara, happy it was time to leave. One by one, funeral goers sadly moved from the chapel.

Nathan Pope sat in the last pew, crying tears of sorrow for his bedridden wife who suffered from liver cancer, and for his best elderly buddy. A few pews ahead, Mrs. Heather Wallace put her arm around her husband Dr. Tom Wallace

Jr. who was solemn and in gloom. Gerald Ballard was one of many who stood in the aisle, fanning his red-eyed wife Florence, who couldn't stop crying for her neighbor. Joe Rutledge and the Lenox Avenue drunkards stood in silence for a minute in front of the pictures.

Jimmy felt spiritless like the mentor he loved, who was spiritless to the world:

"NNNNOOOOOOOOO!"

"It's okay, son! It's okay!"

"He's dead! Slick! He's DEAD!!
THEY KILLED MARTIN!!*It's*
fucked up down south in Memphis!
Cause of the garbage strike! *Those
crackers killed Martin!* **They killed
Martin Luther King! Those fucking
crackers killed him***!"*

"Slick!! AAAH HAAAH! HUUUUH!! HUUUUH!"

Jimmy bawled at the recollection of Al's comforting him inside the stairway on the job April 4th, 1968.

Arlene sat on the other side of the Robinson's crying her eyes out, next to a very somber Aunt Lou, and her traveling nurse of the day. Lou R. Williams silently wept for her nephew, just one tear making its way down her face. Everyone in her family seemed to make it to heaven, and she was still left behind. Losing her nephew Albert hurt on a next level that she never experienced in her ninety-five years of life. He was indeed the last of her family that she felt could ever care about her existence for her remaining years on the planet. Lou's nurse ensured her well-being through the service, whispering concern off and on.

Arlene was given tissue by others as she cried for the most authoritative man she'd ever known. Recalling her own father walking out on the family when she was very young, with Al, all she could remember was good things brewing from him: Love, discipline, courage. Al Carter was truly the father figure she had ever really known. He was hardworking, family oriented, protective of his family and friends. She would always love "Mister Carter", and she was happy that he finally could join his wife and daughter, although the fall was a bit much. She paused on her tears to look around the chapel, discreetly.

"Where's Baby Al? He should've been here by now! Where is he? He's his grandson, Mister Carter loved him! Oh, Baby Al," Arlene thought, bursting into a new flow of tears. Besides Aunt Lou where was Al's closest living relative?

A few blocks away on Lenox and 123rd, Dwayne was isolated inside of a hallway bathroom inside a brownstone turned cheap motel, vehemently refusing to attend his grandfather's funeral. While trying to reason with his incorrigible friend, Patrick lost his religious guard, and kicked at the door.

"How could you miss your own grandfather's funeral?! . . . Open the door! . . . You make me feel as if I'm dealing with a baby! Open up man! . . . I would never miss my family's funeral . . . Look what I've been through myself! . . . You can sit up in this ol' crummy spot like a little sissy and front on Mister Carter if you want to! . . . He was a great man and I'm not missing my final goodbye!"

He kicked the door three more times while the aged stairway creaked with someone ascending to the floor where Patrick angrily begged. Patrick reached his maximum level of frustration and stated: "Later, man!"

"Chill Pat," Dwayne responded. Patrick was relieved with his buddy's muffled response.

Arriving Nicole was stunning as always, hair neatly done, wearing generously sized bamboo earrings, a gorgeous black tight fitting dress underneath her autumn jacket, with high heeled pumps. Patrick hugged Nicole once she reached the floor.

"I'm glad you're here. He still won't come out of the bathroom."

Dwayne snapped from inside, "Damn money why you sweatin' that?! I'll be out in a minute nigga, you giving me a headache! I said chill! I'm going!"

"Dwayne," Nicole called out.

"What?!"

"Honey, I'm here if you need me."

Silence, then came the next muffled response: "Okay."

Patrick gave Nicole a "high five", and said, "I don't know what you do to him Nikk, but you've got the touch."

"Honey, it's all about his recovery. You don't know how many of my clients' funerals, or funerals and wakes of their family members I've been to recently. It's cool. Not a problem, I just like to help. Make them feel like there's others out there who care, that's all."

Inside the bathroom, Dwayne looked into the mirror and ran his hand across his entire bald scalp. He looked down at the brand new black suit and tie. With new "Stacy Adams" shoes to wear, looking spick and span, he broke into a cold sweat, wanting to sell his whole outfit, fiending for crack once again.

"I gotta fight this shit! . . . I gotta fight this crack shit! . . . I got to!"

He turned on the cold water full force, cupping a handful, splashing his face. "No more Pappy." He took a deep breath, walked from the bathroom with head held high, entering the hotel hallway, ready for comfort at any given time.

Patrick extended his hand for a quick handshake that became a tight hug between friends.

"You can do it, man . . . You can do it Dee, through

the blood of Jesus man. Through his blood, with his love you've got strength. You have strength homeboy. Blessed assurance, Jesus is yours; Jesus is ours," he whispered.

"Thanks, high," Dwayne replied. He let go of Patrick and stared at Nicole. She asked, "You need a hit, don'tcha? You need some crack?"

"Um-hum."

"But you're fighting it though. You fightin' it. You with me right?"

He exhaled and nodded again slowly. She touched his hand coming close to him.

"Cool, honey," she whispered kissing him close to his lips. He began an erection which turned sour the moment he thought of Al's head opened from the back upon the sidewalk.

Luckily, Arlene took care of the apartment situation and talked with a few neighbors from 117th days before the service, and Dwayne wouldn't participate or help with Arlene's plans while hospitalized. He would only deal with the memorial service, and in minutes he would be inside these services for his grandfather, Albert Carter.

"The Lord's with you, Dwayne. I'm with you, Nikki's with you, you'll get through this," Patrick stated. Dwayne nodded, in tears once more, while Nicole brushed his back.

The young adults proceeded out of the motel.

Ten minutes later, after the viewing of Al's body, the funeral was over. Kim and Edward marched their parents out of the chapel into the hallway of the funeral home, where a majority of the other mourners were gathering.

"I'll sit with them, go 'head," motioned Edward noticing his sister. Kim wore her "gotta get a cigarette now" look. "Know what I'm saying," she said, winking at her baby brother. She walked out of the funeral home, digging in her purse for a "Newport" cigarette. She didn't cry, but she was still sad for her parents who thought so highly of

"Mister Slick". Jimmy bent forward with his face covered by his hands, still sniffling, while his wife and son continuously patted his back.

"Dad, you okay?"

Jimmy raised his head, red-eyed, looking at his youngest child with fatherly love, putting his arm around him.

"Thanks son. I appreciate you refusing to go to school today after all. I'm glad everybody came. You don't know what Slick meant to me."

Outside, Kim inhaled and exhaled deeply, blowing her tomboyish smoke rings, watching the infinite traffic of Seventh Avenue. She spotted her god-brother Dwayne exiting a taxi with two friends, heading quickly for the funeral home. She stepped on her burning cigarette, bracing herself to give Dwayne her condolences.

"Baby Al, I'm sorr . . ." ; and Dwayne, Nicole, and Patrick brushed past her, barely noticing anyone, while entering the funeral home.

The Robinsons' eyes immediately locked on the threesome entering the lobby, while inside the chapel, Arlene was the last mourner, wiping her bloodshot eyes, saying her final words to a real man inside a closed casket, her hand touching the top.

"I love you Mister Carter . . . I miss you so much already . . . I still don't even know how . . . I'm a tell Nasha and Dante about ya . . . I'll get Donnell to do it . . . I'll never forget you . . . I promise . . . I swear . . . I'll take care of Baby Al . . . I already forgave him, just like you did so many times . . . I forgave him . . . "

More tears ran down her face, ruining her mascara even more. The funeral attendants observed their watches, beginning to get impatient.

"OPEN IT!"

320

The appearance of Dwayne, spirited by his two friends shocked everyone who were exiting the chapel; and quite a few stopped to return and see the final outcome between grandfather and grandson.

After pleading from Arlene and a few others who insisted Dwayne was the last relative, the attendants opened the casket for Dwayne's final look at the grandfather he mentally plotted to kill, who died on his own. Guarded by Patrick and Nicole, Dwayne stood silently for a minute looking at the body of Al for the final time, until people began to approach him with their consoling words.

"He was a great man."

"You alright Baby Al?"

"We gon' pray for ya."

"He look like he sleep."

"You okay?"

"Trust in God Baby Al."

"Still can't believe it."

"Leave him alone, he's alright."

Arlene touched Dwayne's back and smiled at Nicole. "I'm, Arlene Montgomery. Thank you for making sure he arrived. Mister Carter, he was someone who was . . . he'll be . . . we are really going to miss him in our lives," said Arlene, crying.

Nicole embraced Arlene when that second, Dwayne spun on his heel to quickly exit the chapel followed by Patrick, bypassing the people who were reaching out to them.

"Don't worry sister. Everything is going to be just fine," Nicole said to Arlene. "Here, take my card. If you need absolutely anything, do not hesitate to call me. I'll make sure Dwayne is okay."

Nicole hugged Arlene tighter, then she ushered Arlene back to sit at the side of Aunt Lou and her nurse, while more tears ran down Arlene's hurt face. The funeral attendants reclosed the casket lid, and then prepared to exit the chapel with the cold body of scowling Al. Some of the remaining people helped with the flowers and the picture collection, when suddenly there was a commotion outside of the chapel in the hallway of the funeral home.

"Uh-oh, look like they finna fight out there!"

"That's Baby Al! Now that's a damn shame! Acting up, right at his grandfather funeral?!"

"Oh my God!"

Nicole tried to get through the crowd forming on-lookers as quickly as possible. Seemed like each person she tried to move around, more people got in her way, preventing her from exiting the chapel.

In the lobby, Jimmy and Dwayne were ready to lock horns, separated by Patrick and Edward. Jimmy attacked his godson after recognizing him; and Dwayne was ready as always to throw down, never backing down from a fistfight. Patrick ducked, pushing Dwayne away.

"C'mon Dee man! No time to be riffin', not today man," Patrick pleaded. Nicole made it out of the chapel with the rest of the gawkers; and when she spoke her sexy words of wisdom once catching up, Dwayne seemed to calm down while Jimmy kept harassing him.

"Come on honey, stop. Not on the day of your

granddad's memorial service," Nicole soothed.

"You going straight to hell for beating him," Jimmy yelled.

"Dad! Chill! Cool out man!," Edward tried to control his wild father.

Dwayne retaliated, "Fuck you Jimmy! You hear me?! You black ass fucking spasm! Fuck you, you don't know what you talking about! Check it out, you know what?!"

Dwayne broke free from Patrick and ran to Jimmy, punching the mortified man in the face, knocking him from his feet.

"That's my father! My FATHERRRRRR!," Edward roared, going to punch Dwayne in the eye, catching his brow; and Patrick grabbed the teen in a headlock.

"Damn you Baby Al!," Jimmy spat blood from his mouth, on the carpeted floor of the funeral home. Monica went to intervene, as did Nicole and Kim, an expanding melee.

"Get him outta here!"
"Call the police!"
"Beat his ass!"
"Get off me!"
"Take it to the streets!"
"So what's up!"
"Dad! Mom! Get off!"
"Take it outside!"
"Come on, let's get hot!"

Amidst the small pushing and shoving, Dwayne mushed Monica, grabbed Nicole, forcefully pulling her from the chapel lobby out onto Seventh Avenue, while Kim swung at Dwayne's exiting back. She then quickly went to help her family.

"C'mon! We jettin'!," Dwayne growled, unaffected by Kim's punch to his back; he quickly lead Nicole outside to the street to flag a taxi.

"What about Patrick?! We just can't leav . . ."

"Preacher man'll be cool! We out! If I stay I'm going to jail!"

Nicole quickly removed some tissue from her handbag to wipe a bleeding cut above Dwayne's eyebrow when a cab stopped in front of them. Nicole and Dwayne jumped into the car as people-while standing around-gasped seconds later, the doors of Anderson's bursting open with Patrick and Edward throwing up their hands for their pre-afternoon brawl. There was more pushing and shoving from the suit clad men surrounding them to break up the scuffle, and restore order before the police needed to be involved, and to make way for the casket to be brought out of the chapel to the waiting cemetery bound cars.

"Downtown," Dwayne spat at the driver. He continued wincing from minor pain as his drug counselor lovingly soothed his wound. The taxi carrying Dwayne and Nicole sped off heading south towards Central Park, while the chaotic recessional of Al's memorial simmered down, leaving an unforgettable mental experience for all who attended.

Albert Carter was now becoming just a memory.

****

CHAPTER 13

*

"Come on now Dee, man! Why the super-long face homeboy? It's a blessed day, and it's the holiday season! . . . You think Mister Carter would want you acting like this? You think God wants you moping around like this?"

Dwayne sat upright, beneath thick, quilted bedcovers that Nicole picked out for him; he hissed and ignored Patrick, who stood outside his bedroom inside his new co-op apartment. Grasping his forehead and massaging his temples with his left hand, Dwayne furiously changed television channels with the remote control in his right hand.

"I know it's hard, man, but look, God is good; the power of Lord, man, there is nothing in the world stronger than that," said Patrick unzipping his tan leather "Goose Country" v-back winter coat.

"PAT?"

"Chill, my shoes are out front. And don't get loud," Patrick stated, entering his friend's lavish new bedroom.

Much different than his old bedroom, Dwayne's new quarters was fully equipped in an up-to-date style, with added African sculptures and figurines, 25-inch color television on a stand in front of his king sized waterbed with lighted headboard. You were required to take off your shoes at the door of the suite, due to the expensive, white, shaggy carpeting throughout the co-op. Dwayne's move from Harlem to Irwin Avenue in the Bronx was his first major effort to straightening himself out, and Patrick admired it.

Patrick said, "Look, man, I know it's hard, but don't hold it in. I know I didn't come all the way up here to talk to the wall. You cool?"

Dwayne angrily pressed the "off" button, removing himself from under the bedcovers, sitting on the side of the bed, with his head in his hands.

"Pardon me, gee. Just pardon me, my head is killing me."

"You have aspirin?"

"Yeah."

"Take some. Why sit around with a headache when you can take something."

"Come on Pat man, I been popping Bayers and Tylenols all day! This joint had me in the bed all day, like someone holding me down. I ain't never had one like this, high. Word up! I wish I could trade heads!"

"Is that why you have your blinds closed?"

"Hell yeah! The sunlight killed me today."

The phone started ringing atop one of the nightstands.

Dwayne said, "I know that's Nikki checking up on me. Watch this."

He turned back over and answered, giving Patrick the cue that Nicole was on the other end of the line. Patrick chuckled while Dwayne continued his conversation.

"Yeah . . . It's my crib. I answer the phone the way I feel like answering . . . What? . . . But you ain't no big time supervisor, well I take that back . . . Nobody calling me for a job . . . Yeah, whatever . . . Buzz me back in a few, I got company . . . Patrick . . . Yo high, Nikki says hello."

"Tell her hello."

"Call me back, alright? . . . Yeah I still got it, feels like it's going away a little something though, but . . . Aight . . . I'll do that . . . Call me in a few. I'm a take some more and fix some tea now, promise . . . Cool . . . bye."

"What's up with you two, she's your girl now," asked

Patrick.

Dwayne hung up the phone, and went into the bathroom, located inside his bedroom. "I need some Motrin, high. I need 'em bad."

Patrick could hear Dwayne fish around his medicine cabinet, desperate for pain reliever. The headaches he received daily were beyond the migraine stage.

"You didn't answer my question," Patrick yelled out.

"What?! About me and Nikki?!"

Dwayne returned into the bedroom.

Patrick nodded, "Um-hum."

"Yo, what's my name high?! You know I knocked the boots already, had the freak climbing the walls!"

"I think you should take that freak word back."

"Why cause she your girl's cousin? Man so what!"

"Hold up, *rewind*, my fiance's cousin."

"Fiance?! But you just met that chick!"

"Oops wrong! I've known Michelle for years high. She was my sister Cindy's friend from school. She was an angel even then, but we were too busy in the world. She stuck with me through everything. Kept in touch with me when I went back home too. So I didn't just meet her, and I'm blessed to still have her in my life. Glory and thanks be to The Almighty God."

Dwayne hissed hoping that Patrick wouldn't begin another Jesus speech, sitting on the edge of his bed.

"Man, you are lucky that the folks who care about you are covered with the blood of Jesus, and that our Father in heaven loves you enough, to place a young lady, not freak- not chick, like Nicole in your life. Here you have a sister, who has gone above and beyond for you. She helped you find this co-op; she helped you start a bank account, so you can save your money, put her job on the line for you; she buys you things, helped you furnish and decorate this whole crib, you name it and she has done it for you. She totally sticks her neck out for you while you're recovering; she stuck with you after your surgery because General attacked you, and she even got you some new gear to wear. Fly at that! You can't front Dee, we had a great time with her family Thanksgiving over in Jersey, and no matter what my girl thinks, or what I think, or what you say, I know that she is encouraging you in the Lord. And to be right with God is the most important thing for all of us."

"Yeah, yeah, kid. Whatever. Yo, you want something to eat, drink man?"

Patrick followed Dwayne from his bedroom into the luxurious front quarters of his new one bedroom, one and a half bathroom suite. The tropical fish inside Dwayne's thirty-gallon aquarium jumped when the young men walked past. The fish tank was next to a small bookcase against the wall in between the hallway restroom and the co-op door. The large living room stared back at Patrick: the marbled coffee table with end tables for the crystal lamps, a couple of iron crystal chandeliers for the ceiling, ten foot black leather couch, two love seats and recliner chair all purchased from various "Seaman's Furniture" showrooms, plus the angelic white wall-to-wall carpeting, and a humongous stereo rack system. The Sanyo stereo was equipped with two three-feet speakers & two five-feet speakers, featuring a turntable, dual cassette decks and the latest in musical technology: a compact disc player.

Patrick sat on a loveseat and turned on the new floor model television, which was up against the long wall, next to the recliner, other love seat, and stereo. The chairs were placed directly across from the coffee table, second loveseat and sofa; and the sofa was located against the short wall that separated the living room from the walk-through kitchen; and next to the kitchen was the dining room table with four chairs, near the door leading to a terrace decorated with flashing holiday lights, designed inside and outside of its railing.

"How you holding up man," Patrick asked, admiring

Dwayne's tastefully decorated pine Christmas tree, also near the terrace door.

Inside the kitchen, while heating a kettle Dwayne responded, "A little something high. I'm still fighting the you know what. You know, big "C". That ain't so easy, but I'm doing it. Nikk helps a lot. Yo, you want some tea?"

"I'll take some, thanks. So Dee, who helped you with the tree? There's a whole heap of presents down there."

"You know who helped me high."

"Don't tell me Nicole. Word?"

"Yeah man!"

"Wow, you two are really hitting it off. That, is amazing!"

"Man, I told you I be boning her!"

Patrick chuckled, shaking his head.

Dwayne asked, "Why don't you and Michelle come by on New Year's Eve, bring the New Year in with me and Nikki."

"Shell and I will be in church man. You and Nikki should be with us. What are you going to do here?"

Dwayne threw a hiss, entering the living room, with empty tea cups and saucers giving one to Patrick.

He said, "Man, what you think we gon' do here? I got some Moet, and I got a dope slow jam tape with that hot new Shirley Murdock, that other new chick Anita Baker. I got stupid Luther, stupid Freddie, man when that ball drops downtown, my ball's gon' be dropping uptown!"

Patrick shook his head and said, "I know you need Jesus!"

"Word up, high! When that ball drop saying nineteen eighty-seven, Nikki gon' scream EIGHTY seven!"

Patrick said, "Get behind me Satan!"

"It's not me, it's thee. Get behind thee Satan," Dwayne said, challenging Patrick's statement.

"It's me!"

"Thee!"

329

"Me!"

"Thee!"

"Yo Dee, how are you going to tell me, of all people?! Go get my tea chump! H'ear de waatuh ah boil nuh?"

"Oh now you Jamaican all of a sudden?!"

The two friends laughed for the rest of the afternoon while sipping tea, playing music, and video games on the television.

A few evenings later, Dwayne was laid across the couch conversing over the phone, proceeding to light a cigarette.

"You sure Arlene? You sure you ain't mad? I ain't been no angel," he said, into the telephone.

"I'm sure, Baby Al," Arlene began on her end. "I mean, no one is perfect. And I tell you, I sure did want to get your behind locked up a couple of times when you was smoking that stuff. Yeah I was ready to kill you myself. I thought it would take me a long time to get over the things that I've seen you do with my own eyes . . . Couldn't believe how Gwenny's son, my godbaby had turned out, but, there is such a thing called forgiveness, and again like I said, no one is perfect . . . You've been through a lot and it's never been easy. Seventeenth was never easy, even when me and your mama was coming up."

"Tell me more, Arlene! Tell me more about my moms. Man, now I wish Pappy was here to tell me the scoop. I should have listened when I had the chance man; and I don't know enough about that Arnold Mucci character either. My pops, damn! Tell me Arlene, tell me about Gwenny!"

"Child . . . I'm not even the one to tell you about what went down with your daddy, and truth be told Baby Al, there's not much I will say about your mama over the phone," Arlene said, then took a deep breath and continued, "I will say, that, she was very close to me. She was a very special and dear friend; you know we grew up together. She was a girl I'll never forget. But listen, you have my word, we'll get together soon in person and I'll tell you all about it, everything you need to know, okay?"

Dwayne grinned, wishing he knew his mother, and on the other end tears welled in Arlene's eyes at the brief mention of her best childhood girlfriend. She immediately assumed her "godmotherly" questions.

"Well, how's your new place?"

"It's cool. Maybe you can come by, you and the kids, for Christmas dinner."

"You cooking now, Baby Al?"

"A little something. Really, my girl does most of it. I don't think you met her. Her name's Nicole."

"I've met her before."

"You did? Oh, word up! When we did Pappy's arrangements."

"Now wait a minute boy. You mean when I made the arrangements."

Dwayne chuckled and said, "Okay Arlene. You got that one."

"She's the counselor over in Milbrook Projects, right? Near Milbrook I think. Yes I do know Nicole."

"Yeah. She really been looking out."

"We've met before . . . and we have talked a few times. She gave me her business card. She has my number too . . . How's that problem working out?"

"Fine . . . I'll never touch another drug. At times it gets kinda hard. But after Pappy died, and I was in the hospital, I knew I had to leave the drugs alone. Nikki helps me a lot."

"I'm sure she does . . . I like her. She's okay, and I appreciate her caring for your well-being . . . I still think that she may be a little concerned about your money though Baby Al. I know she has done quite a bit to help you, but you just be careful too. Be careful with all that spending you doing with her, and on her, you hear me? Mister Carter fixed it for you to live right after he passed, and you need to be thinking positive, and finding ways to save and flip that money the way you supposed to. I know you have feelings for this girl; she's a very smart, educated young lady. I dig her, but, she has asked about your finances a bit much for my taste. Look like she got her hands all in it too; and I'm not tripping. I'm a woman, and I know what time it is. I'm a just cold let you know what I'm thinking. Again just be careful while you're starting over uptown, hear me?

"Yes."

"And another thing, as soon as possible, I think you need to get in touch with Mister Jimmy Robinson and apologize. You definitely owe him an apology for what went down at the funeral. I know you don't want to hear it, but I have to tell you my feelings."

"But he started beefing with me Arlene! He got dumb loud when I was trying to leave with Nikki and Pat. He said I was going to hell for beati . . ."

"Forgiveness! Forgiveness, forgiveness, forgiveness, the need to forgive! I don't care what he said! He was upset about Mister Carter dying, just like all of us, and he loved your grandfather very much. AND YOU! AND he is your godfather, and has done plenty for you in your life! Call him and apologize!"

"I guess so."

"Boy you a fool! That man OWNS Hamburger Headquarters! Are you kidding me? We just got back not long ago from seeing Donnell's mama down south, and HHQ is up and down ninety-five! Many a drive through, many a state! Look, let me know when you need the number. It is the fair and respectful thing to do Baby Al. He is your godfather, not your enemy."

"You right."

"Good. Well, maybe I'll drop by for a visit next week. I imagine your place is nice."

"I wish I lived higher up. You can see all over the

Bronx up there. I live on the second floor."

"Have you spoke to the nurses upstate?"

"Oh, Ain't Lou? No doubt, I'm getting some wheels next week, so maybe I'll go and check her out. Make sure she's still holding on."

"Wheels?! A car Baby Al?"

His call waiting system line beeped in.

"Hold on for a minute, let me see who that is . . . Yo?"

"Dwayne! Honey, it's me! Nicole!"

"You on a pay phone?"

"Yes."

"Hold on." He clicked back over to Arlene. "That's Nikki now. She's on a pay phone, so I'm 'a talk to her. You need me to call you back? You need anything?"

"No, no, that's okay. Get over to your other line, Baby Al. I'll call you next week. Thanks for the Christmas cards, the kids liked them. Did you get the one I sent?"

"I did. So, I'll call you in a week. Happy holidays."

"Goodnight," Arlene said, hanging up her end. She entered her living room and plopped down next to her nine-year-old Dante, who also sat on the couch playing his tabletop version of Ms. Pac-Man. Without losing an intelligent beat or looking up, Dante asked, "Who was on the phone?"

"Baby Al," replied Arlene. Dante sucked his teeth, a response Arlene had expected.

"What did he want?"

"He just wanted to talk baby, that's all. It's Christmas time. He probably misses Mister Carter," Arlene said, rubbing the bright youngster's back. He instantly stopped playing his game and sat it down on the glass table, and looked at his mother in her eyes.

"I miss Grandpa too. He's gone because Baby Al was mean to him."

"What do you mean sweetheart?"

"I don't like him, Mommy! He was real mean to us, us

and Grandpa. He's mean Mommy! And God took my Grandpa away, and he didn't even hurt nobody!"

Arlene hugged her son tightly and kissed the crown of his kinky haired head, hoping she could smooth the boy's ruffled feathers. She often had to use the same tactics for his father and Dante was growing into a true rebel, a mere carbon copy; yet at times when deeply moved, he displayed her own sensitivity.

Arlene began patiently, "Dante honey . . . sometimes in life . . . we do things out of anger . . . out of hurt . . . we really don't mean to do bad things. We have bad moods, but we don't really mean it . . . Later on, we're sorry for the bad things we do, so we apologize, understand?"

Dante nodded.

"Baby Al has done some bad things in his life, a lot of bad things, a whole lot of bad things, but he will change his ways, and make up for the mistakes he's done. He's doing it now."

"But, Mommy, he made Grandpa cry, and his crazy dog almost bit me! He made all of us cry, even you was scared."

"I know honey, but Baby Al is changing. He's becoming an older man, and I don't think he'll be acting that way anymore. He's sorry for what he's done, he even invited us over."

"Nope," Dante stated, standing emphatically, "Mommy, Baby Al is still mean, and boy is he going to get it! I bet he still uses the words you don't want me and Nasha to say, and he's gonna be crazy his whole life for the mean things he did to Grandpa. I don't ever want to see him. He act like he a crackhead!"

Arlene was astonished with Dante's last statement; how could he know about drugs? Especially when she presided over her children with protection, love, and discipline.

"How do you know about crack?"

Dante answered, "Mommy, everybody knows about crack in the projects! I always see 'em around my school, the crackheads. They don't mess with me though, cause I'll kick 'em where it hurts."
He picked up his game and left their living room.

Arlene thought, "These kids are something else. They too smart for me. I need to talk to them schoolteachers and that principal. What my baby doing seeing some nasty old crackheads hanging around the school, when he's going for an education."

Meanwhile, back at Dwayne's, he finished off his quick conversation with Nicole, who promised more "good news" in person. Lighting another cigarette, he re-propped himself into the recliner, dozing off minutes later.

"Don't just stand there! Get dressed!"

"Ain't gon'e be no graduation if ya' go on with this mess! I'm gettin' old man! I can't take it!"

"Pappy!"

"This my house boy! Hear? It's been my house since nineteen thirty-eight and what I say go!"

"Look Baby Al, I'm over here!"

"Boy, I'm so proud of you. Oh and sorry 'bout this morning but you can't drink out the frigidaire like that, you know that right?"

"So, Pappy, you proud of me huh?"

*"Heck yeah! Baby Al, you real smart
and I know you gon' make it."*

*"Baby Al, I said look!
Damn it, I'm here!"*

*"How did my mother
die?! Huh?!*

"I'm here motherfucker!"

*"You killed her! You destroy
everything you touch! Damn it,
Baby Al! you **killed my
daughter! You killed her
when you was born!**"*

Dwayne jumped inside his dozing daze, recounting the first punch he gave his grandfather, knocking him down the steps; and Al tumbled, tumbled, and tumbled, welts, bruises, and droplets of blood forming. He spun faster, and faster, and faster, until he regurgitated his teeth, brains, with other internal organs, spitting his blood filled liver in Dwayne's face; and drenched Dwayne jumped from sleep at the sound of the downstairs buzzer, almost falling to his shaggy floor, yet bringing him to reality.

"Damn! . . . Goddamn . . . That scared me," he mumbled, panting until he calmed down. He stood up and answered the intercom.

"Yo?"

"It's me, honey!," Nicole yelled from the lobby, and he buzzed her into the building. Seconds later, she rushed in, excited with good news.

"Dwayne! . . . Dwayne! Guess what? Great news! I need you to fill out this application for Transi . . ."

Her sentence was cut short by her client picking her up, planting his lips against hers, kissing her, tonguing her, wanting her, needing her, swinging her around slowly, romantically. Dwayne had totally fallen for Nicole, his first real experience of beginning to love from deep within his soul. He admired her for the way she carried herself, and he loved her for the things she did for him and for others; Nicole had him, hook, line, and sinker.

He passionately kissed her further, carrying her over the threshold through his living room, sitting her slowly on the couch, preparing for an evening of lovemaking. Carefully undoing her blouse and bra, he sucked on her neck and breasts while removing her pumps, with a French kissing dance of circles to her navel, back to tiny pecks all over her face. Moments later, the young adults were naked, engrossed in the making of steamy, sensual love right in front of the Christmas tree with blinking lights, presents beneath, and themselves writhing and riding the physical wavecrests of dual orgasms.

She rested against his chest while they sat in a bubble bath, listening to slow music after Dwayne set one of his three-foot speakers from his stereo, with two candles inside the bathroom. With the music he ran a bar of soap over her body, slowly over and in between every curve with one hand, while with his other, he ran his fingers through her shoulder length hair. She intermittently hummed, and sang Whitney Houston's "You Give Good Love" laying against her newest lover's chest, in his arms watching the shadows and silhouettes of themselves with the flickering candlelight.

They listened to more slow jams, whispering, touching, licking. Although one could cut their sensuality with a knife, Nicole's orgasmic waves eventually became pondering thoughts, scrambled with contrition. What would her co-workers think if they knew she was dating a client, let alone sleeping with him? Did they know? It wasn't the first time she had considered someone who was bouncing back from hardship, only this time she had gone all the way, and this time with a patient from her job.

So quickly and unexpectedly, she had gone from preventing murder as a favor to her cousin's boyfriend, to helping locate and furnish new residences; plus she was helping to manage a new checking & savings account of a drug addicted thug who should be supported as her client only. Dwayne should not have ascended to the level of Thanksgiving dinner guest, to break bread with her family; then again, the God-fearing relationship between Patrick and Michelle provided the buffer, and added more glue to a speeding direction of a blinding love affair she too, was truly beginning to get into. Dwayne was strong, impulsive, sexy, not her average client; and Nicole hoped in this case her "client" would be able to move ahead and leave drugs alone forever, so their union could possibly be forever. Helping out people in need turned her on beyond belief, and she needed everyone to be totally comfortable with her, no matter how much education she possessed. She knew in her heart Dwayne needed a chance, and she was determined to give him much more.

Then again, what would the Ryerson clan think if they knew she was sleeping with an ex-crackhead? The whole family usually criticized Nicole for wanting what they felt was the wrong kind of guy, and they secretly hated her association with "the around the way common folks"; she knew she deliberately defied them this time. Nicole observed a few remarks and raised eyebrows from family members at Thanksgiving dinner; and she answered nearly all of the questions meant for Dwayne about his future goals and education. She did her best to prevent the family from knowing that Dwayne was actually a client. Instead her dinner guest was "just a friend from the Bronx originally from Harlem, who owned his own co-op". They would never approve of Dwayne as her boyfriend, and at this point, as a young woman almost in her late twenties, she knew she didn't care; only her feelings mattered. His past was tragically marred and troubled for sure, but things change and people change. Dwayne Carter was not broke financially; he had some money. He possessed enough wealth to maintain his own co-op apartment, car, and still have cash in the bank accounts she helped him with. If he continued to do the right thing, their money could grow in unison more and more; they would stay together no matter what. Her heart would remain for his welfare, as his woman, friend, and counselor, with no turning back.

"I can't believe I'm here with you," said Nicole.

"This is where you wanna be right?," asked Dwayne.

Nicole added, "Of course. I think I'm falling in love with you, Dwayne. I've always been attracted to you, but I don't know what you've done to me."

He gave his girl a small peck on the cheek, hissed and said, "Oh baby, I know what I did to you. You know what time it is."

"I sure do."

"You like my dope crib right?"

"Um-hum."

"It's the place to be love. No more rats, no more roaches. It's clean, I love it. The neighborhood is dumb quiet. And I thank you, baby."

"I should have tried to find you something closer to me in Co-op. I want you closer to me and my job. So I can check up on you. It is okay around here though. It really is quiet on this side."

He made a humorous attempt at singing, making her laugh. He chuckled, asking, "Yo, why you laughing?! Ain't it romantic when a guy sings to his girl? You can't sing no better!"

"Listen Dwayne, sweetheart you are no Ready For The World!"

"You right! They rock a S curl. I rock a baldie."

"A sexy bald head too, but boobie, you sound like a frog! But you can love me down though." Nicole then sang the rest of her favorite tune in a beautiful second soprano, making Dwayne's heart melt.

They engaged in more foreplay, eventually standing to let the suds drip from their bodies, focusing on their dripping body parts. Making love under the shower was imminent, with loads of oral sex for both. Their guiding candlelight began wasting away as the young lovers came to life. They made love in every area of the suite for the rest of the night.

"Boobie . . . Oh, boobie . . . Psssst! Hey," Nicole whispered in Dwayne's ear, hours later. He slept on heavily, snoring a little. She thought her insatiable desires would be curbed, and she giggled after Dwayne wouldn't budge. She gave him a huge kiss on his cheek and turned over on her side under the covers. She plotted to carnally seize more love at sunrise, the best time for some, the best time for many. Nicole drifted off to sleep while beads of sweat formed on Dwayne's forehead, awakening him. He removed the quilt halfway, and lay with his eyes open. His eyelids rapidly gained weight, and he began to dream.

> *"I'm 'a get ya ass! I'm a get ya ass!*
> *Word up! We all gon' get ya ass!*
> *We dead 'cause of you, Dee man!*
> *We ain't gon' rest 'til your ass is*
> *dead like all of us!"*

The familiar voice of the young man Dwayne heard in his sleep continued to taunt:

> *"Yeah! Sleep on punk! Yeah*
> *uptown pussy! You gon' get*
> *yours! Word to my living Moms!*

You a sucker! Always a sucker!
Always will be a sucker!"

"GRRRRRRRR! GRRRRRRR! GRRRRRRRR!!
GRRRRRRR!"

"You think you chilling now?
Wait a few faggot!"

"GRRRRRRRR! GRRRRRRRRRRR!"

The known dreamy voice changed to a low, dog's growl; and everything went black with a deafening gunshot!

Dwayne awakened again, cold sweat. The sun was moving into visual existence, and the bird groups were already belting their tunes.

"Damn, what the fuck," he huffed. A brand new headache, a million times worse than a migraine's intensity, arrived. "Whew! Where and the hell is this one coming from?" The dog growling resumed with his head pounding, lobes churning, bringing him to tears.

He staggered his way into the bathroom, activating the light.

'GRRRRRRRRRRRRRRRRRRR!'

"Damn, where the growling coming from? Why my head hurting like this?"

'GRRRRRRRR! GRRRRRRR! . . . GRRRRRR'

He knocked some toiletries out of the medicine cabinet until he found a prescribed bottle of eight hundred-milligram Motrin, with one tablet left.

'GRRRRRRRRRRRRRRRRRRRRRRRRRRRRRR'

He quickly flipped the bottle cap, popped the pill, and stuck his head under the sink to wash it down. Then he splashed some cold water on his face, standing up to gaze into the mirror.

'GRRRRRRRRR . . .GRRRRRRRRRRRRRR!'

"Where is this dog? And where in the fuck is that growl coming from?"

He walked out of the bathroom, through the bedroom, past the hallway restroom, to unlock the door. It was imperative for him to meet the mysterious canine that constantly growled outside of his suite.

'GRRRRRRRRRRRRRRRRRRRRRRRR!'

Dwayne opened the door and the growling ceased, with the headache stopping also. He stood in the hallway in front of his suite looking in both directions, and then he re-entered his place.

"Damn, I'm bugging," he said, closing the door. "Man, I'm going to sleep, I don't know what the hell is going on," he chuckled, creeping back into the bed to snuggle up next to Nicole.

Less than an hour later, Nicole cradled Dwayne's head while he cried out, rocking him as if she gave birth to him.

"It's okay. Boobie, don't worry. Boobie, Nikki's here. You don't need no more crack, no more crack baby. You understand me! Dwayne, YOU WILL FIGHT!"

She spoke firm as she could, patterning her job routine; she had to be strong for him, to help him overcome this addiction. With every positive response from Nicole came a negative reaction from Dwayne. Shaking his head like a spoiled child, the 21-year-old crack fiend whined, cried, blowing mucous bubbles from his nose.

"I need it . . . I need it, Nikki, please baby, please love . . . I need that shit . . . It fucking got me man! . . . It got me," Dwayne sniffled, "You don't know, Nicole . . . Word up! . . . You don't understand, know what I'm saying . . . tell this pipe shut the fuck up! . . . I don't have it no more and it keep following me . . . just a hit love that's all, so it can stop calling me . . . it will make this headache go away too . . . It keep fucking wit' me! This pipe is calling meee, get that fucking pipe to stop calling meee . . . I need to smoke for this headache! . . . just a little hit, just a little pull . . . it ain't gon' hurt . . . I won't be back hooked cause of one hit . . . I won't be hooked!"

She continued rocking him in bed, never letting him out of her warm grasp, thinking, "Damn, how I'm 'a tell him about the job I hooked him up with, if he freaking like this?"

With her many connections in society, Nicole pulled strings and landed Dwayne a railroad clerk's job with the New York City Transit Authority. She would get with her connections and postpone his starting date. Dwayne was still sick, in his case similar to heroin, and he needed her constant expertise.

Time marched on into the New Year. Patrick and Michelle became man and wife, exchanging wedding vows on Valentine's Day. The families of the bride and groom grinned, smiled, but secretly abhorred the idea of their union. Patrick's relatives disliked Michelle shortly after her amplification in his life upon his return to the United States. They thought of her as too bossy and governing; and sadly, the Ryerson's detested the fact that Patrick was still recognized from his family's massacre a year and a half prior. Regardless of how their families felt, Patrick and his girl tied the knot at their church with eighty guests, on a freezing wintery Saturday. Patrick's family threatened total absence if Dwayne was present, so Dwayne's invitation was null and void. In his heart, Patrick wanted Dwayne as his best man, especially since Michelle had Nicole as her maid of honor. It was a choice between Dwayne attending or the Livingston family attending, in which Patrick chose the latter.

In spite of Dwayne's anger at being barred from Patrick and Michelle's nuptials, his union with Nicole continued to grow, and love seemed to conquer all. She moved up the ladder to the coordinator of affairs position at the rehab center, and he reported regularly yet discreetly for his check-ups. A few months had passed since he held a freebasing pipe or laid eyes on a crack vial. Dwayne's weight increased by twenty pounds, giving him the most solid look he had in years; he felt good to be off the drug and eating properly.

Shortly after his twenty-second birthday, he started his job as a railroad clerk on the day tour, working his shift duties from eight o'clock in the morning until four o'clock in the afternoon, right before the rush hour. After purchasing a two door red 1987 BMW 325i Cabriolet convertible with black leather top and interior directly from the showroom, along with the furnishings and other expenses of the co-op, Dwayne needed a job; and he loved Nicole for helping attain work. Punching a clock, instead of laying around at home was absolutely breathtaking for him. He didn't even question her connections this time. With Nicole in his life permanently, his current possessions, and 10,000 leftover in the bank, Dwayne's life was on an upswing, for good.

True positivity emerges from the ugliest of negative situations; and for every ounce of positivity one is blessed with, a huge chunk of negativity is headed their way, speeding toward its destination.

Dwayne and Nicole enjoyed the beauty of their ascension for the remainder of spring into the summer's dawn. The young lovers simply painted the town red. She even deserted her quaint sanctuary in the Co-Op City section of the Bronx and spent the last portion of her vacation helping him decorate his co-op further. There was decreased family time with the Ryersons in New Jersey, and increased time at Dwayne's place, with no verbal turbulence from her parents. She was surprised they never questioned, although the entire Ryerson family knew "Nikki's secret", via Michelle Livingston. All family questions, concerns, gripes, and complaints were routed to her answering machine at home, barely checked because she was never there.

One summer afternoon at his apartment, when Dwayne called from work, Nicole requested that he bring home some "syrup for her ice cream". She giggled, thinking of Dwayne's aggressive sexual appetite, and she prayed he would be up to par after dealing with subway patrons for eight hours. While Channel 7's Eyewitness News blared through the living room, draped in her sexiest "Victoria's Secret" lingerie, Nicole began to worry; it was close to seven o'clock, and Dwayne usually reached home by six. She threw on her floor length, lavender satin robe while slurping on a spoonful of Haagen Dazs' butter pecan ice cream, and she waltzed onto the terrace. She could faintly hear the elevated Broadway train line rattling blocks over in the distance, beyond the songs of the birds. The humid wind blew her hair while she looked over the terrace railing, hoping to see the BMW come slowly sailing down Irwin Avenue.

"I hope nothing happened," she thought, returning inside the air-conditioned suite to watch the rest of the news. She heard some keys jingle, locks turn. Dwayne pushed the door open and slammed it. Nicole jumped from the recliner, relieved at his arrival, but concerned about his peculiar acting entrance.

She asked, "Boobie, what's wrong? What happened? Did you get the syrup?"

She walked towards him while he angrily took his shoes off.

"Do it look like I got some syrup, Nikki?! I forgot the damn syrup!," Dwayne shouted; then he stormed from the living room.

Nicole followed her boyfriend into the bedroom. Dwayne was sprawled across his bed on his stomach in his Transit Authority uniform, resembling a blue suited, disgruntled ship, sailing troubled waters. Nicole came over and rubbed her hands on Dwayne's back, then climbed on top of him, and she mashed her face next to his.

"What happened honey? Let's talk about it, okay," she said, easy.

"Let me turn over love," he replied.

Dwayne turned on his back, and Nicole snuggled into his arms, the last fitting piece to an enigmatic puzzle. Holding her tightly, he stared at the ceiling, with a new headache setting in.

"Dwayne, let's talk about it."

The headache arrived and was worsening by the second, making Dwayne feel like someone was trying to slit a hole through his crown and remove his brains. After a few deep breaths, eyebrows permanently connected, speaking listlessly he said, "I just saw this dude snatch an old lady's bag . . . slam her to the ground . . . and run."

"Oh no! Did she get hurt real bad? Did someone call the police? Jesus! So then, what happened?"

"I chased him down and caught him love."

"That's good! So why are you upset honey? You did a good deed." She gave him a peck on his cheek then his lips; and Dwayne gazed into her eyes.

"I ain't no different, baby," he said, "A year ago I was

doing the same thing . . . It never leaves you. Nikki, it never leaves . . . There's always something there to remind me I was a crackhead . . . The wicked stuff I've done ain't gonna never leave me . . . I ain't no different than any other crackhead."

She kissed him on the cheek again, and he returned an intense French kiss, then squirming because of the torturous head pain.

"What's the matter honey? Another headache," Nicole asked, gently rubbing his temples.

"I keep telling you, these bad boys ain't no headaches I had before. They unreal! And Motrin not doing jack shit for me! Listen, you know I love you right?"

"Yes."

"Yes, word to mutha, do know that I love you, and the whole nine, but I need to be left alone right now."

Trying to bypass an attitude, Nicole gave her last peck of the evening to his forehead. She went for a large glass of grape Kool-Aid, hoping that it would do some good. Once she returned, Dwayne was sound asleep. She placed the glass on the dresser and left the bedroom for a hot shower, thinking of her wonderful evening turned sour.

"My baby feeling bad now because of some ol' crummy thief. He'll be alright," she thought, while the room steamed itself to sauna proportions.

The next morning, Nicole slowly came to her senses with Dwayne's playful voice in her ear; she opened her eyes, nostrils filling with the aroma of breakfast close by.

"C'mon sleeping beauty, wake up . . . Wake up sleeping beauty . . . I love you baby . . . Get up sleeping beauty," Dwayne whispered. He prepared a giant bed tray of pancakes, eggs, bacon, with glasses of milk and O.J.

"Oh wow, Boobie, breakfast in bed, what did I do to deserve this honey?," Nicole murmured, coming to life.

"I figured since you wouldn't let me knock the boots

last night, I would mak . . ."

"Excuse me, mister headache himself? Headache, remember?"

She sat herself up, wiping her eyes, happily staring at the food.

"I want to brush my teeth, honey, can I?," Nicole whined.

"Go ahead, cause ya breath is most definitely kicking," Dwayne teased.

"WHAT?! Don't even try it negro, cause you sure did try kissing me just now!"

She moved out from under the bed tray to go to the bathroom, throwing one of the pillows at him. "That's too much food for me anyway!"

Nicole entered the bathroom while Dwayne, fully dressed with a shirt, slacks, and tie, lay back on the bed. He toyed with the remote control flipping television channels, his favorite hobby.

"I didn't hear you get up! . . . Where are you going so dressed up? You're dressed nice for once, instead of like a hoodlum!"

"I'm going downtown to check out E-zo! I'm a show him how I'm chilling!"

"E-zo?!," asked Nicole, while brushing her teeth, yelling over the running faucet.

"Yeah! My man from back in the days, Eric Martinez! . . . His moms is giving him a party cause he leaving for the service, so me and Patrick going, downtown around the old way!"

"Wow! Becoming a serviceman is a major step, in the right direction! My dad was in the Air Force, and I have other family who served the country! Just enjoy the party! Be nice, and be careful honey!"

"Feel like that headache trying to come back! I couldn't even sleep last night love! My head was killing me all night!"

Nicole re-entered the bedroom, fresh and ready for breakfast in bed. She said, "Well, you could've fooled me. Right after my shower you were fast asleep."

"I thought that headache was really going to take me outta here. Here, let me help you," he said, moving the tray back so she could slip under the covers.

After saying grace, she began eating.

"Hmmm . . . not bad. Not bad at all. The food gets better and better."

"Pardon me for not getting you up earlier. I know it's back to the center on Monday. So I figured my baby should get to sleep long as she wants."

"Awwww, thank you honey. You so sweet."

"You know what time it is."

Nicole finished half of the meal, and Dwayne removed the dishes and tray, carrying them out of the bedroom to the dishwasher.

"Nikki," Dwayne yelled from the kitchen.

"Yes honey?!"

"Do you know the people next door, you ever seen 'em?!"

"No! Why?!"

Dwayne returned to the bedroom, and kissed his girl.

"Cause, I know you be hearing the dog."

"Dog? What dog?"

"What'cha mean what dog? The motherfucker growled all night. Every night! How can you sleep through that?"

"Boobie, come on now. That's all you hear, is dogs barking around here, all day, all night. It's okay really. You have a lot of private homes around here. You're on the second floor; now if you lived higher up, you wouldn't hear them."

"No this dog is dumb loud, growling, and barking and shit. It was right here in this bedroom last night. That's how close. You had to hear it. Not the dogs outside in people backyard, no this dog is inside this room Nicole."

"I didn't hear a dog. Definitely didn't hear it while I was sleeping. They may have a dog next door. I'll find out, then again, why am I getting all into it? I don't live here," she said with sarcasm.

He lovingly stared into her eyes.

"Baby, you know I want you here for good. I love you. All you gotta do is say the word, you know that."

Nicole smiled, her heart at ease. Dwayne said, "You here twenty four seven anyway. I been wanted you to stay. Will you stay here with me, Nikki?"

She giggled, and then she shrugged her shoulders.

"Maybe."

"Stay."

"Maybe."

"But you know I need the hottest chick in New York with me right now. Promise me. Don't you want to stay here with me baby?"

"A little something, something."

"But I fixes you breakfast in bed though Nikk."

"Yeah, I guess I could get used to getting breakfast in bed. Just don't change that big daddy."

Dwayne winked at her, and puckered his lips; and she winked back, puckering her lips for a smooch.

"Oh, and don't forget to do me that solid," Dwayne said.

"What?"

"The neighbors. You know you crazy friendly, and I might come out my face. Just find out who that kid was cursing all night too. Bet? And don't forget to find out what type of dog they have over there. Okay?"

"Okay, my sexy bald headed man."

He winked again, she winked back. He retrieved his shoes from the bedroom closet with his suit jacket. Then he leaned down to her and they again kissed passionately, making their evening promises. He stood from the bed, and was out the door, ready for his day, and she was turning underneath the bedcovers, anticipating his evening's arrival.

****

CHAPTER 14

*

Just when she thought she was having a horrible day at the office, a large bouquet of long stemmed red roses was delivered to Nicole in a beautiful arrangement. She created a space for her floral guests on top of her desk. While the deliveryman admired her search for a vase, after finding one, she signed for the flowers. The frustration of the center's short staffed day was whisked away by the lovely aroma of the flowers as she sniffed, noticing a small card inside the gift that read: "IN EXACTLY TWO MINUTES, THE LOVE OF YOUR LIFE WILL ENTER THE ROOM."

Three minutes later, wearing a silk Gucci short set with matching Gucci shades, Dwayne entered the room flaunting a wrapped gift inside a shopping bag. He walked over to Nicole while she stood hunched over the flowers.

"Dwayne, you didn't have to do this," she said, with a cheerful look on her face.

"You like 'em?"

"What do you think," she playfully spat. The deliveryman exited after he was tipped by Dwayne.

"How did you get up here past the guard?"

"They know me, it wasn't hard. I told them I was sending the flowers. Me and the delivery man met at the same time. I planned it that way."

"Why aren't you at work today?"

"I called out sick. The doctor couldn't find nothing on them headaches neither."

"Why?"

"I don't know. You asking me?"

Nicole sucked her teeth, giving a "yeah, right" head gesture. She stood to file away some folders. While she had her back turned, Dwayne took the opportunity to sneak up behind and grab her lovingly.

"What, you . . . what are you doing, Dwayne?"

He knew she couldn't resist his masculine charm that much. He couldn't resist her deep femininity either. It wasn't a day that passed, where he would miss thinking about her.

"I brought you this," he said extending the gift. She opened the bag to find an identical silk outfit, matching his.

"You like that right? Always a Dapper Dan fan baby," Dwayne said, sticking his tongue inside her ear.

"Look, Dwayne, you can't be acting like this, not in my office. Not while I'm on the job. Somebody might come in!"

The door opened and in came one of the receptionists.

"Nikki, I'm sorry, but you have a client downstairs for Taylor that insists he's on her schedule for today. I told him we're closed for the day."

Dwayne backed off Nicole. "Send them up, it's okay, I'll handle it," Nicole said, embarrassed. The receptionist left.

"See what I mean, now's not the time. I'm busy today. We hardly have any staff. It's Wednesday," Nicole whined.

"But you're an assistant supervisor; I thought you was a big shot?! What you doing having clients," asked Dwayne.

Nicole sucked her teeth. "My how we forget! No matter how big time I get, Mister Dwayne Albert Carter, I'm still for my people. And I am coordinator of affairs, sir! I beg your pardon, of all the nerve. If you needed help, I'd help you. I did help you!"

"Man, fuck this," Dwayne mumbled, and he snatched Nicole into his arms, kissing her hungrily. She responded to his advances, participating in the tongue fight for close to two minutes. Their kiss was cut short by some knocks on the door.

"It's three-forty-seven, love. Why don't you jet from this joint and hang with me for the rest of the day," he said passionately.

"I don't know, I just don't know about that, I ca . . ."

Someone knocked on the door again.

"Just a minute," Nicole yelled. "Look, Dwayne, I'm busy! You have to leave!"

Intensifying the embrace, his crotch to hers, he stared her eye-to-eye. "Yo, I'm not leaving until you tell me you're spending the rest of the day with me."

"Dwayne," whined Nicole.

Dwayne insisted, "Tell me you love me, tell me you don't want me."

"Honey, I do, but . . ." Someone banged on the door hard this time.

"Look, okay. Okay! We can do this; oh, you make me so sick! Wait for me outside, I'll be out in fifteen minutes!"

Nicole was angry with herself, being unable to resist his charm.

"Bet! I'll be outside," Dwayne smiled, ecstatic. Nicole shook her head, and Dwayne quietly pulled the door shut after Nicole's client entered.

They rode in the convertible, leather drop-top down, and found a legitimate lot for parking; and then, walked City Island Avenue in the City Island section near Pelham Bay. Dwayne and Nicole admired and took in the sights of the nostalgic fishing village, home to a host of fishermen, their families, seafood restaurants, and romantic eateries. Hand in hand they strolled, ironing out their differences, squaring away petty insecurities, planning on an even brighter future for their lives together with the sunset.

With Dwayne leading the way, the young lovers

approached and entered one of the many marinas. The plan was an evening sail for two on a yacht through the waters of Orchard Beach out into Long Island Sound. With the appearance of the moon inside a starlit sky with different shaped clouds, they continued pouring their hearts out to one another; and Dwayne was full of more surprises, and love games. He pulled a note from his pocket, balled it up and put it into Nicole's palms; the note instructed her to close her eyes. Once her eyes were closed, Dwayne reached into his other pocket and pulled out a diamond ring.

"Keep your eyes closed love, and give me your hand."

Nicole giggled, extending her right hand.

"Gimme the other one," he laughed.

"How was I supposed to know, I didn't know!"

On the ring finger of her left hand, Dwayne perfectly slid on a three-thousand dollar two-karat diamond ring.

"Can I open my eyes now," she asked, bursting with excitement.

"Go ahead."

Tears rushed to Nicole's widened eyes as she stared at her wondrous engagement ring. She covered her gaping mouth with her other hand, overwhelmed with joy.

"You like it baby?"

"Like it, oh Dwayne, I love it so much," she said, beginning to cry.

All she could do was reach out and hug her lover, embracing him tightly.

"I did it because I love you and I wanna be with you, forever," Dwayne said.

They kissed, to seal their commitment; and Dwayne asked, "You accept my engagement? Huh? You love me? You gon' marry me love?"

"Yes! And I'm moving in! To stay! And I'll love ya forever! And ever! And ever! Yes," she shouted in his face.

They indulged in another hungry kiss, and she playfully stopped cold. Nicole paused a second and gave her lover a sly grin.

"Okay, Mister Carter, I might have to change my mind though. Ummm, I think we, can get married, possibly, maybe . . . maybe on one condition," she stated.

"What? Now what's your condition," he laughed.

"Please, let's change that living room around. It's busted! Wack! It's tacky honey!"

Dwayne laughed along with his girl. "We will. You can count on it, love," he said planting a smooch on Nicole's lips. The star crossed lovers gave the signal for their captain to return to the marina; they were in love, ready for love, but hungry for seafood.

Two smitten months quickly passed since Dwayne and Nicole's official engagement. Nicole rented her co-op to her younger sister Nefertiti as she spent her days and nights permanently on Irwin Avenue with Dwayne. With the exception of Nefertiti, the rest of the Ryerson family chided Nicole the moment she left her home to reside with one of her "street clients". At the center, she was the subject of many gossip flavored conversations. She abhorred her family and co-worker's beliefs and viewpoints about her relationship with Dwayne. All of the gossiping brought them even closer together.

In spite of their domestic merriment, continual days and nights of fiery sex, with the total curtailment of his drug usage, the headaches and voices continued; and Dwayne was reluctant to include Nicole in on his issues, seeking counseling at his nearby hospital emergency room even. He refused to be admitted in order to receive the proper x-rays and cat scans for further investigative treatment. Then, the level came when he could hide no more.

One night while massaging each other in front of the blaring floor model television, Dwayne fell asleep at Nicole's side.

"And this is my posse! Let's give 'em a hand! . . . Aw come on

now! Y'all can do better than that!," Arsenio Hall commanded his studio audience, and Nicole nudged her snoring man, sucking her teeth.

"Wake up! Why are you so sleepy all of a sudden?"

Nicole waited until the commercial before she tapped Dwayne when he sat straight up like a jack in the box, yelling, "What the fuck was that?! What the . . . Yo . . . What the fuck . . . Yo, you said something?!"

Nicole quickly turned on the lamp. "You okay, honey?"

Dwayne began to groan, rubbing his temples.

"No, I'm not okay . . . Baby, it's my head . . . my head, Nicole. It's too much man. I got a headache that's killing me. I feel like the train is running over my brains. My head is the fucking third rail and the train track! I don't know what's up," he said listlessly.

"Maybe you should see a doctor honey. Let me take you to the hospital, boobie. I'll wait with you. Didn't you tell me once that your grandmother used to have a lot of headaches?"

Angrily cupping his forehead, Dwayne hissed, "And didn't I fucking tell you the goddamned one train is running over my head?! Why twenty fucking questions Nicole? I been to the motherfucking doctor a billion times already! They can't find shit! They never find nothing! They didn't find nothing at North General, and they can't find shit up here! And I'm not going to keep letting them quack motherfuckers tell me a bunch of bullshit, stick they fingers up my ass and experiment on me!"

He instantaneously sprang from the couch and went for his shoes, hissing further.

"I'm outtie like Curt Gowdy! I need some air . . . I'm sorry for yelling sweetheart," he said, before opening and closing the door to the suite.

Nicole didn't bat an eyelash, the winded scenario happened so fast. It was if a foreign force changed his personality and snatched him from the apartment.

Hours later in bed, Dwayne burst into one of his night sweats.

"WOOF! WOOF! WOOF!"

"General, come here boy!"

"Sic 'em! Fuck 'im up!"

"Grrrrrrr! Grrrrrrr!
Grrrr! Woof! Woof! Woof!
Woof! Woooo! **Grrrr!**
Woof!"

Dwayne sat up in the darkened bedroom alone, panting heavily; and Al looked directly at him, bleeding from his gums, with a toothless smile. His right eye was missing from the socket with his projected brains dripping down his face onto his bloodstained lumberjack shirt. Dwayne froze, cowering under his bed sheets, exposing his eyes only when Al jumped on top of him.

"Aaaaaaaah! Aaaaaah! Pappy, get the fuck off meeee! Nikki!," Dwayne subliminally screamed.

His yelps and moans caused Nicole to awaken, always prepared for a screaming attack. Nicole usually felt that she could rescue and elevate Dwayne in his time of need, mental or physical. In the beginning, her omnipresence in his life seemed to be treasured, and she believed through her discipline, love, and diligence, the relationship with Dwayne would always grow. Things were suddenly changing.

Nicole touched her lover's forehead in the dark, while Dwayne moaned and groaned, louder and louder. His added sound effects made her overly concerned; there was more sniffling, there were gurgling noises, there were the louder cries, and the extreme dampness of his pillow worried her. She jumped out of bed in search of a wet towel for his forehead. When she returned to the bedroom, she turned on the lamp, and shrieked at the sight of teary-eyed Dwayne, reddened face mashed against the smeared pillowcase, nostrils pouring blood.

"OH MY GOD! **Boobie!**," Nicole screeched, panicking. She ran for some extra towels, and when she returned, she covered his nose and sat him on the edge of the bed. He crouched over with his face in his hands, spitting, with blood bubbles coming from his nose.

He asked, "What time is it?," while Nicole continued rubbing his back.

"Honey, it's almost three. Dwayne, baby, why are you hurting like this?"

Nicole kept her arm around Dwayne, squeezing him tightly with all the love and patience that reluctantly remained in her heart. Dwayne himself was mentally transported back to his childhood on 117th Street, and to his grandmother Mattie. At times like this, Nicole's love and tolerance reminded him of Mattie, rocking him after one of many spoiled tantrums as a child.

"Honey, I don't understand why your doctor couldn't find anything wrong. I'm calling an ambulance; you'll be at Montefiore in no time," Nicole said.

"No. Hell no Nikki! It was just a dream that's all."

"A dream?!"

"And I'm not sitting up in no hospital emergency room all night again. My grandfather just broke my nose in a dream, that's all . . . and it turned stupid real. Ain't no thang!"

"Stupid real?! Look at your pillow! Look how you've been bleeding! Look at the blood on my hands Dwayne! You need a real doctor!"

"I'm NOT GOING!"

"Fine!"

Nicole sucked her teeth and left her bloody lover in search of new bed linen, and to wash his blood from her palms. After cleaning up and returning to the bedroom, she observed him for more bleeding and his routine accompanying beads of sweat. With no blood in sight, she was relieved, but still concerned and angry. Minutes of bewilderment passed while the young lovers stared at each other. After relieving himself, Dwayne returned to bed; and Nicole questioned herself, until she drifted off to sleep.

Their backs were glued until dawn for the first time.

A few nights later, Nicole drove the BMW slowly and silently while Dwayne rode the passenger side after a light grocery shopping. Each time he asked her a question, she turned up the volume of Public Enemy's "Rebel Without A Pause", and when he stopped talking, she decreased the volume. The couple left turned the corner of 236th and Irwin, and then hooked a right, sailing into their parking space at the co-op apartments where they resided. She continued to playfully ignore Dwayne, laughing to herself because she knew disregarding his questions drove him up the wall.

"Oh! So you ain't talking to me now, huh?"

"Hmmmmmmm! Hmmmmmmm! Hmmmmmmm!"

"So you wanna keep ignoring me now?!"

"Terminator X! Rock the Wwwooooooh! Terminator….!"

"Why you buggin', Nicole? See if I ignore you, you catch an attitude. Alright, I'm a remember this bullshit! Watch!"

Nicole walked ahead of Dwayne, entering the building and elevator before him, but waited for Dwayne with the key in the suite's door. She said, "Oh! So now you're mad?! You've been snapping at me a lot lately, and it is not too cute Mister! Like I'm supposed to keep getting yelled at, and keep getting dissed because you are having unexplainable headaches! I tell you, I'm upset about what happened to Scott La Rock, isn't it horrible? You tell me, I don't know shit about hip-hop! I just ask you a simple question in the store, like what do you want Jif or Skippy, and you bite my head off! . . . Boobie, you keep ignoring what the doctors tell you to do at the hospital. You ignore everything I tell you to do when it comes to those crazy headaches. Dwayne, all I can do, is love you, kiss you, and try, really try, to make you feel better. Look, would you like try some Midol instead, for the pain?"

"Midol?!," Dwayne exclaimed. They laughed together for the first time in weeks, pushing open the co-op door. Nicole flicked on the lights of the suite, and the couple looked around perplexed. The entire living room was rearranged completely.

The couch was changed from the short wall in front of the walkthrough kitchen to the long wall. The floor model television had been changed from the long wall to the short wall. The two love seats were facing the apartment door, sitting below the windowsill near the terrace door. The recliner sat alone in a catty position near the couch. The marble coffee table still sat in front of the couch while the marbled end tables with crystal lamps sat on both sides of the couch, as always.

"Okay! I get it. I truly get it you! Now, this living room is fly," Nicole said, admiringly.

"Yo! Now, YOU REALLY buggin' the fuck out," Dwayne snapped, his malevolent tone whisking Nicole from her daydream.

"What? I like it. I like it baby. The living room is nice now."

"I know that! You ain't have to go all out without telling me!"

Nicole took on a look of confusion, while Dwayne hissed, "Now you got amnesia right? If you wanted to change stuff around, you coulda let me know. You know how you get with your surprises."

Nicole was befuddled; things were not adding up for her. What was Dwayne talking about? Why did he yell at her for changing the furniture around, when she didn't do it? She was thinking he rearranged the room to her liking as a surprise.

"This living room looks nice for a change, and I didn't change no furniture!," she answered aggravatingly, revved for a first argument.

Dwayne said, "So who changed it?! Shit just don't move by itself, Nikki! You buggin'!"

"I'm telling you I didn't do it, Dwayne! Are you sure you didn't do it?"

"Yo love, check this out, I'm going to bed. Forget this. You need to let me know when you gon' just start touching my shit, and switching it around! And put the groceries up!"

Dwayne left the living room, and left his girl staring at their bags of groceries on the white carpet. A spooky feeling came over Nicole as she held out her hand, looking at her gorgeous two-karat diamond engagement ring with question. Weird things were happening, and she loathed the fact that her tabooed excitement and euphoria was rapidly dissolving. With her birthday weekend steadily approaching inside the emergence of autumn, Nicole convinced herself that Dwayne must have surprised her, and granted her wishes for a better, more sensibly arranged living room. She remembered how the living room looked before they left for the supermarket and compared it to the present arrangement.

Nicole thought, "Guess he's right about questioning one thing, how can furniture move by itself? . . . It just doesn't sound right . . . he had to change it around, it's impossible for Dwayne to think it was me . . . when would I have time for that . . . he just doesn't want to admit it . . . but he had to move the furniture around . . . he just had to .

. . he probably had Patrick or some other guys he know come over and do it while we were gone. Like the story he told me about surprising his grandfather with a new bedroom set, back when he sold drugs."

She took one last look at the remodeled living room, shaking her head, giggling; and in the bathroom, getting undressed Dwayne was in deep thought, seriously thinking.

"Damn! How the furniture move around like that?! . . . Nikki love playing games . . . why she can't just come out and say she moved my shit around without telling me . . . she better not had no dudes up in my crib moving my shit around . . . she couldn't move all that stuff in one day by herself, let alone two damn hours! Who and the hell was in my house when we went out?! . . .. Damn! . . . Women! . . . Swear they gotta run shit . . . Can't live with 'em, and can't live without 'em."

He hissed, then grinned while turning on the water, leaving the doors open for his lady to eventually join him inside the shower as usual.

Subway trains roared through the 49th Street/7th Avenue station, uptown, downtown, on express and local tracks. Subway patrons hustled and bustled about, as the station crowded with more rush hour folk. Tokens were dropped every three seconds or less, turnstiles spinning infinitely with people entering and exiting the New York City subway system.

"So how ya like them Giants, Carter man," Dwayne's older relief asked, while they prepared their end of shift changeover inside the railroad clerk's booth.

"Tonight?! I bet you they get taxed by them 49ers, slayed by San Fran," Dwayne exclaimed, helping with the tally of subway tokens.

"You have a point about that young brother."

"Yeah man! I'm glad that little strike they had is over. It didn't last. That's making them dumb hungry now, and they been busting chops this season anyway. Them 49ers been ready to go off at the drop of a dime. They strictly taxin'!"

Dwayne loved rooting for any of the football teams, ecstatic about the game on TV after a brief players strike. Nicole was fixing dinner for their invited guests Patrick and Michelle. Patrick happened to be a Jet fan, so he and Dwayne usually kept a whole heap of noise rooting against one another, Giants versus Jets, versus any team.

Dwayne put his walkman headphones on his ears, staring out at the hustle and bustle of the subway riders.

"Carter, we running short on ten packs ain't we?"

"Yup," Dwayne replied, digging into his Benetton carry case for his "RED ALERT" mix audio tape, mistakenly dropping it on the floor.

"Damn man, you nervous 'bout that game tonight?"

"Hell no! What I say man? We want our New York team to get busy true indeed, but look at how San Francisco been coming off though?! They doing damage tonight homeboy."

He crouched down to pick up the tape.

"Sir, we have no more ten packs of tokens, so I'll count these out for you," he heard his co-worker say to a patron.

Dwayne stood and went into a frightened shock because of the patron, eyes opening wide, mouth gaping. He dropped his whole Sony cassette walkman this time, its door breaking off with the batteries and cassette tape sprawled all over the token booth floor. His co-worker's transaction went over his head, while Dwayne froze in complete horror! His dead grandfather Al Carter stood in front of the booth, purchasing tokens for an afternoon subway ride.

Al slipped a twenty-dollar bill under the thick plastic partition for his fare. Dwayne stared incredulously, while the other clerk shelled out ten admitting tokens. Unlike the battered, terrified Al, this Al looked radiant. He was powerful, strong, cunning, without his spectacles. His hair was cut into a small white afro. He wore a familiar looking church suit with a fall trench coat. With his favorite derby cocked to the side, Al also carried a briefcase with an umbrella. Dwayne couldn't believe his eyes. The grandfather that he physically abused was alive, and a customer riding the New York City subway.

"Damn Carter! Man, you'd better hope that thing works after a fall like that," the other clerk said.

"Thank you Mister," Al said, once he received his ten tokens and change. He winked at his grandson and walked away to catch his train.

"No! It can't be," thought Dwayne, hyper. "It just can't be! Pappy is dead! I saw him dead! What the fuck is he doing riding the double "R" train uptown?! Nah, NO! **It can't be!**"

Leaving his walkman and all of his belongings behind, Dwayne left the token booth door open stupefied, looking to follow Al. He had to see where his grandfather was going.

"Hey, Carter! You're leaving your stuff! What happened, man?! You seen a ghost or something?! . . . Later on then, coulda closed the door."

"Hell yeah . . . I did," Dwayne mumbled, going through the exit gate. Looking ahead on the platform at various ages and genders, he tried to locate Al amidst the many trench coats worn by traveling businessmen. He felt a large gust of wind, and a local train whisked into the station, headed the same direction Dwayne trailed his grandfather.

"There go Pappy! I'm 'a talk to him; fuck that! How and the hell did he come back alive? I know I'm not crazy!"

Dwayne walked quickly to catch up to Al who was blending into the multi-racial crowd of waiting passengers.

"**Pappy**!," Dwayne yelled.

Al ignored him, waiting for the crowd of exiting patrons to pass before boarding the train. He entered the crowded subway car, while his frantic grandchild bumped, tripped, and pushed his way up into the end of same car he boarded.

"NEXT STOP WILL BE FIFTY-SEVENTH STREET! WATCH THE CLOSING DOORS," the conductor announced. The chime bell sounded, and the doors closed; the train proceeded out of the station.

Dwayne continued moving through the packed subway car as quickly as possible to catch up. Al stood calmly at the opposite end, blending into the visual scheme of passengers who were sitting, standing, and holding onto poles and steel straphangers, swaying with every natural bump of the train.

"Where did he go?! I know I seen Pappy get on this train," Dwayne thought reaching the end of the car. He then searched his way back midway in the opposite direction. Looking back and forth, he proceeded back to the other end where Al originally boarded, looking around, and anxiously back towards the other end. No Al.

"Where is Pappy, I saw him get on this train!"

Dwayne walked to the door leading to the other subway cars, checked, and it was locked.

"Pappy got in this car! Where did he go?! This door is locked, and he's nowhere on the train! Where is he, what's up?!"

"So, a duppy is a dead person?"

"Nah maan it's like a ghost."

"A spirit like."

"Yo y'all, I'm going to get my jeep.

Y'all bugging out."

Snapping out of his daydream, Dwayne exited the train at the next station to return one stop back to his place of duty to retrieve his belongings. He fixed his walkman, bidding farewell to his co-worker for the final, more coherent time and headed home. Climbing out of the subway to the packed streets of Times Square, he returned his headphones back to his ears.

'Milk is chilling! Gizmo's chillin'! What more can I . . . !'

Dwayne lip-synched and bobbed his head to the thumping hip-hop beats trying to shake off what he visually experienced while crossing Seventh Avenue. He headed towards the parking lot for his ride.

Hours later, Dwayne laughed repetitiously at his dining room table. The "awesome foursome" enjoyed a meal of oxtail, peas and rice, with a salad. Reluctant Michelle squirmed amidst the clique. She could barely digest her meal around the worldly profanity. Patrick and Nicole shook their heads, baffled by Dwayne's nervous antics.

"Word up! **I got to be seeing shit! And hearing shit!** Pappy asked for a ten pack! **Word to God it was him!**"

"I hear ya man," chuckled Patrick, shaking his head.

"Ain't my boobie crazy, Shell?," Nicole giggled. She was breathing easier now that Dwayne's headaches and nosebleeds had ceased. They continued their meal while the football game roared from the television set.

A week and a half later, Dwayne and Nicole double dated with her sister Nefertiti and her boyfriend Corey, going out for cocktails, and a night of dancing far from the Bronx.

They grooved the night away at Club Zanzibar on the crowded dance floor, and as the club became more crowded, the couples mistakenly separated. Tired of dancing, Dwayne and Nicole found a spot to cuddle and smooch, nursing their drinks; Nicole had her favorite Strawberry Daiquiri, and Dwayne drank a double shot of gin with soda.

Nicole held her drink for a half an hour, while her man returned to the bar twice. Although she hated to make a scene, Nicole cringed at the thought of being the designated driver. She didn't want Nefertiti to see Dwayne in an inebriated state of mind. Nefertiti was another black sheep in the family, and she took a liking acceptance to Dwayne only because of her older sister, and Nicole wanted to keep it that way. Dwayne's sauntering trips back to the bar soon became staggering returns, and soon he was red with intoxication.

On his fifth return with another double shot of gin and soda, Nicole took his glass away. He snatched the glass back with a look that would make the strongest weak with fear.

"Please give me the car keys!," she yelled sternly, over the loud music.

"No!"

"Dwayne, you've had enough!"

"How the fuck you know what's enough for me?! You a fucking psychic?"

"Stop cursing at me!"

"So mind your business!"

She watched him gulp down his entire drink within seconds. A year ago, when he was a struggling crackhead, her presence was influential. Now, it seemed as if her touch meant nothing to Dwayne; it was like her love was taken for granted.

"Boobie, please! Please don't drink anymore! Promise me!"

"I'm not into promises!"

"What?!"

"You heard me!"

"Boobie! You're drunk! I wish I didn't have to leave you, but I can't hold it another second; I need to go to the ladies room!"

"So go! Bye!"

Nicole quickly moved away with mixed emotions while Dwayne hissed, and stumbled back towards the bar, mumbling, "Fuck that, I'm drinking!"

Dwayne drank two more double shots of gin with soda. Things were hazy and his speech was slurred until finally he glued his forehead to the edge of the bar counter.

After time lapsed, he mumbled, "Yo, where my fucking girl at?!"

He lifted his three-hundred pound muddled head, and left the barstool to look for Nicole. The mission became much more difficult than expected. Dancing couples multiplied, becoming swaying silhouettes of six, and the dark setting complete with booming music and flashing lights, mixed with mist, developed a persona of its own. Dwayne bumped into different clubgoers, yet managed to make a path for himself, stopping to regurgitate, splashing his suede "Bally" shoes and matching shirt; he still crept about the club on special assignment.

"Watch it man!"

"Pardon me duke!"

"Yo!"

"Excuse me!"

"Girl look at him!"

"He just threw up!"

"Yo money! Watch where you going!"

"ILLLL, he stink!"

He made it to the restroom area and spotted Nicole chatting away with a well-suited male. Dwayne was livid, extra furious. No wonder she took so long to return to him; she wanted to rap to other guys. He was ready to kill when he saw three more guys come up, stand around Nicole, and she kissed every one sensuously on the cheek.

Dwayne heatedly thought, "I can't go nowhere with this bitch! . . . Look at her! I'm tired of this shit!"

When Nicole pointed to her engagement ring, one of the guys said a word and the rest laughed. With Nicole included on the joke, Dwayne flipped. He stumbled towards Nicole and her friends. Dwayne got in Nicole's face, yelling at the top of his lungs, and her friends came to her defense, forming a circle around the couple; thus a scene was created.

"Who this Nikki? Huh! Who the fuck are they!"
"Yo, money!"
"Get the fuck away from my girl!"
"Nikki, who this clown?"
"Clown?! I'll beat yo' motherfuckin' ass!"
"Yo this nigga drunk! You know he don't want none!"
"So what's up?!"
"C'mon! Punk motherfucker!"

The arguments died down after the club security got involved. Dwayne and Nicole were escorted to another area, and he vomited onto the carpet of the discotheque a second time. Nicole's friends laughed while the other clubbers turned up their noses.

Nicole shouted, "I told you to stop drinking! Those were friends from my job and guys I knew from school!

Why did you embarrass me? How are you supposed to drive us home?! What about Nef and Corey?"

"Bitch suck my dick! And fuck Nef and Corey! Everywhere we go, you always in a motherfucker's face!"

"Don't be calling me no bitch! You crazy?! Cursing at me?! You're not hardly my father!"

Dwayne wiped his mouth with the back of his hand, inhaled deeply, and smacked Nicole, knocking one of her bamboo earrings out; and she gasped in shock, pain, and embarrassment. The first, stunning slap from her man would surely lead to more violence she started thinking, with tears rising then spilling from her eyes.

"You don't never raise ya motherfucking voice to me! You supposed to be going to take a piss! Taking all goddamn night! Then I see you playing the wall with five niggas around you like a fucking trick bitch!"

The droplets of hurt and humiliation streamed down Nicole's face ruining her makeup; a welt formed against her cheek. She wished she could disappear for a few minutes while everyone near the couple stared at them, expecting more of a scene. Some of the women frowned, giggled, shook their heads in disgust, and the men shook their heads also, but no one intervened. She turned back to her inebriated lover, whose shirt was wet with vomit and eyes red with eyebrows connecting.

"I want your shit out my fucking crib tonight," he shouted. With his last words, Dwayne tried to walk a straight line away from sobbing Nicole, leaving her, Nefertiti, and Corey stranded at the club without a ride.

A forty minute late night car ride on the freeway became an hour and fifteen minutes. Dwayne made it back to Irwin Avenue from deep in the heart of Newark amazingly without crashing his car, parking the ride catty-cornered, missing the space.

"*Jim Browskeeee! . . . That's what . . . it is . . . got to get . . . it!*

. . . Got . . . got to . . . into you . . . yoooouuuu . . . Jim Browski . . . Jim . . . badder than the . . . badder . . . baddest rope ch . . . baddest rope chain . . . Word up! . . . Word up! . . . Word up," he mumbled, staggering with hiccups, first stopping, then walking as straight as possible while bypassing some exiting neighbors, before entering the high rise. Leaving a lake of vomit on the elevator floor, he took a few more toddler steps to his front door, fumbling with keys in hand, he entered his place.

"Home sweet home," Dwayne thought closing the door, locking the top and bottom locks. Deciding to put the chain on, he suddenly heard some heavy breathing, other than his own. He froze in his tracks, turning slowly to face his intruder. He caught a glimpse of gray hair, a familiar flannel shirt, with some gray trousers.

Dwayne spun around, shut on the chandelier lights, and standing in front of him was Al, with his fists clenched. Dwayne's mouth gaped in horror, seeing his grandfather once again, and this time, Al was in his apartment! He began to have his doubts about seeing him in the subway; and now, he realized that he did see his grandfather, but how could he be alive? How did he get inside the co-op? Where did he come from? Al was supposed to be dead, how did he return? The once battered senior citizen stood in the middle of Dwayne's living room, gazing directly at him. He wore his last outfit after Dwayne sold his clothes for crack. Without his glasses, he stared at his grandson, exhaling angrily.

Al creeped towards Dwayne; and he frantically thought, "Oh shit, here he comes! . . . Does he talk?! . . . I wonder if he talks . . . But Pappy's dead! . . . He was broke up in front of the building . . . Is he gonna say anything?!"

"Who the hell say you can stay out so goddamn late, boy?!," Al yelled, voice bellowing with coarse venom, sounding much more evil and stronger than his grandson ever heard.

"Oh shit! He talks," Dwayne thought backing up slowly, until he was up against his apartment door. Al came closer, repeating his question with strict malevolence.

"Answer me! Goddamn it, answer me! Where were ya! You don't listen! Who say you can stay out so goddamn late?!"

Al smacked Dwayne then backslapped him in one swiping motion. Then he grabbed Dwayne's entire face and mushed his head forcefully against the door, breaking the peephole and doorbell.

"You gon' learn motherfucker," Al yelled, scooping up his grandchild's entire body in a suplex, slamming him to the floor. Dwayne lay dazed on the carpet, suffering from pain and visual confusion. Before Dwayne could part his lips to speak, Al jumped on him, banging his head against the floor until he was unconscious.

"What goes around, comes around," Al shouted prophetically, once his attack was finished.

Sunday, 2:37 p.m.: the next day. Dwayne finally regained his senses. For most of his life, he was oblivious to the hopeless feeling of being attacked, until now. His body hurt all over. His head, back, rib cage, along with his legs, were in agonizing pain. His face felt extra heavy for some reason. He took some hard blows from Al-which blew his mind-with his head and face pounding in discomfort. Too strange to be true, too crazy to be true. Al was dead for a year, how could he come back and beat up someone? There were no such things as ghosts, or were there? His subliminal pandemonium returned with vengeful additions. The dog growls jumped around in his mind, and now there were several voices:

"Ha! Ha! Your punk ass got fucked up!"

"Ya seen that last night, Mama?! Ya

seen what happened?!"

*"Oh honey! I saw it! But why so bad?!
That ain't like my sugar dumpling!"*

*"Mama! Look at all he's done! Do you
think he deserved it?!"*

"Not like that, honey!"

*"Yeah he do! Good for that sorry,
uptown punk motherfucker!"*

Using all his strength, Dwayne picked his face up from the floor, flipping himself onto his back. From the corner of his eye, he could see the wide space of dried blood that continually leaked from his mouth through the night. He crawled to the recliner and used it to stand on wobbly legs as he glanced at his surroundings.

Slowly and methodically, he limped his way from the living room, past the aquarium and library into the hallway restroom. Dwayne looked in the mirror and was shocked with the reflection of a face that was completely disfigured, assuming the look of a defeated boxer. His left eye was swollen, blackened, and bloodshot. His right eye was swollen. Along his forehead were welts and lumps. His lips doubled their original size, split open with dried blood. He touched his enormously distended lips, attempting to open his mouth, giving him excruciating pain. Tears welled in his eyes when he noticed his two front teeth were knocked out, incisors gone with wobbly, reversed canines remaining.

Dwayne mumbled, "My teeth . . . they're gone . . . How? . . . How did this happen? . . . It's impossible . . . Pappy's dead."

He exited, stopping short overhearing someone putting a key in the top lock, then the bottom lock. He watched the door open, but bounce back shut because of the chain lock.

"Dwayne! . . . Dwayne," Nicole shouted from the hallway, banging hard on the door. He was relieved hearing Nicole's voice, after thinking Al was returning to beat him up again.

"It just can't be! Pappy is dead! I couldn't't've been that drunk yesterday," thought Dwayne with increasing head pain.

Nicole kicked the door, sounding furious like never before.

"Dwayne! . . . Dwayne! . . . You in there?! . . . **Open the door! Now!**"

"Alright," he mumbled as loud as he could, removing the chain. Nicole burst inside with two suitcases setting them down, removing her pumps. She quickly walked past Dwayne stating, "I just came to pack! It's cool! You want my shit out?! You've got it!"

Dwayne peeked into the building hallway. Outside his door with looks to kill were Nefertiti, Corey, and his brother Antoine joining Nicole for back up. She talked them out of running up into the suite and killing Dwayne; only if he violated her again, they would have permission. Antoine drove them over, escorting the distraught young adults the same way like when they were stranded at the club by Dwayne.

After being smacked and humiliated, Nicole decided to leave her man. Dwayne was acting loony, moody, and Nicole knew she exceeded her call of duty as his woman. She had totally cleaned up his act for him, and a slap to the face was the thanks she received. For Nicole, this was indeed the last straw. They needed time apart. If Dwayne was unable to handle their separation, that was his problem. He kicked his drug habit and remained clean in record time, but he was slipping suddenly, and it wasn't good.

Dwayne walked and sat on the couch, with his face in

his hands. Fifteen minutes later, Nicole had her bags packed and was standing at the door, passing her bags out into the hallway.

"Where you going Nikk man," Dwayne mumbled, face still covered.

"Outta here! Nerve!! You fucking bastard! Who do you take me for?! You think I'm one of these stunt skeezers from the street that you're used to dealing with?! How dare you, after all I've done for you!"

She threw her house keys into the den and reached down to put back on her shoes. She paused, after noticing the large bloodstain that ruined the shaggy white carpet where the keys landed; and she noticed something red and white resembling a tooth yanked from its root, in the center of the stain. Coming closer, near the stain's borderline, she observed another tooth and Dwayne's route paved dirty footsteps, prints she never thought she would see because of the suite's "shoe rule". Nicole asked, "What happened to the carpet?"

Dwayne removed his hands from his face, making Nicole gasp.

"What happened to your face?"

She quickly removed her shoes a second time, and rushed over to her bruised lover. She sat next to him, touching his wounded face gently like she would, argument or not. Dwayne flinched in total discomfort from Nicole's touch.

"Oh my God, Dwayne, what happened," asked Nicole.

"Somebody . . . somebody in the apartment," Dwayne painfully responded.

"Someone broke in the apartment?!"

"I think it's the same person who switched our stuff around Nikk."

"Huh?!"

Outside of the suite, Nicole's entourage began questioning her whereabouts. Corey and Nefertiti were still very angry that Dwayne abandoned them at the club the previous night; and Antoine stayed ready to pounce because of his very own undying crush on Nicole.

"I wonder what she's doing, her bags is out here, all the stuff is packed," said Nefertiti.

Antoine shrugged his shoulders and Corey spoke up.

"Tell her it's time go! What she gotta say to that lame ass nigga?!"

Nefertiti walked up to Dwayne's door and peeked inside. "Come on, Nikki," she shouted.

"I'll be right out, Nef. Just hold on," Nicole replied, doing a one minute gesture.

Her favorite sister sucked her teeth and walked from the suite. "You know she's sitting in there with him?!"

"Nah! You lying," Corey exclaimed. Antoine laughed, shaking his head.

"My sister so damn stupid! Always been! Nicole Maria with tons of book sense, but common sense, zip-a-dee-do-DUH! Now I see what Mommy and Nadia mean. He should slap her ass again!"

Meanwhile inside the suite, Nicole called the police, then Michelle, who in turn contacted her husband who was visiting his grandmother in Harlem. Once Nicole made her calls, she gave an announcement to her backup crew, sticking her head out into the hallway.

"I'm coming, there's been an accident. Gimme a few minutes."

"What accident?! Look like he got his ass kicked before we did it," Nefertiti snapped.

"Okay, I'll be out! Don't leave without me, I just have a few more things to say to him."

"How long, damn! You shoulda been ready, girl!"

"You'll be okay," asked Antoine. Nicole nodded and smiled partially. She said, "Just take my things down to the car, please."

"We going to Mickey D's, cause I want some fries. Hurry up! Just be careful girl," Nefertiti instructed her older sister.

"I will. I will. Go and come back," Nicole said, shutting the door; and they carried her suitcases and bags away, out of due respect.

A half an hour later, a husky white police officer questioned Dwayne at the door while his black partner looked on. Also standing outside Suite# 2E was Nefertiti, Corey and Antoine. They returned from McDonald's to continue waiting for Nicole. She stood next to Dwayne with her shoes in hand, and Patrick sat on the couch, watching T.V.

Dwayne explained to the police his situation the best he could without sounding bizarre. He wanted to tell the police that his grandfather Al was the guy who forced his way in and beat him up. He knew everyone would think he was crazy, so he kept the news about Al to himself.

Once the police left, Nicole put her pumps on and proceeded out of the door.

"Wait," Dwayne said touching her shoulder. "You sure you wanna do this?"

"Dwayne, I love you and I'm truly sorry about what happened to you but, we need time apart. You hurt me."

"I'm sorry, baby. I've been under crazy stress, honey."

"We're all stressed! That doesn't give you the right to slap me, curse at me like a dog in the street, or call me a bitch in front of people. No, I'm not trying to hear that!"

"Please. Please, baby. Nicole, let me make it up to you. Things'll be okay, I promise!"

Dwayne touched her face passionately and Nicole

angrily jerked away.

"We need time apart Dwayne, I'll call you," she retorted coldly. She walked out of the suite, and out of his life.

Dwayne looked at his closing door, hissing sadly.

"Damn, Pat! Damn! Damn! Damn! I fucked up! I pissed her off!"

Patrick, ten pounds heavier, munching on a bag of dried plantains, changed channels with remote in hand.

"Cheer up, man, you just had a little fight. Me and Shell have 'em all the time. You'll be back together in no time," he replied confidently.

Dwayne walked over and sat on his recliner. "But yo, I smacked her last night man when we went to Zanzibar's. She had all these niggas in her face. I was ready to fuck up all of 'em!"

Patrick couldn't help but stare at Dwayne's bruises. He never saw his buddy look like this ever. It must have been a gang of hooligans that attacked Dwayne; he got beat up pretty bad.

"Dwayne, you can't remember the guy who attacked you?! One guy actually broke into the apartment?"

"Yeah! He was in here. He rushed me! But I was drunk."

"What did he say?"

"I can't remember."

"Just one guy made you look like this?! No homeboy, not you," Patrick said with total disbelief. "No high. You have never gone out like this, ever! Are you sure you didn't get jumped? You must have been jumped to look like this."

"I didn't get jumped."

"One person though man? Was it Hulk Hogan or Superfly Snuka? How did he look?"

"Man Pat," Dwayne began, "I was crazy drunk, and it happened so fast . . . he was an old man like . . . the dude was about my height . . . he had gray hair . . . a dark-skin dude man . . . I couldn't really see, cause when I saw him in here I backed up and shut the lights off by mistake . . . and he . . . smacked the shit outta me . . . body-slammed me."

"Dee, man, I'll pray for ya. It sounds too weird to me man."

"Would you think this is more weird, if I told you my grandfather did this to me? Would you believe me?"

"I would say crazy and weird. And no, I wouldn't believe you."

"Other weird shit been going on too, man."

"Chill with the language."

"Chill my ass! I'm stressed out Pat!"

Dwayne explained to Patrick about the rearranged furniture.

"Somebody might have keys to your place, get your locks changed," Patrick said.

"I might have to, cause the same thing might happen again, and I ain't going out like a sucker this time. The last time I was drunk but the next time, I'm 'a try to have some iron, so I can blast duke!"

"That's not the answer," Patrick said, shaking his head with emphasis.

"So what's the answer then?"

"You know what I'm gonna say."

"Yeah, I know, PREACH!"

Patrick happily revved the motor for his used blue 4-door 1984 Volvo while Dwayne hopped into the front seat passenger side.

"Man what's up with this car? How did you get this car," asked Dwayne.

"I keep forgetting to tell you, and you forgot to remind me," Patrick began, "God is so good man, and it's a small world after all just like the song. One of my father's employees, a good brother, who kept in touch with me and my family, this guy has sold me this car and I can make payments to him whenever and however I want."

"Word?!"

"And guess what else? We're about to go half on a deal where I'm going to own my very own properties man. Right around the way. This dude already owns a building on sixteenth and Lenox, and in that same building, he has hooked me up with an assistant manager position. Guess what I'm managing? . . . ASSOCIATED!"

"Associated? You mean the supermarket?"

"Yes!"

"Around the corner from where I live?! I mean, where I used to live?"

"Right around the corner, my man. It's no joke. It's rough sometimes. Lots of familiar faces that know us. I stay in the booth most of the time, but when I have to check on something sometime I get people who stare, because they remember. Mostly people recognize me for trying to get past it all, those who remember my family, it's cool though; people just deal with their shopping, deal with their groceries. I'm busy in there."

"That's crazy. Associated on sixteenth round the corner?! You should get me a job around the way."

"You will never make it with my cousins in the same store high, and I'm interviewing them for positions next week . . . That's right. The cousins that you have beef with."

"But I sent your family a check for five hundred. I paid them ba . . ."

"I know Dee. But you still thiefed from the house. They're not forgiving as me. Don't sweat it though. Besides, you're making crazy loot with Transit, don't play yourself homeboy. Look how you're living now. Your co-op is dope! And that's the Lord reminding you to give thanks, give him all the glory! Dee, we've both been through a lot, but we can't make it without Christ. And wouldn't have made it without Christ . . . Are you sure you don't want to go for a spin? I say let me drop you at the hospital. You need to get checked, your grill is damaged up homeboy."

"Nah man, I'm 'a get back upstairs. Maybe I can buzz Nikki at her crib, and talk some sense into her."

Patrick replied with a smirk, "C'mon Dee man. You know that will never happen. You'll be talking to her answering service. And if she is chilling with her parents or Nadia, you can really forget it. Her folks won't even let you through."

Patrick stuck his hand over for a good old soul five.

"Dwayne, if you have any more problems, call me. I'm serious. Whether I'm around the way or home in Brooklyn, I'll be right over."

"How's the new crib?"

"Babies live in cribs."

"Har-dee-har-har! You know what I mean!"

"God has blessed me and Shell with a nice home. It was a blessing for her parents to leave us the house. It's great. Her dad needed to be sure I was worthy that's all. Her parents have their own property to tend to in Florida. Trust me, my wife and I needed our own space. It was time, ya understand me? Now she can complete her studies. She's already a practical nurse, and by next year she'll be an RN. We're still thinking of renting the top floor apartment though."

"Damn, I guess you need this ride. All the way in Brooklyn though man? That's dumb far."

"Not really. I have other family out there. I'm getting used to it. It's just big out there. Like Queens, having the same street names over and over. At first, I had a hard time finding where we live, but we're on Jefferson Avenue, not Jefferson Street. And what's crazy is that they're not all that far from each other, just a few miles. I'm used to it now, and I'm closer to carnival now."

"Man, better you than me. I'm staying uptown."

Patrick tried not to gaze at his friend's face, and Dwayne noticed his buddy's discomfort with glaring. He slapped him five and shook Patrick's hand.

"It's cool, high! I'm 'a be aiight. So you think my grill tore up right? You never seen me look like this."

"Never."

"Cause you know the time! You know I'm nice with the hands Pat; we both nice with the hands since we was young downtown, but I just don't know B . . . I just don't know . . . See how my grill is? I guess I gotta rock shades now."

"And you need to rock ice on your face. But more than anything, you have to ask the Lord for deliverance, for him to rock with you through your ordeals, ya understand me? I'm serious, Dwayne. You should come to church with us when you get a chance."

He nodded while Patrick continued: "You gotta repent my brother. If I didn't love ya, I wouldn't tell ya. We're in the last days man. Everything that's going on right now is in Revelations. Armageddon is right around the corner and when those saints go marching in, I'm gonna be in that number! Hallelujah!"

"Thanks, money. I'm glad about you and Michelle's spot, I mean home . . . and I'm glad you came by," Dwayne said, slapping five again.

"You know it! Now get out my car chump, so I can get home!"

Patrick pulled off while the dusk set in.

Dwayne watched Patrick's car get tiny in the distance while walking; and suddenly the warm wet drops falling against his hands and chest made him look down. His nose was a faucet of pouring blood and he was frightened, embarrassed. A few neighbors saw Dwayne run up into his building out of the windy November afternoon with a nosebleed that saturated his messed up face and shirt.

He ran up the stairwell and out into the second floor hallway, approaching the suite. He reached for his doorknob, baton styled, and when he entered he could hear the popping and frying noises emerging from the kitchen. Dwayne quickly snatched a towel from inside the suite's restroom and provided a dam for his bleeding nostrils, holding his nose shut. He crept across his living room towards his dining room afraid of what he would find.

That second Al appeared, dressed with his chef's apron and hat; and he placed a neatly decorated plate of fried chicken, macaroni and cheese, string beans, with a square of buttered cornbread onto the dining room table. Al went back into the kitchen.

Still holding his nose with the towel, Dwayne peeked around into the kitchen to see his grandfather standing over the stove, turning more frying chicken in a pan with a fork.

"Chicken and the meal is almost done Baby Al," Al said.

The statement made Dwayne drop his towel, holding his breath scared stiff. Dwayne's first exhalation of shock made him cough with a blood clot flying from his nose, blood trickling again; and the thought hit him to run for his life, to sprint for help. Dwayne ran to the door of his suite and snatched it open to find Al standing outside in the hallway.

"Get yo ass back in that house now! Get to that table and eat," Al yelled and pushed Dwayne to the floor, making him hit his head. Al then dragged his kicking grandson by his neck through the living room, picked him up and sat him at the dining room table. The room was starting to spin with a dizzying, frightening head pain setting in for Dwayne, causing him to squint while he desperately focused his vision to track his grandfather's next moves. From his chair at the table, Dwayne watched Al finish with the chicken, turning off the stove, and then he fixed his own supper plate identical to Dwayne's.

Then Al came to the table, placed his plate of food down, pulled out his chair and sat down; he bowed his head to say grace. Al looked at his grandson who stared incredulously, continuing to panic. He scowled at Dwayne and pounded on the table making Dwayne jump.

"What the fuck you looking at Baby Al? EAT!," Al shouted.

Dwayne, frightened eyes wide, with blood running faster from his nose, sat frozen unable to move, in terror.

Al stood from his side of the table and walked around to Dwayne's chair. Standing behind his grandson, the once battered senior citizen grabbed both cheeks of the young man's face with sheer odium. Al, venomous eyes bulging with the intent to hurt, started smashing Dwayne's face into his plate of food. His face being pummeled one too many times made Dwayne stand on reflex, leaving a blood sauce over his meal, the macaroni and vegetables smeared on his face. He was painfully floating in a cloud of faintness, with the motions of a marionette.

In a split second, Al punched Dwayne in the jaw, knocking him clear to the floor a second time. The volatile insensibility of his living room slowly began to fade, but not without Al walking into Dwayne's dimming vision. Al's face was decorated with extreme rage while approaching Dwayne's sprawled body; and he threw the rest of the food at Dwayne, hitting him in the face with the plate.

He looked down on his injured bloody grandson who lay writhing in pain, unable to scream for help, fighting for air to breathe with darkness settling into his frantic mentality. Stepping on Dwayne's neck until his flesh went from pale to blue, Al laughed, "Ya reap what'cha sow, Baby Al!"

****

CHAPTER 15

*

After the last attack from his grandfather, Dwayne took a copy of the police report from the first assault to the hospital emergency room for treatment. He gave the triage staff a performance of being mugged inside his apartment twice, with an addition of loud, profane threatening neighbors and their barking dog. Once his vital signs were taken and he saw a physician, he was diagnosed with dehydration; and Dwayne was hooked up to an intravenous to get more vitamins and fluid back into his system for the blood loss. After three bags of Lactated Ringer's, with his one day discharge, Dwayne was awarded medication for the headaches, the severe nosebleeds, and a doctor's note for time off from work. He was also given instructions for the care of his face, and dates for oral surgery. Once returning home, he popped as many pills as possible to sleep, to deal with the permanent dog growling in his mind. The aggravating scratching, rustling barks, groans, and whining moans were in the walls of the bedroom, and only at night.

The following afternoon after a minimal amount of morning sleep with the meds, the growling subsided with the return of a brand, new agonizing headache. He squinted at the time on the digital alarm clock.

"Damn, it's crazy late! Four eighteen, it's going to be dark soon! **Fuck**!" Dwayne took a deep breath, turned over in bed to his nightstand to pick up the telephone. No dial tone, just a dog's growl with scratching noises.

Dwayne pushed himself out of the water bed as quick as he could to shower, dress, and go out into the street to get some answers to his domestic insanities. While inside the shower out in the bedroom, the telephone began to ring; and the phone continued ringing for the duration of the shower.

'I thought the goddamned thing didn't have a dial tone!'

Shutting off the water, he exited and crossed his bedroom to the still ringing telephone and snatched up the receiver.

"Hello?!"

The response was the same repetitive scratching, whining nightly canine sounds. In a flash, Dwayne yanked his telephone from the wall jack and threw it across the room like a pitcher expecting a batter to get a strike. The phone smashed into the wall, leaving a dent that would need eventual plastering.

He dressed for the coming December weather quickly and left the suite. Bypassing a few unreturned "good afternoons & good evenings" from entering and exiting neighbors, Dwayne walked the sidewalk with lone chirping bird sounds and more dog barks outside of his mental. He entered the parking lot, approaching his car, and the automobile started on its own, motor revving.

'WHAT THE FUCK?!'

Dwayne unlocked the door of the convertible, and jumped into his seat, looking around incredulously, feeling his car running. "Damn, I don't have to put the key into the ignition," he wondered. He tried to shift from park, to neutral, and it wouldn't move. The motor continued to run, with the radio coming on suddenly.

"Damn! KISS-FM?! Why am I listening to Chuck Leonard and I didn't even turn him on? . . . And how is this motor running with no key?!"

Dwayne put the key into the ignition and the car shut itself down, motor stopping, radio dead! Minutes passed with unsuccessful attempts to start his automobile, pumping the accelerator futilely and the car would not start. He punched the steering wheel, snatched the keys out of the ignition and left the BMW.

"No car, no phone! . . . shit is getting crazier and crazier," Dwayne grumbled.

"You have reached the home of Patrick and Michelle Livingston . . . We're not in to answer your call right now . . . Please leave us a message after the beep and we will return your call . . . Have a blessed . . ."

"This nigga not even in his crib," Dwayne said, slamming the pay phone receiver down on its hook. He angered thinking of his defective phone line and kooky acting car, while he blew on his hands and rubbed them together. His fading mind pondered another plan, because time surely was running out.

"Hold up . . . That's right! Patrick said he working at Associated. Time to take a run around the way! . . . A cab from Irwin and 231st to 116th and Lenox? . . . Nah, I'm a save this bread, I'm running low . . . Iron horse here I come, and phone company tomorrow."

He headed downtown. Destination: Patrick's new place of business, the "Associated" supermarket around the corner from the tenement where he was raised. He rode the Broadway local to 96th and transferred to a crowded uptown express, which went out of service at 110th Street. He exited the subway and walked Lenox Avenue, looking at his old neighborhood. He saw Harlem Hospital in the extreme far distance; he passed a dilapidated building at 113th Street that served as his boyscout meeting place across from the projects; he extended his middle finger towards a row of tenements he had been married to during his crack days. Cold equivalent sensations of doom set in as he crossed 116th and Lenox. He thought of the first time he had met Scheme from Brooklyn, and he thought of their first conversations about making big money.

Dwayne snapped out of his daydream upon entering the warmth of the familiar busy six aisle supermarket. Filled with rush hour travelers and neighborhood shoppers, many were buying their turkeys and other goodies for the holidays.

He approached one of the cashiers and asked, "Pardon me miss . . . is Patrick here? Patrick Livingston?" The turban wearing young lady shrugged her shoulders.

"He's gone for the day. He closes tomorrow," another cashier added.

"Damn," thought Dwayne. Exhaling then plotting the next move, he walked out of the supermarket back to the hustle and bustle of the neighborhood. That second, Dwayne thought of the old house on 120th Street. The mission of the evening continued. He needed to find his best friend and talk with him and his family's sole surviving grandmother immediately. The Livingston family and their spirituality was the only thing he felt could help his grave situation. The Livingston's input on ghosts was imperative.

Hooking a left on the corner, Dwayne headed to Patrick's old house, hoping that his best friend would do the meritorious, like visiting his grandmother after work, before going home to his wife. And Dwayne was hit hard as he passed the corner of the block where he spent three quarters of his life. Of all the people in the world, he thought of Barbara Nelson as he crossed 117th. He wished it were summertime, or any other season where it would be warm enough to stop in to check on her. Although they fought as neighbors while he grew up, part of him was concerned about her. How was she spending her Thanksgiving and upcoming holiday season?

His old block seemed so lonely; he wondered if she

were still living. He thought of Aunt Lou, and some of the many elders who disappeared from his life after his turnaround due to the money with the move uptown. Apparently, big money never awarded him any happiness because his pockets were nearing depletion once again, similar to the weeks of his teenaged crack awakening. The moment he could get back to work, he planned to stay at work, to keep his pockets lined with as much green as possible.

The temperature dropped as he continued Lenox with the wind blowing even harder. The chill of the evening setting in, he stopped at the corner of 120th, thinking about Patrick's relatives. It was only one year ago that he stole from their home, and the rest of the family still hated him with a passion, even after he tried to pay them back. They also detested the fact that Patrick remained Dwayne's best friend, and was proud of it.

Dwayne proceeded around the brisk corner, thinking, "I know they don't want to see me, but I got to find the nigga Patrick! . . . He knows about shit like this. Pappy is dead! What he doing buying tokens to get on the train?! . . . Why he changing the furniture around in my living room, and cooking in my kitchen?! Knocking my teeth out and shit! Nah B!"

He stopped in front of the Livingston brownstone, looking up at Patrick's old house. The house knew nothing about happy times, standing proudly as always. It was once full of life with Patrick's siblings. Even though Una Livingston had returned after the tragedy with more relatives from Jamaica and England, the place still wasn't the same.

"Well, here it goes," Dwayne said, running up the front steps to the second floor entrance. He rang the bell, shivering after being hit with a new gust of wind.

"Damn, hurry up, shit," he thought. He heard the familiar locks unlocking with subsequent slam of the inside door while his back was turned. He spun around and saw Patrick'sgrandmother peeking through the glass door pane.

Una Livingston looked completely different from what he remembered. After her family was murdered, she became sickly, aging considerably. The once salt and pepper shoulder length hair that she always wore in a neat bun was a frizzy snow white. She walked with a cane, and there was noticeable weight gain. She couldn't recognize Dwayne at first with his back turned, but once he came closer to the glass, her eyes opened wider than the spectacles on her face. She sucked her teeth Caribbean style, shaking her head and hands angrily. She turned around to go back inside when Dwayne tapped on the pane.

"Please, Miss Livingston, I need your help! I need to find Patrick! Is he here?! Please!," he yelped. Una ignored him, opening the second door, proceeding to re-enter the house. "Miss Livingston! Please!"

Dwayne knocked hard on the glass pane and rang the bell frantically; he yelled, "No! No! No! Don't go! Please! I need to find Patrick."

Una sucked her teeth again, turned around, and returned to the front door. "T'cha! . . . T'cha! Wha' ya come roun' 'ere fa? Ya na' 'ave nuh business 'ere! Go 'wey! T'ief! Go 'wey! Ya nuh' 'ave business 'ere, ya' k'no'! Go 'wey!"

At the sound of Mummy Una's angered cries, nephew Carlton appeared, vexed at the sight of Dwayne. He soothed, "Mummy. Relax no'uw! Doan't worry ya'self!"

Carlton comforted his great aunt, guiding her back into the house, then he turned around to face Dwayne, having waited years for the moment.

"Wha ya trouble mi Mummy so?! Eih?! G'wan for mi bust yi raatid poosyclaat! G'wan nuh maan! Pahtrick nuh live 'ere nuh maan! Cleear ouwt!"

"Yo man! I need to see your fucking cousin man! Fuck that!," Dwayne fired back.

The haunting, as well as the weather, was beside him

now. The accelerated wind gusts promoted a drop in temperature by nearly fifteen degrees. Possible snow was in the forecast for this year's Thanksgiving.

"C'mon man! I need to see Patrick! Open the door, you fucking monkey!"

Carlton reached into his pants and pulled out his nickel plated, nine millimeter; he snatched open the door, grabbed Dwayne by his neck with one hand, and with his other fist mashed the iron into Dwayne's nostril.

Carlton taunted, "Ya waan caal mi mounkey no'uw? Poosyclaat yenkee bwoy?! What no'uw?! What no'uw?! Wha'?! . . . Mi fuuckin' cousin Pahtrick! . . . H'im a eeidiot ya' nuh! Eeidiot nuh maan! Fi be friends dem wit' de Yenkee bwoys dem poosyclaat!" Carlton let out a hearty laugh while Dwayne's eyes opened wide, quivering from cold winds and the fright of the gun.

"What . . . wha . . . what you gon' do with that," Dwayne stuttered, his eyes glued to the barrel.

"Ya see?! Ya see?! What goes around comes around! Ya fuckin' poosyclaat Yenkee bwoy . . . Teke h'an' t'ief from ah mi yaard?! T'ief from mi Mummy . . . Get de fuuuck ouwtta 'ere! Baambeclaat! Wha?! Wha?! Wha' 'appen?! Wha' a' gwan maan?! . . . Get da' fuuuck ouwtta 'ere! Poosy!"

Carlton pushed Dwayne down the stoop of the brownstone and simultaneously let off a gunshot into the moonlit gusty air. Trying to use his arms to break his fall, Dwayne hit the pavement of 120th Street, listening to guffawing Carlton who stood at the top of the steps. Seizing more opportunity to heckle Dwayne further, concealing his weapon, Carlton disappeared into the house. Seconds later, he returned throwing eggs at Dwayne, catching him each time.

"G'wan tuh ya' bed! Poosy! G'wan! Bloodclaat! G'wan!"

Wincing in pain, Dwayne used the stoop railing to

stand. Dripping with egg yolks and whites, he staggered away from the house, limping in the direction of Seventh Avenue.

Carlton laughed all the way into the house, telling Una and the rest of the family what he'd done to Dwayne. After scolding hot headed Carlton for indiscreetly busting shots, and for wasting valuable eggs, Una and the rest of the Livingston family burst into laughter. They hoped the news wouldn't get to Patrick or the neighborhood precinct.

While a few NYPD cars perused the neighborhood, due to a couple of 911 calls about "overhearing gunshots", Dwayne walked through Harlem back to the subway to head home sadly. Some passengers gawked at the sight of his appearance; he was looking as if he had been jumped. He cursed the New York City Transit Authority, the onlookers, and himself.

After the humiliating incident at Una Livingston's and a couple of days spent at home, with plenty of ice packs to the face and codeine for body aches and pain ingested, Dwayne returned to work. He wore big dark shades to cover up his black eyes; and although his mouth and face swelling went down with the ice packs from the hospital, he tried not to smile because of missing front teeth. There was nothing to smile about anyway. He had been literally thrown down the steps in front of the Livingston brownstone by one of Patrick's cousins; and his grandfather he abused had returned to haunt him in a horrifying way, taunting him daily in the exact manner in which Dwayne had abused him, and there was nowhere to run, and nowhere to hide.

On his first day returning to his clerk duties at New York City Transit, the morning through lunchtime went well and uneventful. It was the afternoon that would soon turn to hell. Like clockwork, one of the many northbound "R" trains entered the station; and as the patrons boarded and left the train, Al also exited the train. He looked around and saw his grandson working and approached him. The elderly man was dressed familiarly, ripped multi-colored flannel shirt with missing buttons, and gray trousers, opened rip in the thigh with flesh and tissues exposed, with a missing zipper and brown urine stains in the crotch area. Al came through the exit gate and sauntered over to stand behind a patron who was asking Dwayne for directions.

"SHIT!," Dwayne yelled. The middle-aged gentleman returned a bewildered stare to Dwayne's outburst.

"Mister, I'm sorry! Just cross over to the downtown side to get to South Ferry. Take this block ticket so you won't have to pay! And hurry up!"

Dwayne was afraid for Al to stand near his customer while Al grinned at his delirious grandson sitting inside the token booth. Dwayne screamed for another patron.

"That ain't the way to talk to a paying customer on your job now Baby Al! Where's ya manager?! I wanna make a complaint," laughed Al.

"You're not real! Leave me the fuck alone! Next! **Next!**," Dwayne yelled.

"Oh yeah Baby Al? We'll see about that."

"We not gon' see about shit Pappy! YOU ARE DEAD! And I'm not scared no more!"

The line of disgruntled token buying passengers watched Dwayne burst into a new shouting match with himself. A few had even complained to the Transit Authority and their personal community boards about the bizarre railroad clerk who talked to himself daily. Some were afraid of him, apprehensive to purchase tokens, while Dwayne remained tortured. They were relieved during his time off and away from the booth, but the return to work with the days ahead would prove to be more bizarre. Every day at work was a day like most, harassment from Al, frightened people backing off, and then, poof! Al was gone. At night, the assortment of voices, growls, migraines, and mind games returned and increased, at times, to nightmarish proportions. Nicole, the love of his life, remained estranged after walking out on him, adding to his woes. What a difference a year made, with the previous Thanksgiving being spent with Nicole and her family as a recovering drug addict, striving to bury his violent, poignant past with an assisted, enthusiastic effort to turn life around. The Christmas/New Year turnover, fresh money and new love turned out to be the vital energy for forward movement.

A year later, the one hundred eighty degree difference was preparing Dwayne for a new lease on his existence. There was no Nicole, no Thanksgiving, just work with overtime hours; and the Christmas/New Year turnover found Dwayne working through the holidays as well. Dwayne frequently tried to call Nicole in the beginning of the separation, but after she threatened to file harassment charges against him for the phone calls to her job, he simmered down. There were only gifts sent to the job and to her place in Co-op City every two weeks, coinciding with paydays.

He kicked it to a couple of new female conquests he met during work hours, trying to block out Al's return and consistency of following him home every day. The new friends with benefits and "booty calls" filled a physical void only with Dwayne, but as Valentine's Day passed by, he found himself missing his fiancé more than ever. No woman on the planet measured up to her.

Like the previous holidays, to keep his mind occupied, Dwayne became accustomed to working and securing overtime in one shift for "time and a half". On President's Day, after his relief came at the usual time, Dwayne retrieved and calculated subway tokens for his end of shift duties, and started home. Once he reached his beloved place, he did the lonely usual.

"Junk mail," he thought, opening his mailbox. "Bill . . .

Bill . . . Bill . . . Bill."

He slowly exited the elevator examining the mail, walking the second floor hallway, down to Suite#2E. He truly didn't know what to expect now that Al was back physically visiting him. His grandfather's latest pattern shifted from following him everywhere through the subway system, still buying subway tokens every day, to leaving profane, threatening, phone messages on Dwayne's answering machine.

Dwayne unlocked and opened the door, praying his grandfather wouldn't be inside. Once entering and seeing things were clear, he turned on the lights and moved to shut the door behind him when he heard glass shatter inside the suite. Leaving the door ajar in case he had to run, beginning to hyperventilate, Dwayne crept into the kitchen. There was no Al, but the cabinet doors were open, and two wine glasses were shattered on the floor. With his coat still on, Dwayne swept up then trashed the glass and headed back into the living room. The carpet rule was now void thanks to Al returning. Dwayne had scrubbed his carpet with the top brand of carpet cleaners, and the blood stain still remained.

"Thank, God," Dwayne said exhaling, relieved there was no real sign of Al.

Grabbing the TV's remote control, he plopped onto the couch and took off his coat. "New York's Live At Five" came into existence, and Nicole's educated gentle presence was instantly longed for.

"Damn, Nikki's favorite program . . . She love Sue Simmons . . . Man, damn . . . I wonder what she doing? . . . Where she at? . . . I wonder if she got a new nigga?"

After the countless bouquets of roses, other floral arrangements sent to Nicole's job, and several calls to Nefertiti's before, during, and after the holidays, Dwayne was at wits' end without his fiancé. She usually "wasn't home" at her own co-op, or he received the Ryerson family's favorite gift at the sound of his voice: the dial tone; and it was going on three months later.

Dwayne did come to a point where he felt he wouldn't beg Nicole back, but he still missed her so.

"Damn, Nikki! Why you had to leave me," Dwayne said, walking into his bedroom. He sat on the edge of the bed, turning on the bedside lamp. Frowning at the bed's temperature, he turned up the heat of the water. He opened a drawer beneath the bed frame and removed a framed picture of his lady with himself in an embrace, taken days after he proposed. Dwayne glared then shook the portrait with aggressive love.

"Damn Nikk, when you gonna come back?! I need ya, word is born! Come home! Damn!"

Holding onto the picture, he checked his answering machine messages, turning up the volume: 'You have six messages.'

The first message was from Patrick: *". . . What's sup, Dee! It's Patrick, man! Sorry you haven't heard from me in the longest while . . . You sure you want to be married? . . . Guess who I ran into around the old way? I ran into Art! Arthur Boyd man! He wants to get in touch with you! I didn't give him your number or nothing like that! He says he has a record coming out, wants us in a video maybe. I don't know about all that, being down and all. Shell will be riffin'', because of the church, you know that . . . Gimme a call when you get in! Later! . . ."*

"Damn, Art got a record coming out, and you didn't give him my digits," Dwayne grumbled shaking his head.

The next message was from Dwayne's unhappily married new friend Kaeemah: *". . . Hey . . . Missed you this morning, I was hoping you were home by now . . . I missed my boat, so I was running late, took the 1 train instead of the R, then the express at Chambers then back to another local because it was right across the platform waiting . . . I just couldn't hear my boss's mouth after all of that . . . I should have saw you this morning anyway . . . couldn't get away lunchtime . . . it was sooo busy today . . . I miss you daddy . . . I really do . . . Did you get to press charges on those guys who jumped you, and tried to rob your apartment? . . . Thought about you all day Valentine's Day . . . I'm a try to call you later . . . I need to come back to the Bronx to see you, I'm getting off this island for real . . . In the morning with me heading to work, five minutes here, five minutes there when we can is not enough for me . . . I need to feel you again . . . I'll call you later Dwayne, I hope I can get away . . . "*

The next message was from Al: *". . . Mo' glasses gon' get broke up hear?! You fixin' to piss me off boy . . . You ain't got shit to eat or drink in this house . . . Cain't make us die no more of thirst, and ya sho cain't make us starve to death neither . . . thanks for letting us back in here though . . . We sho' do wish Nicole would come back home . . . Damn Nikki! Why you had to leave me and us!! . . . See you soon Baby Al!"*

Dwayne felt the tears of fear welling in his eyes while the next message came in from Arlene: *"Baby Al, I mean Dwayne, sorry, it's your godmommy . . . Gotta remember you a grown up man now, over twenty-one . . . Hope all is well, haven't heard from you in a while, can't seem to catch a hard-working man like you, hope your New Year been good . . . The kids, Donnell, and I are fine, just touching base with you . . . Maybe we'll do lunch . . . I should be downtown tomorrow in the area where you work . . . Call me okay, stop acting like a stranger . . . Bye now."*

The next message was from another new friend named Ada: *". . . Sit down! I said sit your . . . sit your asses down NOW! . . . **Now!** . . . Sit the fuck down before I knock your asses into next week!! Oh shit . . . Um hello . . . Dwayne?! . . . Why you never home when I call boo?! . . . Wait . . . Leave your sister alone! . . . Give her that ugly fucking cabbage patch doll before I snap your fucking neck like a goddamn chicken!! . . . I'm on the phone! . . . Dwayne, I'm tired of leaving you messages over and over, your finger not broke, call me back! . . . Just like all these other no good niggas out here, give 'em some ass and never hear from 'em . . . Leave that damn VCR alone boy! . . . Touch it again and I'm a FUCK YOU UP! . . . I'm not gon' keep calling some nigga who act like they think they all that, and don't want to be bothered . . . Nope! Trust me boo-boo . . . one nigga* *loss is another nigga gain . . . SIT DOWN DAMN IT!! . . . It's not even right that I always be leaving you messages and you don't return them . . . this is my last time calling! . . . YOU SPILLING JUICE ALL OVER MY MOTHERFUCKING FLOOR!! . . . ooooooh these KIDS!! . . . Dwayne, call me back!! Go get that MOP before I hurt you . . . What?! . . . I'm the Mama 'round here . . . DWAYNE CALL ME BACK! . . ."*

The last message was from Nicole: *". . . Hello . . . Dwayne it's Nicole . . . I've been trying to get in touch with you for a while now . . . Your machine is always on, so I don't leave messages . . . I need to talk to you . . . Give me a call at home, or at the center tomorrow . . . I'm still at Nef's . . . talk to you soon . . ."*

"Ah yeah!"

He excitedly punched his hand with his fist. "My girl called! Yeah!"

Dwayne's ecstatic feelings scrambled, and he began thinking, "Damn what's up . . . She must be missing me too, just as much as I'm missing her after all . . . She telling me to call the center or call her at Nef's crib . . . but Nef's crib is her crib . . . that means she must be coming back here then, cause she would say, call me at home, or call me at my Moms . . . But Nikki said call her at Nef's crib; she gotta be thinking of coming home to me! . . . My baby coming back here with me. Yes!"

Grinning at the portrait of himself and Nicole, with his free hand he took off his shoes and then began to dance with the portrait next to his chest, crooning. "Nikki, called me, cause she need someone to talk to; Nikki called me, satisfaction guaranteed; Nikki, called me, cause she need someone to talk to; Nikki . . ."

"I coulda told ya she called," Al said, standing in the doorway. Dwayne stopped his cover-record dance routine, and frighteningly turned around to stare at the grandfather he knew was deceased. Al bopped into the bedroom, pimp style; and with each footstep, the closer he came, Dwayne's eyes expanded until they were petrified, saucer sized.

"What's the matter Baby Al hmmm? Ain't think I'd remember to tell ya who called? Whatcha gon' do to me this time?"

The absolute terror of seeing his grandfather return from the dead possessed Dwayne's soul completely. Al was dressed differently this time, no flannel shirt, soiled trousers, or even the suspenders Dwayne sold for three dollars. His entire outfit matched with his pinstriped derby and suit, featuring jingling metal clamps, cufflinks and spats, with brand new patent leather shoes, topped off with attitude. This couldn't be real. How could defenseless, old, decrepit Al return so strong, so violent, dapper?

Dwayne fearfully muttered, **"Get out of here! . . . Get outta here! . . . Get outta here, you're not fucking real!"**

Dwayne ran wildly, talking a swinging punch in Al's direction, refusing to let the senior citizen attack him again and get away with it. Al blocked the punch with tripled muscular strength, grabbing Dwayne's neck with his other hand. He choked his defenseless, terrified grandson down to the floor, straddling him, staring him face to face. He squeezed Dwayne's neck until he was blue again, letting go of his neck just in time. Dwayne gasped frantically for air when Al grabbed him by the neck a second time, breathing in his face a horrifying speech:

"I'm not fucking real huh?! . . . You feel my hot ass dead breath in ya face?! . . . **I should kill yo' hateful ass now so we all can rest in peace . . . But no . . . You gon' suffer! Like I suffered! Like yo' mama suffered! Like yo grandma, my wife suffered! Like you gon' suffer Baby Al** . . . You cain't kick my ass no more when I call you that . . . From this moment on, I do all the ass kicking 'round here. Cause you beat me . . .You beat on me . . . YOU BEAT ME! . . . When I Gave You My life! . . . and I tried to crawl out that window, to save my life, when I GAVE **YOU**MY FUCKING LIFE! . . . Baby Al . . . **I WANT YOURS!!"**

Al's clammy hands grasping his neck, actually choking it was horrifyingly real. The phone rang with the answering service picking up the call. Patrick's voice re-entered the stillness of the bedroom.

"I . . . I . . . I want to talk . . . wanna talk to Patrick," Dwayne stammered, gaining enough air to speak. Al cackled raucously, showing him no mercy. The terrifying intimidation of this haunting was unnerving, and Dwayne knew his grandfather was going to kill him this evening.

Al began strangling his grandson again, whose eyes were already going upward in their sockets with shock, and his complexion began to pale. Al taunted Dwayne with a new dialect, taking on a mid-western drawl he never heard his grandfather use.

"Lawd! . . . Help me Lawd! . . . Help me! . . . Don't kill me Pappy! . . . Whaddya wont Patrick fuhr boy? For what? . . . To tell him I'm back! . . . If ya' tell anyone that I'm back, yo' zebra ass is dead! Ya' got that Baby Al?"

Dwayne hoped and believed that his savage grandfather understood his nod, hoping Al would loosen his grip, but it was too late. His bedroom, with its receding furnishings, had already faded to black. His earlier un-connecting punches helped him none, along with his frantic kicks.

Al finally loosened his grip, once Dwayne passed out again.

After finally regaining consciousness the next day, unbeknownst to skipping work, Dwayne went to his bank for some cash. Luckily catching his institution before closing, he removed $1,100 dollars from his savings account. His next mission was a date with Harlem. He left for his old neighborhood, determined, with a weighty goal in mind. Dusk set in while Dwayne headed south behind Dyckman Projects onto the mouth of the Harlem River Drive. This evening's return around the way was for some well needed acquaintances. The decision to comb the streets until he found what he needed was his and his alone. Riding Second Avenue after exiting the freeway, bumping the sounds of Keith Sweat, he needed his re-connections to the old hood to be instantaneous. Luckily, the habit of smoking crack disappeared with the past, mixing with his sudden need to be strapped again. Dwayne lit a Newport, took some deep drags and stopped his cassette tape, turning on the radio abruptly caught by a red light.

'. . . *Feel the music pumping hard like I wish you would, now push it!* . . . *Push it good!* . . . *Push it realllll good!* . . . '

"Damn, fine ass Salt . . . and Pepa bad too, damn . . . Man, Art Boogie or Boogie Art whatever Arthur calls himself, he need to introduce me to them," Dwayne thought, hissing.

He made a right turn on 121st Street to jet to his native west side for some information. He refused to return to the Bronx without security, and his pockets were filled with just the right amount for the heat he needed. After stopping by a couple of barber shops including Billy Harten's, and seeing a few folk who feigned admiration for his quick turnaround, Dwayne acquired the details he needed on where to get an easy nickel plated Colt .45 special or a quick 9 millimeter glock. He frowned at the notions of "deuce-pounders" or anything he considered small. Dwayne was set on a weapon that would blow his grandfather away for good and kill him on contact in case he attacked again.

Subsequent arrangements were made from a few phone calls at the barber shop and a couple of pay phones; and Dwayne found himself parking his car on 104th and Fifth Ave. Checking his watch, he hissed. Ten more minutes passed with another hiss from Dwayne's mouth as his thoughts scrambled: 'What's taking this cat so long man? . . . It don't take a year to drop off a burner, goddamn!! . . . It's a good thing I'm going for that surgery tomorrow, cause they taking crazy long . . . word up, least I'm a get another doctor's note for work . . . Can't believe what happened again last night . . . Pappy tried to fucking kill me . . . I gotta get Patrick to listen this time, to understand . . . I gotta make him understand . . . damn, FINALLY . . .'

A big, dark Oldsmobile sedan pulled up alongside Dwayne's BMW with its motor still running. Dwayne started his car and got out to go around to the driver side of the other car.

"What's up kid," said the familiar guy, heavyset, covering his braided head with his hood while exiting his car.

"Let's make this quick homie. Hold up, do I know you," Dwayne asked digging in his pockets for his wad of money.

"Dee it's me, Fat Jazz?!"

"12th Street?"

"YEAH!"

"OH SHIT!"

Dwayne slapped five and embraced another hood affiliate.

"Let's do this quick though man! It's dumb cold out here! But how you," asked Dwayne.

"I'm chilling! Just came home, you know how that is. Gotta get this stinking ass cheese indeed! They told me I was going to see you, cats at the shop. You aiight?! What some Brooklyn cats run up on you again or something?!"

"Nah B."

"Oh, aiight! Cause I know a few of them Decepticons out there, Scourge, Rumble, Cy, Badness, the nigga Saur, Devastater, they family though! I can tell by your face why you need to do this tonight. Let me know if you got beef! If this ain't enough, I got you. And we know niggas, just like you do! But how you been? You looking good though, just a little lumped up. Never seen you like this high. I like that whip you pushing!"

"Just working for Transit B. Good looking out though."

Their conversation continued with the quick, even exchange of money, ammunition, and firearms inside a gift wrapped shoebox, just the way Dwayne liked it.

"No question Dee. No question homie. Haven't seen you in a long time, maybe even since Wadleigh."

"Oh yeah! That's where I know you from! 12th Street Jazz! Couldn't run laps in gym. That was dumb long ago. Been a few years!"

"Yeah cause E-zo and the rest of the crew, you, Shawn, and the West Indian dude went uptown to school. I went to Brandeis downtown. I forgot duke name, the West Indian cat; what's his name again, the one that went to school with us? Ya man!"

"Patrick."

"Right, right! Yo his sister went to school with me, but she graduated ahead of my year. That's messed up about what happened to them, I heard about it up North. You seen him?!"

"He doing good."

"And sorry about your family too. I heard about what happened on 17th Street."

"I want to say it's over with, but right about now it's COLD, like freezing man. I gotta go! Good looking out man. Old 12th Street Jazz! Fat Jazz from back in the days! Next time I see you, we'll chill money. Thanks for coming through."

"No doubt Dee. Get out these streets with that. It's crazy cold, but these streets is crazy hot, y'no I'm sayin'?! Take my number though. It's 212, 876, . . ."

"Not now B! Jazz, the same way we caught up tonight, we'll catch up when it warms up homeboy. Dig?"

Dwayne slapped five and hugged his chubby buddy and ran back to his warming car. 12th Street Jazz jumped into his antique automobile and sped off. Dwayne followed suit and headed for the FDR. He drove back to his co-op excited and as fast as he could. Victoriously cruising through the pitch blackness of the Harlem River Drive north of the George Washington Bridge, he kept grooving to the sounds of Biz Markie.

Entering his parking lot, he shut down the motor of his car and turned on his overhead light. He tore the paper off the shoebox, opened and removed his latest toy, a black .45 automatic-colt-pistol with a brown handle. He felt inside the box for his accessory clip with a few rounds. Examining the barrel, and assembling his around the way purchase the way he was accustomed, Dwayne shut off his car light.

"Yeah! Ya know what I'm saying? Protection," he said aloud, slapping in his loaded magazine. "I'll be damned if I let Pappy kill me . . . I'm a kill him first. This time he's dying for real. When I'm done with the motherfucker, he dying twice!"

Dwayne kissed his weapon, and left his car, slamming the door remotely locking it. He was ready for the climate of his warm suite indoors, with protection, if needed.

****

CHAPTER 16

∗

On the first floor of a modest three floor brownstone inside a huge den a few nights later, Mrs. Michelle Livingston napped with her chemistry book in her lap, sitting in a recliner with her feet up. After church, while studying for an exam that would take place in school the following evening, the earnest young woman snoozed while her husband Patrick added the finishing touches to their Sunday dinner. Wearing only sweat pants, bare chested and barefoot, Patrick prepared a meal that was just enough for two. He peeked in at his wife whom he left studying, and he chuckled after hearing the random snore from Michelle. Shaking his head, he smiled deep within his heart, still in love deep inside, for what he felt was a strong, happy marriage.

"Mi queen tired. Why am I not surprised," Patrick thought returning to the kitchen, hungry himself. First Patrick set the table, with wine glasses of sparkling cider. Then he fixed Michelle's china plate of jerk chicken, plantains, rice & peas, cabbage, and two dinner rolls. Patrick brought the plate of food inside the living room and over to sleeping Michelle and held it in front of her face. He rotated the plate for her nostrils to behold so she could awaken to the aroma. Five seconds and Michelle jumped, opening her eyes, making her chemistry book fall to the lacquered, hardwood floors of the brownstone.

Michelle said, "I could have knocked that food out of your hands . . . Who told you I want chicken? Jerk chicken at that!"

"You want this here angel?"

"No, I'll come inside to the table. Sorry honey, I've been so tired lately."

Patrick returned into the large kitchen and sat Michelle's plate at her end of the dining table, a table which accommodated six to eight people. Michelle stood from the recliner and yawned, stretched, retrieved her textbook and went to join her husband. Patrick waited with his plate of food, with an extra dinner roll, and sat close and catty cornered to his wife. He took her hand when she entered the kitchen sitting at the table, as they bowed their heads to give thanks for the meal.

"Our Father in heaven . . . we ask for your continued blessings . . . as we give thanks for this meal . . . for the nourishment of our bodies . . . in your holy name we do pray Father God . . . in Jesus name . . . Amen."

"Amen," Michelle responded to her husband's prayer.

"How does it taste?"

"Let me taste it honey . . . I'm not a glutton like you," Michelle said with sarcasm, beginning her meal.

"How is it Shelly Thunder?

"Like jerk chicken. And don't call me no Shelly Thunder, Patrick Swayze!"

Patrick began to devour his plate of food while Michelle dealt with her morsels of food meticulously. "This is too much food on my plate. Why you overrun my plate with food all the time, I'll never know. You're succeeding in making me fat-ter," said Michelle. She removed the rolls from her plate and put them on his, while he continued eating, smiling at her.

"With your new job, according to you, you won't become fat."

"You sure are right about that! I should have stayed at Delpeche, then finish these final semesters. Careful what you wish for babe. I wanted to get my feet wet as a nurse, and they work me hard."

"I know angel I know."

"I'm actually starting to miss going to the office. Working at a seventh floor nurses station in Woodhull Hospital is much different than taking two elevators, one to the seventy-eighth floor and transfer to another . . ."

"Like you're on the train," chuckled Patrick.

"Yes! I'm telling you right, transferring on seventy-eight between two elevators, to go up to the 100th floor. And mind you, I did that every day since the eleventh grade. I kinda miss the office now. I was there almost five years. I grew into womanhood at that desk."

"I know."

Michelle, with a twinkle in her eye, pointed her fork at Patrick, pursed her lips and stopped eating. Patrick began to sip his cider and grinned.

"What? Why are you looking at me like that?"

"Glory be to God, I had to marry you! You goon! And it's not because you can cook either! And it wasn't because of Cindy! I mean, she is part the reason, because we wouldn't have met but, you would drive your brother's car to see me on that job. Remember?"

"Yes my angel. To drive you all the way back out here, just to attend Friday night service with you."

"Oh no you did not Mister! You liked to try and get fresh with me in that long elevator ride up and down!"

"No I didn't!"

"Yes you did! Sometimes you wouldn't even let me off the elevator! You made me ride back up to seventy eight, then back down and back up, you howling wolf! It's a good thing people would get on the elevator. You wouldn't let me off!"

Patrick laughed at the playfully flirtatious memory of his wife. The recollection was purest in truth. At the time, to escape the marginally violent daily lifestyle of the penthouse, once in a while when he could, Patrick would spend time with his older sister and younger siblings. One day over the phone Hyacinth complained to Patrick of crying at school after receiving a C for a project; and a saved, sassy American girl, freshman to be, prayed with her inside of the study hall. Hyacinth would proceed to spill her guts after the prayer about being separated from her immediate family, to move alone in Brooklyn near to a few cousins, yet still missing the good times she once shared at home. The young lady prayed with her again for a cohesive family life that would end the dissension the Livingston family was experiencing.

Patrick was very attracted to Hyacinth's friend from college upon meeting her. He admired Michelle's spiritual drive, and Hyacinth spoke highly of her. Hyacinth liked her so much that Patrick met them both one afternoon for shopping purposes at Michelle's afterschool job. This was the second time in his life since elementary, he would go downtown inside of the Twin Towers; Patrick, with specific directions through the World Trade Center concourse, found 2 World Trade. He entered the building, looking for the elevator bank marked "1-78", bypassing the "1-40" and "43-74" banks. His stomach dropped with speeding anti-gravity and his ears popped with the altitude change, during the fast two minute elevator ride into the sky. Transferring at the seventy-eighth floor, Patrick passed the "80-90", and "90-100" banks to get an express car in the bank marked "100-110".

At 2 World Trade Center, 100th Floor: "Delpeche, Hart & Sands Company", receptionist Michelle Ryerson waited with her friend Hyacinth Livingston patiently, for Hyacinth's younger brother she heard so much about. Once Patrick arrived, he escorted the young women out of the office, and off the premises for the day. For the evening they went to dinner, and the trio went to a crowded movie theater to check the blockbuster film "Mad Max Beyond The Thunderdome". Once Michelle called her parents informing them she was with Hyacinth and a "responsible relative", they were relieved. Patrick wound up driving the girls to Coney Island for an extended night of fun and back home, getting Michelle's telephone number for "future prayer".

The young couple in Christ laughed together quickly, both remembering how the future prayer briefly became occasional "in-person after work floral arrangements", until the tragedy that befell the Livingston family.

"I miss her too, "said Michelle.

"I know angel, I know," Patrick replied starting up with his food again. "Your food is getting cold, and you always complain about how microwaved food is no good."

"Okay. I was just having a moment. I mean, don't get me wrong. Cindy was hoity-toity around City Tech now . . . And you know I love my Jesus and I'm a woman of God . . . But I'm a let you know, honey you are not all that! The guys at school were cool, but them worldly girls had to go! But when I saw Cindy crying that day, I just needed to let her know that God loved her, and there is nothing too heavy that the Lord would place on her heart."

Patrick finished his plate of food, stood and kissed his wife on her forehead.

"I love you angel. Are you finished?"

"No."

"I figured that."

Michelle continued with her meal, watching her husband clear his area of the table; then he began washing his plate and glass.

Michelle continued, "Just like Pastor Davis preached today, God is our number one everything; and the Lord is not going to put on you more than you or your heart can bear. It's right there in Luke, in that new testament."

Patrick added with his back turned, "Yup, yup. Luke 1:37 angel, for nothing is impossible with God. I hear you."

"I know you hear me, but are you hearing the Lord? I

loved the sermon today. The holy spirit was all over me."

"That's why you're tired too, all that shouting you did. It's not only your new job. It's church, school, work at the hospital, it's everything. It's me."

Michelle detected the familiar desolation in her husband's voice. The usual turn of emotion happened the moment any of his slain relatives were mentioned in a conversation.

"No sweetheart, never you."

Patrick stopped the water from running. He went back to the table to sit with his wife.

"Angel, I'm doing the best that I can. I just want them back you know . . . If I had to do it all over again, I would have never sold drugs, and I would have fought against Uncle Barry and Uncle Ezra, bringing that type of lifestyle to the family. I would have stayed out the game. My mother was right all along. It's just that, I didn't understand back then, why she really kicked her own brothers out of the house, and why my father allowed them to stay away . . . and when she kicked me out of the house for letting them visit, I had nowhere to go . . . I was so into the world, we all were . . . And word to God I can't front, it felt real good! Had a birthday party that lasted for three days straight . . . in a penthouse we had designed, just for us. We made so much money . . . And then, it was like . . . Everybody started dying . . .

"We all kept shooting, and getting shot up . . . Shell . . . I just miss my little brother, I miss Andy . . . he was so smart, and so talented, he was young . . . and I want my Sharon and Rosie back, I want Cindy back, I need my sisters back to protect them and I need my father . . . yes the Lord blessed me with holding onto Nigel, I'm grateful . . . but I miss Frankie's laugh, and I really want my Father, and I need my Mother . . . I'm trying to keep them alive in memories . . . Memories when we were together, before all the drugs took over . . . if people really only knew how drugs and alcohol destroys families . . . Shell, I wish my parents could have met you, their daughter in law . . . I want my grandmother to be enough for me, and all my cousins from overseas, but sometime they're not enough angel, they're not!"

"Hear from God honey," Michelle interjected holding Patrick's hand.

"Yes angel, there you go! Like, when I'm at Associated around the way now, sometimes it's so painful, because I can't bring back them back! I really can't bring my family back! . . . But as long as I keep God and you in my life, I'm a be good. Look, don't feel like you don't have to speak about Cindy around me. My sister was beautiful, and she still is. At least you met her and she was instrumental in bringing us together. I can hear her voice every day in my heart and mind, all my brothers and sisters . . . my Father, Mother."

"Just hear from the Lord honey."

Patrick smiled at Michelle and said, "See this is why I love you. Thorough-thorough-thorough woman of God, you are so anointed."

The telephone started ringing, and Michelle stood to answer it.

"Hello." Her face and body language instantly took on a new persona.

"Yes, how are you . . . he is . . . he's busy right now with our dinner . . . What? . . . Excuse me?"

Patrick removed Michelle's plate from the table knowing she wouldn't finish the rest of her food. He whispered to her: "Who's on the phone?" She didn't respond, continuing her discomforting conversation.

" . . . Lost?! . . . We go to church on Sundays . . . he's BUSY! . . . Look I can barely hear you, what? . . . You know what?" Michelle hung up the phone.

Sucking her teeth, huffing, she sat back down at the table. Patrick began scraping the leftovers in a plastic container.

"What's wrong angel? Who was on the phone?"

Michelle wouldn't respond with her arms crossed.

"Uh-oh," Patrick began. "Wha' Mummy sey to you?"

"Your grandmother is fine. She is respectful to say the least."

"Don't bother fret them, you have to finish studying, and I have to massage your feet."

"Then, I won't be able to study Mister."

The phone started to ring again. Michelle started back to the phone, and Patrick stopped her.

"Wait now. You, put the food away for tomorrow, and I'll get it."

"You should let the answering machine pick it up Patrick. I can't stand him!"

Michelle indignantly rose from the table to continue packing leftovers. Patrick shook his head inhaling, then exhaled and answered the phone. "Hello."

"Yo, ya fucking wife hung up on me B!! Where you at nigga I'm on Jefferson," Dwayne yelled from the other end.

"Whoa, whoa, whoa, calm down money, hold up, calm down! You need to chill with that . . . Dee I can barely hear you! What?!"

"Pat I'm out here in cold ass Crooklyn looking for your crib! I need your help right now! I can't take this shit no more! I'm not trying to die! You gotta help me! Where your crib, I'm on Jefferson Street and . . . um . . . Bushwick?! It's crazy factories over here!"

"That sounds like the wrong Jefferson man!"

"Where's your crib Pat man?! PLEASE!"

"I think you have to stay on Bushwick further down, until you get to . . ."

Michelle shouted, "OH NO YOU DON'T!" She stormed over to Patrick and depressed the button on the telephone, disconnecting the call.

"Shell!"

Michelle stated, "No honey. No way jose! He is NOT coming to my house! You go back to Harlem with that type of worldly filth!"

Patrick took a deep breath, needing to choose the right words to deal with his wife. "Now angel . . ."

"Don't you now angel me! He cannot come here! I do not appreciate his tone! I won't put up with him, his tone, or his filthy mouth! You don't call MY house and demand to talk to MY husband when I tell you he's busy! Talking about he's been calling us all day! Save that mess for someone who's trying to hear it!"

"Sweetness," Patrick started again patiently, "We've just finished speaking about the love and power of God. I truly don't think it's cool to go from speaking the word, to hanging up phones on people, twice. Two wrongs don't make a right. Dee's never been easy, you know that."

"Don't you even try it Mister! He is not coming to MY HOME!"

"OUR home, and what you're doing and how you're acting is not of God right now."

"Don't give me that! So I'm supposed to let one of Satan's crew up in here Patrick?"

"God doesn't neglect those in need Shell. It's right in Psalms, I think it's Psalms 9:17 or maybe 9:18; for the needy shall not always be forgotten, the expectation of the poor won't perish."

"How do you know he's in need? Anytime something happens to DWAYNE you go off running!"

"He must be in trouble angel, or he wouldn't be in Brooklyn on Jefferson Street looking for Jefferson Avenue."

"Leave him over there!"

"Would Jesus do that?"

The phone started ringing for the third time. Patrick put his finger to his lips and stated, "The brother is in trouble and we won't be the ones to judge angel. We leave the judging to The Almighty. That's for God to deal with."

Michelle rolled her eyes at Patrick while he picked up the phone.

"Hello . . . Wha' 'appen Mummy? Wha g'wan? . . . Eih hih, h'ohw ya keepin todey? . . . Eih? . . . Mi jus' fill mi belly fulla de jerk chicken . . . Mummy! . . . Wha yah ah chat 'bout? . . . Mi nah bring de chicken coume, too far nuh maan . . . H'ahrlem not 'round de cahrner ya 'nuh . . . fat jus in ah mi belly . . . eih? . . . Gaan ah church todey, yea maan . . . Meeshell h'allrite."

"My grandmother says hello," said Patrick, covering the mouthpiece of the phone.

"Saved by my grandmother in-law, cause your boy not coming here!"

"Mummy, h'old de line nuh . . . Mi 'ave anuddah call dem ah coume . . . Yo . . . Where you at son?!"

After listening to Dwayne's questionable location, Patrick covered the mouthpiece again. "Shell, are we near Gates and Broadway?"

Michelle began humming one of her favorite hymns, while scraping the food from the pots into the plastic ware, ignoring her husband's question.

"Gates and Broadway is near Jefferson, but not where we are," said Patrick. "You must have taken the Williamsburg Bridge, I used to get lost over there too, it's two Jeffersons . . . if you see someone out there, tell them you need to get to Jefferson and Stuyvesant, and we're on that block. We are Jefferson between Reid and Stuyvesant."

On the other end of the line on a functional pay phone, Dwayne was chilled to the bone, spiritually and mentally because of the haunting, yet physically because of the frigid evening temperature.

"Yo answer your phone man if I call again . . . you know I don't know shit about Brooklyn, but Pat you the only one who can help me! Jefferson between Reid and Stuyvesant?!"

"Yeah man, I'll look out for you. Hurry up though because my wife and I have things to do."

Patrick looked at Michelle and she hummed louder after his last statement.

"We'll not go back . . . we'll not go back . . . we'll not go back in the world . . . we'll not go back . . . we'll not go back . . . we'll not go back . . . to the world."

Patrick quickly finished the conversation with his grandmother after clicking back over. Giving her his love, he put the phone receiver on the hook. He chuckled watching his wife wash the rest of their dishes and pots, drying them with her humming, pretending to ignore him watching.

"We'll not go back . . . we'll not go back . . . we'll not go back . . ."

"Are you sure the song goes like that angel?"

"We'll not go back . . . we'll not go back . . . we'll not go back in the world . . . We'll not go back . . . we'll not go back . . . we'll not go back, to the world."

"So you trying to igg me I see."

Michelle finished drying the pots and walked past her husband announcing, "He goes, 'I need to massage your feet angel-honey'! When your boy get here, you make sure you massage his feet! I have a chemistry test tomorrow, and *Meeshell* has to work!"

Patrick shouted playfully: "PSALMS 9:18 though! . . . Or is it 9:17," he pondered.

Twenty minutes later, the doorbell rang the second time, and Michelle exhaled aggravatedly from her position in the living room. Patrick went into their foyer and opened the door and then unlocked the black iron front gate, pulling it back.

"Good you found a place to park. I would have left the front open, but we don't play that out here Dee," Patrick said, slapping Dwayne five and giving him a hug.

They walked into the living room.

"Yo my bad Michelle for getting loud, but it's bleeding outside! And I'm in big trouble, and it's getting ugly. I need Pat word up! At least to talk this out and find out what I need to do!"

Michelle looked up from her book at the two men, re-pursed her lips shaking her head, and looked back down into her test material.

"Where's your courtesy homie? Take your hat off in my house and give me your coat for a minute man," Patrick said, helping Dwayne with his belongings.

"Pat, this shit can't wait man, I came all the way out here to Crooklyn for your help, so you know what time it is!"

Michelle rose from the recliner, giggled, and said, "You want something to eat Dwayne? Are you thirsty?"

"Nah. Thanks. Good looking, I appreciate it, but yo Pat. We need to talk."

"Sit down, man," Patrick pointed to the couch and went to hang his buddy's coat in the hallway closet near the door. Michelle sauntered her way from the living room, yawning, shaking her head.

"Massage the feet of the world," Michelle stated prophetically, stopping short when she noticed the brown handle of Dwayne's black weapon peaking above his belt. Patrick came back into the den and noticed what his wife saw.

Dwayne said, "I know what you thinking, but I already told you the deal Pat! That stuff that went down at my crib, before the holidays? You know I'm not going out like a sucker no way! I told you Pat! I told you!"

Michelle threw up her hands and went up the stairs, and Patrick became livid. He was angry for being put on the spot in front of his woman, with having many worlds collide in front of him, inside of his home where there was no escape. Patrick needed an explanation from Dwayne for his current antics.

"Dee, what's up with you, and what's up with that!," Patrick said furiously, pointing at Dwayne's gun. "You bring a joint in my home? . . . In front of my lady man?! . . . What in heaven's name is wrong with you? I'm saved man, and you know I don't roll like that no more! I don't care what my cousin's stay into, or what they do; but I'm not with the guns, and the knives, and the drugs anymore, and you know this! . . . Why you come all the way out here with a burner telling me you need help? And you frighten my wife!"

"Nigga I'm not trying to hear that! I'm being haunted by a guppy! And I'm a kill it!"

"WHAT?!"

"That shit that happened in my crib months ago! When I got hurt that night after the club!"

"Dee what are you trying to say? Have you lost your mind?"

"What is that Jamaican ghost shit that haunts you? Your Pops told us about it!"

"What? A duppy?!"

"Is it guppies or duppies?"

"Guppies are tiny, harmless fish man! You should know B! You have an aquarium with tropical fish in it! Are you talking about a duppy?"

"Yeah!"

" It's duppy. D-u-p-p-y, not g-u-p-p-y."

"What you know about them? What's the difference between a duppy and a real ghost? Whatever the fuck it is, I got one, in my crib and this iron right here . . ."
Dwayne pulled the gun from his waist pointing at it, and Patrick froze, eyeing his friend wondering his next move, becoming more vexed.

"You see this four-five in my hand Pat? YOU SEE THIS?! That thing you call a duppy, or a guppy, puppy, duppy, whatever the fuck! That DUPPY, put this here burner in my mouth tonight and tried to pull the trigger, and I ran! And I had to get to you Pat cause I'm tired of this shit! I'm a kill it, before it kills me! And I need to know what you know!"

Patrick took a deep breath, furious, but poised while being unarmed. He did recall Dwayne speaking of a few sightings and descriptions of Mr. Carter's return; however, there were no such things as a duppy, or a ghost. The only spirit he chose to deal with was the "holy spirit". Patrick was well aware of the real story. He heard of the recent tale of his cousin Carlton pulling out his nine millimeter on Dwayne because of Dwayne troubling his grandmother. His family would never forgive Dwayne for making the evil choice of breaking into their home and stealing, after they first welcomed him inside.

Glancing at the weapon his boy brandished, Patrick wanted no part of the new wave of gun violence brewing, which would be the total opposite of his subtle married life, and the new path of positivity he was learning to embrace. He had to persuade Dwayne out of the house immediately, and this time he pondered if their friendship, a kinship that seemed life-long, had run its course. Dwayne continued his terrified rant.

"Word up kid! What you know about them shits?! Please tell me?! Do they disconnect your phone?! That's why I can't get through to you, and the phone company can't find nothing wrong! The duppy stopped my phone line! Do they keep attacking you, and beat the shit out of you, and come to your job, and ride the subway and shit?! Do they beat you down like this, where you gotta go out and get a burner for protection?! Pat tell me what you know about ghosts! Tell me what you know about duppies! This nigga ain't no Casper the friendly ghost shit at all . . . Tell me wha . . ."

"**DEE!** . . . All I'm going to tell you, and what I know, is you're going to make me lose my religion! CALM

DOWN, HOMIE, IN THE NAME OF GOD! I'M TELLING YOU B! I don't know jack about duppies! It's a back home thing! I'm raised here like you, basically. My grandmother might know about that."

"Call your grandmother now!"

"I just spoke to my grandmother. No man!"

"But you said you would help me, and I hate to admit, but I'm fucking scared of this shit! Ghosts not supposed to knock your teeth out! I have a duppy on my case!"

"A duppy on your case?! Man, come on! Dee, you're a Yankee boy! I'm Jamaican and if I don't know that much, you definitely don't know nothing! I mean, before I came here to live, back home when I was a shorty, I think I hear the grown-ups them say Rollin' Calf coming down from de mountain . . . or Old H'ag peeling off de people dem skin, or the white witch of Rosehall, kill her husband . . . but I never paid that stuff any attention!"

Patrick tried to cool his temper unsuccessfully, still noticing Dwayne holding the handsome black .45 ACP, with the barrel pointing at the floor.

"Dee, you need to put that joint away or leave my house homeboy, straight up and down! Shell is probably calling the cops. And you know me, nor you, need that! I love The Lord, but I love no cops. You don't either."

Dwayne tucked his weapon back into his waist.

"And calm down," Patrick said. "Make this quick because you have scared my wife. And I need to make sure she's okay."

"So what you gon' do for me kid? This duppy shit is important. I need to know! Remember how it changed all my furniture around? I thought Nikki did it, she thought I did it?"

"Yeah and I told you then to change your locks."

"Change my locks for what Pat?! You know that duppy ghost broke in changed my shit around, and did what he did anyway! And you know who it is too!"

"Who?"

"It's my grandfather!"

"What about him?

"He's the one! He's the duppy ghost, or whatever you people call that bullshit!"

"We people?! Yo Dee, moneygrip, yo check this out . . . ," Patrick stood and went for Dwayne's coat, losing the last barrier on his cool for the first time in years. He returned to the living room, and passed the coat to delirious Dwayne.

"You not gon' help me?"

"Transit has you bugging crazy hard! You need a vacation Dee, you flipping out!"

"This duppy shit got me flipping out," said Dwayne, slowly putting on his coat. "Call your grandmother! You can't call your grandmoms back for me?!"

"I'm not calling my grandmother! I was kicking it with her, and your call interrupted the line. When I get a chance, I'll kick it with her later about it! Sometime this week maybe, but not tonight!"

"Nah B, you fucking up! No, no, you are fucked up. This is not a good look! This is NOT A GOOD LOOK PAT! Word up!"

The two friends glared at each other negatively for the first time in history, with Dwayne gradually becoming an enemy inside of Patrick's vision, and Dwayne returning his energy with darkened eyes that were virtually devoid of pupils, hissing while putting on his hat.

"Yeah nigga . . . This shit is COLD SEX! If I was a Jamaican nigga B, you would do it! This is fucked up Pat! **This is not a good look!**"

"What do you mean?!"

"Fucking coconuts! I been telling you I need help with this ghost shit! You know Pappy been following me for months trying to kill me! I been by 20th, and your sucker ass cousin pulled out on me again and kicked me down the steps! I drive way out here to Brooklyn from the Bronx in the bleeding ass cold, tell you again my grandfather put this fucking pistol in my mouth! Pappy damn near pulled the trigger, and you know the nigga beat my ass a coupla times, and you can't even call your grandmother for the information I need! I know what's up though . . . I know what time it is! . . . See, it's only cause I'm American! And cause I'm an American, because I'm a fucking YANKEE BOY, like you people call it, you think I'm fucking crazy!"

"Yo Dee hold up! What the hell is up with this yankee-coconut business, you people bullcrap?! What's up with you man?! Disrespecting my house?! Disrespecting my wife?! Yankee, coconut, nah son! We boys first! What's up with this bullshit," Patrick yelled.

"What the fuck! I'm talking to a wall or something nigga?! My grandfather is a duppy! I'm telling you he's trying to kill me! See I know you playing stupid cause of your cousins that hate Americans!"

"What are you talking about Dee? You've lost it!"

"Yeah right Pat . . . Bet if I was a coconut you would hook me up! All you motherfuckers like to call niggas like me a yankee! A LAZY, CRAZY YANKEE! You ain't shit though! Word to MUTHA! All you coconut motherfuckers done took over everything any fucking way, and you won't help nobody but yourselves! I gotta be Jamaican for you to help me nigga?! You won't even call your fucking grandmother to ask about ghosts! That's FUCKED UP PAT! Fucking monkeys only help your own people! Taking over everything! Taking everything like a fucking plague!

Patrick lost his temper with Dwayne which was the absolute wrong thing to do, equivalent to bull versus bull, scorpion versus scorpion, lion versus lion, etc.

"Get the fuck out my house!," Patrick yelled. He then shoved Dwayne towards the front door.

"You get the fuck out my house, **you thief punk bitch! And doun't coume baack! BAAMBECLAAT**

YENKEE BWOY! BAAMBERASSCLAAT YE POOSWUUH!! Mi never h'ask fi coume dis blaastid country, supposed land of de free, houme to dem POOSYCLAAT BREVE! Bloodclaat yenkee bwoy t'ief eiidiot, baambeclaat yenkee bw . . ."

In the blink of an eye, Dwayne pulled his weapon out, pointed at Patrick's forehead and pulled the trigger to a click drowned out by Michelle's blood curdling scream; and Patrick ceased his backsliding rant of profanity, grateful for the inhaled breath of life that flashed before his very own eyes. His ceaseless, everlasting prayers to the universe proved divinely for his past, present, and future, for it wasn't time to re-join his family yet. And Dwayne had his very own life flash in front of him also, grateful that his weapon had stalled with a faulty clip of jumbled rounds, after being taunted continuously by disappearing Al, who he knew threatened to pull the trigger the next time Dwayne pulled a loaded gun on him. Dwayne, Patrick, and Michelle were frozen in time for a moment, with a simple gratitude for life; yet with the ticking of subsequent seconds, there could be no turning back for their previous actions.

Dwayne stormed out of the brownstone leaving the front door and gate open with nothing left to say, and Patrick tended to his sobbing hysterical wife who curled into in a terrified ball at the bottom of their staircase. The individuals still clung to life, but their relationship achieved death within seconds, from a speeding, invisible bullet to their souls from a damaged automatic weapon that jammed.

There was irreparable damage between the three young people, an unforgettable moment that would plague their spirit when mentally visited for the rest of their lives.

****

CHAPTER 17

*

Refusing to return to his suite, Dwayne stayed in the BMW overnight, still with voices and rumbling growls, dealing with his mental state until the twilight of the dawn. He nodded through sunrise until mid-morning, and when fully awakened, he drove through the streets at random, deciding on another next to last resort. Scrapping his original idea of going to Co-op City, in case he would have to shoot Corey or Nefertiti for interfering, Dwayne decided it would be the center where he would convince Nicole to come home. Besides, she had called him and wanted to talk a few days prior, and it would be better to contact her in person. It was just the reverse of luck that he found a parking space a few feet away from the entrance of the rehab center, a place he knew all too well. Before entering the center, he took a deep breath, patted his weapon's placement, and entered the building, with its hustle and bustle of a Monday schedule.

After exchanging words with a receptionist and a few security guards, Dwayne stormed his way through the halls on the warpath for Nicole. No one would stop him from seeing his woman, absolutely nobody! Two security guards angrily trailed behind, ready to pounce. Dwayne stopped at her original space on the first floor, took the stairs to the second floor, searching, casing the entire building until he found the closed door to the large room with the carved wooden name "NICOLE M. RYERSON M.S.W" on the outside.

Dwayne burst into Nicole's new office, startling her while she was on the phone sitting behind her desk. The guards followed him into the room ready to seize their enemy.

"Wait fellas! It's okay," she said, placing the phone receiver to her ear after dropping it. One security guard was still ready to grab Dwayne when the other stopped him.

"Hey! I said it's okay! Really," Nicole stated with a commandeering look.

"You sure?!," the aggressive guard asked.

"Honey, I'm sure . . . You, Mister Carter, pull up a chair and sit down."

Dwayne found a steel chair and unfolded it in front of Nicole's desk. The two guards exited, one giving Dwayne the meanest look he'd ever created.

While Nicole finished up her telephone conversation, her man admired the new office that was awarded, with her latest look. Her hair, usually permed, curled and shoulder length had blonde & black extensions braided up into a bun; she wore an electric blue cashmere turtleneck sweater with jeans, black leather boots above the knee, with pearl earrings and light lip gloss with a bluish tint. On the other end of the phone line, warning Nicole of forthcoming trouble, was the same receptionist Dwayne had exchanged words with. The entire staff hated him, especially after he and Nicole became engaged.

Nicole continued into the telephone, "Yes . . . everything is okay up here now . . . Yes, I do appreciate your concern . . . I'm fine . . . Thanks. It's okay, really. I'll let you know . . . No he did not call you that, not out of your name . . . I know . . . I'll get to the bottom of it . . . Awww, thank you . . . Thank you, that means a lot. Don't worry . . . Bye now." She hung up the phone, took one of her deepest breaths ever, and focused her attentions to her fiancé.

"How are you," she spoke sternly.

"Okay," Dwayne replied. "I got some new front teeth, see," he smiled, pointing at new partial top dentures. He wanted to tell her the truth, he was far from okay. The teeth and oral surgery was the only successful move over the last few days. He wondered how to break the news that Al had really returned from the dead. Al was the culprit behind his facial bruises, missing teeth, and mental pandemonium.

Nicole asked, "Did you get my message?"

He nodded and said, "I like this office, big college girl. You moving up in the world. Rocking MCM bags now. The center is starting to hook you up."

"Well, they know I'll have doctor in front of my name like my Mom and Dad. I've started classes at Lehman, in your neck of the woods, you know to get this Ph.D. They have faith in me like I have faith in myself. I'll be vice president here once I receive my degree . . . Coffee?"

"Nah. Thanks but no thanks."

"So why you haven't you called me?"

"The phone's been fucked up. The line is tied up and the phone company can't find anything wrong, they can't do nothing and it's bugging me out," he said shrugging his shoulders, staring off into space. If he could just explain how Al had destroyed the phone line. After a few seconds passed, she fixed a cup of coffee and sat back down to face him.

"Why aren't you at work today?"

"I'm on a vacation. I had to take a few days off. I was exhausted."

"Growing your hair back I see. It's really been a while. I'm seeing a lot of gray up there Mister Carter. Quite a bit, excuse me. But it's cute . . . Handsome if you will, distinguished."

"Should I say thank you for a gray hair compliment?"

"Your face is healing pretty well. You look better than the last time I saw you."

"I'd look even better if you come home with me, and I

would feel a lot better once my ring goes back on your finger. Think I ain't see that right? I'm 'a get you back, Nikk, if it's the last thing I do, word up! I miss you in my life so much. Come home baby, I need you."

Nicole put her mug down and folded her hands across her desk. She took a deep breath while she felt her tears coming. She looked at the ceiling, and then looked at her naked left hand.

She wanted to be back in Dwayne's life as much as he wanted her to, but she was afraid of the erratic mood swings, aberrant behavior, and denial that something may be wrong; things may worsen between them. The easiest thing to do would be to go inside her new purse, and return the diamond to its rightful place on her left ring finger; and the hardest thing to deal with was the reality of who and what she faced sitting across her desk. His rescue mission to prevent murder was her sole purpose originally, and to reach out and touch others and encourage hurting souls to rebuild themselves was still her makeup, and still part of her job description.

Yet, she finally acknowledged the violation of the wrong choice she made, allowing her own ignorance for the sober boundary of counselor and client to be crossed; it was a border that should have been professionally cast in stone, with each and every patient, including the difficult man on the other side of her desk, who removed his hat and shades to reveal a newer, beckoning intensity in his eyes. She looked into the rapidly healing face of a troubled man, a man whom she sacrificed her professionalism for, a man she unfortunately allowed herself to be sucked into becoming a deeper part of his existence, into becoming a woman to his total being. Her time was beginning to run short to make the decision in continuing the relationship.

Nicole wished she never knew Dwayne could possess multiple sides of fiery passion and caring tenderness. To lie in his strong arms at night, on a good night during the good times, was what she craved and missed; and to participate in the freaky games of love, flavored with orgasmic colors, humor, and layers with his forceful habits of sensuality was what she needed. Dwayne Albert Carter regrettably turned out to be the perfect match for Nicole Maria Ryerson in bed. If she could just undo the hands of time to be blind to the feelings that zoomed through her soul, heart, loins, and mind. Perhaps there was a chance, a random thought that made him need to relax, which is why today's appearance at the office was so crucial for them both. In the beginning, he was a decent listener, he was thoughtful and spontaneous, he was open, receptive, and in synch with her direction and generous with his entire body, especially with the lovemaking in and out of bed.

Dwayne slowly reached across the desk while she undid her hair barrette, to allow her braids to fall, just for her man to see; and their hands met in a loving grasp on top of the desk. Dwayne and Nicole identically thought, perhaps just one kiss, one kiss should assist and cure this twinkly moment of truth and need. Her need to be strong enough to separate from him, for her illuminating future, and to not wind up in the throes of lustful, steamy intercourse inside her office; his truth to have her home as a loving bodyguard, to be a shield from Al, and to resume their loving union.

She despised the return of crisp, deliberate lies about his whereabouts. To make matters worse, Michelle had called the office with a warning cry and her version of what she and her husband experienced in their home, less than twenty-four hours prior. Nicole was adrift once again, inside of Dwayne's strong touch, attempting to pull her hands away thinking of her frantic cousin's cautionary pleas, but Dwayne held onto Nicole's beautifully smaller hands for dear life. And the warm electricity that always radiated from his large, strong hands was the gateway to the opening tune of their feelings that led to the routine caressing of their bodies.

"Please come home baby," Nicole thought she heard her lover repeat, while lost in emotion. He rubbed her empty left ring finger saying, "Don't worry . . . I'll put it back on for you, and this time, when we make up, I'm going to prove my love to you."

As badly as she missed Dwayne in her life, Nicole still acknowledged her growth apart from the man that she briefly loved with every ounce of her femininity; and the grasping knowledge of this surge and advancement hurt more than the shameful slap inside the club, or any of the embarrassing situations and moments, that her choice to deal with him in a relationship placed her in. To return to life with Dwayne would be a step back. Her instantaneous attraction to him was severed with the perceptive discovery of Dwayne's violent nucleus. The night fits to bad temper snaps were one thing, the hallucinations another red flag; then, simply having her staff and family prove that their love would turn wrong was also discomforting.

And now Dwayne was terrified of being alone. He knew in his heart having Nicole back home would help. Even thinking of Al gave him the jitters. At first, Al was just in the co-op waiting for him every evening, or he would ride the subway with the rush hour crowd. Now, his evil grandfather was everywhere, and he was deteriorating more and more with each of his savage recurrences. The elderly flesh was rotting away, exposing subcutaneous tissue, cells with thriving maggots; Dwayne squirmed just thinking about it.

"So will you come? Tonight . . . please?," he begged.

"Is everything okay with you?"

"Yes, and no."

"How is that? What's wrong?"

"I'm losing my mind. Well, I can't really say that I'm losing it, but I'm not so good. Things ain't good love."

"Dwayne, it is way too early in the morning for this. I

mean, you're asking me to come home to you, then, you're telling me things are not good because you're losing your mind. What's up with that?"

"I'm bugging out over you though."

"So explain."

"I can't," he snapped mistakenly, thinking of Al.

"Please, Nikki, come home with me. I can explain everything at home! . . . I love you. We're engaged to be married. You my woman, I'm your man, and I need you home with me!"

The buzzer sounded on Nicole's desk phone indicating she had a call.

"Ryerson."

Dwayne loved watching his girl's serious facial expressions and different behavior on the job. At work, she was in total control, standing tall and looking good, queen of Hollywood inside of her new office.

"Okay," she said, hanging up the receiver. "I have an important meeting in about five minutes." She picked up her cascading braids, pulling them together to make a new bun.

"Listen, I'll call you. Later on tonight, okay?"

"Don't front Nikk. Come on baby. Put the ring back on at least."

"I'm not making any promises. We're taking this one step at a time," she said, sternly.

"Ya miss me," he asked, trying his usual post-spat mannerisms.

"What do you think?"

"Call me boobie."

"Look, we'll discuss those things later. I have a meeting to attend!"

"Put the ring back on."

Nicole stood from her desk, politely paying him no attention digging inside her purse. She pulled her office keys from her bag, instead of the engagement ring, opening the door.

"You'll have to excuse me, Dwayne. But I will call you."

"I need you to put the ring back on before I leave."

Nicole took a deep breath, and looked at the floor. She quietly responded, "No."

"Nikki!"

"I can't right now Boobie, I just can't."

Dwayne became reluctant to leave, now that his plans to tempt Nicole fell through. He tried not to become more upset, dropping his head with a hiss, seeing the uniformed trousers of two security guards joining Nicole out of his side eye.

"You sure you alright up here Miss Ryerson? You cool," one of the men asked.

"Yes ma'am! Baby Al ain't giving ya no trouble is he," Dwayne heard the voice of the second gentleman.

Dwayne snapped up his head to see his grandfather completely dressed in a security guard uniform, identically with one of the guards from earlier. Petrified, exasperated, and irate, Dwayne stared at Al who stood next to Nicole.

"I'm fine. Mister Carter here was just leaving. I have another meeting I have to run to. Meetings, meetings, meetings all the time, that's what we do here at Roberto Clemente. Right fellas?"

"Sho' nuff do fine baby! You can say it again," Al said, licking his lips, "All we do is meetings all day! Shiiiiiit! A cat like me need to be in all them meetings, meeting wit'cha! Givin' ya' some meat to meet!"

Al groped his crotch through his uniform pants, sticking a dark, mottled tongue out in Nicole's direction, wiggling it back and forth. He licked his lips, then he looked at his maddening grandson.

"Good god almighty Baby Al, I see why you been tapping this, but she need a real nigga like me to hit it! I know this pussy good, cause she sho' nuff do smell good."

Nicole noticed the antagonized change in Dwayne as he glared at her and the security officer, ferociously. With Dwayne not budging, she rolled her eyes, and sucked her teeth.

She began thinking, '*No, not now with this jealous mess now Boobie . . . God no . . . He's flipping out . . . He must be using again . . . If he can't respect my job then we can't be together . . . He just will not change for the better . . . Look at him staring at Mr. Torres like he wants to kill him . . . my God just like the club that night . . . He has to go . . . I'll try later . . . maybe . . .*'

"Bye, Dwayne," Nicole snapped. "I have to go now!"

"Nikki . . . Yo . . . I . . .," Dwayne began to stutter with eyes fixated on Al and his partner as they flanked Nicole.

She put her hand on her hip, angrily patting her foot with the knowledge of only one guard standing with her. In her mind's eye, Nicole was transported back to Club Zanzibar's which constituted a violent smack across the face, and the recollection confirmed her decision of prolonging the engagement.

"Listen I can't leave you in my office right now Mister Carter. I've asked you to leave several times, and you just sit there and keep staring!"

The security guard pulled up his pants, took a deep breath and started walking towards
Dwayne. "Sir, you're going to have to leave this room immediately."

"Tell her! Tell this fine smelling, juicy piece of puss in boots I'm just a coward ass nigga being haunted!,"Al yelled, beginning to laugh; and Dwayne sprang into action.

"Shut up," Dwayne hollered at his grandfather, standing with his weapon pointed and squeezing off a gunshot at Al. The booming blast of the .45 shockingly stopped movement in the entire building, with the exception of security officer Torres, who after walking into the fired slug that ricocheted through his body, did his last two step and fell dead.

Dwayne shot Al two more times, the rounds being heard from the top floor of the rehab center to the basement. Al disappeared, and was hopefully shot and finally blown away for good Dwayne hoped. Nicole screamed for her own life at the turn of events, with her co-worker shot to death in front of her, her fiancé being the killer. Her arms, lifted up in distress and total horror, were shaking with her life flashing in front of her; and in a flash, Dwayne seized his crying, frightened girl before she could run amok like the rest of her co-worker's and staff inside the building.

"I got his ass yeah!! Yeah!! SEE YUUHH!! SEE YUUHHH!! I smoked him baby!! Yeah, but we gotta go Nikk! We gotta get out of here! Come on," Dwayne yelled with victory, jerking Nicole by her arm. Proceeding to quickly exit the center, he kept his hot pistol pointing in the direction of anyone who came near to prevent them from trying to leave the premises. The lingering, incognizant staff and clients ran for cover at the sight of murderous Dwayne abducting Nicole from the center.

"Look he got Miss Ryerson!"

"Oh shit, duck down!"

"Oh my God! Nikki! That maniac, he's got her hostage!"

"He used to be here! Yo that's her nigga?! OH SHIT LOOK OUT!"

"We're gonna be killed!"

"Call the police!"

"Move! Oh no here he comes! He's taking Miss Nicole!"

Dwayne bopped past the stares of fear and dread, with the gun straight ahead, pulling Nicole along while she yelled and cried out loud for her terrified life.

"Nikki will you fucking chill out? You got to play this shit off baby! Chill boo! Calm the fuck down," Dwayne angrily whispered in Nicole's ears, after putting her in a headlock with the weapon to her head.

The couple shuffled out of the center, and out into the freezing February morning. Dwayne pulled Nicole with all of his frantic strength, taking the .45 away from her head, still yanking and tugging her along. Before they could get a few footsteps to the car, they were approached by a homeless man. In his eyes and mind, the destitute fellow believed the advancing hustler with his harlot exiting the center would have money, after working one of his girls all night.

"Hey bruh? Hey! Say bruh man, can ya spare some change sir," asked the vagrant. Dwayne paused, and looked at Al holding out his hand asking for money. The quivering gentleman was shot through his windpipe at point blank range, with another high pitched scream from Nicole. Then Dwayne saw Al sitting in the back seat of the BMW, motioning for him to get inside.

"You see who I see," Dwayne shouted to Nicole pointing at the backseat of the car. "I keep shooting this motherfucker, and he still alive! Shit! Now what I'm 'a do?! . . . Damn, I'm bugging out! . . . Nobody's gonna believe this shit! Damn, Pappy! Why you keep fucking with me?! Today of all days! . . . It's bleeding out here," Dwayne shivered with blood and mucous spreading across his top lip.

Dwayne lugged Nicole around to the passenger side, opened the door and stuffed her inside. Slamming the door, pointing the gun at her, he ran around to the driver's side and jumped into the car. The car amazingly started right away, and heavily cloaked individuals hurried and scurried about, pointing in the direction of the screeching BMW.

Dwayne zoomed off towards the Bruckner, taking every light that he could without crashing, just to get to the expressway. Between heckling Al, and hysterical Nicole, Dwayne was beginning to feel as if he would lose his mind. In the front seat passenger side, Nicole cried, taking deep breaths, desperately wondering what she could do, that would aid in her escape from someone she should have never met. Al let out a hearty laugh in the backseat, taunting his grandson more by soothing scared, unaware Nicole.

"Okay baby . . . it's gon' be alright . . . don't cry lil' doll baby . . . Baby Al ain't gon' hurt'cha . . . not while I'm here . . . Don't cry baby . . . don't be scar . . ."

"SHUT THE FUCK UP!!"

With one hand on the steering wheel, Dwayne shot Al again, this time shooting out the entire backseat passenger window. Nicole screamed again with the deafening sound of the gunshot inches from her face, complete with a misty spray of shattering glass bits spraying into her lap, and behind her in the backseat. Feeling as if she would faint, she pleaded with her man instantly.

"Dwaaayynnee!!! Pleeeasse!! **Please! No more! Oh my God! Please don't kill me**!! I'm Sorry HONEY!! **I'm sorrryyyyy!** I'll do what you need! I'm sorry baby!! Please don't ki . . ."

"I'M NOT GON' KILL YOU NIKKI!"

"Please Dwayne! Pllleeeease!"

"It's not you baby! I love you! It's my grandfather! I have to kill him before he kill me!"

"Oh my God Dwayne!! NO MORE!!," Nicole screamed, with a new stream of flowing tears, knowing the backseat was empty. And it tickled Al to watch his grandson sense imminent danger, misery, and anguish; he knew Dwayne was terrified of him, and he enjoyed every minute of it. To make Dwayne feel all the pain, mental horrors, and anxiety that he once endured was something the senior citizen craved.

"Hey bruh! Hey! Say bruh man, can ya spare some change sir," Al laughed, mimicking the homeless guy Dwayne murdered in a duplicate voice. "Sike! Still trying to kill me huh?! And I just won't die! After ya kicked my ass like there was no tomorrow, you wanted me to die then, and you want me to die now! The good Lawd knows, it's a damn shame!"

"Pappy what the fuck do you want from me?! Huh?! Nikki SEE?!! Pappy is right here with us?!"

"What do I want from ya," Al asked. "What do you think? Ya think I'm here for my health, Baby Al? I want your soul. I need it. We all do, so we can rest in peace."

Dwayne gazed into his rearview mirror while Al continued ghoulishly: "We ain't gon' rest in peace until you die. I hope ya disobey me, so I can bus' yo' ass again. Maybe this time, I think, *I'll kill YOU!*"

Nicole tried to regain a hold of her situation one more time. There must be a chance for her to escape. Perhaps if she behaved the total opposite of her current state of mania; she decided to use the very tactics that caused them to fall in love in the first place. The writing was on the wall for the duration of their relationship, with her beau seeing visions of his grandfather since his death. Nicole decided she needed to get into Dwayne's head and pick his brain about Al Carter. Taking deep breaths of trepidation, she attempted to change her swagger.

"Dwayne . . . Please . . . stop running Boobie . . . don't run, just find a place to pull over . . . Your grandfather is not going to harm you, just pull over."

Al burst into an evil, hoarse laugh that made the hairs stand on the back of his grandson's neck, nearly drowning out Nicole's soft pleas. Dwayne looked at Nicole. Her mascara destroyed with braids unkempt, her eyes were super red, with tears dropping, yet she still kept her new poise.

"Oh my God . . . Boobie, if you love me like you say you do, you would pull over and talk to me. **Please honey!**"

Before entering the Bruckner, Dwayne pulled over on a service road near some abandoned factories. Nicole covered her mouth and began to cry again, extremely cold after her kidnapping from the center without a coat or hat, with the car window being shot out. The brunt of Al's sardonic rancor passed, with quietness in the back seat. Dwayne checked his rear view mirror and saw the senior citizen sleeping. Nicole's sobs were loud enough to be heard over the zooming trucks passing them.

"Stop crying Nikk! Stop crying! Shut the fuck up and listen to me! My fault baby! MY FAULT! I don't mean to scare you like this, I love you boo! Word is fucking born! I love you, and I would never do nothing to harm you . . . You helped me get off drugs, you helped me get a job! All that, word up! Chill! I would never do nothing to harm you! Stop shaking!"

"I'm cold Dwayne . . . I'm cold."

"Yo put this on," Dwayne started taking off his coat to give to Nicole.

"Dwayne . . . Boobie . . . you are going to have to turn yourself in."

Dwayne did a double take hearing his girl's statement. She truly didn't understand what he was going through with Al sitting in the backseat of the BMW. He felt the chill once his black leather "Goose Country" came off. Glancing at Al, ensuring he was sleeping, Dwayne draped his coat over Nicole; never letting the pistol out of his hand.

"Better now baby? Okay? Let's go home and talk about it. I'll tell you what you need to know."

"I'm so afraid Boobie. Oh my God, Dwayne, you have just killed two innocent people . . . Dwayne, you're going to have to turn yourself in! Oh my God!"

More tears ran from Nicole's eyes while she tried to maintain her composure. Michelle was right this time. Dwayne was truly on a rampage to kill anyone who stood in his way. Her teardrops were ceaseless due to Dwayne's murderous oblivion, and she still feared for her own life. She watched him keep looking at his backseat as if someone were sitting there.

"Yo, I didn't pull over for you to be talking this kind

of bullshit Nicole! Let's make this quick baby! We can talk about whatever's bothering you at home!"

"Dwayne . . . do you . . . do . . . do you know what you've just done?"

"Hell yeah! I shot my fucking grandfather baby! And he still won't die! Don't you see him sleeping in the backseat?! Huh?!"

"Dwayne I love you, but you have to stop this!"

"Stop what?!"

"These stories, about your grandfather . . . oh my God . . . **Dwayne he's been dead close to two years now**!"

"No he's not! He's alive! What the fuck is your problem?! Don't you see him," Dwayne yelled at Nicole, pointing at the empty backseat. Once he raised his voice she knew she was fighting a losing battle. She started praying subconsciously while continuing to figure a way out of the car, and away from Dwayne.

"Nicole! He's been following me, and following me, and following me! Nikki my grandfather is alive! He's real! Real eyes! Real hands! Real feet, legs! Real fucking false teeth, dentures damn it! **The motherfucker real!**"

While Dwayne spoke about Al, Nicole continued to cry, and her loud whining sobs awakened Al. Dwayne tried to carefully explain his beliefs to distraught Nicole.

"Look baby. He's the one who switched around our stuff at the crib. Remember?! We couldn't figure out which one of us did it?! My grandfather did it! Remember how bad I was looking after the club?! Nikki, he did it! That's why I got the burner, cause he keeps threatening to kill me! And if you come home with me, everything will be okay!"

"Stop begging! You ain't supposed to beg a woman," Al interjected.

"Mind your fucking business!"

"Make me!"

"Suck my fucking di . . ."

"**DWAYNE**!," Nicole yelled, snapping him from his

argument with Al.

"Now you see right?! Do you see," Dwayne asked Nicole.

"Dwayne, but . . . but . . . honey . . . I can help you Boobie! I really need to help you. Remember . . . this is me now, remember me? Remember me Dwayne? Baby it's me, your darling Nikki, just like Prince?"

"Prince?! . . . BITCH! This ain't no fucking game! *Look, let's go!"*

Dwayne went to shift the car into drive.

"WAIT BOOBIE!"

Dwayne growled and shifted the gear back to park, and Nicole took both his hands, and stared him eye to eye.

"Boobie, you know I love you right?!"

Dwayne nodded, hyperventilating with the arrival of a new, excruciating headache; and Nicole continued her new strategy, trying not to shake, unsuccessfully.

"Dwayne, I am coming home with you. And when I get there, I'm going to make sure that I take super-duper good care of you, the best care for my Boobie . . . You've been through a lot, so much over the past two years; and I refuse to turn my back on you now . . ."

"Go on girl, "Al shouted.

"I'm a make sure you get lots of rest . . . I'm a cook for you, and take care of you how I used to, how you need . . . We'll even take a vacation together daddy . . . But I need you to be honest with me baby . . ."

Al started tapping Dwayne on the back of his head; and Nicole watched Dwayne angrily break his attention span, still holding her hands.

"I'm trying to work shit out with my fucking girl Pappy, die nigga shit!," Dwayne shouted to the backseat.

"Dwayne you need some rest," Nicole continued, "Your mind is not right. It's your mind Boobie. Trust me. And if you let me go back to the center . . ."

"She 'bout to say you smoking crack again," Al chided

emphatically.

" . . . and let me start you up on a new plan, a new treatment plan baby, let me set it up. Sweetest heart, I gotcha covered, cause it's your mind baby. You need to come back to the center, it's all in your mind. I love you and it's okay. I know you're back to smoking cra . . ."

In a flash Dwayne smashed his weapon twice into Nicole's face, beating his frightened point into her painful torment of gloom, mixed with her blood curdling scream seeping into her consciousness.

"I'M NOT ON NO FUCKING CRACK!! MY GRANDFATHER IS AFTER ME!! HE'S AFTER MEEE!!!"

"Don't you **touch that gal no more**," Al yelled, grabbing Dwayne's neck before he could hit Nicole a third time with the gun. He froze in place the second Al grabbed him. Al then let go of Dwayne and pushed up the front passenger seat with Nicole hunched in it, and opened the door, and Nicole fell from the car to the cracked pavement, unconscious.

"Oh shit," Dwayne caught his breath, snapping out of his raging stupor. He jumped out of his side of the car and went over to Nicole who lay on the pavement, blood faced and lumped up.

Al shook his head and said, "It's a cold, cold world out here Baby Al. I told you ya destroy everything ya touch. That gal turned yo' life around, and now look at her! Look what you've done!"

"She dead?"

"You better hope she ain't. Three strikes, and yo ass is out! She breathing I reckon. You see her breath in the cold like she smoking! But you best get out'chere, cause them cops is coming!"

Al returned to the backseat of the car and closed the door. Dwayne looked down on Nicole who began to moan, spitting blood from a once beautiful face. He covered her again with his Goose Country as she lay on the freezing sidewalk.

Dwayne ran to his driver's side, jumped in the car and began the trek back home, unable to shake Al, taking off without Nicole who lay on the ground semi-conscious. He entered the Bruckner Expressway again, and Al continued the routine heckling.

"Real bitch move boy! . . . Beating on that fine woman and leaving her out there in the middle of the street cold as it is . . . I ain't train you like that . . . Man oh man, ya got it easy now, thanks to me dying. If I could do it again, live my life over, I'd cut yo ass a loose! You wouldn't have a pot to piss in! . . . Damn, I ain't been over this way in a while. This Major Deegan sho' is smooth . . . Know what I mean!"

Dwayne couldn't deal with the frightening delusiveness of his world anymore. Al had to be stopped. Was this reality? Were ghosts really real?

"Patrick," Dwayne yelled aloud, then recalling the previous night's twist of fate.

"What about him?," Al asked.

"Nothing."

Al shook his head. "Lord have mercy, it was a crying shame what happened to his people. I sho' hope he's holding up."

Dwayne drove on silently, angry.

"That cornball holding up! Him and his family won't tell me shit about duppies!"

"Huh?"

"Ghosts!"

"OH! You want them to tell you about ghosts huh? You want to tell him about me?"

Dwayne ignored Al and he repeated his question.

"You hear what I ask! Whatcha gonna see him for? Huh?! Ya wanna tell him about me?! . . . Answer me! . . . What you wanna see Patrick for?!"

"None of your business, Pappy! Shit!"

Dwayne saw the BMW letters with car logo quickly rise into his vision in a flash when Al cupped the back of his neck with one hand, and smashed his head into the horn blowing steering wheel with the other. Dwayne screamed, painfully and blindly panicking, as the vehicle swerved out of control. He regained control of the car, finally capturing his direction after having his life flash in front of him.

"Pappy, what the fuck you doing?! **You trying to get me killed?**," Dwayne yelled, still painfully refocusing his vision.

"Still cussing at me boy? We taught ya better than that! When I asks ya question, ya give me an answer, hear? I'll make you crash this motherfucker!"

The car speed increased: 65, 75, 85, 95, 105 miles per hour; and Dwayne dodged trucks, vans, other cars from lane to lane with skill until the video game dream became his reality.

"Faster Baby Al," Al bellowed with his coarse voice, while his grandson pressed the brakes with every ounce of frightened strength. The laughter now coming from the backseat was the exact replica of the ghoulish chuckles Dwayne heard during his worst crack stupors. And the laughs came from Al, whose face had deteriorated even more this time, and his grandson's heart pumped even faster.

The car had a mind of its own reaching 108 miles per hour once Dwayne got the brakes to kick in. Tires screeching for the South Bronx to hear, the car swerved into the left lane sideways, head on, hitting the divider, causing it to bounce back into the middle lane. In the next two seconds, the BMW was hit by a moving van, causing Dwayne to smash into a school bus filled with children, thrusting a few of them from their seats. A four car pile up began after the initial mashing, right at the 149th Street/Stadium exit; and this is where the car finally stopped, after grazing the right lane divider.

More blood dripped from a new gash in Dwayne's forehead because of no seat belt. He retrieved some tissue from the glove compartment for the wound, hissed, looking at the backseat; no Al again. Frightened, guilty, and embarrassed, he lightheadedly exited his mangled pride and joy.

Amidst the echoing cries of the injured children, distant salsa, and the imminent ambulance and police sirens, Dwayne briskly walked the exiting ramp towards 149th Street. As he descended, he gave a last look to the car. His automobile sat lifeless, the culprit mixed up in an afternoon jam. Traffic was backed up for miles throughout the South Bronx, slowing down movement of service up into Pelham Bay, all because of the delirious, bleeding operator of a mashed up ordinary BMW; its remains leftover for the authorities to investigate upon their arrival. The front of the left side was mashed up, with a broken headlight and twisted bumper. There was a giant gash by the driver's door, with several big dents, scuff marks, and chipped paint on both sides.

While walking the ramp he thought, "Damn! Damn! Damn! Shit! What the fuck's wrong with me?! Pappy is dead! . . . **The nigga is dead!** AAAAAAH! . . .**The nigga ain't real! What's wrong with me? The motherfucka ain't real! He AIN'T REAL!**"

Looking at the bleak sky with spring on the horizon, shivering, Dwayne discreetly but victoriously flagged a taxi, mumbling listlessly, "God . . . help me."

Tears escaped his eyes like steaming parachutes landing to the cracked pavement.

He rode home in a dazed silence; everything had gone wrong. He was a fugitive, wanted for murder. Everything, all of the bad was beginning to catch up to him. He desperately needed anyone.

"Get 'im boy! Grrrrrr sic 'im!
Grrrr sic' 'im! Get this old black
motherfucker boy! Grrrr sic' 'im!
Get 'im!"

"Why you doing this to me,
Baby Al, why?. . . I've done all I
could for you . . . Please don't
hurt me no mo' . . . I love you
. . . That's why I raised
you . . . I love you . . . You
my grandson . . . I . . . I
. . . can't go on like this!"

"I can't either. I can't go on like this either, Pappy," Dwayne murmured, shivering, coughing. The neighborhood was quiet except for the elevated Broadway train, and the hustle and bustle of the cars and buses traveling 231st Street. Not too many people loitered about the streets like in Harlem, except for Dwayne who brought an enigmatic energy to the peaceful street of his co-op. The taxi turned the corner onto the street where he lived. He reluctantly entered his building, although he was grateful for the warmth of the complex; and the moment he reached the second floor, the rustling began immediately.

"Damn, No! No! Shit!," he cried with the loud returning dog growls. His anxiety swallowed him whole, as he stumbled into the suite. The dog growling went from loud, to medium, to soft. The co-op was hot, humid, perking more than 120 degrees Fahrenheit. Dwayne walked through his den with the temperature of hell and opened the terrace door to the sounds of sirens in the outside air, with the hope of letting the cold draft into the sweltering suite.

Looking right at the entrance of the kitchen, his heart

jumped in his throat at the sight of Al, smiling with no teeth, face deteriorating once again since their last confrontation before totaling the car. This was true hell, eternal damnation. He wanted to run, but couldn't. He wished he could escape, but where? Where could he go now? Maybe he should challenge Al, but that would mean a definite brawl, and the fight could be fatal.

"Well do you?"

"Do I what?"

*"Believe in spirits?
Ghosts?"*

"You bein' haunted?"

*"Can't you answer the
question, Pappy?!"*

*"Naw . . . I don't believe
in no ghosts . . . I know
there is life after death,
ah reckon . . . Say it is . . .
I believe ya' do unntah
others as they do unntah
you . . . ya' reap what'cha
sow . . . wha' goes around comes
around I guess; why, we got
ghosts 'roun' here?"*

Al guffawed heartily, shortening Dwayne's daydream.

"Just look at 'cha! Staring at me! Breathing hard! Ya gettin' sweet on me boy?! Getting' sugar in ya' tank?! Ya' getting' weak in the wrist?! Whatcha lookin' back in here so hard for? Seen a ghost or something?"

He laughed once again, and Dwayne coughed at the sudden urinary and fecal stench that reminded him of an Al he knew way back when, only this time the smell was a million times more powerful.

"So how does it feel, Baby Al?"

"How do what feel Pappy?!," Dwayne yelled, struggling to catch his breath.

"How does it feel . . . to get the shit beat outta you . . . to be punched at . . . kicked at . . . laughed at when ya didn't even ask for it?"

Dwayne said nothing while Al kept on.

"I told ya, ya reap what'cha sow! . . . I told ya . . . I said it over and over again, but ya didn't listen . . . I gave you all I could, all my life! . . . I did right by ya . . . I raised ya!"

"Why you never told me who Gwenny was? You lied about my mother! You shoulda tol . . ."

"SO WHAT! She was MY BABY GIRL ya high yella' faggot! I ain't tell ya' who yo' mama was! I LIED! Big GODDAMN deal! . . . I needed to tell it when I felt the time was right! . . . Ya always been selfish!"

"Pappy, you know what? Fuck you! Cause I know you ain't real. You're dead! I saw you in front of the building!"

"And what a fall it was! All because of you and that damned CRACK! Yo SORRY ASS even MISSED my goddamned funeral, and you ain't even COME to my burial! . . . After I raised you, and my wife ain't want yo' half white cracker ass at first! After she lost her life to love you! After ya mama lost her life to love ya!"

Al turned away and walked into the kitchen, sad after mentioning his wife and daughter. Dwayne followed him inside and saw two pots, one medium and one very large, steaming on top of the stove.

"Pappy?"

"You went by Patrick's last night, didn't ya," Al asked, with his back turned. Then he gruesomely chuckled, shaking his head.

"Ya been running around town, pulling that gun out on people since yesterday, killing mo' folks! You cain't kill me Baby Al, you don't know that boy?! You don't know that?! Told ya', ya' gon' reap what'cha sow boy! Just wait a while boy, you ain't seen nothin'! **You ain't feel nothing!**"

Dwayne hissed loud enough for Al to hear and said, "Word? That's what you think, Pappy."

"Still wit'cha fresh ass mouth I see!"

"Fuck you!"

Al turned, and glared at Dwayne. "What?"

"You heard me!"

"Oh yeah?!"

"Yeah! Fuck you! You ain't real!"

"Says who?!"

"Says me! You ain't real Pappy! You're dead!"

"GODDAMN IT! There you go again!," Al yelled, pounding on the counter next to the stove. The amplified growl started again.

"You better believe I'm real, Baby Al! Until you die we gon' stay real! Wherever you go! I'm a be there! I'm a be inside, outside, and aroundside yo' ass!"

Dwayne pulled out the pistol to shoot, and was greeted with clicks of an empty clip. Al roared in laughter, non-stop chuckles in amusement. He watched with glee as his grandson ran about in the apartment looking for the shoebox with more bullets. Once the box was found, Dwayne was down to two rounds. Returning to the kitchen, he loaded the magazine in front of his grandfather, then slapped it in, aimed at Al and stopped.

"So you real huh Pappy?!"

"Yep."

Dwayne squeezed the trigger and shot Al for the umpteenth time. Al started snickering with the hilarity of being popped with more bullets.

"You ain't real, Duke! Ya see! It's my mind, Pappy! I just shot you, and nothing happened! Cause you not real!

You dead! It's my mind!"

Dwayne pointed at his temple, "It's my mind, Pappy! Got it?! Cause ya ain't real!," he painfully retaliated.

"I'm not real, Baby Al?!"

"No you not!"

"How's this, FOR REAL!"

Al grabbed the larger pot of boiling water and threw it on Dwayne, and pushed him to the floor, covering his entire head to his shoulders with the pot; and Dwayne gasped while being scalded, kicking and screaming at nothing.

"You gonna die sucker! Just like I did when your grandpops is finished with your punk Harlem ass! Ha! Ha! Ha! Ha! **PEACE! See yuhh! See yuhh!!"**

The hot pot fell off Dwayne's head as he crawled blindly about the kitchen.

"Help meeeeeeee! Pleeeeeease! Somebodyyyyy! Pleeeeease," he yelled.

Dwayne reached the aquarium to regain his terrified, painful balance. The infinite growl became louder while Dwayne ran for his life, screaming his way through his suite. Once he reached the hallway restroom, he splashed cold water over the maroon colored wounds that were forming over part of his neck and chest. He glanced up and saw Al's laughing face in the mirror looking down on him.

Dwayne froze in place, while his grandfather grabbed him from behind.

"Noooo! Noooo! NOOOOO!! NOOOOOOOO!! PAPPYYY!!!!!," Dwayne cried.

Al yanked Dwayne's elastic band in his underwear, lifting his entire body, wedgy style. Grasping the back of his head with his other hand, Al banged Dwayne's destroyed face into the bathroom mirror until glass chips were embedded in his skin.

"**You!!** Destroyed everything!! **You ruined everything!! Baby Al!! I'm a kill you**," Al yelled, with each head bang.

The gushing water overran in the sink. The knocking sound of Dwayne's head, gunshots in the suite, and Dwayne's screams caused a few neighbors to alert the nearby neighborhood police precinct, just an extra squad of cops on their way to apprehend the sniper who was wanted for killing two people, and injuring many others. Some of the tenants peeking from their peepholes and chained doors witnessed the tormented young man flee for his life, running from his demented soul. They heard about him on the news via the radio and television.

"**Noooooooo! NOOOOOOOO! HE'S GONNA KILL MEEEEE**," Dwayne yelled, running from his suite and down the hallway towards the stairs. His face bled heavily, like someone sliced parts of skin away with a knife. Smearing the second floor and the staircase walls with blood, he sprinted sightlessly from the building with his pistol drawn unknowingly from terror; and he ran smack into the NYPD forming standoff.

Dwayne was oblivious to the instructions of "**DROP THE WEAPON!!**" from the law enforcement while pointing his weapon at Al for the last time, his grandfather dressed completely in NYPD regalia standing with two partners with their guns drawn, at the bottom of the steps.

The three policemen with back up arriving to take him into custody fired seven excruciating rounds into advancing armed Dwayne, knocking the taste, air, and saliva out of his mouth and body. He instantly felt and saw hot bloody darkness, body smashing to the pavement, hitting his head on the concrete. And serene Irwin Avenue was full of action, turning a quiet, winter afternoon in the neighborhood into a summer type of semi-war zone with sirens, lights, and gunfire.

Time passed in slow motion, and some minutes later, EMS intervened; and all watched the EMS workers apply oxygen and whisk mangled, lifeless Dwayne Carter onto a backboard, up into an ambulance, with its motor revving. He was identified at the scene, as the fleeing killer who murdered two people on the other side of the borough, and wounded many others including his girlfriend counselor in the process.

The colorful, glaring eyes of the NYPD and EMS lights spun madly against the on-looking pupils of the curious ones behind their frozen windowpanes. The yelling cry of the sirens and screeching tires of the Montefiore trauma bound ambulance with trailing police cars, echoed into existence with awaiting ancestry needing a verdict of mortality.

****

CHAPTER 18

*

Time waits for no one, and while spring steadily moved its way into being, Dwayne lay hospitalized for the second time since Al's death, with forty stitches in different areas of his face. His face, head, and upper torso, horrifically decorated with first and second degree burns, joined a few healing gunshot wounds to the arm, chest, back, and thighs. The nineteen hour emergency surgery to fix the massive internal bleeding was mildly successful, after being shot by the police seven times in front of his co-op high rise.

There were at least three leftover bullets inside Dwayne's body, too close to vital arteries and organs to be removed. There were also two leftover police officers: one, guarding the operating room while surgery was performed, and the other stationed permanently at his bedside, while Dwayne was placed under arrest for murder and assault with a deadly weapon.

Obliviously awaiting conviction after being nursed for a month on the surgical intensive care unit, Dwayne-with an NYPD guard-was moved to his isolated, private room on a ward after his bed became available. The nursing staff, with the assistance of the police guard un-cuffing one of Dwayne's limp wrists from the bedrail, would continue to try and turn him every two hours to prevent forthcoming bed sores. In order to give him the medication to sustain his life, the nurses and police would have to wear full isolation gear, in the forms of outer gowns, gloves, and masks; Dwayne contracted pneumonia, with his incontinent, inert body lying inside a coma. His life support ventilator was preset for eight to twelve respirations per minute, to give him the necessary artificial breathing, for life marches on and on.

"The Lord is my shepherd, I shall not want . . . He maketh me to lie down in green pastures . . . He leadeth me beside the still waters . . . He restoreth my soul . . . He leadeth me in the path of righteousness for his name's sake . . . Yes . . . though I . . . I . . . Yes though I walk through the valley of the shadow of death . . . I will fear no evil . . . For thou art with me . . . Thy rod and thy staff, they comfort me . . . Thou preparest a table before me in the presence of mine enem . . ."

"Excuse me . . . excuse me . . . forgive me for disturbing your prayer, there is another visitor for Mister Carter inquiring at the nurses station," the nurse said.

Patrick, totally engrossed with his mission of absolute mercy, did not hear the nurse enter the room, after the creaking, and closing of two sets of thick double doors. They smiled at each other, and the nurse said, "I actually should be praying along with you, but I have to run!"

"You are more than welcome to pray with me anytime," Patrick replied.

"I will," the nurse said. "Just have to start more rounds. I'll pray with you one day. I just needed to give you that message. Mister Carter is only allowed two visitors at a time. Just the rules for the isolation patients."

"I'll be right out."

The nurse exited the room, and Patrick continued his recitation:

"Thou preparest a table before me in the presence of mine enemies . . . Thou anointest my head with oil, Halleujah! . . . My cup

runneth over! . . . Surely goodness and mercy shall follow me all the days of my life . . . and I will dwell in the house of the Lord forever . . . and ever, and ever, and ever, and ever man . . . Yo man! . . . Eh yo man! . . . Hey! . . . Yo, Dee! . . . Hey, Dwayne! God bless you brother . . . Happy birthd . . . Happ . . . yo Dee, God bless you on your birthday man."

Patrick moved closer towards the bed, observing Dwayne; and the grisly disfigurement of Dwayne's appearance scourged Patrick's vision. All of the stitches remained visible, and Dwayne's maroon charred skin had permanently closed his right eye, his skin extra fleshly in blotches, looking similar to a slice with extra mozzarella. His right wrist was handcuffed to the bedrail. Patrick extended his hand to touch Dwayne's scorched, stitched up skin, drawing his hand back quickly because of the grotesque roughness. Dwayne was motionless; his respirator tube placed and taped inside his mouth, only moving with the mechanical breaths of the machine, not a care in the world of the living. Patrick touched his opened eyelid, attempting to close it. It jumped back, startling him.

"Hang in there, Dee. Just hang in there brother," Patrick said. He left the room, re-entering the small vestibule before the two sets of double doors leading back into the main hallway. The anteroom was equipped with a sink, and an area for donning the isolation gear. Patrick removed his protective equipment as per the nursing instruction signs, trashing the mask, and tossing the gown into a large bin.

Lathering his hands while washing, Patrick shook his head thinking of Dwayne being handcuffed to his hospital bed while in a coma; and a tidal wave of bittersweet memories flooded his brain.

> *"Fucking monkeys only help
> your own people!! Taking over
> everything! Taking everything*

like a fucking plague!"

"Get the fuck out my house! You
get the fuck out my house, you
***thief punk bitch!** And doun't*
*coume baack **BAAMBECLAAT***
YENKEE BWOY!!!"

"A WHAT?! Get the fuck
outta here Pat. A three-day
party?! That shit is fly!"

"The party starts at eight on
Friday the twelfth and it
goes straight through to my
birthday! Bring Shawn and
E-zo. We got stupid catching
up to do! Remember, your code
name is Baby Al!"

"Yo . . . Hold up! Gimme
another code!"

"Umm, nope! See ya at the party!"

"WHAT!!!"

"Damn high, you answer the
phone like that?! Damn!"

"Yo, high! My grandpops
threw away my shit!! All my
shoeboxes is gone!"

"Word?!"

*"Word is fucking born! I
could kill him!!"*

Alas, the shuddering recollection of the abuse, with memories of unfortunate intra-racism and being part of the world. Patrick had always been the least to suspect that Dwayne ever raised a hand to his grandfather. These days he wondered if the cruel turn of events in Dwayne's life was the sometime sweet, but horrifying revelation of universal law, rearing its ugly head like a jilted beast.

"Maybe he was right. Maybe there is a duppy," thought Patrick.

*"Word up! I got to be seeing shit! And
hearing shit! Pappy asked for a ten
pack! Word to God it was him!"*

Patrick needed more information about duppies, because if Dwayne was actually being haunted, was it really the spirit of Al Carter? The spirit of his grandfather couldn't possibly cause this type of physical wreckage, or could it?

Considering himself a saved man of God, Patrick wanted to dismiss his thoughts about ghosts, yet after seeing Dwayne's deterioration first hand, from the first alleged haunting to his current comatose state, Patrick pondered heavily.

". . . It sounds weird to me man."

*"Would you think this is more weird
if I told you my grandfather did
this to me? Would you believe me?"*

"I would say crazy and weird.

And no, I wouldn't believe you."

"Duppy," Patrick said aloud.

Patrick dried his hands and entered the hallway giving a head nod to the police guard. Hearing the speed of heels clicking in a "matter of fact style", he turned in the direction of his fast approaching wife, heading towards them. Patrick mentally geared himself for his zealous wife.

"What's up angel," Patrick announced. Michelle, hands on hips, inhaling/exhaling with the pursing of lips and the raising of eyebrows looked at her watch.

"I really did not expect to be in the workplace all night, when I'm supposed to be off," Michelle snapped. "We should be home getting ready for church tomorrow, not celebrating the birthday of a criminal who destroyed my cousin and her career, who even tried to kill you honey!"

"Shell, we went throu . . ."

"I get it sweetheart! You're a man of God. I know, honey, I know this already. You struggled with forgiveness the last few weeks, and you decided on the right thing. You wouldn't let me rest until you got here to read Psalms twenty-three to a twenty-three-year-old murderer on his birthday. I get it! But I want to go home Patrick!"

The couple continued walking in the direction of a lounge area near the elevators, past the nursing station full of staff. Patrick and Michelle received a few stares while Michelle continued fussing.

"There's this woman asking me a bunch of questions, saying she's his godmother, and she's getting on my last nerves! I just want to go home, so I can relax! I should have followed my first mind and stayed home, because you can take care of yourself honey; then you said, we would visit with your family in Harlem today, not come up here to see a murdering criminal!"

"Angel, "Patrick started in a stern tone, "We are

leaving right now, and I appreciate you trying to understand my need to forgive."

Michelle sucked her teeth. "I should have never called Nikki this morning! But I'm worried about her and this mess she's in with the D.A., thanks to your so-called friend! Jesus that girl is just so worldly and hard headed! If she would just listen to the family, and just cooperate and listen to her own attorney, press charges against that maniac; and you should too, so he can stay behind bars where he belongs! This is one grand mess, and my Uncle Craig and Aunt Noella are worried sick. We should be in New Jersey right now making sure Nikki is doing okay or maybe in Harlem with your grandmother, but not here! You didn't even know it was his birthday, and if you didn't eavesdrop on the conversation I was having . . ."

"We were in bed, and you woke me up!"

"Well where was I supposed to go?! I was on MY phone in MY bedroom!"

"Relax! And keep your voice down."

"We are all common knowledge Patrick! And if you're not careful, which you're not, they'll be dragging you right into this case too, with all the back and forth!"

"Calm down angel. If I'm called as a witness in court, I'll just tell the truth about him. But they're not calling me because Nikki's going to keep you and me out of it, she said she would. Now, is she the lady you're speaking of?"

The couple came closer to a lounge area filled with couches where Arlene and her 14-year-old daughter Tanasha were waiting; and Patrick recognized her immediately. He always remembered the sweet smelling woman from his childhood, meeting her through Dwayne on different occasions. These days their paths crossed frequently each time Dwayne was in trouble. Her daughter briefly reminded Patrick of the many young women who tried to hold court at the penthouse, before the tragedy. He immediately snapped himself from his current trance, extending greetings to Arlene and Tanasha.

Arlene continued detecting a pushy, combative air in the young man's wife. Michelle reminded Arlene of a stockier Barbara Nelson, and recalling Barbara took her to the character of a wicked spider, weaving webs of trickery and deceit inside the old house on 117th Street. Arlene felt Barbara despised her to this very day, still affected by the memory of having Barbara for a past neighbor, and being the mother of her ex-fling Floyd. Arlene and Michelle's eyes negatively met again. Michelle sarcastically looked at her watch, sucked her teeth then looked at her husband. Still aware of her mission, Arlene asked, "Are visiting hours still going on?"

"Wow, yes they are," Patrick said, "Allow me to apologize. I was caught up with saying the twenty-third Psalm to Dee for his twenty-third birthday. Sorry for taking so long. I'm sure the nurses will le . . ."

"The visiting hours are practically over, if you want to see him you need to hurry up," Michelle interjected.

Patrick said, "Come, I'll show you a fast way by the nurse's station to get to him."

"Patrick, she doesn't need an escort."

"Are you coming along too?," Patrick overlooked Michelle, speaking to Tanasha.

"Nasha stay here, I'll be back," Arlene said to her daughter.

"Honey, where are you going," Michelle called to her husband.

"Nowhere, just back to the room, chill! I'll be back," Patrick replied, stepping off.

Patrick and Arlene started into the ward while Tanasha put her walkman headphones on immediately, determined not to converse with Michelle who was fuming after being ignored by her husband.

Once inside the ward of diminishing morbidity, Arlene felt the extreme spiritual and mental chills she always felt when entering hospitals. For the first time ever, her psyche was deluged with guilt. There was so much that had happened, and a small part of Arlene felt that she dropped the ball in explaining to Dwayne what she knew about his history. Arlene was totally engrossed in her own life, dealing with her own mid-life crisis. She continuously faced a strained union with a man whom still hadn't asked for her hand in marriage, and the raising of her growing children fathered by this man. She dealt with a daughter in high school, with a son in middle school; and Tanasha & Dante quizzed her daily with tons of life questions about any, and every single thing.

As much as Arlene tried to manage her history with the Carter's, there were always recurring situations igniting the fiery ties that bind. While Arlene knew that no one could block her maternal bond with her children, the obligatory ties to her childhood friendship with Gwendolyn Carter existed in every ounce of her being; and Donnell her beau, refused to acknowledge this bond. Arlene tried to make it easy for his understanding, which never manifested for him. It was about blood being thicker than historical water with him, and he refused to believe in Arlene's need to love people who were not her blood. No matter what Donnell thought, or how he felt he put his foot down, it never worked, because Arlene's history with the Carters of 117th Street would remain in her heart.

If the hands of time could be reversed, she would have made more time for her godson, even if it meant bringing Tanasha and Dante along kicking and screaming for her to have her head examined. The children would never understand their mother's loyalty to Dwayne either; and Arlene kept her maternal past with the raising of Dwayne personal. Dwayne Carter was Arlene's first child in increments of his early life before her own children were born. She named "Dwayne Albert Carter" at the discretion of his grandparents, after being finalized as his godmother.

After Mattie's death, whenever Al allowed her (god)motherly side to flow, Dwayne was always regarded as Arlene's first born in her heart. With the bond still mentally existing, Arlene was finally given an opportunity for a triumph, post the tragedy that struck 117th Street with Al's death.

Everything seemed to be going well for her godchild each time they spoke after the funeral; he had even listened to her instructions, making amends and establishing a degree of closure with Jimmy, according to Monica Robinson in conversation. Things were quiet in all of their lives until out of nowhere, Dwayne and his twenty-four hour tumultuous binge became the subject of local news. Dwayne's story was the top of discussion for nearly three weeks, on the local television news and in the newspapers.

Testimonies poured in from witnesses inside and outside of the Roberto Clemente Center, commenting on the loving, unarmed security guard murdered in cold blood; and there was "Pop" from the neighborhood, begging for his drink year round before noon, who was shot to death in the winter's cold, put out of his misery finally. There was the report on finding Nicole pistol whipped near the Bruckner, to the few injured fourth graders heading for their school trip at the Judaica Museum via the Major Deegan Expressway. Bystanders in the quiet neighborhood of Irwin and 236th spoke to reporters of seeing the terrified young man running from the building, after hearing several gunshots from inside the complex. The frantic gun wielder had blood spurting from his face and nose, with weapon in hand, running outside a couple of feet into a barrier of police who opened a vortex of defensive fire; with the lawbreaker in the center like a spinning top, falling down the few entrance steps on his head after being shot.

Arlene remained shocked about the story and the many tales surrounding what happened; and after seeing the pictures of Nicole found battered by Dwayne via the media, and hearing that he killed two men inside and outside of her work establishment, Arlene attempted contact with Nicole through the center. The powers that be refused to disclose information. Then before she knew it, Arlene was subpoenaed to court by the Bronx District Attorney for the ongoing case developing against her godson who was still unresponsive in a coma for more than five weeks, remaining under arrest.

Patrick and Arlene approached Dwayne's room; and when Arlene saw the police officer she stopped walking.

Patrick asked, "Are you okay?"

"No," Arlene replied, eyeing the cop and taking a deep breath. Patrick pulled Arlene a few steps back before speaking.

"You need me to go inside with you?"

"It's not that," Arlene said, gulping down more deep breaths. "I'm just . . . All I'm just . . . I'm just saying, Baby Al's in a coma. Must they be standing outside his room like that? Damn! What, do they think, he's going to jump up, run out and start shooting people again?"

"I hate it too, but it's real this time. This is no TV hype. This madness going on with Dwayne is crazy deep right now. He's even handcuffed to the bed inside the room and the whole nine."

"Are you serious?!"

"I'm serious. Say look, if you need to pray before going inside we can. I'm not crazy about five-oh either, but what can we do? Dwayne is really, really messed up now."

"It's too much! Do you know, we have to go back to court again in a few weeks? Nicole, poor girl, she really don't want Baby Al in jail. Me either really, you just don't know! But MY GOD, I just can't believe how he terrorized all them people that morning at that center! Nicole is so devastated, confused! She got permission from the D.A. for me to testify about Baby Al, you know, how I know him and Mister Carter. I'm not crazy about none of this at all!

Lord knows, I don't know how that girl do it. Those pictures they showed of her on the news!"

"Yeah man, Nikk is definitely traumatized by everything. I know she's been trying to chill in Jersey and put it all behind her, but with the case still going on, it's hard. It's a lot at stake right now. Nicole and my wife are first cousins. This is how I get the scoop on everything."

"Oh okay."

"Everything is going to work out though, I can feel it in the name of Jesus. God is good. There's some evidence Nikki believes that's in the other hospital he was in, after Mister Carter passed. Dwayne really hasn't been himself since then."

"None of us have. Lord knows me and the kids miss Mister Carter so much."

"Yes, he was a very nice man. Long as I can remember from way back, very nice man. Dee was lucky to have him . . . You think you're ready to go inside now?"

Arlene nodded and took another deep breath, and they proceeded to Dwayne's room.

"You'll have to wear a mask and slip a gown over your coat before you go all the way inside," Patrick explained, with the police officer clocking their every move. "Inside this first room, you'll find everything you need, but you may want to remove your coat, because I was sweating in there, big time. It's extremely hot inside, with the machines and everything."

"Thank you, Patrick? Am I right?"

"Yes. Patrick Livingston."

"Okay. My mind is not totally gone. I'm Arlene again, and I am the godmama! And I remember you, definitely from the funeral."

"Forgive me for that day . . . I was a bit out of character."

"I'm not one to judge anybody. But I remember you now. A little bit from the neighborhood too. Always sticking with Baby Al, God surely will bless you."

"It's just what Jesus would do . . . and please forgive my wife. She really means no harm. She's very overprotective."

"I'm sure she's worried about Nicole. The things we do for love, family, and friends. The situations we put each other in, take each other through. Look how we're here in this hospital on a Saturday night, after all that's happened. My family, my children, they insist I should give up on Baby Al. They say I run behind him too much, and I'm too concerned."

"I know how that is."

"**PATRICK!**"

Patrick turned away from Arlene in the direction of approaching Michelle.

"Excuse me, let me have a word with my wife. We both will be out here, waiting for you."

Patrick met Michelle halfway, and pulled her over to the side for a few choice words, while Arlene canvassed the entrance of Dwayne's room. After reading the instruction sign for visiting with the full isolation patient, Arlene pushed open the doors into the first room to wash up, then geared up to view her godson.

She quietly entered Dwayne's new space, nothing like the lavish co-op he described, his isolated hospital room with electronic machines and monitors being the complete opposite. As she stood looking over her best friend's son, she mumbled sadly, "Ol' Baby Al . . . I sure hope you gonna be alright . . . Really I do . . . Life is something else."

"GWENNY! Oh my God, you're
bleeding!"

"Please! Get my mama! She upstairs! . . .
My baby! I can't lose my baby! What's
happening? What's happening to me?!"

"It's gon' be alright! Calm down girl! . . .
Look, let me get an ambulance! I'm gon'
call the operator! . . . Take some deep
breaths and you stay right here! . . . Don't
you move a muscle girl! You gon' be alright,
you hear me?!"

"It's about time you woke up!"

**"*What the fuck you put General in*
your room for, huh?!. . . You
always! Always! Always! Is
fucking with something you ain't
got no business fucking with!"**

"And then that damn dog jumped on the table,"Arlene remembered shaking her head, recounting two of her godchild's birthdays.

"Baby Al, my prayers are with you. I love you," Arlene said softly. She quietly left Dwayne's room.

"Is everything okay," Patrick asked, the moment Arlene stepped from the room. He knew different when Arlene nodded, yet exhaling herself into a torrent of tears. Michelle dug into her purse and gave a handful of tissues to the sad woman.

"Thank you," Arlene said, as she dabbed her made up eyes, then blew her nose.

Patrick asked, "What's going on with him in there? Is he okay?"

Arlene continued wiping her face, and said: "Oh I don't know, you're asking me? I'm sorry, Patrick, and Misses Livingston."

"Call me Michelle."

"Please . . . You'll have to excuse me . . . In spite of all the terrible things Baby Al did to Mister Carter . . . and I guess to other people . . . he's still my godson. I was very close to all them Carters, especially his mother. And . . . They're all . . . they're all . . . they're all dead!"

She fell into more silent, breathy tears. Patrick and Michelle took her by the hands, and Arlene shook her head quickly, gently letting go and pushing them away.

"No, no, I'm fine . . . I'm fine. I mean . . . just to see Baby Al like this. I haven't seen him in a while, in a long time. He was doing so good with the new job and his new place . . . then I see him on the news, and in the paper, oh my God . . . It's his skin, his face, it looks so terrible! . . . It's just terrible . . . They're all dead! . . . And Baby Al is near dead! Why on earth must he be cuffed to a bed?! My God! Does he even know he's in this world?! I don't mean to look so foolish in front of you, this is just getting to me, you know!"

Michelle looked at her husband who was just as shaken, and the police guard continued staring in space, unaffected. It was times like these Dwayne's entire life mystified Patrick, totally. His mother died giving birth to him; his father died during a sixties school riot; his grandmother died on Christmas Eve when he was nine-years old, and his grandfather fell to his death, practically in front of him; and now, he lay in a coma on his birthday. Then, there were the drug binges; the bouts with cocaine, marijuana, crack, alcoholism; the ongoing fight with bi-racial heritage, another subliminal struggle.

"Well, I'm leaving, but I rushed over as soon as I could," Arlene said. "I hope to see you again. We'll probably run into each other again, right here. Thanks for sticking by my godson. If Mister Carter was here, I know he'd say the same thing."

Patrick grinned and exhaled at Arlene's statement.

"Yeah I know. I sure do miss old Mister Carter."

"You know I do. He was like a father to me. Shoo, all

those years? I think about him every day! Sometimes, I feel as if he's still here, like he's never left," Arlene said.

"Word up! I got to be seeing shit! And hearing shit! Pappy asked for a ten pack! Word to God it was him!"

"I know what'cha mean," Patrick said, looking at the floor.

"Take care of yourself. I'll see you soon."

"Arlene . . . My wife and I were wondering how you arrived here? Would you like a lift home?"

"That would be very nice of you, thank you! My car will be out of the shop next week; I really appreciate it."

Patrick walked away with Michelle and Arlene, briefly thinking of his very own life, which had been just as painful.

During the car ride, Arlene exchanged numbers with Patrick & Michelle, and they agreed to keep each other informed about the "New York State vs. Dwayne Carter" case, and Dwayne's condition; especially after Arlene was appointed to being Dwayne's sole health care proxy by his hospital social worker and health care team. Michelle tried her best to be cordial with Arlene, after Patrick talked to her about the importance of respecting her back at the hospital.

After Arlene and Tanasha left out of the backseat, Michelle refused to speak to Patrick because of their hospital episode in the visitors lounge. He knew that after church service and Sunday dinner the following day, Michelle would soften up. The car ride home was totally quiet, only the low sounds of a gospel cassette accompanying their ears.

Once they reached home and made it to the bedroom, Patrick tried to kiss Michelle good night; and once she refused, he criticized her for what he felt was immaturity. They argued about themselves, bickering over Dwayne's misfortune until Patrick feigned sleep; and after his repulsive wife dozed off, his mind still flooded with questions, needing answers. Patrick hardly slept a wink, part bewildered, slightly fearful, and perplexed. It was no use talking to Michelle about duppies, or any other West Indian oriented folklore because she wouldn't understand, and wouldn't want to.

He found himself thinking about duppies and the mythical stories surrounding them. He often heard as a lad in Jamaica how "de duppy dem come fi ya'", or how absolutely no one wanted to deal with certain duppies like the infamous "Rollin' Calf". Hours into thought with sleep finally setting in, Patrick dreamed about his older siblings, always longing for the good ole days with Nigel, Franklin, and Hyacinth. They cherished the duppy stories, and also feared the humorous tales. If he could just bring the deceased back to life, back into existence, because as time went on he realized that he never recuperated from the massacre, now just two years fresh.

Yes, the love of God and the blood of Jesus saved his mental, to a degree; yes, the rigid affection of Michelle filled certain gaps; yes, he was on the verge of making business deals with owning property in Harlem, and managing businesses in these properties; yes, his cousin Grant became his assistant manager after he moved into the store manager seat after a vacancy became available; yes, his English side of the family stepped right in after the hardship, taking control of the brownstone on 120th. Although, his current kin were blood relatives, Patrick realized they would never replace his family that was slain. It was a true blessing to have the one surviving family member, their beloved matriarch Una still around. She would know everything, from beginning to end about duppies.

Awakening the next morning, after dreaming of Jamaica all night, Patrick thought, "Mi need fi chat wi Mummy . . . Make that move right back to twentieth street . . . Sit with her, and talk with her," Patrick thought.

Hours later during the church service after the offering plates were passed throughout the sanctuary, the men of the congregation were summoned down to the pulpit area for personally needed prayer. Pastor Davis laid his hand on each kneeling male, praying in spiritual tongues with individualized prayer for each man within range, while the organist played the appropriate music for the moment. And when the preacher came to Patrick on his knees, with head bowed and palms outstretched to receive annointing, Patrick prayed aloud with his pastor for all of his family, past, present, and future. Patrick prayed for Michelle, while she watched the large three rowed cipher of men in prayer surrounding her husband. Patrick prayed for all his staff and friends, including Eric who was stationed in Germany with the United States Army. Patrick prayed for the strength of the women he was close to, especially Michelle, Nicole, and Arlene; he also prayed for the increased strength to get through the abrasive "New York State vs. Dwayne Carter" case.

Once the week got off to a start, other business at hand took precedence in Patrick's life, such as the thorough spring inspection for the supermarket he managed. There were long hours on the horizon for Patrick and his entire staff as they prepared to clean the store from top to bottom. All shipped goods entering into the store were thoroughly examined by everyone, checking expiration dates, price tags, plus making sure their customers were not overcharged for items. The mission was handled with a fine tooth comb and magnifying glass, because the Consumer Affairs Department, along with other big boy inspectors from the Department of Health, and the Department of Agriculture & Markets were coming to look for the smallest error, to slap the store with fines and violations; and Patrick refused to have it. His goal was to have his "Associated" supermarket on top, with high ratings.

For the duration of the month, Patrick became thoroughly engrossed with the current inspection of the store, and when alone, he chuckled about forgetting to pray about the amount of long hours he began to put in. When he reached home Michelle was always asleep, and he would leave early in the morning to open up the store with Carlton and/or Grant, before his wife was awake.

He worked weekends and even missed church, angering Michelle, just to do proper record keeping and paperwork. The gates of the store wouldn't come down until, he knew everything was together, which seemed to never happen, even after a seventeen hour day. Knowing that at any given time, the food inspectors could anonymously appear as shoppers kept Patrick driven. The inspectors would pretend to shop, asking questions to other consumers about the in-house goods, looking for dirty equipment, soiled, soggy vegetables, expired products, opened canned goods, boxed, or dried goods, etc. Exterminators had to be called for a vermin free environment, along with the cleaning services for the mopping, buffing and waxing of floors. The refrigerator and freezer temperatures needed to be monitored, everything down to the staff restrooms being maintained properly. With the rest of the April showers, there was a noticeable roof leak near the meats & poultry aisle that needed attention. All of the preparation to pass the necessary inspection, plus seeing customers for the regularly scheduled shopping hours kept the entire staff on pins and needles. There were petty arguments amongst themselves, settled in the boss's office usually with small talk, the offer of prayer, the offer of overtime, or all three.

The day finally came for the inspection and the store passed with a great score. The word was out that Mr. Livingston was calling a meeting at 8am the following morning with staff to congratulate everyone. Those able to attend would be paid overtime; and those unable to attend would have the word passed along via a survey of what they desired to eat all day long for free, rewards for pulling together at the time of need. And the morning after, while certain staff members embraced each other, Patrick, Carlton, and Grant explained their high ratings, and what they intended to do to keep the standard.

The happy vibe remained for the day while business was at its usual pace, yet less pressured because the inspection was done, until the next seasonal one for the summer.

Patrick helped around the store with the staff as they tended to their duties, and he was interrupted by Grant while he was slicing meat for a customer.

"Listen 'ere sir! Someone 'pon de foune," Grant said to Patrick. "In ah de h'office. Ledy neyme *Ei-leen Munt'gum'ry.*"

"Mi nuh k'no' H'eileen Munt'gum'ry . . . Why ya nuh teke de message?"

"Ol 'eap a dem deh pon de desk!"

"Mi nah k'no'; weit nuh?! Eileen? You mean Arlene? . . . Coume, teke dis ova! Mi soon coume baack."

Grant relieved Patrick behind the counter in the meats & poultry section while Patrick hurried to his office to take the call. He unlocked his door, entering the medium sized neater space, because of the inspection. Grateful to be in the confines of the office away from the hustle and bustle, Patrick quickly picked up the receiver on his desk phone:

"HELLO?!"

"Patrick, it's Arlene . . . finally I've caught you. I been putting a lot of change in this phone."

"Arlene, hey, how are you? We had a big inspection this week! Thank the Lord we passed and it's over. How have you been? How's things at the hospital? How's Dwayne?"

The line went quiet except for the routine background and scratchy pay phone buzz; then it sounded like Arlene was sobbing.

"I've been trying to contact you all week Patrick," Arlene replied with tears. "I've left you messages at home with your wife, and I've been calling you there at the office. People keep taking my messages and they won't give them to you. I been trying to get in touch with you since Monday when we all went back to court."

Patrick glanced at six different messages from Arlene on top of his desk, shaking his head.

"I apologize Arlene, really. I have truly been busy . . . talk to me though, what's going on?"

There was a knock on the door. "Come in, it's open!"

One of Patrick's female cashiers brought him covered double paper plates of food, with an opened D&G Kola Champagne.

"Right t'eere so," he instructed his employee, with a head movement toward his desk.

"T'ahnks . . . Excuse me Arlene. So are you okay? What's the matter? I have all the messages right here. Again I apologize; if you only knew what we went through to rock this inspection. You okay though?"

Arlene continued weeping: "I . . . I . . . I came by to see Baby Al the other day, and he was talking!"

"Praise God! Praise his holy name! Are you at the hospital now?!"

"Yes. Vacation from the job, and the way I spend it, Donnell hates it . . . but your prayers . . . maybe your prayers worked . . . He's not on the machine . . ."

"Please deposit five cents for the next three minutes."

"Hold on . . ."

"Thank you, you have twenty cents credit toward overtime."

Patrick said, "That's great news Arlene! The Lord is pulling him through! So he's not on life support, and he talked to you?!"

"Yes," Arlene replied, "They just have an oxygen mask on his face and he's not on isolation anymore but . . . it's when he spoke, and Nicole knows . . . because of court . . . Patrick didn't your wife tell you?! She was there, this week Monday in court . . . your wife and the rest of Nicole's family was there with her . . . You don't know?!"

"I sure don't. I've been that busy, it's crazy! When I get home sometimes it's after three in the morning, and I'm out the door sometimes by five. I don't disturb my wife; I let her sleep."

"Patrick a lot has happened with the case . . . I was so uncomfortable in that court room, but I had to tell what I knew about Baby Al and Mister Carter . . . the doctors from North General got subpoenaed too, and they came up in there with all kinds of X-rays and cat scans and MRI reports . . . Patrick I can't believe your wife didn't tell you anything! That is really not a good thing! We went to court four days ago!"

Patrick took a deep breath while listening to Arlene. Continuing her report, Arlene described her godson asking for Patrick at the bedside, strangely fading in and out of consciousness with complaints of "his Pappy trying to kill him", and he also complained of some guy named Scheme having General biting after him; with increased concern about Mister Carter's alleged reappearances. Arlene experienced all of it with her own eyes she explained, and Patrick could hear her elusive pain.

"I'm sorry to say this Patrick, but . . . I believe she didn't say anything cause she mad Baby Al might beat the case . . . None of Nicole's family wants him to beat it . . . The doctors that was there said it's something else really wrong with him, that made him shoot those people . . . All of them said it, even his counselors that Nicole told him to go see, the psychiatrist from North General got subpoenaed, his health records from here, there . . . and that D.A. is really fighting for Baby Al . . . everything and everybody getting subpoenaed left and right, even the Montefiore doctors . . . and they all been testifying trying to cover up their tracks, cause Baby Al really been sick for a long time . . . and, the doctor saying he's in and out of consciousness . . . And his old doctor even said, he would keep making up stuff, like he was, hallucinating . . . he called it organic, like an organic psycho disease . . . I don't get into all that fancy medical stuff . . . Nicole said Baby Al been suffering for a long time too, that's why she looking like that; and he just stopped breathing they said . . . Nicole, she . . . she . . . she gave me the engagement ring, and she told me she hated to do it . . . I know she did, and I know she wants to do more, poor thing; and ain't nothing we can do now . . . We have one more court date . . . Nicole said she still going to come up here to see him, that she's thinking about it, and her family broookkke on that child so hard! . . . and I don't know about that other one."

"I'll talk to my wife."

"Don't say nothing to her. She has her reasons for wanting to protect Nicole; it's about family, and I understand. She know you don't want Baby Al to go to prison, and that's why she didn't say nothing to you about it. He really been sick, don't tell her I told you. And I understand what she's doing, don't say anything to her."

Patrick could hear the sorrow in Arlene's voice again, while he pondered what to say to Michelle for keeping developments of the case from him.

"Please deposit five cents for the next three minutes."

"Patrick, Baby Al has been asking for you to stop Mister Carter from trying to kill him . . . It's terrible! He keep saying it over and over again. Lord knows this is a nightmare!"

Patrick held his forehead while listening to Arlene after she added more change. He took a deep breath and uncovered his plate with two rolled curried goat rotis, with a side of cabbage. Taking a giant bite of the roti to ease the tensions of his hungry stomach and bewildered thoughts, now that the inspection was over, his grandmother's brownstone on 120th Street became an imperative stopover. Patrick was adamant again about the duppy information because of Arlene's story. Still, he knew his family would feel his motives for helping Dwayne would be proven futile. Patrick knew he was justified by God for caring. It was easier to let go and let God Patrick taught himself; and if he was about God, especially with his works of life outside of the church, then he would remain a friend to the end. He still constantly faced this issue. To know that Dwayne finally emerged from the coma after two months, Patrick thought he was well on his way to recovery. Arlene's information said different.

"Tell you what Arlene," Patrick began. "Please forgive me for chewing in your ear."

"That's fine."

"Tell you what . . ."

"*Please deposit five cents for the next three minutes.*"

"Tell you what I'll do. Tomorrow, I'll go to the hospital in the morning first thing. I'll go straight uptown before I even start work. Okay?"

"Yes."

"I'll see what I can find out. And I'll be sure to call you tomorrow before I leave there."

"I'll be hom . . ."

"*Please deposit five cents for the next three minutes.*'

"Call me at home. I'll be looking to hear from you."

"And don't worry, I won't say anything to Michelle. I was super busy with my store, but she still could have let me know what's up."

"*Please deposit five cents for the next three minutes or your call will be terminated.*"

"I'm glad I finally caught you."

"I'll call you tomorrow Arlene."

The call disconnected on its own while Patrick took a sip of kola champagne. He leaned back in his rolling chair and opened his bottom right side desk drawer. Removing his Bible, he turned immediately to the book of Matthew, Chapter 7. Still enjoying lunch with another bite of roti, he skimmed until he found what he was looking for.

'Even so every good tree bringeth forth good fruit; but a corrupt tree bringeth forth evil fruit . . . A good tree cannot bring forth evil fruit, neither can a corrupt tree bring forth good fruit . . . Every tree that bringeth not forth good fruit is hewn down, and cast into the fire.'

After he finished reading Matthew 7:17-19, Patrick compared the verses to Dwayne and Michelle. Deleting his wife first, Patrick thought, "Nah, not my angel . . . I know what she has up her sleeve . . . I'm alright . . . It's cool . . . But my boy? . . . I don't know . . . I have to keep praying, and I'm going to pray for me . . . Heavenly father keep me in check!"

After a few more minutes in prayer for himself and everyone, Patrick returned to work.

The next morning after dropping Michelle off to her 8 to 4 shift at Woodhull, Patrick high-tailed it to Montefiore to see Dwayne, and to hopefully meet with his doctors. He turned up his brand new "Take 6" cassette tape in the dashboard to help with not backsliding because of the road raging New York City traffic. Once arriving at his destination, finding an uneasy space, he parked almost three blocks away from the hospital, nestling between a Chevy Nova and a Honda Prelude.

There was a big difference in the hospital life and its traffic on a weekday. The tranquil motivation of relatives visiting loved ones during the weekend was replaced with a hustle and bustle similar to that of the Wall Street Stock Exchange. The serenity of offspring and kinfolk stopping by for idle chatter becomes serious business, outnumbered by packs of staff from all areas of the medicine business. Some earnest visitors like Patrick come for information, which becomes fateful at times, or they come for simple support. Support and encouragement was on the young man's mind as Dwayne's room door opened slowly, and Patrick stuck his head inside. The room was dark, with dancing images of limited light, because of the rented television set hanging from the ceiling.

"Pssssst!. . . Eh-yo! Eh-yo," Patrick whispered quietly to his sleeping friend. "Yo Dee! . . . hey . . . it's me, it's Pat homie! I heard you been asking for me . . . Hey Dwayne, wake up brother! . . . Yo, I'm a keep praying for you homeboy, word up . . . May God give you the strength you need brother man to come out of this . . . We all praying for you, and I know Nikki is coming through to check on you too . . . she'll be here soon man . . . I don't know when, but I trust Nicole will come to see you . . . God loves you, we all love homie . . . Arlene and Nikki loves ya man."

Dwayne didn't budge, resting on heavily. Patrick crept into the room and shut off the blaring television.

The life support was gone, replaced with a lime green oxygenated mask that practically covered Dwayne's whole face. Still hooked up to cardiac monitors, indicating a heart rate of 114 beats per minute, Dwayne's youth had disappeared into a hospital room redolent of waste and death. The silver handcuff remained in place with the addition of two hospital wrist restraints, tying Dwayne's arms to join the handcuff on the same side. Ensuring that the doors didn't slam, Patrick exited the room.

"Excuse me officer, should both of his hands be tied together like that, with the handcuff," Patrick asked the police guard. The hard gum chewing officer shrugged his shoulders, chuckling.

"Maybe he's praying," the Caucasian officer replied.

"Is the doctor around?"

The policeman shrugged his shoulders again; and Patrick walked away, again desperately trying not to backslide. He approached the nursing station, busy with staff.

"Excuse me . . . Hello? . . . Excuse me, I'm visiting Dwayne Carter, is his doctor around," Patrick asked the nursing station clerk. The obese, auburn-haired Caucasian woman nastily pointed towards one of the doctors, scribbling inside a green loose-leaf binder.

"Thank you kindly," Patrick smiled, thinking, "Gotta kill 'em with kindness . . . Excuse me, doctor . . . doctor?"

The young brown-haired Caucasian male wearing scrubs, lab coat, complete with spectacles and black yarmulke paused, looking directly at Patrick. "May I help you," he asked.

"Yes, I'm visiting Dwayne Carter, and, I'd like to find out how he's doing," Patrick stated emphatically.

"Great! I'm Doctor Katzberg," the doctor replied, extending his hand.

"I'm Patrick Livingston."

"I was jotting a few notes on Mister Carter, what a coincidence," the doctor tried to be cordial. He stood and walked from behind the nurses' station eagerly, carrying a binder with "CARTER" spelled in black ink on its side margin. The doctor led Patrick towards the lounge area for visitors.

"Come this way. What relation are you to Mister Carter," the doctor asked, entering the area of love seats.

"I'm a life-long friend," said Patrick, sitting across from the gentleman, establishing eye contact.

"Great."

"So how's he doing, doctor?"

"As far as his physical recovery is concerned, he's made a mediocre comeback. His face is healing well with the stitches, and his wounds finally healed. I'm sure you understand there was no way to remove the other bullets that were close to his heart and lungs; doing that would have resulted in a blood clot in his major artery, which could result in death, but he'll live, he'll do okay. I believe, he'll continue to progress."

"So, when is he getting out of the hospital?"

"Well," the doctor paused, "Mister Livingston, have you spoken with the family?"

"Doctor, I am family. His girlfriend's cousin and I are married . . ."

"So you've been to trial and you're aware of what's happening then."

Patrick exhaled and said, "No, unfortunately I haven't been to court doctor. What does going to trial have to do with my question about my friend going home? I was told by his godmother who has been frequently visiting, that he's not on life support anymore and that he's been talking and asking for me. So now, what's up? Why does he look like that? And why on earth is he still handcuffed and tied down at the same time?"

"Well, you know, there's been some problems."

"Like?"

"Once he came out of the coma, he yanked out a lot of tubes, his breathing tubes, his nasogastric feeding, so he was restrained, and sedated . . . We've done several cat scans, and other tests, and your relative has something called an epidural hematoma; and this why he is going in and out of consciousness. An intracranial bleed . . ."

"A what?"

"Intracranial bleed, the epidural hematoma, it's pretty much the same thing. Sir . . . Your relative has been bleeding on his brain for quite some time now; he has a lot of blood in his skull, beneath the tissue membranes of his scalp, there's really a lot of bleeding . . . This is what we found with his most recent MRI that was done yesterday. It matches the information from some of his lost records and notes. Several arteries and blood vessels inside his brain have ruptured, and we're looking to repair that. It's a little out of hand at this point, but we'll do the best we can to stop the speed of the bleeding. I understand he has had several traumas and blows to the head . . . There was a report that he even fell on his head after being shot; then, I'm understanding that he was in a huge auto accident on the same day of the shooting."

Patrick nodded, exhaling deeply. He tried tuning the doctor out at this point, but couldn't.

"He has been bleeding on the brain for several months, according to the records from another hospitalization that was overlooked, and he's been to our emergency room several times with the same symptoms. His brain has even shifted position, a rare case, but it happens unfortunately, you know with all of the bumps and knocks to the head . . . With the burns, he may need skin grafts . . . there's lots of things stacked up against him. There is also the possibility of a stroke, because of how long he's been bleeding with the brain shift. And you're aware of the court case, what's happening?"

"My wife has been there with her cousin; her cousin was injured that day . . . My wife informed me of a few things, but not everything; we've been missing each other, due to our schedules," said Patrick, hating to bend the truth, subconsciously praying for forgiveness.

"There is no way humanly possible that Mister Carter will be able to stand trial . . . The other hospital he was admitted into for treatment, prior to being treated here, was contacted for his case," Dr. Katzberg began again, "A psychiatrist and some former physicians have compared their treatments with our diagnosis, and his records were found and brought in . . . We all find that Mister Carter is suffering from a medical condition we refer to as organic hallucinosis, coupled with organic mood disorder, all forms of an organic psychosis, so to speak. He seems to think that someone is following him, or that someone is trying to harm him. It's his grandfather that passed away two years ago? Fell out the window to his death right?"

Patrick nodded uncomfortably to the doctor's

question.

"It's because of the intracranial bleed, your relative is having delusions if anything; and apparently, he has been suffering from this delusional disorder for a long time, because of the amount of blood we saw on the MRI. Again, we'll do what we can to stop the bleeding; his will to survive is going to help. The organic hallucinosis is partly drug induced also. We know that Mister Carter was abusing drugs, but with his misplaced records, he told the other physicians he'd been clean for some time. Some drugs differ with certain cases, drugs, alcohol, which drug was Mister Carter abusing, wasn't it cra . . ."

"Crack doctor! Get to the point!"

The doctor was taken aback by Patrick's sudden change in temper.

"I'm sorry. Doctor, I truly apologize . . . I'm just upset. I'm real worried about him doc."

"Well, like I said before, the organic hallucinosis, can be drug induced, so when you say that he was a crack abuser, it seems perfectly logical. He'll even beat himself or harm his own body, because of the delusions with the organic mood disorder. It's because of the consistent bleeding on the brain. The brain shift may have led to seizures along the way, with visions of things and people who don't exist, smells, taste, different things he hears. Sort of in the same light as paranoid schizophrenia, but not exactly the same attack on the five senses."

Patrick and Dr. Katzberg rose to their feet. Modern medicine was great, but ancient customs still stood the test of time. The duppy theory still upheld its importance. Patrick's plan of wanting to check his grandmother remained; and he hoped he wasn't violating God by leaning to his own understanding, by still desiring his grandmother's opinion. He needed time alone with her before the rest of the family could wake up for the day in person, and not over the telephone. It was almost two years since Albert Carter's death, and his recovered thug-now near death-grandchild claimed his re-appearance more than once. Perhaps there was still more to the phantom mystique than meets the eye.

"So what now? What's next for him," Patrick asked, re-establishing eye contact.

"Well after we stop the bleeding, depending on the verdict of the case, he'll be admitted into a long term care facility, sorry to say, for the rest of his life. He will need to heal from the intracranial surgery, plus he needs ongoing medication and treatment for the organic hallucinosis and mood disorder. If there was no bleeding, then his hospitalization would have lasted maybe, four months, perhaps up to a year even . . . BUT if he were not bleeding, then he would have to do possible life in jail. Know what I mean?"

Patrick looked at the floor and nodded, "I guess so."

The doctor hoped Patrick could handle the last part of the news. It wasn't the easiest thing to tell a friend, or a relative, that their loved one-who escaped death many times-was being considered for possible placement in a mental institution. In his years of practice, he saw many patients deteriorate at the speed of sound in those places. Dwayne Carter would have his tenth life sucked from him in a psychiatry ward; and as far as his current physicians were concerned, Dwayne had deteriorated to a state where he must be considered for the long term psychiatric treatment.

"Doc, is he really gonna be put away for the rest of his life?"

"Listen, it's just rehabilitative therapy until he eventually heals, with lots of observation. Don't worry, optimism is the key. He's responding to lots of medication; and he's responding well."

"Thank you, doctor, for the information. I appreciate it," Patrick said, extending his hand, and the men shook hands.

"No problem," the doctor replied. With his stethoscopes swinging to and fro around his lab coat, Dr. Katzberg walked from Patrick back towards the nursing station.

Patrick walked in the opposite direction towards the elevator bank. Catching the down elevator to the lobby, he found the closest available pay phone. Putting his quarter in the slot, he felt a small tear manifesting in his eye.

"Hello may I speak with Arlene please . . . Hey . . . Yes, it's Patrick . . . Good morning to you also Arlene. How are you today? . . . I'm okay, I'm about to head to work now . . . Yes . . . I did, I sure did get the rundown . . . Yes, I saw him too . . . No, he didn't say anything, I just talked to him, but he didn't respond . . . What can I tell you Arlene? . . . You were right . . . Now I see . . . I understand now . . . I understand why you cry Arlene . . . I understand why you cry."

****

CHAPTER 19

*

In the early morning rain, at 5:30 while family members slept on Mother's Day Sunday, Patrick entered the other brownstone he knew all too well. With jingling spare house keys on his key ring, and wet bags of groceries in case the household was running low, he entered his old house prepared for the breakfast menu he already planned to fix for the holiday. Giving morning greetings to Grant, who awakened at the sound of an extra person squeaking around in the home, Patrick gave his assistant managing cousin a head nod.

"Gwan fi sleep nuh," Patrick whispered, "Mi gaan cook brekefast fi Mummy Una h'and de howse. Nuh bodder, 'nuh fret, 'nuh maan g'wan drop h'asleep. Weke up, fill ya belly leytuh."

Grant nodded, returning groggily into the living room that was completely rearranged into extra sleeping quarters, because of the many relatives inhabiting the house.

Patrick sat the groceries at the bottom of the staircase. He stuck his hand in one of the shopping bags and took out copies of the Sunday New York Daily News, Caribbean Life, and the Sunday Gleaner of Jamaica; then, he hopped and skipped up the stairs to greet his grandmother who he knew should be awake.

Upon his arrival at her bedroom door in the familiar quarters, Una had practically cursed him. And once she lovingly chastised, she ordered her grandson all over her bedroom, out of loneliness for Bradley, Dora, and the rest of the children from her original family. She contemplated returning home to Jamaica for good, for there was no use for her in the United States. Most of her time these days was spent worrying about church duties, social security benefits, her diminishing household presence amongst her "new" relatives, advancing technology, and the day when she would finally get a visit from Patrick. Once in a while the household vibe with her English nieces, nephews, and cousins living in the brownstone was similar to the good old days; however, the glory days of her arrival in the United States, living with her son Bradley and her vexed daughter in-law Dora, remained in her heart.

"Kiss mi neck baack, ti raatid! Wha' hoppen nuh bwoy? W'ere de briefcyese, it h'urly in de marnin'," Una said, excitedly to her grandson.

"Mummy! Teke de peypers fi read, 'n' g'wan dress. Mi ah cook fi ye right nouw! H'appy Mudder's Dey! Mi love ya. Mi gaan douwnsteirs in de kitchen!"

Patrick hugged Una then kissed his grandmother on the cheek, giving her the newspapers. He returned downstairs to the second floor, picked up the groceries and went down the hallway into the kitchen. Once he set out all of his items, he thoroughly washed his hands, and put his artistic, culinary skills to work. The surprise breakfast of ackee & saltfish, bammy, fried plaintains, boiled banana, yam, callaloo, fried cornmeal dumpling and cornmeal porridge, sausage, with homemade sorrel to wash down the meal, was for the women of his former household on the holiday. The miniature tidbits of the meal he carried to his grandmother touched her heart just the way he planned it. After she finished eating, Patrick returned her plate downstairs to the kitchen, gave Mother's Day greetings to a few cousins who had awakened as they thanked him for preparing breakfast.

Patrick carried a mug of hot tea upstairs to his grandmother's bedroom, sporting the biggest smirk he wore in months. Seemed like old times after a while with Patrick's surprise meal for her; and Patrick knew he picked the right time for the visit. He would make it back to Brooklyn in time for the second service at church with non-speaking Michelle. For the time being, it felt very good to be at his home away from home.

He re-entered the comfortable bedroom he remembered. Una sat in her favorite chair, large enough for two people with her swollen feet propped up on a matching stool, catnapping while the television watched her, papers sprawled around her lap.

"Mummy," Patrick called out.

"Coume," she responded, snapping back to reality.

Patrick thought, "Mummy stay wanting hot tea. That's Mummy for ya. Love her death."

He handed his grandmother her beloved mug of tea, opened her drapes then kneeled by her ankles, and began to massage her feet.

"Praise God . . . Halleujah," he chanted to himself repetitively, feeling truly blessed to have his father's mom at his side again, and in a semi-healthy condition for her age. He nodded his head in the blinded, overcast sunlight thinking this was the perfect time to find out about duppies. After a surprise Mother's Day breakfast in the bedroom, while Una's feet were being massaged would be a great opportunity. While she sipped her tea after eating most of her favorite foods, her guard was definitely down. It was now or never.

"H 'ow's mi fevorite grandson? 'ow ya keepin'?"

"Mummy . . . Tell me what'cha know 'bout duppy," Patrick said quickly.

Una stopped sipping, with a raise of her loving eyebrow, and a puzzled look on her face.

"Uhm?"

"Tell me what'cha know, Mummy . . . 'Bout duppy."

"Mi nuh k'no' not'ing 'bout no duppy mi pickny! No'uw fix ya faece," Una regally snapped at her grandson, seeming offended.

"Whoa! Why so feisty," Patrick thought. "Just like an old school Jamaican woman."

He decided to coax the information out, because she had to know about duppies. Everyone from Jamaica knew about duppies, spirits, spooky things of that nature. Even other West Indian countries were familiar with them.

"Let me try her again," Patrick thought, continuing to massage her feet; he even kissed and hugged her calves like Hyacinth used to do. He let a few minutes go by until she finished her tea. She passed the empty mug to Patrick. "Res' it, deere," Una motioned Patrick towards the bureau.

Patrick put the mug and saucer on Una's bedroom dresser, resuming his duty of rubbing her feet.

"Mummy, mi wan' no 'bout duppy," Patrick insisted.

Una looked at her grandson with loving eyes, and the stern pursing of her lips transformed into a humorous smile with flawless dentures. She kissed her teeth Caribbean style, and Patrick stopped rubbing. He knew that she knew, especially after the look she gave with added sound effects.

"Mummy! Wha' ya kiss ya teet' up nuh' fa? Come on. Ya tell mi someting, mi small maan! Bac' 'ome in ah Maanchester? Eih . . . Remember?"

Una giggled at her "Americanized" grandson. How could he remember things from "J-A"? Patrick was too small to remember anything that went on in Jamaica.

"Rubbish . . . Go 'wey!," Una snarled.

"Y'ah maan! In Maanchester, Mummy, ya tell mi. Ya ah coume from de bush near de houwse near de kitchen."

"No maan! Eh-eh," Una started her wonderful duppy memory, "Listen 'nuh . . . Mi deh in ah mi bedroom fas' h'asleep, and h'all of a sudden, mi jus' feel someone h 'and, it ah coume cross mi shoulda. Mi sat up, mi look! Mi sey eh-

eh! An'd mi look, an' mi see mi faddah stand righ' by mi bed. Eh, Pahtrick?"

Patrick's eyes widened with his grandmother's account. Her friendly encounter with her father's ghost mystified him; he needed more duppy information.

"Yea' maan! Mi h 'ear. So h'all dem duppy nah evil?"

"No maan, soume evil, soume good. Duppy kno' who fi frighten ya nuh," Una replied, then paused, rolling her eyes and pursing her lips. Patrick answered her mental question before she asked; he could tell by her puzzled look that she needed some answers. He also knew that she knew he may be on a mission to help Dwayne.

"Mi friend dem catch up wit' an evil one."

"Wha' ya ah talk seh? Wha' friend ya a chat 'bout?," she asked incredulously.

"Mummy, it's Dweyne," Patrick said.

Silence, while Una tried to figure out who Dwayne was.

"Dweyne?"

"Eh-heh, Y'ah maan, Dweyne. You remember Dweyne, Mummy?"

She let a few seconds pass when suddenly, Una remembered her grandson's evil American friend. The troubled, Yankee boy who stole her money and house keys, with the intent of confiscating everything for the drug crack. Family rumor had it that her grandson was fretting about, on a mission for his Yankee friend who Carlton tormented months prior. She remembered the rest of the family laughing about how Patrick would be contacting them, out of desperation, out of revenge for the trick that Carlton played on Dwayne, as well.

The family was telling the truth. The wicked Yankee had even been on the news, and inside the city newspapers for killing innocent people. Una too, detested the fact that Patrick tried to remain close to Dwayne, but she decided to let go and let God, being true to her faith. She recalled the night when Dwayne came by the house looking for Patrick. He seemed like he was being chased, even tortured.

"De tief? De crack one?! Eh," Una shouted, sitting upright with a sarcastic temper. De blaastid crackhead k'no' 'bout duppy?! H'im ah smoouke dat blaastid crack 'til 'im big h'ead drop h'off! Dem raas yenkee pickny k'no' not'in 'bout duppy ya' 'nuh!"

"Mummy, h'im grandfaddah duppy coume back! H'im 'freid fahr h 'im ya 'nuh."

Una kissed her teeth. She knew in her soul and mind Americans knew absolutely nothing about duppies, so once again *de yenkee bwoy* was lying. Even Patrick, of Jamaican descent, knew nothing about them, so how could Dwayne know anything! Patrick told his grandmother the entire story about Al Carter returning, rearranging furniture, playing pranks, and abusing Dwayne.

"Listen 'ere Mummy . . . H'im a chat seh 'im granfaddah lick 'im h'aard in 'im faece two time, and trow 'im pon de ground . . . H'im try fi seh de duppy ghost in 'im yaard Mummy; h'an' de duppy jus' trow 'im 'boaut de plece maan, but mi nuh k'no' Mummy, mi nuh k'no'," Patrick explained to Una with disbelief.

Una burst into laughter, eventually making Patrick chuckle. As an adult, Patrick liked to hear his grandmother laugh, but as a child she would scare him. Una laughed like a witch.

"Mummy! Wha' ya laughin'?"

"Heeeeee Hee! Hee! Hee! Hee! Hee! Hee! Hee! Heeeeeeee! Serve dat DUHTY YENKEE BWOY T'IEF RIGHT! Hee! Hee! Hee! Hee! Heeeee! 'Im granfaddah duppy should ah kill 'im! Hee! Hee! Hee! Hee! Heeee!"

Patrick was shocked at his grandmother's cold heart. Obviously she didn't know how much Dwayne was suffering since Al's death.

"Mummy. Ya nuh k'no'. Ya nuh unnastand."

"It's h'allrite. Mi k'no', mi unnastand . . . Mi unnastand

mi pickny . . . Coume . . . Nuh boddah nuh fret . . . Coume 'ere maan . . . coume beby . . . coume," Una said, with her arms outstretched, scooting over to allow her Patrick to sit with her. Things happened for a reason, in its divine order, the elderly woman thought as she embraced her grandson. Patrick favored her deceased son so much when he became worried. He was never too old to be embraced, because he truly worried, so much like Bradley Livingston, cool and detached, but inquisitive, and overprotective of family, friends, and loved ones, such a man of the cloth.

While Una hugged and held Patrick tight, like during his pre-adolescent youth, Dwayne awakened in his hospital room to French toast, cheese eggs, link sausage, grits, hash browns, and toast with butter and marmalade. Also added to the deal were the fresh fruit, and freshly squeezed juices. The succulent aroma of his breakfast combined with a luscious feminine smell; and Nicole entered his room, and kissed Dwayne on his forehead.

"Happy Mother's Day, honey, and many, many, many more! Even though you're not a Mother, but Happy Mother's Day," she shouted, untying his wrist restraints, beaming with joy. "You see honey, what goes around, comes around. You've fixed me breakfast in bed lots of times. Now it's our turn sweetheart."

She walked around his bed wearing a long black trench coat with a white leather Louis Vuitton purse with pink lettering hanging from her shoulder. She smiled at Dwayne; and he smiled back, removing his oxygen mask, slowly with excitement. His heart rate monitor displayed a rapid, steady beat at 94 beats per minute.

"I heard the really good news, that you are doing much, much better, so I came to get some of that real good news myself," said Nicole. She smiled her flawless smile and started unbuttoning her coat; and then she removed it, for Dwayne to witness her transparent Victoria's Secret white negligee. She tossed her coat and pocketbook onto the windowsill, and stood with her hands on her hips, with her dark nipples hardening while she winked her eye at her mate. Dwayne, in awe of his current state and surroundings, was amazed at his woman and her antics. He did hear Patrick's voice saying that Nicole would visit him, but standing virtually naked as the day she was born inside his hospital room was seriously bold on her part, yet intriguing.

Nicole said, "Well boobie, how does it feel to be twenty-three?"

"I don't know baby, the same way it feels to have been twenty-two. I guess I feel the same. But Nikk . . ."

"Well, you still look good as you did, cutie, mmmmm," Nicole said, licking her lips.

Dwayne thought to himself, "Look as good as I did? But, I . . . I . . . I got shot by five-oh . . . and . . . Pappy burned, burned me . . ."

He patted himself down in a bewildered frenzy with his left hand, trying to pull with his right, unable to move. Then he touched his face, rubbed his skin, and there were no stitches. He pushed the breakfast tray to the side and kicked away his bedcovers, surprised.

"Now, I know we didn't make that big old breakfast for nothing! If you're not willing to eat, you can at least look at me Boobie. Aren't you hungry," Nicole asked, as she grabbed both breasts and sensuously squeezed, pointing her nipples in his direction, a routine Dwayne loved back at the suite.

Dwayne's hands were still agitatedly busy, one being glued to his face like a magnet, and the other cuffed to the iron bedrail stuck like a magnet. He touched at his skin and there was hair, plenty of hair; the hair follicles inside his scalp were filled with long thick strands like the days of his youth, suddenly kinky, and nappy. He grabbed at his Afro, which was what he had unexpectedly, an Afro big and nappy.

"NIKKI!!"

"*What?!* You're so damned **ungrateful** all the time! Breakfast in bed on Mother's Day, and . . ."

"Please love," Dwayne cut her off, his voice shaking, "Please . . . please bring me a mirror."

Nicole shook her head, smiled, and put her finger in her mouth; she turned to the windowsill to dig in her purse. Five seconds passed, and Dwayne started hyperventilating.

"**Nicole!**"

"Okay, okay, I'm coming," she giggled, returning with a hand held mirror.

"What's all that noise?!"

A lot of people started gathering outside of Dwayne's room. There was the sound of a very live party. The fiesta effect was equipped with the sounds of music, cooking, complete with the sounds of clanking pots and pans, and the jovial noise and sounds were all coming from the vestibule outside of his hospital room. Dwayne snatched the mirror from Nicole's hands and his eyes opened wide, frighteningly.

"**What the fuck is going on**?"

Dwayne's head and chest burst with pain, and his fist clung tenaciously to the plastic handle of the mirror, for he was Al. He was his grandfather inside the reflection in his hands, no destroyed fair skin, but the familiar caramel colored complexion with wrinkles. Their bruises were now identical, and the hair he now unbelievably pulled was his very own snow white, uncombed Afro. He called out to Nicole, and she laughed and ran from the room.

"**Nikki!! Comeback!!** Yo!! Come here!!"

Dwayne inched himself to the side of his bed, with his breath coming in short spurts. The taste of his blood was bitter, trickling immediately from his nose; and he spat out more of his blood, moving his entire body towards his bedside, with the exception of his cuffed wrist.

"Nikki!! . . . Please! . . . Please!! . . . Don't leave me,"

Dwayne begged, as he swung from his bed to stand by the bedside, with his wrist reddening, and cutting into his skin. He turned his head, noticing he was a few centimeters from the doorway, suddenly vomiting thick clots of blood, when a pair of slime ridden bony hands reached for his throat from behind him.

"Get the fuck off me! Get off! Get off," Dwayne tried to yell, but the pleas were stifled as his eyes rolled back to see Al choking him again. Adding to this terror was Al's occasional fist, punching Dwayne in the head while he squeezed his grandson's neck with his other cupped hand; and his grandson tossed, turned, and shook inside his karma weaved net, like any wicked hunter shockingly entrapped by their own game of universal law.

"Shut up! Shut **UP!**," Al bellowed, and he kicked Dwayne's ankles making him fall from his limited, hunched balance. Dwayne's body flipped opposite from his wrist that remained in place, cuffed to the bedrail. Al let out hoarse, ear piercing laughter that could be heard for miles, watching the dislocation of his grandson's right shoulder. There was only enough stamina for Dwayne to focus on his shoulder pain while venous blood was dripping from his nose and mouth, coloring his grandfather's bare feet and ankles. Al kept his foot implanted against Dwayne's chest, mushing his grandson 's trunk against the side of the bed, while his slicing wrist also began seeping blood.

"Ya always wanted a surprise party boy! Now ya got one! **SURPRISE!!** Get up! Get up! Get up right now I say! I got people here that been waiting to see you for a long time Baby Al, **GET UP!**"

Al moved the entire bed with his connecting grandson into another angle to be viewed by a multitude of arriving guests.

"Nnnnnn . . . Nnnn . . . Nn . . . Nikk . . . Nikki!," Dwayne muttered, needing his love to rescue him from his repetitious distorted reality of pain. Although his head

swam at this point, he noticed the silence of the room door creaking open simultaneously with his twisted dislocated shoulder that would soon break. The blood from his face and nose trickled faster, forming an expanding pool on the floor, while Dwayne tried to breathe without his mask. Through his vision of blood, he managed to glance at the entering calves and trouser legs of his company while the sounds of the party escalated to a deafening volume.

Dwayne looked up and saw the security officer he shot from The Roberto Clemente Rehabilitation Center holding the door open to the vestibule. With the name tag "Torres" still in place, his stained uniform had a hole in his chest. Al shook hands with Security Officer Torres while exiting the room and stated, "See he ain't want no breakfast; guess it's time for his supper then." With the hospital bed centered in the room with Dwayne's writhing body connected, he heard a starting bell ring, and Al announced while passing through the crowded vestibule, "I believe that boy supper's 'bout ready now . . . GO ON, and start the PAR-TAY!".

People began entering Dwayne's room one by one, along with the aroma of a Thanksgiving feast. The arriving people conversed, interacting with one another like most soirees. Dwayne's rented television popped on by itself, along with loud radio waves filling the entire room with 107.5 WBLS. As the familiar people entered, they all began to circle the bed. Coughing, spitting with excruciating head, chest, and dislocated shoulder pain, Dwayne's heart rate increased while continuing to vomit blood; and the room slanted with anti-gravity, with other arriving guests. With desperate thoughts feeling trapped again, Dwayne was unable to run, his wishes and first time prayers un-granted. Not only had Al returned to hatefully haunt and taunt, but this time there were others. There were more spirits who wanted a piece of him.

With dizzying vision, Dwayne saw Officer Torres with a bullet hole to his chest holding open the door for more and more arriving visitors. The room soon became uncomfortably packed with those whose mortal lives were touched negatively by Dwayne.

The homeless fellow with bloody throat exposed removed a pint of vodka from his coat and poured it on Dwayne. The splashing vodka caused Dwayne to burn with his pain. Then there was a young lady wearing rolling skates with half of her neck. With her exposed meaty bloody breasts inside her ripped open blouse, she had a crushed torso that was black and blue. She held onto a muscular guy with a Jheri curl, sporting entry and exit wounds to his chest and back, a ripped black tight t-shirt with patterned rings designed around it, in an emblem style with the word "SATURN" on the front.

An older Caucasian male was well-suited and smoking a cigar, whispering to a middle-aged, reddish haired Caucasian woman, entering the room. The woman wore a blouse with a rip, advertising a giant bloody gash between her breasts; and the bloody hole was an open wound, as if the woman was just stabbed. The man kept whispering to the lady, and she pulled along a young, angry acting Caucasian male in his twenties. The young guy tried to find space inside the room with the couple; and they sat on the windowsill. The younger Caucasian with his pissed off head, sat with a bloody throat cut, exposing his entire trachea and esophagus.

Through Dwayne's vision, the young man looked familiar, and he resembled the older couple; he was possibly a son or a nephew, but why were they in his hospital room? Why were all these people in a room that could only accommodate three visitors comfortably, and the amount of people now entering the room was up to eight, with more joining the festivities looking for space.

Dwayne thought, "Damn that cut looks nasty . . . All these people look nasty . . .Where's Nikki . . . Damn, I must know these people, but from where . . . where do I know them from?"

The room faded away and Dwayne fainted, only to awaken numb in his bed minutes later with more guests crowded around him, staring.

"HEY-HEY-HEY! THE GANG'S ALL HERE," Al shouted from somewhere nearby. Dwayne was unable to see his grandfather inside of the room now packed with nearly thirty extra people squeezed together. The door of the room had to remain open there were so many people filled to capacity, all familiar faces leading out into the anteroom. Dwayne's tears began to roll seeing Patrick's family again for the first time in nearly three years. Mr. & Mrs. Livingston stood uncomfortably in the crowd, with Uncles Barrington & Ezra, Franklin, and Hyacinth peeking in with her nursing cap and uniform. Andrew was staring, with deejay headphones, Rose & Sharon with their jump ropes in hand; and the entire family had dried blood over their heads, chests, necks, and backs.

"Move out the way so I can bring that boy his supper," Al yelled with the many visitors shifting and squeezing out the way.

The Chambers-Livingston family moved uncomfortably, started shifting, rearranging their standing positions to accommodate Al bringing in a new rolling bedside table covered with Dwayne's new meal. The other table with the untouched breakfast was shuttled out, while the visiting party continued to change their standing positions.

Leaving four other white men huddled together near the window, the Caucasian couple with the young white guy made their way to the right side of Dwayne's bed. The woman came to his head, the older gentleman with the cigar causing others to choke and fan their noses, hunched in the middle grinning, while the angry young man, with piercing eyes and one connected eyebrow from right to left, was squeezed and placed at the right foot.

More peering faces crowded and surged toward the people who surrounded Dwayne; and he was extra nervous, feeling near death more than ever. With waves of nausea, he began to regurgitate more blood, slowly but surely recognizing the faces of his spooky guests who glared at him from the first row. On his right, he gazed at the Caucasians and figured out they were his unknown paternal side: The Mucci's.

Next to the Mucci family, a young thug stared hard, angry, and deadly at Dwayne, pushed against the right foot of the bed by six bodies; three of the men wore masks, and the other three heads were uncovered with familiar faces, flanking their cousin, nephew, uncle, and friend rolled into one: **SCHEME**! Brooklyn Scheme's presence at the party made Dwayne remember all the dirty tricks he pulled on his ex-partner.

"Oh shit," Dwayne gasped, for in the center of Scheme's forehead was a giant hole, large enough for all to view the gunned down peddler's brains moving around inside. Scheme eyed Dwayne with hate, still smiling, chuckling aloud while rubbing his bloodstained knuckles together.

More tears rolled from Dwayne's eyes, seeing Shawn Young squeezed next to Scheme, shaking his head chuckling with his gold tooth gleaming, cracking his knuckles in his trademark fashion. Wearing a furry "Kangol" hat, his intestines and liver were exposed while wearing his favorite Gucci sweat suit with jacket open. Next to them at the left foot of the bed, huffing and puffing was a familiar heavyset black woman in her late fifties or early sixties.

"That boy still HONGRY I bet'cha!," Dwayne heard Al yell. The obese woman replied, "Sho' is. He ain't touch his breakfast. But I reckon he gon' be hungry; we all is . . ."

Al now wore his apron and chef's hat, bore every bruise, welt, and the resident black eye, from the heyday of the abuse.

"Wooooh-wee, it is a *BEAUTY* inside this here! Wait 'til everybody get a load of what's on this platter! I still ain't lost my touch," he yelled happily.

His grandfather managed to wheel in the long, skinny table without knocking over many of the items. The table was covered with a small white cloth, beautifully decorated buffet style, with plenty of Negro delicacies that covered the entire thing. There was a covered main course on a raised tray in the center, with a small Cornish hen, sausage dressing, ham, pot roast, black-eyed peas and rice, mashed potatoes, corn, collard greens, macaroni and cheese, candied yams, assorted breads, salads, gravies, etc.

"Gee, dinner smells delicious," the redhead to the right stated. The gentleman mumbled to his younger clone, "Yeah, she's a fucking nigger lover anyway . . . Why don'tcha shut you's face already Helena, will ya?"

A mini argument ensued between the couple, and they were quieted by Al. Then Al held the table in place, because of the crowd, and put his arm around the woman crushed next to him; and Dwayne recognized her at once, with tears welling in his maddened eyes.

'It's Grandma Mattie! This shit is gettin' crazier and crazier!'

The dog growling that haunted him for months started again, once Dwayne looked into the eyes of the young, pretty light-skinned black girl squeezed at the head of the bed on his left side. With her hair done in a 1960's beehive style, she smiled down with eyes of love at Dwayne, looking extremely familiar, but Dwayne wondered where he saw her. She wasn't Nicole, for sure, and she wasn't an ex-girlfriend, or any of the young women who flocked to him during his teenaged tenure of black money; she wasn't anyone who was caught in a crossfire of bullets, or anyone he had mugged while he was an impenitent, bloodthirsty, crackhead; she was infinite beauty. She was all the girlish good stuff: sugar, spice, all that could ever be nice, and they resembled each other; they favored each other in the same fashion as everyone around the bed, with the exception of Shawn, Scheme, the trigger men, and many others. Just as Dwayne realized the young man at the bedside was young Arnold Mucci, his father, he realized who she was.

'GWENNY!!'

Everything fit into pieces like a puzzle, and Dwayne tried to fight his tears to no avail as he mustered up courage to continue his family reunion. Each person in the room had died, and each individual was tied to his life, and reason for existence. The horrifying daydream was becoming too much to bear.

'I don't believe this shit! This is crazy, I'm know, I'm not crazy! These were the voices I was hearing all these months . . . I couldn't sleep at night cause of them . . . The girl voice and the lady voice was Grandma Mattie and Gwenny . . . The guy that was popping shit was Scheme . . . But this can't be . . . they're all, they're all . . . dead.'

He burst into uncontrollable tears looking at all of his company, and screamed, **"Pappy, why are you doing this**?!"

Al's proud smirk switched to an angry glare.

"Ya know, it's time for you to stop being selfish boy! It's a holiday and you gotta enjoy it! What better way to enjoy Mother's Day? What better way to celebrate, than with friends, family, and yo' MAMA! We cain't let death leave you out neither! See, Baby Al, this how we all died. We're all dead! And it's all because of you boy! Happy **Dead** Mother's Day!"

The hysterics climbed to a next level when Gwenny unlatched the top left bedrail and jumped up onto the bed to embrace and comfort her son. The floral print dress she wore was spotted with bloodstains in her vaginal area as if she were menstruating without protection. Dwayne yelled out to nothing when he noticed more dried blood smeared on his mother's calves and ankles.

Gwenny embraced her child, and Dwayne flipped at the touch of his mother's ice cold bosom against his neck. Her arms and hands were freezing; she was a most beautiful zombie straight from the grave, not an ounce of blood pulsating through her veins whatsoever. He wanted her to let go the more she lovingly squeezed.

While Gwenny held her son by his neck, blood poured from Dwayne's mouth, and his nose this time, dispensing meaty clots of blood. The canine growls escalated with more waves of nausea, and most of all, the recurring, intolerable head pain. Things began speeding up, like going from a 331/3 r.p.m. record to a compact disc rotation, with a hypertensive heart rate of 113 bpm, gaining speed by the second. All hell was breaking loose with hysterical, Dwayne mixed right up in the middle. The frustrated, uncomfortable party began arguing with one another. Mr. & Mrs. Mucci started a fresh argument, without whispering, and Arnold bickered with Gwenny over Dwayne's bloody welfare, eventually trading racial slurs. Mattie and Scheme joined the verbal brawl, and the dog growling reached proportions that practically shook the room.

"I'm dead cause of that nigger bitch!"

'GRRRRRRRRRRRRR! GRRRRRRRRRRRRRRRRRR! Grrrrrrrrrrrrr!'

"Kiss my ass! My whole black ass! You see our son needs attention! You wouldn'tna been no damn good no way! You're a dirty rat bastard rapist!"

"Fuck you! Nigg . . ."

"I'm glad them colored boys slashed your throat at school!"

'Grrrrrrrrrrrrrrrrrrrrrrrrrrrrrrrrrrrrrr!

GRRRRRRRRRRRRRRRRRRRRRRR'

"Leave 'im alone, Arnie calm down! I died in jail with the spooks! Y'ull catch a heart attack, hey will ya!"

"Shut up! You stabbed me, your own wife trying to kill only one spook!"

"Niggers!"

"Crackers! You honky ass punk!"

'GRRRRRRRRRRRRRRRRRRRRRR!'

"Your stupid ass stood in the way when I told ya's to move!"

"It's wrong Sallie honey! She's a mud shark so what! Christ! He's your grandkid too!"

"It's his fucking fault I'm dead!"

"You shouldn'tna had him snorting that damn cocaine! Good for you! Those West Indian boys shoulda shot you!"

"They shoulda shot you! He made you have **stupid** headaches 'til you kicked the bucket!"

'*Grrrrrrrrrrrr! GRRRRRR! Grrrrrrrrrrrr! GRRRRRRRRRRRRRRRRRRRRRRRRRRRR!*'

"Now wait a goddamned minute young buck! **That's MY WIFE!**"

'*GRRRRRRRRRRRRRRRRRR! Grrrrrrrrrrrrrrrrrrrrrrrrrrrr! GRRRRRRRRRRRRR*'

Dwayne was becoming short of breath without his oxygen mask, unable to see clearly because of imminent shock and the power of duppy scrutiny. The covered main course platter shook in the center of the table, like a boiling pressure cooker ready to blow its stack.

'*Nikki...Please!...I'm dy...dying!...Help...Help me ...Nicole...Hel...Help me, Nikki!...Nikki!...Help me!*'

"Look at him! Mo' spoiled than goddamned two month milk! Baby Al! Ya spoiled! See Mattie! I told ya not to spoil him and ya wouldn't listen! And Gwenny let go of that boy and get outta that bed front of all these folks!"

Gwenny did a doubletake at her father's merciless command.

"But daddy, he's bleeding, and Baby Al needs . . ."

"Damn it! I'm running this show! **Let the boy SUFFER! LET HIM GO!**"

Torn between obedience and the responsibilities of motherhood, Gwenny clung to her son for dear death.

"Get out that bed Gwenny! So he can join us! See Mattie Mae! I told ya not to spoil him woman!"

"Oh Albert, please," Mattie fired back at her husband.

"Man! The boy need to eat! And join us grandson! JOIN US GRANDSON!! JOIN US!!"

'Nikki . . .Please! . . . I'm dy . . .dying! . . . Help . . . Help me . . . Nicole . . . Hel . . . Help me, Nikki! . . . Nikki! . . . Help me!'

Dwayne and his duppy party hungrily listened to his braggard grandfather.

"Man, Baby Al, you's lucky! Fixed everything you like! Mashed 'tatas, sweet 'tatas! Pot roast! Got'cha birthday cake in the oven! Grape Kool-Aid in the frigidaire! Sweet potato pie in the icebox! And most of all, I got yo' favorite!"

Al removed the top from the platter; and Dwayne let off a blood curdling yell, with eyes rolling upward in their sockets, because on top of the platter lay the split open head of General, his beloved pit bull. With a tomato in his mouth and quivering nose, the steamed alive dog skull in halves bit down into the tomato and started barking on contact.

They all watched Dwayne Albert Carter wallow and writhe to hell, screaming in horror, as General's grotesque head still wound up in front of him growling and barking. Dwayne continued regurgitating mucous and blood until everything was depleted, while fresh canine blood and brain oozed from the busted skull of the 1 ½ year old pit bull he endearingly nurtured from birth, yet brutally killed.

'Nikki! . . .Nikki! . . .Noooooo! . . .Nikki! . . .Somebody!'

And Nicole heard her lover's cry for help, rushing as fast as she could to his aid. She was guilty but innocent of the sickening party she initiated with visiting guests in Dwayne's hospital room, well over the maximum violated room capacity. Once she squeezed past the younger Livingstons, re-entering the room, murderous Scheme stood and pulled out Franklin Livingston's nickel plated nine millimeter, and shot Nicole at point blank range, blowing her throat and windpipe against the wall, getting her blood into Gwenny's eyes and hair.

The impact of the gun blast caused General's half head with one popped eye to catch Dwayne by the neck with its jaw, sinking his teeth into his master's jugular veins and tendons, as if his neck was the juiciest steak on the market. Oblivious to his broken shoulder, Dwayne was thrust from his hospital bed in terror.

The increasing light of the darkness found Dwayne on the floor of his hospital room, face down, with his urinary catheter and nasogastric tubing ripped out again, intravenous lines lassoed around his neck in chaotic disarray. Fading into unconsciousness, his right side disappeared while he tenaciously held the help button for patient assistance, while his heart rate remained at 148 bpm.

By the time help arrived, Dwayne looked like a cross between a suicidal pet fish out of its aquarium and a paralyzed tortoise. Bleeding thick, meaty clots of blood profusely from the nose, mouth, and penis, the staff tended to a patient whose horrifying dream had become his terrifying reality, as the physician's fearless predictions came true. The remaining internal blood clots did shoot to his shifted brain, resulting in a cardiovascular attack for the young man.

Before the end of Mother's Night, 23-year-old Dwayne Carter was rushed a second time to emergency surgery for a runaway intracranial bleed, unable to talk or move, with a twisted, ruined face, a moderate to severe stroke, with a dislocated shoulder and broken arm to add to his other presents for life.

****

CHAPTER 20
*

Late August, 1992. Another sunny Sunday. Beautiful assorted trees whisked by, along with deep rivers, tranquil lakes, farms, cornfields, and vegetation. There were farm and forest animals, and brown and green covered mountains, both tall and small through curved hilly roads in the distance; all part of the pastoral scene, with an air-conditioned black Nissan Pathfinder heading west on the interstate, filled to the hilt with thumping hip-hop beats.

Patrick lifted the mobile phone and followed the instructions of the jeep's driver for use, reclining his seat a bit, gazing out the window. Patrick said to the driver, "Man, are you going to turn down that music? I can barely hear the busy signal! You're lucky I'm putting up with this. I don't listen to that worldly stuff anymore. What about the little people back there?"

"Awwww come on now duke, don't sweat that! Don't you know who I am; I'm touring with Aaron Hall and Bobby Brown next month! And last month I performed with Special Ed, Naughty, and my beautiful black Queen Latifah. Don't worry about them in the back. Once we get our eat on, they'll be knocked out. They're used to daddy's joints pumping anyway. Yo E-zo, you aiight back there?"

Eric Martinez, dressed from head to toe in his Army dress green uniform, replied, "Yo, I'm good brother! Real good! I knew you was going to make it! Last time I was home, I couldn't believe when I turned on Pump It Up and saw you up there on TV, I bugged out! . . . It's just good to be home with my peoples around some real hip-hop, and not RAP MUSIC! . . . yo high, I'm straight!"

"Pump It Up eh," the driver of the jeep asked. "OH YEAH, with bad ass Dee Barnes. That was a long time ago. She definitely one of my boos. I need to see how she's doing."

In the driver's seat, a frown came to the face of Arthur Boyd once he raised his shades, noticing the one lane traffic congestion they were about to hit.

"Damn! Does it have to go down like this? On a weekend, way out here man," he complained. "If my peoples found out what I was doing, they would get on my case. I'm supposed to be back in the studio by six; I have to lay tracks all night, plus I'm flying to the coast in the morning. It's never sleep on my agenda anymore!"

"Don't worry about it, our exit is coming up. The cemetery is over there to the left," Patrick said pointing.

"Yo you wilin' Pat! Do you really want me to take my eyes off the road?"

Practically slaving himself to death as a gopher in the music business after college, Arthur had finally struck gold in 1989, landing a recording deal with a big label that had major distribution. A few of the sides he recorded had charted on Billboard's rap chart, and the video he shot was well on its way to number one. The "new and improved" Arthur dealt big money, and big numbers of women. He had grown to six foot four, and he exercised frequently to compliment the musical persona created for him. Still wearing contact lenses, these days for strict business purposes, he was name brand from head to toe, with gold gracing his neck, wrists, and fingers, but mostly in his mouth. He was in New York City for the weekend, and called Patrick, who in turn contacted Eric.

Eric coincidentally was home on leave from overseas, in between the transferring of duty stations. The young men agreed to get together for old times' sake. They learned by their early twenties that tomorrow was never promised to anyone, therefore, the time was the present Sunday to spend the afternoon together. Arthur brought along his two sons, Richard and Jason ages 7 and 8, for the ride with his childhood buddies.

"It will be a year before we get to this exit," Arthur said, while his beeper went off constantly.

"Relax," said Patrick, "It's right there!"

Arthur reached over into his glove compartment and pulled out a "White Owl" cigar. "Pardon me Pat," he said digging into his pocket and producing a bag of reefer; and Patrick did a double take.

"Yo E-zo," Arthur yelled, "Take this man, and lace this up for me." Arthur tossed the bag of weed and the cigar to Eric in the backseat.

"Damn Arthur! YOU CHANGED B! Is this what having records out do to folks? You puffing lah-lah kid," Eric asked, bursting into laughter.

"Just lace that up son! You'll see what's up! It's a forty of Private Stock in here too!"

Patrick shook his head as the jeep finally entered the ramp to exit the highway.

". . . but lead us not into temptation . . . but deliver us from evil . . . for thine is the kingdom . . . and the power and the glory . . . forever and ever . . . Amen," Patrick concluded his prayer.

A few seconds passed, and the sudsy beer hit the soil, partly splasing the gray headstone that read from top to bottom:

"You Were Created To Fly With The Angels Of Heaven . . . We Love You, But God Loves You Most . . . SHAWN GREGORY YOUNG . . . SUNRISE: OCTOBER 26th, 1965 . . . SUNSET: AUGUST 3rd, 1985 . . . *A Beautiful Son . . . A Courageous Nephew . . . A Loving Father"*

Patrick took deep familiar breaths, with tears slowly

rising. He rubbed the back of crying Eric.

"Yo my bad," Eric said wiping his eyes, "I just feel bad cause I'm never going to see him again in this life . . . and I never been out here B . . . I miss my homie so much . . . DAMN! . . . I wish he could have stayed running with Zulu word up! . . . Shit! . . . He would be alive today man!"

"I understand brother, "Patrick said. "Man, you have to cry E-zo. Let it out . . . They tell us men not supposed to cry, and that's a whole heap of crap . . . E-zo, Shawn was our boy, and he got killed with my whole family, trying to help my family, you know what I'm saying? . . . I have never stopped crying for Shawn . . . or my whole family . . . I just bawl every other day brother man . . . you owe us no apology E."

Arthur poured the entire forty ounce of beer on top of Shawn's grave. Then he took his Timberland boot and formed a small a tiny hole with some medium dry dirt.

"Where's that blunt," Arthur asked Eric.

"It's in the whip, in the backseat. Why?"

"Aw man! YOU better hope my boys not smokin' and tokin' up them trees pretty please," Arthur said, running through the aisles of graves back to his jeep. Patrick and Eric looked at each other peculiarly, and shrugged their shoulders.

"Times change and people change," Patrick said, slapping Eric five.

"I don't know moneygrip! I think it's all that high profile Hollywood-Hollyhood celebrity BULLshit!"

"Hey, what can I tell you, Boogie Art is Boogie Art."

"Yeah right!"

Arthur started the jeep then returned to his high school boys at the graveside. He crouched and put the cigar filled with weed to stand up straight, then covered the dirt around it until the blunt stood on its own.

"Gimme a light one of y'all," Arthur asked, standing

up with his hand out. "COME ON E-ZO! You been blackening your lungs since Wadleigh junior high school duke! Gimme a light!"

Patrick laughed while Eric passed his green "Bic" lighter to Arthur.

Arthur re-crouched in front of Shawn's headstone and said, "Yo Shawn, it's me Boogie Art . . . Remember me? I'm here with E-zo and Pat Livingston man! . . . I know you looking down on us . . . You laughing, ready to smoke . . . I still don't smoke though . . . I know you rocking with me anyway though . . . You been with me from up top . . . This el is for you."

Arthur lit the blunt buried in the ground, and the flame began to smoke by itself; and the guys burst into laughter.

"See, this is how you remember people," Arthur stated emphatically.

"OH MY GOD! YO PAT! THIS DUDE ARTHUR IS BUCKFUCKINWILD NOW," Eric laughed loud and hard.

"Yes . . . We all have definitely changed," chuckled Patrick.

"Cool? You aiight," Arthur asked Eric. Eric nodded.

"Bet! Let's be out, I have to feed my sons. I know they are hungry, and we need to get to see Baby Al."

Arthur headed for the jeep with Patrick and Eric pointing at him, leaving Shawn smoking his blunt in spirit.

The guys were back on the road again with the thumping hip-hop of the day, including listening to tracks from the upcoming "Boogie Art" debut album. Minutes after riding the highway, they passed an exit advertising a choice of restaurants in which the boys decided they wanted chicken.

After their much needed eat and rest stop, the guys continued their trip, landing right back in the middle of another interstate traffic jam that moved like a funeral procession with millions of cars. Sure enough, Richard and Jason fell fast asleep, covering themselves with an abused 8-ball jacket, while their father cranked his latest effort that was bulleting up the rap music charts; and Patrick contacted the Mary Morton Center.

Arthur said, "See Pat, what I say? My boys are used to the hip-hop and hanging out, when I'm not touring."

"Dwayne is ready," Patrick said, passing Arthur the phone. "When we get there we have to ask for Miss Ross, the charge nurse. It's funny how you keep referring to Dwayne as Baby Al after all these years. I haven't heard anyone use that name for Dee in the longest while. Maybe just his godmother Arlene. I wonder why I never called him that as much as we've been around each other."

"Me either, said Eric. "We all go way back like a spinal cord and shit. I never called Dee that. I remember he used to hate that name. He bit off me. Man, call me Guillermo if you dared; you will be swallowing teeth."

Arthur said, "But remember, I used to rest on 17th and Lenox before we moved up near Edenwald. Me and Baby Al lived on the same block, 17th between Lenox and Seventh, and those were . . ."

"Definitely the good old days," Patrick cut him off.

"Maybe for you kid. Baby Al used to bust my ass and take everything I had, all the time, since first grade."

Arthur turned down his booming system, a gesture that caught them by surprise. They subconsciously noted the changes in each other's personalities ever since meeting up, after many years. Luckily Patrick had Arthur pick him up on 120th because he knew Michelle's mouth would be wide open, witnessing her husband jump into a jeep with loud, "worldly" music.

They made it through another traffic clog of one lane traffic, due to an accident. Arthur activated his radar detection system once the lanes became clear, and the conversation struck up again. The guys spoke about their current occupations:

"Well, you know I have two supermarkets now. 16th Street, and my cousin Grant and I manage a Gristedes downtown on 86th. Thinking about getting another one around the way though, maybe uptown closer to 25th; that's where the ducats is at, so you brothers know the deal, whenever you need to do your food shopping . . ."

"Yeah my Moms told me Pat," Eric said. "She told me you hook her up every time she sees you at Associated. That's a good look man. I appreciate that, looking out for Ma Dukes when I'm not around. I'm thinking of making the army a career anyway."

"Word?"

"Yeah! I made my rank real quick because of Desert Storm. At first I was thinking of going for my E-6, but I have the chance to go OCS at my new duty station. I want that real bread B!"

"Isn't OCS officer school," asked Patrick.

"Yeah man!"

"E, that is DOPE! Praise God homie, praise God!"

"Cool," Arthur said. "It's good you know about all that military stuff Pat. Now back to this free food though. I know you better give me some free food when I come through."

"Art, man, are you crazy? You're the man now. I know you clocking all the girlies making records. If you can't buy your own groceries, then all the girlies you clocking can buy them," said Patrick.

"Yo, Pat, please do us a favor and don't say nothing. You taking me back to eighty-four with the stuff you saying," Arthur laughed. "If I keep hanging with you B, I'll be rhyming like Sugar Hill or somebody! ALTHOUGH, they're still one of the many great pioneers of this hip-hop game. And I love being a part of this kid. I just want to make quality music. You hear this jam we listening to? My joints, the work I do have to be music my children and my family can be proud of man."

Arthur started bobbing his head to the current beat, and Patrick snickered, shaking his head.

"You like that cut, kid? You sweating that right," Arthur asked.

"Man if we didn't go way back, I would **make** you put on this gospel tape I have in my pocket. But your record, it sounds, ummm, it's dope," Patrick grinned.

"Get ya slang right they're not saying that anymore!"

Eric laughed and added, "Man, I can't keep up either. I've been over near Hamburg, Germany for a minute!"

"It's phat, understand, phat! P-H-A-T! Phat is all that, and homie, phat is where it's at! But it's the thought that counts my brothers, and for that compliment Pat, you get to be in my next video," Arthur said, reaching over to pinch one of Patrick's chubby cheeks.

"Hey, hey, hey!," Patrick playfully shouted, giving Arthur one punch in the chest, which made the vehicle sway just a bit. At the same time, the radar detector gave off the warning of the police nearby.

"You need to slow down anyway," Patrick laughed, going to playfully tag Arthur a second time. "Dwayne might trip out when he sees you man, you used to be a straight up nerd!"

Arthur laughed and returned the hard punch. "Ah shut up! But who's a nerd now nigga?," he asked amusingly; and they both pointed in the backseat at Eric.

"I know neither one of you is pointing back here at me! Nerd?! Don't let this Martinez-Delacruz nametag on my chest fool you! You can take a real dude out the hood, but the real hood stays in that dude! I'm always E-zo from Foster! I do gats, and smoke cats, but it's round the world now! You already know the deal!"

The next serious topic the boys discussed was children, and love: "Damn, Art, I'd never think I'd see the day when you'd have some sons, man," Patrick said.

"We're old men now, hear 'em snoring back there," Arthur replied.

Eric laughed. "Yeah Art. They inhaled that KFC man, and they been out cold ever since! You and Michelle have kids too duke?"

"I must be old then too," Patrick added, and pulled out a wallet sized photo of his 3-month-old daughter Unasia. After Patrick's blue-faced pleas, Michelle named their daughter after his grandmother, still giving the name a current twist. Patrick showed Arthur and Eric the picture.

"She's beautiful B."

"She's my heart, man. She looks like me and Shell," Patrick then showed Arthur the photo, and he glanced.

"I can't front, Pat, man. I'm scared of marriage B!," Eric stated.

"Word to mutha," Arthur added, "Ain't no type of love in this music industry. A cat like me, I can't front, I'm just sticking and moving. I give it to brothers like you if you can make that marriage thing happen, man. Your daughter is very pretty."

"I'll get there," Eric said, "I'm going to marry my oldest kids Eriq and Eriqua's Moms, if she'll come and join me; bring the kids out with me to my new base, but I'm doing my OCS first. Get that bread, so I can take care of them all. Get mine out of this concrete jungle. I almost didn't make it, if it wasn't for the military. We'll see what happens," said Eric, checking his own vibrating beeper.

"You do want to provide that domestic stability of two parents man. I still say it's Jesus. You think me and Shell coulda made it without the Lord? You never heard that saying, a family that prays together, stays together?"

"No doubt," said Eric.

"So okay then. Same with a marriage. I love my wife and my daughter with all my heart. But I must put the Lord first. Love my heavenly Father with all my heart especially, and he's keeping us," Patrick proudly stated.

They continued to reminisce, laughing about the old times, the good, the bad, the happy, and the sad.

The guys spoke on education: "I have my G.E.D., man again, thanks to the military but that's not enough for me," Eric said. "I should've kept on hanging with you guys in high school, and I would've passed. I was too busy doing graffiti. I can't front though, I like how they consider it art now; and I'm going to get some bread from what I can do. But not until I get this OCS, and get more and more degrees."

Patrick added, "I like what you're saying E! I mean, I've been telling myself for the longest while that I'm just twenty-six, ya understand me? My wife and I can work together with our family, so I can go back and get my associate's, and then we can keep it moving. I realize now that I'm not too old. It will be hard work, but with God all is possible, and it's not too late."

"It's never too late for you to go back to school kid!," Arthur interjected. "It was crazy old heads with me up in Albany State, but some of those old school cats helped me screw my head on straight. Fellas, I kid you not man, at one point I wil'd out with mad chicks, but I graduated. If I catch a class here or there outside of my music, I'll get my master's. Word is bond! But you brothers should go for it. Keep going for your dreams! Now that you have your G.E.D. E-zo, and Pat man you been had your diploma from G-Dub, you brothers get into some programs somewhere, some schools, quick as you can!"

The guys spoke on drugs: "My parents, may they rest in peace, now I completely understand why they put Uncle Barry and Uncle Ezra out of the house . . . I have a better understanding why they didn't want Nigel and Frankie around either . . . Man if I wouldn't have started getting into selling drugs my family life would be so different now altogether," said Patrick.

Eric added, "Art man, you were the only one who didn't do drugs, who never participated into that type of thing. Look what it got you and look where it got us."

"I hear you duke," Arthur said. "Look how drugs affect us all, especially as a community though."

A small tear rolled down Patrick's cheek, and his voice became distant.

"My whole family got murdered man. Because of drugs . . . Drugs . . . Drugs destroyed my family, and it sent me crazy . . . and there were times, several times when I felt, I should be locked away too. Maybe dead like everybody else."

The guys continued speaking about death: "Don't talk like that Pat. I'm glad we're all alive to make a change! We lost a lot of heads along the way; plenty of dudes that's gone who could help with the change we should make as a community," Arthur said sadly.

"I'm sorry about your whole family B. Pat you know we was all family at one point," said Eric.

"Man . . . If you woulda knew the things that ran through my mind, when I saw Andy run up the steps with Sharon, and I saw the two of them get blown away . . . Right in fronta me . . . Sharon was my baby sister . . . Andrew was our baby brother . . . Rosie, I can't even remember where she disappeared to, or my Mother, and Cindy never became the nurse she wanted to be like our Mother . . . just gone in a flash," Patrick's voice trembled, while a few more tears jumped from his eyes. He took a deep breath, letting out one long sigh.

"Yo, I got some tissues if you need some Pat. You cool," Arthur asked. Patrick nodded, quickly wiping his face with the back of his hand.

"Thanks man. I'm okay. I talk about my family and what happened to my wife. I rarely get the chance to truly vent. Growing up with Shawn on 20th was fun for us. He was our boy. We have to thank the Lord for this opportunity today, the opportunity to celebrate life. Father God, me and the brotherhood thank you for giving us this opportunity to be together. Wow, we're almost there . . . The Mary Morton Center is a few more miles."

Patrick, Eric, and Arthur slapped each other five; and Patrick turned around and held Eric's hand in a firm grip.

Patrick said, "I have to speak the word of Jesus and praise God's holy name. It's only right."

"Got'cha."

"It's funny how we're older now and how we knew each other since we were in junior high school," said Patrick, turning back around in his seat.

"Word! I told you I knew Baby Al since we were like, what, I think about five years old, kid! That's like twenty years plus," Arthur added.

"We have to thank God that we are still here to talk like this."

"Word, we're losing people. My Moms is still crying her eyes out over La Lupe. The Queen of Latin Soul. She was dope," Eric said.

"I heard of her. She contributed a lot to the game, mad people don't know about," Arthur continued, "Alex Haley passed, Miles Davis gone . . . I should have been on that doo-hop tribute about him, and I still can't get over Troy."

"Troy? Who was . . ."

Eric cut Patrick off. "Aw Pat, where you been. Even I heard about T-Roy in Germany!"

"I'm still sad about that, even now one of the Boyz died. Heavy D and them, man. I loved Trouble T-roy. Troy was my man," said Arthur. "My peoples in Mount Vernon working on a hot tribute to him, should be out by now. Damn man. Death. It sure ain't easy. Just to think we all have to go that route. Ain't none of us no strangers to it . . . I still can't believe Shawn is dead. MAN!! Shawn was the only one one out of the crew who never really picked on me. Pat you were cool, but out of the hoodlums in the crew

. . . ," Arthur chuckled, pointing at Eric, "Shawn never really picked on me. I'm making a dedication record for him too, cause I miss him."

Patrick added, "Think I don't? We lived on the same block at opposite ends, just like you and Dwayne. I heard little Shante is the spitting image of him . . . he died the same night, with all of my family. I'll never forget how he was my family."

"He woulda just been 26, too. Damn, he been dead a long time; he died at 19 years old."

"With all my brothers and sisters, my moms, pops," Patrick became listless again.

"And Mister Carter fell out the window, damn, that's some more ill type shit," Eric said.

The friends were quiet after Eric's last statement; even the cassette tape stopped turning.

Patrick spoke, breaking the silence, once again wiping his face with the back of his hand: "You know, I know it's been hard for Dwayne. I've seen what his life has been like firsthand . . . I know you know the deal."

"We heard."

"It's been so hard for him these last few years with Mister Carter being gone . . . And his girl, after this last time what went down years ago, she really couldn't take it anymore."

"She broke out," Arthur asked; and Patrick nodded.

"She had to, lost her job . . . I mean she smart, real educated. She's doing good. Married to this other guy now. My wife is jumping for joy though about that, but I always felt Dwayne and Nicole were made for each other. They really loved each other."

They were silent for a few seconds, then Arthur said, "He didn't treat him right Pat man, you can't front . . . Even I know what went down on the DL, cause heads around the way used to tell me."

"What do you mean? What went down on the DL?"

Eric spoke up, "Pat come on now. We men now! You know what's up famm! Dwayne used to FUCK his grandfather UP! And it was all LIES in the spot that night, cause my cousins Julio and Paco told me before I got locked up; you know, that bullshit that went down with Scheme, my man from Brooklyn . . . I'm just saying though . . . Your sister would be a nurse, Shawn and your family, would be here now, Pat if you only knew the real deal . . . Dee is always my man-fifty grand, but he did a lot of foul shit you know, pardon my language Pat . . . Art, I'm sorry."

"Nahhh, I'm not mad at you E, "Arthur added, "Even after we moved uptown off the block, I still heard. Mister Carter was a very kind man. He tried to do for everyone around the way. They told me Baby Al was smoking that bullshit, wilin' on everybody, especially Mister Carter . . . It's horrible the way that man died on the block. My family still devastated! I was upstate at the time in school; but we all had to remember Mister Carter the way he was, just a great man that loved everyone, on the real!"

"Well, if I'm going to be a true man of God, I can't judge Dwayne for the mistakes he's made, because we all make them," said Patrick. "I can say that he probably wishes Mister Carter was still alive, so he can tell him he loves him, and that he always loved him . . . and I know he is suffering. You brothers haven't seen him in dumb long, but I'm warning you now, I'm telling you straight up Dwayne will NEVER be the same guy we knew. I'm about that forgiveness, like my father in heaven. There's nothing harder than life itself, that's the real deal, and Dwayne is still paying. I wasn't no angel in the game either."

"I guess we all have done our share of bad . . . We all do in this life . . . Positive, negative, positive, negative . . . Both my boys have different mothers, I'm not that proud of that," Arthur said.

"Art, at least you have access to your sons man! Out of my six, I only really see Eriq and Eriqua. My other three are over in Germany, with two of their mothers, and my other son is in the system. Who knows if I'll ever see him," Eric said, sadly shaking his head.

Patrick sat up straight, adjusting his seat to direct his say to his boys.

"Look, bust it . . . Remember this my brothers . . . I'll tell you like I told Arlene, Dee's godmother when she had to close his co-op, sell his ride, handle all of his business . . . and it's the same thing I told Dee after Mister Carter fell out of the window, and Dee almost missed the funeral, not wanting to go . . . it's what I felt, when Dee stopped me from blowing my own head off after what happened, happened . . . it's the blood of Jesus, it's his blood and his love, and through those two things, you've got strength. We all have strength. Remember that man. It's gonna be alright, because God will really take care of it. No matter how you perceive him, once he's first, he takes care of it. Those two things brother, makes the equation for us all, all God's children; love and blood equals strength."

They roared past the sign they were waiting for.

"The Mary Morton Center, next exit. We finally here! I'm seeing Baby Al after all these years. I really haven't seen him since college. I have a surprise for him, and I can't wait to show you guys," Arthur said.

"What? Free show tickets?! I know I'm good for that," laughed Eric.

"Oh no question! You already know the deal on that, you down with Boogie Art! Anything I do you guys will be a part of it whenever you want to get down; but I have an even bigger surprise! Baby Al is going to flip!"

"Well now, we all will get our wish, praise God," Patrick added, and they slapped each other five, exiting the interstate.

Nurse Diane Ross, draped in a big white lab coat covering her summery slinky pantsuit, walked with vigor and great news about her most interesting young patient. The stethoscopes inside her lab coat hip pocket jumped up and down like an ecstatic human being, while she briskly walked the bright, long, modernized hallway of the psychiatry division. Nurse Ross was wired about her patient's bombshell, yet she had butterflies about the collateral of his visitors.

She entered the ostentatiously rich lobby of the Morton Center which resembled a grand hotel. There was wall to wall carpeting with lots of sofas, antique furnishings, plants, modern art with thespian-type paintings on the walls. Patrick, with his head thrown back against a cushion of one of the many sofas, noticed Dwayne's nursing practitioner heading their way.

"Here she comes, the lady with all the info on our boy," Patrick said to Eric and Arthur. The three men stood to greet the energetic nurse with her hand outstretched.

"Hello I'm Nurse Ross. Hello to you, hello to you, and welcome to you! Off the record, I need you to autograph this for my daughter, thank you very much," she presented a rolled "Rap Masters" magazine to Arthur, "WOW. You were not kidding Mister Livingston. You do know this guy Boogie Art. My daughter is going to go crazy when bring I this home. I told her I would eventually meet you, thanks to your friend here."

"I brought along another one of Dwayne's buddies from school too," said Patrick.

"Hello. I'm Eric."

"Hello. I'm Diane Ross."

"And I'm Arth . . ."

"Boogie Art!," Nurse Ross cut Arthur off, " And I'll hear about this magazine for years to come. My daughter's name is Hope. Thank you."

"Miss Ross, Richard and Jason are my sons," Arthur said, signing the magazine.

Richard and Jason held out their hands to shake Nurse

Ross' hand.

"Ohhh, they are too adorable. Well mannered. Nice! . . . Okay guys, so we need to get outdoors as soon as possible! Has Mister Livingston shared the great news, or would you like it to be a surprise," she asked.

Arthur passed the autographed magazine back, and looked at Eric, both shrugging their shoulders.

"Well let's get out back," Nurse Ross stated.

Dwayne's visiting entourage left the lobby. They followed Nurse Ross down another long hallway towards the exit.

"I have great news about your friend. And I know he will be glad to see you all at the same time! You went to school together? All school chums, wonderful," she said.

"We went to middle school and high school together," said Patrick.

"Hold up," Arthur said stopping the progression before they could exit. "I want to show you my surprise."

"Art what's up," Eric asked, chuckling, shaking his head.

Arthur dug in his pocket and came out with a photo, and showed the picture to Patrick, Eric, and Nurse Ross.

"OH WOW! That's when we graduated from . . . that must be Wadleigh!," exclaimed Patrick, "That was back in the seventies! Where did you get that?"

"Baby Al should like this picture of me and Mister Carter. He got to get a kick out of this!," Arthur grinned.

Eric burst into laughter looking at the picture, "DAMN ART! You have come a LONG WAY! I forgot when you used to rock them coke bottles on your eyes homie!"

Nurse Ross added, "I think I agree with your friends Mister Boogie Art. And the older fellow is . . .?"

"That is Dwayne's grandfather in the picture," said Patrick.

"I've met him years ago. Yes, yes. I remember him,

Mrs. Williams' nephew! Miss Joseph and Mrs. Williams always said nice things about him! Interesting picture, this will be a surprise for your friend. He will be glad to know about it. Well, my surprise is, today Mister Carter finally learned to stand up, and he wants all of you to see, so let's go!"

Nurse Ross entered the August afternoon, followed by Patrick, Eric, Arthur and his sons, leaving the air-conditioned building.

He turned a bit, and attempted tossing a little, dreaming dreams of his good life yesteryear at the dawn of a clear, very cold summer day. The subliminal haze filled with shaking fists of dice amidst the blunt smoke and champagne, were rolled by many of his comrades in crime. Split second transformations of bleached jeans, Rucker games, Godfather, Ski, and Kangol Beaver hats mixed into innocent deejay battles for recreation. There were plaid suits, sweat and silk suits worn, and Playboy sneakers.

Dwayne inhaled, exhaled, inhaled, exhaled; he breathed into the freezing mist of Benetton bags and shirts, and the Diadora sneakers on his customers; he breathed into the memorable images of Latin Quarters, Underground-Union Square, The Fever uptown in Boogie Down Bronx, the packed, sexy scene downtown at The Tunnel, and women spilling out of the Red Parrot; plenty of rope chains with medallions, jammed with random pilgrimmages to Albee Square Mall and other Brooklyn points.

His sub-zero mental filled with the rollercoaster aromas of medication, cakes, breakfasts, and the sounds of gunshots, chirping birds, and tranquil streams. There was the chilling spiritual of riding a ten speed bicycle to nowhere, just riding, and riding, and riding, on a winding road towards Aunt Lou's home where she resided, therefore adding her feeble whispers to the many sounds plaguing the lobes of his brain.

In the real world, Dwayne underwent surgery on his head to decrease the pressure of the intracranial bleeding. The stroke on the left side of his brain, with blown blood vessels, practically left him a rotted vegetable. After many months of investigation, Dwayne was finally given a bedside arraignment for the case titled "New York State vs. Dwayne Carter", in which he plead "not guilty by grounds of insanity". The verdict was due to the amount of evidence supporting the medical diagnosis of Dwayne: an ongoing epidural hematoma-bleeding on the brain, ruled out by the organic hallucinosis, organic mood disorder, resulting in a moderate to severe cardiovascular attack; there would be no jail time served. Many were still very angry at the outcome of the case clearing Dwayne of all charges, starting with the Ryerson family and the families of the victims he killed.

The young man who was responsible for crashing a two door red 1987 BMW 325i Cabriolet convertible into a full school bus, fleeing the crime scene, bypassed the pending lawsuits from the angry families of the shaken up children. It was proven that Dwayne's delusional disorders were at an all-time high before, during, and after the Major Deegan accident, therefore Dwayne was free from the laws of the land again; but still bound by the wrath of universal law.

It was agreed that he would be admitted into a long term care facility. With the concentrated cooperation between Montefiore Hospital, the court, Arlene, and Nicole, he was shipped to the expanded "Mary Morton Hospital & Morton Center of Psychiatry & Rehabilitative Research". The Morton Center became his permanent residence and home to the dreams that transfixed themselves into easier and more tranquil thought patterns, with round the clock medication. At first it was a mental and physical fight for survival. His life flashed repetitiously before him like automated photo slides. The dog growls raged inside his soul; and General's head tossed itself back and forth inside his vision.

There was increased hideous laughter from Al, mixed with Gwenny's intrepid maternal pleas for freedom of her son's mind and body; and the freedom to forgive and forget. And under the strict care of the Morton Center staff, he emerged slowly but surely from yet another catastrophic state. His body mechanics and basic functioning skills renewed themselves in microscopic chunks. For years he could only half-smile at Arlene's gentle touch, or Patrick's encouraging voice, after they would travel miles to see him when their schedules permitted. They would watch, tearfully at times, as he stared into space with an occasional flinch or grin, once they asked him to move or smile. He eventually collected enough strength to hold a paper cup, and he even wore diapers, unable to contain himself. He soon became eligible for Medicare, bound to a wheelchair, with a permanent attendant to do the pushing. And the rest of his days were to be spent as a permanent resident in the psychiatric division of the Morton Center.

Footsteps away from the entrance of the gazebo, Patrick stopped walking.

"Miss Ross, let me have a quick word with the brothers. We'll be there," Patrick said.

"Okay, let's not be too long. Time is almost up for Mrs. Williams and Mister Carter. There are other patients who need time in the gazebo. I'll let him know you're here," said Nurse Ross.

"Don't mention me or the picture okay? Let it be a surprise," said Arthur, looking a few feet across the grass towards the gazebo. "Did Baby Al get there yet? I see another nurse over there, and there's two elderly people over there."

Before Nurse Ross could speak, Patrick cut her off,

"I'll explain to him. We'll be right over."

Nurse Ross looked at her watch, and looked at the men, popped her eyes and then continued the winding path towards the gazebo.

"Yo Pat man. What's up? It's two old people over there! Where Dee at," asked Eric.

Arthur added, "Yeah. I thought you said he was ready to see us. I showed you how to use my jeep phone. I'm running out of time kid. I even turned my beeper off. I have to get my sons back to their Mothers and then get to the studio. All I want to do is see Baby Al, show him this picture of me and Mister Carter from back in the days and then we can bounce. This place is giving me the he-bee-gee-bees now."

"I tried to tell both of you the deal on our way up here," explained Patrick, "Dwayne is right there. He's wearing the dark glasses."

"Pat, that little old lady over there is feeding that old blind dude! Look like they on some married type shit," Eric chuckled.

"That's Dwayne being fed by his aunt over there!"

"Getttttttt the fu . . ."

"NAH," Arthur exclaimed, cutting Eric off before he could incredulously finish.

"Aight. Seeing is believing. Come on, let's make this quick," said Patrick, walking towards the gazebo followed by Eric, Arthur, and the boys.

"Hey old man," Patrick said, entering the crowded gazebo first. He gave Eric and Arthur the "pause" sign before they entered. Nurse Ross and another attendant stood with two of their clients as their parked wheelchairs faced each other, divided by a rolling table with a plastic tray of lukewarm baby food and applesauce for dessert.

Aunt Lou patiently shook, lovingly trembled, trying not to drop the spoonful of pureed carrots, while she stretched to feed her great-nephew some lunch.

"Come in guys while there's still a little time left. Mrs. Williams is feeding Mister Carter before he shows us his surprise," Nurse Ross said; then she spoke to Dwayne, "Mister Carter, your friend Mister Livingston is here to see you on your big day, and some others."

Dwayne nodded slowly, coughed and spit up onto his bib. Aunt Lou's attendant wiped his mouth, and Nurse Ross smiled.

"This is great. How are you doing Mrs. Williams? Is your nephew eating okay?"

"He alright . . . sho' is lil' hungry," Aunt Lou said to Ross.

"I sure do hope I have your type of strength Mrs. Williams when I get your age. May I tell them how old you are?"

"What'cha say?"

"Your age ma'am, can I say it?!"

"I'll say it . . . I am one . . . hundred and one. I am 1-0-1 . . . praise Jesus," Aunt Lou said.

"Yes!," Patrick exclaimed, "Praise the Lord! Praise the Lord Dwayne! Only the blood of Jesus can bring you back to us like this. Only the blood, brother. Only, the blood! Only the blood of Jesus can bring you and your grandfather's aunt together. Got a surprise for you outside. Big time Army soldier and a big, big time rap star drove me up this time. Brothers come on in here!"

First Eric entered the gazebo, speechless, gazing at the 101-year-old elderly woman doing her best to feed one of his ex-partners in crime, who had drastically changed. Dwayne had aged more than sixty years in Eric's vision.

When Arthur entered, he froze in horror. He realized that he truly hadn't seen Dwayne since high school, because the emaciated caricature of a man in front of him surely wasn't the Dwayne "Baby Al" Carter he knew from the street they were raised on in Harlem. Before his sons could enter he quickly stopped them.

"Wait!!"

Arthur left from the gazebo and took his sons back up the path a bit. Patrick boasted, "You see what the blood of Jesus can do for you brother? Blessed assurance! . . . Yo E, why don't you say something?"

Eric opened his mouth to speak, but his words would not form while glaring at Dwayne being fed by his great aunt who could barely feed herself.

Patrick rambled on, with nervous excitement: "Eric Martinez is here Dee! E-zo, our boy from around the way! He's home from the army brother!"

Patrick was used to Dwayne's hideous appearance at this point, and he liked to encourage him the best way he could. Patrick looked at Eric and shook his head, giving Eric the "calm down, it's okay brother" look. They saw Arthur approaching a second time without his sons, and he entered the gazebo.

"Will they be okay all the way over by the hospital," Patrick asked.

"I only have to say things just once. They don't mess with me. I didn't need them in here, you know what I'm saying?"

"I need to get out of here. I'll watch them, "Eric said, and waved at everyone, shaking his head leaving the gazebo.

"It's a football in the whip! Get it for 'em! Tell them I said play for a minute," Arthur announced to Eric; then he tossed him the jeep keys: "Catch!"

"I got you homie," Eric yelled back, continuing on the path after catching the keys.

"Start up the whip, we're on our way!"

"Does that voice sound familiar Dee, "Patrick asked.

"Yo, yo, yo! What's up, Dee Nice," said Arthur, desperately trying to regain control of himself.

"See man, it's Art! Arthur Boyd from your block, 17th Street! He went to school with us man!," Patrick explained,

"He has records and videos out now. Remember Arthur?!"

"What's up, bab'y pa'?," Arthur mumbled slowly, and went to hug Dwayne. "Yo man, I haven't seen you since high school! How you been? I brought you a picture of me and Mister Carter from when we graduated from Wadleigh!"

Dwayne grinned slowly, exposing limited teeth, forming his mouth to speak. Arthur noticed a small tear sprint from Dwayne's left eye, making its journey down to his once smooth fairskinned chin, but disintegrating into the flappy first layers of scarred, gross tissue, face and skin still disfigured, burned. With no front teeth when he smiled, wearing shades because of being legally blind, he had patches of long gray hairs popping up all over his ruined scalp, a complete double of the elephant man. He was deaf in his left ear, having it sewn closed because of the burning in his co-op. He wore a short sleeved shirt, trousers with suspenders, and his body leaned unstably to the side.

"Damn, Baby Al looks just like Mister Carter now, even older," Arthur thought.

Shaking in spite of the summer's heat, Dwayne puckered his two-toned chapped lips, and sucked some applesauce off the shaking spoon given by Aunt Lou. They watched Dwayne struggle with the last spoonful, of his own strong will, legally blind and partially deaf.

Aunt Lou's female attendant and Nurse Ross smiled at Arthur.

"Mister Carter can't see the picture, but show it to Mrs. Williams! That picture is worth money," said Nurse Ross.

Arthur gave the picture of himself and Al to Aunt Lou to hold with her nursing attendant. A twinkling began in Lou Williams' eyes, and a smile came to the elderly woman's face.

"That's my Albert . . . my sistuh Jessie Bell son . . . I sho do miss my Albert . . . but I have Baby Al with me now

. . . and Baby Al is exactly . . . the way . . . I re . . . member my nephew. Just like my . . . Albert."

"I'll get a copy of the picture for her," Arthur said, "And for you too love." Aunt Lou's attendant began to blush. "And Pat, make sure they get the copy."

"You know it homie."

"Muh . . . Ross . . . Uh . . .Th . . . Th . . . thank you," Dwayne stammered. "I . . . I . . . wah . . . sur . . . ppprr . . ."

"Sure. Okay," Nurse Ross began. "Well, Mr. Carter is ready, to show us, surprise us, and all of his loved ones with the amazing progress he's made. This is why we allowed this to happen today . . . We usually don't allow our psychiatric patients outdoors, however, Mr. Carter and his family and friends," she winked at Arthur, "are the exception for this joyous occasion today. Mister Carter has finally learned to stand on his own!"

Nurse Ross, Patrick, Aunt Lou's attendant, and Arthur clapped. "And now Mr. Carter will show us!"

Patrick and Arthur carefully rolled the table from between Dwayne and Aunt Lou first, then passed a four prong bottom-aluminum cane to stand next to Dwayne; and then Arthur reached out to help him, when Dwayne pushed his hand away.

"What's wrong Baby Al? You don't want any help, can you make it," Arthur asked with concernment.

"Ih . . . Ih . . . cooool . . . Uh . . . do . . . mah . . . self."

"Whatever you say, my man. Do your thing," Arthur chuckled.

Dwayne struggled with all of his might to stand, resembling a human earthquake 9.5 on the Richter scale; he moved with snail speed, but with the willpower of the average ram. Within his mind, he felt his new lease on life.

It took nearly four minutes for Dwayne to stand up in place.

The moment Dwayne stood, hunched over still

shaking, yet standing, he received his thunderous applause. Nurse Ross, Patrick, Arthur, and the nursing attendant clapped for half a minute; and Aunt Lou clapped three times.

Eric puffed a Newport Light, standing against the jeep's driver side parked a few feet away from the ramp of the front entrance. Richard and Jason played with their football on the grass nearby. The moment he heard the automatic sliding door, and Patrick's Bible toting voice, Eric stubbed out his cigarette. His two friends for life came around the front of the jeep with Arthur sternly beckoning his sons, "C'mere! Chill y'all, come on! Game over! We're about to leave. Come on! Get in the ride, NOW!"

The boys obediently listened to their father. Jason carried the football and Richard snuck in two extra cartwheels. They ran to the jeep and around its rear and climbed inside. Arthur smiling at his growing boys then asked Patrick, "You ready to do this? Ready to say your prayer?"

"You know what? I would, but nah, we going to take it back. Remember the way we used to get down? Only this time, in this cipher we not passing the blunt with trees, we passing the word of God, cipher style. You wit' it E-zo?"

"With what," asked Eric.

"Lord's Prayer," replied Patrick, "And we doing it cipher style."

The three men, one 27-year-old with two 26-year-olds locked their arms and shoulders, bowed their heads in a cipher, and did a "round robin" styled prayer with everyone saying a verse. Like any team when victoriously prayed up, planned, and done, they broke their cipher hard with a growling "**YEAH**!!!" in unison.

"Well, let's bolt then, we out," Arthur said.

Once everyone was loaded, Arthur sped away from the Morton Center grounds.

"New York City here we come! We can do this," Arthur said, bobbing his head to the beat.

The Pathfinder soon roared its way down I-87, cruising smoothly towards the city limits.

Arriving back into the hoods they knew and loved, Eric and Patrick rode with Arthur to return his sons to their different mothers. And everywhere they traveled Arthur was approached, sometimes swarmed for autographs, while Eric and Patrick remained in awe.

Deciding to take a quick spin through his very own stomping ground before dropping Patrick off, the jeep turned onto 117th Street from Lenox Avenue, and Arthur took it slow, reminiscing, stopping in front of his old building. A few of Arthur's followers, asking for autographs, said they would always buy his records, being he supported and hung out around the old way with his lifelong friends.

After Boogie Art finished his autograph session, with blasting tracks from his upcoming debut album, the guys drove off. Arthur picked up speed a bit when Patrick yelled, "**WAIT**!," grabbing the steering wheel.

Arthur slammed on the brakes, stopping the jeep short. Angrily putting the ride in park, he spat, "What the hell is wrong with you man, you trying to get us killed?!"

Eric said, "Damn we just finished getting the shock of our lives with Dee, and you want to chill in front of his building too? What the fuck?!"

Eric shook his head as Patrick watched the elderly man look directly at him, smile, then cross in front of the jeep, and step onto the curb. He crept slowly towards his old residence of 128 West 117th Street.

"Lord have mercy! That's Mister Carter," Patrick thought, nearly in shock.

Al was well dressed, in church going attire. He stopped creeping and somberly stood, looking up at his and

Dwayne's building.

"Pat you alright man? I know you're a religious fanatic but damn! You about to catch the Holy Ghost or something duke," Eric sarcastically asked from the backseat.

Patrick glanced back at the spot where Al was standing, and he was gone.

> *"Mi deh in ah mi bedroom fas'*
> *h'asleep, and h'all of a sudden,*
> *mi jus' feel someone h' and, it*
> *ah coume cross mi shoulda. Mi*
> *sat up, mi look! Mi sey eh-eh!*
> *An'd mi look, an mi see mi*
> *faddah stand righ' by mi bed.*
> *Eh, Patrick?"*

> *"Yea' maan! Mi 'ear. So h'all*
> *dem duppy nah evil?"*

> *"No maan, soume evil,*
> *soume good. Duppy kno'*
> *who fi frighten ya nuh!"*

Patrick smiled, thinking about the conversation he had with his grandmother about duppies once on a Mother's Day morning.

"Mummy, mi love you," Patrick said aloud.

"You's about a crazy Jamaican nigga B!," laughed Eric.

"Hey! Hey!," Patrick playfully shouted. "We're not niggers!"

Arthur said, "Now you sounding like you belong in a Spike Lee movie."

"We're all brothers man. Yenkee bwoy! Rican! I'm too righteous to call E-zo a spick."

"Yeah, yeah, whatever. Look, we gots to get out of here now. I had enough of 17th Street when I lived on it.

Hey you back there. You still rolling with me downtown right," Arthur asked Eric, looking in his rear view mirror.

"Yeah black!"

"You might get on some new tracks with me," Arthur said, then he asked Patrick, "Where you want to go?"

"20th, between Lenox and Seventh."

"The hood, kid?"

"The hood. I'm getting my car, say goodnight to my family, then I'm out to Brooklyn. I'm going home to my wife and my baby."

The friends slapped five and shook hands, and they pulled off.

Patrick decided with each breath he breathed, his grandmother Una Livingston would be certain of his love for her, and the rest of his family would be thoroughly cognizant of his adoration for them as well. He refused to have his life end up like his friend, Dwayne "Baby Al" Carter.

Unlike his friend, Patrick and his relatives cherished their grandmother, whereas Dwayne brutally abused his grandfather. Sadly, the majority of people who abuse others-spiritually, mentally or physically-get away with the dirty deed; however Dwayne's situation was slightly different.

In Dwayne's case, he was forewarned by others, friends, foes, neighbors, relatives. They repetitiously told him the adages: "What goes around, comes around", "You reap what you sow", etc. Anyone with a conscience cannot hurt others, without being subconsciously haunted, again mentally, physically, or spiritually.

For those who believe in the Caribbean duppy mystique, you know Al physically abused Dwayne during his vengeful haunting; perhaps the spirit of Albert Carter even called others out into the deal of retribution.

For those who don't understand the duppy mystique,

or even refuse to, you know that Dr. Katzberg's diagnosis rang 100% true; Dwayne did suffer from delusional disorders, ruled out by organic hallucinosis, because of the brain shifting of his runaway intracranial bleed. This very diagnosis caused Dwayne to bring harm to himself, and others, leading him to a crippling stroke at age 23. For those who believe in, and understand basic karma-universal law, relative to the saying "what goes around, comes around", you know that the belief holds a strong significance. Everything Dwayne did to Al and other people came back to him, in some form or fashion, the stroke with bullet wounds included.

Like Al mumbled over and over, when his grandson nearly stifled the life from him, simply tossing his body atop the carcass of his loving pit bull: "YOU REAP WHAT YOU SOW". This Bible verse in Galatians 6:7, can perhaps be distantly related to the intensifying mystic power of ghosts, duppies, karma, universal law and/or the conscience. The adages are biblically derived, strange, but true; seriously deep and ostensibly powerful. You reap what you sow; what goes around comes around. Do unto others as they do unto you (Matthew 7:12) . . . you must, according to the good book . . . Because **THE CONSCIENCE CAN KILL.**

THE END

ABOUT THE AUTHOR

Ronald Haynie is a veteran of the United States Regular Army & US Army Reserve, and a former student of Marymount Manhattan College, majoring in English with a minor in Theatre Arts. He is published in the military anthology "Afterwords: Bring Down The Walls".

As an actor/orator, Mr. Haynie is the first to perform the Nobel Peace Prize winning "I Have A Dream" speech-made famous by Rev. Dr. Martin Luther King, Jr.-in Spanish by memory.

"DUPPY: Ya Reap What'cha Sow" is his first novel.

Have you enjoyed this novel? Please share your thoughts and comments, and interests in future purchase and support:

RONALD HAYNIE
P.O. BOX#564
NEW YORK, NY 10034
(646)535-6170
Haynie.Ronald@gmail.com

Printed in Great Britain
by Amazon.co.uk, Ltd.,
Marston Gate.